AFTER THE END

Trapped Days

Fractured Days

Final Days

Grace Hamilton is a pen name created by Relay Publishing for co-authored Post-Apocalyptic projects. Relay Publishing works with incredible teams of writers and editors to collaboratively create the very best stories for our readers.

Cover Design by Deranged Doctor.

www.relaypub.com

AFTER THE END BOOK TWO

FRACTURED DAYS

GRACE HAMILTON

BLURB

The old world is gone. And it's not coming back...

It's been eight days since the lights went out for good. Eight days of surviving chaos and the worst of humanity. Eight days for the truth to sink in: the survivors are on their own.

Shannon Grayson has escaped from the massive retail center where she was trapped, but a festering bullet wound in her shoulder requires medical care. In the aftermath of society's collapse, doctors and medicine are hard to come by—and her infection is getting worse.

Meanwhile, a chance meeting with an old military brother brings Dennis Sullivan and his traveling companion Kim Nakamura to an unexpected sanctuary. The town of Humboldt seems to be a haven of law and order in a world that's falling apart.

But as Dennis grapples with his addiction, Kim begins to suspect that Humboldt isn't quite as safe as it appears. The town militia provides security and order. In return, they only ask for one thing—absolute control.

CONTENTS

1

BILL WHEELER

"Well now, that's a problem and a half." Bill Wheeler stared out the front window at the toppled-over truck blocking the two-lane road a few yards in front of him. Beside him, his partner on the road made a noncommittal noise. "Looks like we need to find another route again."

"What's the best way?" Shannon's voice was scratchy and harsh, even after nearly a week of healing. Bill looked sideways at her.

Despite her naturally tan skin, Shannon's face was pale, with clearly defined dark shadows under her eyes. Her skin had a sheen of sweat on it, despite the cool temperatures both inside and outside the truck cab. She looked hollow and exhausted.

"Bill. What's the best way?" Shannon glared at him, impatient with the delay in his answer.

Bill turned his attention to the map spread out on his knees, knowing questions or observations wouldn't be welcomed—not at the moment.

They were on Highway 79 just outside Humphrey, but not far back, he'd seen a turnoff. He traced it on the map. "We could take Route

152. It goes south, then east, then hits Highway 165 up to Stuttgart and rejoins the larger roads there."

"Works for me." Shannon shoved the truck into reverse. Her expression twisted with pain as she moved, and her eyes went glassy for a second.

He was no doctor, but if she wasn't running a dangerously high fever, on top of pain, exhaustion, and infection, he'd eat his boots without salt. "You all right?"

"Yeah. Gear's just sticking a little." Shannon shook her head sharply as if to clear it, then began to back the truck down the road. Her hands were shaking on the wheel, and in the rearview mirror, Bill saw the back end was perilously close to an SUV.

"Shannon…"

"What?"

"SUV on your right. You're getting a little close."

"Crap on a cracker." Shannon swore and adjusted the wheel with a series of jerks. Bill breathed a sigh of relief as the trailer cleared the SUV with a foot or so to spare. "Anything else?"

"No. You're good for now." The road wasn't all that wide, and it hadn't had a lot of traffic on it when the EMP event just over a week ago had killed every car made since the dawn of the new millennium.

The truck continued its slow, crawling rumble backward. Bill alternated his attention between watching for the designated turnoff and watching Shannon.

He knew neither of them looked their best after more than a week without bathing—hair oily, skin grimy, and clothing dirty from the struggles they'd endured at the South Central Retail Supercenter only a few days before. But where he was only accumulating the normal wear and tear of days on the road without wash water and fresh clothing, Shannon was on the fast track to being one of the nameless deceased people in the criminal dramas his wife had loved to watch.

The bruises on her throat and the side of her head—bruises sustained fighting off a lunatic days before—were still a dark, ugly purple color. They ought to have been healing to a lighter blue-green by now, unless the damage was worse than he'd thought. Even that wasn't nearly as worrisome as the arm she kept tucked close to her chest in a makeshift sling. That was what Bill was really worried about.

He'd tended the bullet wounds she'd sustained in her confrontation with Langmaid as best he could with the supplies he'd been able to access at the supercenter, but he wasn't sure it had been enough.

The shoulder had gone red and swollen, and three nights ago, it had started looking infected. Bill had done what he could—and what Shannon would let him do—in terms of cleaning out and draining the wound, but the medical supplies they had were minimal, and Shannon's condition was getting worse.

Her hands were constantly shaking, and every adjustment she made seemed to be more difficult than it should be for a driver with Shannon's experience. She was breathing hard, breath rasping in her bruised throat. Bill knew the effort required to control the rig shouldn't have affected her so badly.

He wanted to offer to take over, but there was no space to turn the rig around, and he was too unskilled a driver to back it along the road. Thanks to Shannon, he could now handle the rig under normal circumstances, but he wasn't confident enough to try reversing over any stretch of ground.

They backed slowly over a few miles until Bill spotted the turnoff for Route 152. Bill directed Shannon's attention to it. She backed up a few more yards, then began the process of making the wide right turn onto the new road. The truck shuddered through the turn, and Bill frowned.

Shannon was an expert driver, but the turn was as rough as one Bill might make. Shannon's face was twisted into a grimace as she pulled the wheel around. She was wheezing, and her face was getting paler by the second. She looked like she was about to pass out or throw up, though he knew for a fact she hadn't eaten much over the past few days. Neither of them had, given that their only options were what they could pull off the rearmost pallet in the back of the truck and prepare over a fire they made—or rather, Bill made—with the lighters they'd carried in their pockets from the supercenter.

Bill watched her straighten the truck out with mounting concern. "Shannon—"

He didn't have time to say anything else. The movement of the truck pulled the wheel straight, jolting Shannon's wounded shoulder as the tire hit a large bump in the road. Shannon cried out, then went limp and folded over the steering wheel.

Bill had just enough time to register that she'd fallen unconscious when the truck veered right and began to run off the road and into the ditch. Bill scrambled to loosen his seat belt enough to try to stop the truck. He worked himself loose, lunged awkwardly sideways toward Shannon, and tried to grab hold of the wheel to straighten the rig out.

But another hard jolt cracked his head against the dashboard and sent him crashing into darkness.

2

KIM NAKAMURA

Humboldt wasn't much different from any of the other small towns they'd passed through during the past week. Kim Nakamura was fast running out of patience with her companion's determination to linger and inspect every single building they passed.

She watched as Dennis Sullivan, until recently her Witness Security contact for her mother and now her travel companion, limped steadily from one storefront of the abandoned strip mall to another, peering at signs and into windows with focused intensity.

"Supply hunting" was what he called it. But there was food in both their packs, they'd scavenged clean water earlier in the day, and they were each carrying at least one change of clothing. There was no shortage of cooking fuel and other burnable items for making meals. There was only one thing Dennis was looking for: drugs.

With a sigh, Kim crossed the cracked pavement to his side. "Hey, there's nothing here." There were several assorted stores, but none that were carrying any useful items.

Dennis frowned at her and adjusted the single crutch they'd snagged from the clinic at Murray State University to help take the weight off his badly injured knee. "We can't be sure until we check each of the buildings."

"Oh, come on, Dennis. It's a nail salon, a tax accountant, a karate gym, and a bunch of other random businesses. There's not going to be any food or water or anything else we can use." There wasn't even a pawn shop or an outfitter where they might have picked up ammunition for the two guns Dennis carried, or other weapons.

"You never know." Dennis's jaw went tight, a stubborn expression on his face.

"Sure. Because every business keeps pain pills and narcotics behind the counter or under the cash register." She saw the guilty expression on his face. "That's what you're really looking for, isn't it? You're hoping to find more drugs, and there aren't any."

"That's not what I—" Dennis cut off at her scowl. "You know my knee and hip have been bothering me. The pain pills take the edge off so I can walk."

"I know you've been popping pills every hour whether we're walking or not. You're practically stoned most of the time, and you stagger as much as you walk." Kim curled her lip. "Face it, you're barely functional, and you're too addicted to care. Now you're slowing us down so you can try to score more meds."

"I can't keep going without my meds." Dennis winced as he shifted his weight. "You know that."

"I know you believe that." Kim said. "The way you take those things, you have more Vicodin than water in your system, never mind food. Mutt's eating more than you are." The big dog barked softly, as if in agreement, from behind Dennis.

6

Dennis sent a halfhearted scowl in the dog's direction. "Mutt's a bloody trashcan. She eats anything and everything, and more than both of us."

"Fine. You eat less than I do, and I'm a college girl used to watching my weight and my budget." She folded her arms. "I get that you need your meds for pain, but even I know you're taking way over the daily recommended dosage. You've got a problem."

Dennis's glare grew tighter, but underneath she could see a bit of shamefaced agreement. He knew she was right, she was certain. He just didn't want to admit it. "With the way we're walking, and the mess my knee is in, taking a few extra pills here and there is expected. Once the swelling goes down, or whenever we get to Memphis and a place to rest, then I can cut back some—"

"You won't, because there'll be another reason, I bet," Kim huffed. "You know what, you do whatever you want. I'm going to see if there's anything actually useful nearby." Before Dennis could respond, she turned on her heel and stomped away, back across the parking lot and down the road.

When Dennis had showed up at her dorm room a week before, dirty and battered but determined to see her safe, she'd thought it was a good thing. Traveling with a former Marine and US Marshal, a man trained in survival in war zones and worse, had seemed like the safest way to go. She'd been relieved to have her protector nearby, with everything that had happened. The large dog he'd brought with him had helped.

The last few days had changed her mind. It wasn't that Dennis was slower than she was. She could live with that. It was the drugs, his dogged insistence on taking them whenever *he* felt he needed them, which was far more often than anyone could possibly need to take any sort of narcotic, even if they'd just had a limb amputated. Worse was his determination to pretend the pills weren't a problem when she saw how groggy they made him and how they affected his coordination and movement.

Dennis blamed the pain. She knew better. It wasn't pain that made his eyes glassy and his speech short. It wasn't pain that made him eye every town they passed, looking for another score.

He'd admitted he might have a drug problem that first day in her apartment, after he'd recovered from his collapse at her door. But it seemed like he'd forgotten his promise to do better and to take care of her in the days since then. He gave her advice when she asked, but most of what she'd learned about surviving the post-disaster world they now lived in and walked through had involved her own observational skills and common sense.

Yes, he had the map, and he'd helped her determine the best route between Murray and Memphis. He'd told her what to pack so she would be prepared, and how to balance being prepared with what she could carry over long distances. He'd given her a crash course in packing lightly but wisely, with items that were lightweight, small, and could serve multiple purposes or be used multiple times. He'd showed her his water bottle, his canteen, and the iodine pills he used for water purification as examples.

On the other hand, learning to build a fire had been largely a matter of trial and error, as had learning to set up a campsite on the road. Dennis offered tips but didn't do much of the work, citing too much pain.

The same was true of learning how to manage traveling itself. She'd never been into hiking or long-distance travel. He'd told her she needed good hiking boots, but not that she needed two layers of socks. At the end of the first day, she'd had horrible blisters. It was only then that Dennis had passed along some tips for reducing the chance of further pain. A little late, in her opinion, even if he had provided bandages, antiseptic, and antibiotic ointment to treat the blisters that evening.

That was Dennis every step of this trip—and for a lot of the time she'd known him. Too little, too late. He helped her out sometimes, but she felt like his only reason for looking after her at all was because her mother had made it a condition of her cooperation. She'd found it frustrating to the point of infuriating during the five years she'd been under his care while her mother was in WitSec, but she was about ready to leave him by the side of the road one night and try to make her own way.

Or maybe, maybe it would be best if she just took off right now. He'd never catch up to her if she left town while he was busy looting the abandoned stores for pills, even if he could be sure which route she'd taken out of town. It would be tough going the rest of the way to Memphis on her own, but she was pretty sure she could do it. She had the supplies, and she could find more food when she needed it. She'd certainly make better time. Dennis had the map, but there were places she could get another one, like an abandoned gas station.

Footsteps behind her intruded on her thoughts. Kim gritted her teeth. Of course Dennis would catch up to her before she had a chance to act. He did seem capable of moving quickly when she least wanted him to.

She turned, a sarcastic question ready, only to choke it back with a gulp.

The man standing behind her was Dennis's age, or close to it, but he most certainly wasn't Dennis. He was burly, with worn jeans and a heavy jacket, his tanned face surrounded by short salt-and-pepper hair and a beard that looked like it had been started on the day the EMP hit.

All of that she noticed later. The first thing she noticed was the shotgun pointed squarely at her face and the gruff voice that echoed in her ears. "Who are you and what are you doing here?"

3

LEE KINGSTON JONES

His split lip and left cheek ached fiercely. Lee resisted the urge to prod them with a finger. He knew from long experience it would only hurt worse if he did. 'Course, it was going to hurt either way, but that was life, wasn't it? He only knew two ways of living: hurting or waiting to be hurt.

Well, no more of that. Lee hunkered down against a wall, wrapping his arms around himself as he renewed his vow in a low mutter. "I ain't going back. No, sir. He's not gonna get a chance to use me as a punching bag for his bad temper again, no way. I'd rather starve on the streets. I'd rather get gunned down by a gangster. Anything's better than being home with that jerk."

For as long as he could remember, he'd been the favorite target for his father Max's temper and drunken rages. Slaps upside the head and kicks to the backside had been his lot when his father was in a good mood. And when Max Jones was in a bad mood—which was more often than not—Lee had taken a lot worse.

The beating last night had been the last straw. His ex-cop father had been raving about his days on the force, and how "nothing like this happened when he was a cop." Though what "this" referred to, he hadn't said, and Lee hadn't asked. Lee had waited until his father passed out from cheap booze, then he bolted. He hadn't really planned anything beyond getting out of the house and as far away as he could before the sun rose.

He'd run until he couldn't run any more, then squirreled himself away into a back alley and hunkered down. The night had been cold and unpleasant. Every little noise woke him up, but he was okay with that. At least he wasn't listening for his father's footsteps in search of a punching bag. Once he'd woken, he'd scrounged water from a neglected decorative fountain in someone's backyard, nasty as it was, to ease his thirst. He continued down the streets, taking back roads until he made his way out of town.

Now he was on one of the small community roads between Tunica and White Oak, huddled up against an abandoned and boarded-over gas station, cold and hungry, with nothing but the clothes on his back and the pocketknife he kept in his jeans pocket. It was still better than being at home with his hot-tempered jackal of a father, but it didn't change the facts. He needed food.

He didn't have any money, not that money was worth crap ever since the world had gone crazy almost two weeks ago. But he didn't have anything else he could trade for food, and he had no idea who he could trade with even if he did find—or steal—something. He didn't dare go to any of the places he knew cops might hang out. Any officer of the law who spotted him would know his father and immediately haul him back home. That was the last place he wanted to go.

He could try robbing a store, but that would require going back toward town, where there might be more officers. Plus, breaking into a building might draw unwanted attention. He didn't know how to pick a lock. He also wasn't sure he wanted to encounter any other looters. One of them he might be able to handle, but a gang of them would beat him bloody and steal the clothes off his back before he could blink twice.

On the other hand, there were other scavengers and looters roaming the streets. He had a knife. It might not be too hard to roll some guy or girl traveling alone for whatever they'd managed to gather. Once he had food in his belly and some supplies, he could decide what to do next.

He just needed to wait by a popular travel path, like one of the main streets. Lee pushed himself to his feet and loped his way toward Highway 61. It was the main road for most small towns around here and the most likely place to find a wanderer or a scavenger.

He made it to the road without incident and hunkered down between a couple beat-up cars, knife in hand and belly growling sullenly with hunger. He hoped it wouldn't take too long for someone to show.

He wasn't sure how long he'd been crouched there when he heard the tread of feet and soft humming. He looked around the edge of the car and gulped.

The guy was dressed in dusty but good-quality clothing, a bag over one broad shoulder. He was dark-haired, tan-skinned, and more importantly to Lee's eyes, huge. The man must have been at least six feet tall and more muscular than most of his father's cop buddies. His expression was relaxed, even amused, and he strolled along as if he didn't have a care in the world.

Lee's stomach was rumbling, aching with the need for food, and the guy didn't look like he was that much of a threat, aside from his size and apparent strength. Lee didn't see any weapons, and he didn't have the wary, cautious look most people did. Maybe he was one of those guys who thought his size was enough to see him through confrontations and didn't care about anything else.

If that was the case, Lee would teach him that size wasn't everything and give him a little something to worry about besides.

He waited until the guy was almost past him and leaped out, knife extended in a threatening posture. "Gimme your food or lose it the hard way, old man!"

The man stopped, the humming dying away as he slowly turned to face Lee. "Excuse me?"

His face wasn't so placid now, but Lee had already committed to his plan. He wasn't about to back down just because of a stern look. He brandished the knife and tried to sound tough, the way his father did when he was giving orders. "You heard me! Gimme your bag, or I'll put this knife in your ribs and take it!"

"Will you, now?" The man hummed. "Are you really certain this is what you want to be doing with your life, boy?"

"I'm no boy, and you got ten seconds before I stick you!" Lee made a stabbing motion in the man's direction, hoping to scare him into dropping the bag.

He never saw the man move. One moment he was menacing the man with his blade. The next, his knife-wielding arm was slapped aside with bruising force, the blade skittering away from fingers that felt painfully numb. Then the man's hand grabbed his arm in a vise grip, clamping down until the bones ground together and a scream clawed its way from Lee's throat. Then he was on his knees, arm trapped in a grip that threatened to crush the bones to powder, and the man was looking down at him with a bored, faintly bemused expression.

"Well now, whatever shall I do with you? Self-help experts say you should never leave problems unsolved, and a boy like you trying to rob me is very much a problem."

Lee swallowed hard and gasped out choked words. "Dude, I'm sorry. I'm sorry. I'll never—"

"Oh, I know that. I'm simply deciding what to do with you. After all, you threatened to kill me for my food, for my belongings. By rights I should do the same to you, but it's obvious you have nothing worth taking. So, should I kill you on principle? Or break your arms and legs and leave you at the mercy of others and the weather?" The man's smile was empty as he studied Lee, seemingly trying to decide which way to go.

Chills struck down Lee's spine. The air of violence, the casual talk of killing, and the way the guy fought—there was no way he was some random vagrant or scavenger. He was something else, and Lee thought he knew what.

Police bands still worked sometimes, and he remembered his father cursing about news that had come in on one of them about a breakout at the Mississippi State Pen. It had, after all, been another reason his father had taken a fist to him, and he'd ranted about it while he was whaling away at Lee. Some convicts had broken out after the power went down, and no one knew where they'd gone. That was enough to tick Max Jones off.

Lee had a feeling he knew where at least one of them was.

"Well, boy, what should I do? I could start by breaking your arm to help you decide." His hand tightened.

"Wait." Lee croaked the words out. "Wait! I can help you!"

The man laughed mockingly. "First you attempt to rob me, now you claim you can help me? A fairly dramatic change in position." His fist clenched a little more, and Lee gasped. "Why should I believe you?"

"'Cause I know who you are. You're one of those guys out of the prison down south, right? Did you know they're putting up police barricades to try and catch you guys?" The pain was blinding, and the only thing that kept Lee talking was the knowledge that if he didn't convince the man to let him go, it was going to hurt a lot worse. He'd run away from home to get away from pain, not to have his bones broken by a complete stranger.

After a moment, the man's hand loosened just a little, to the point where the pain dropped from agonizing to bearable. "Barricades? I was under the impression most towns are rather lawless."

"They are. Were, I guess. Are. I don't know. But my old man's a cop, and they were talking about setting up barricades around Tunica—between Tunica and North Tunica, I think. In case anyone from there comes up this direction." Lee heard himself babbling the words. "Look, I can help you."

"You've already said so. But words are not actions, and I have no reason to trust you."

Lee swallowed hard. "I know, I know. But dude, just don't break my arm, and I can show you how to get around them. I know the area. I'm from around here. I can show you the back roads or how to travel cross-country to avoid the cops."

"How do I know you won't simply betray me to them?"

Lee looked up, letting the guy see his bruised cheek and bloody lip—and his glare. "I told you, my old man's one of them, and he's the one who did this to me. I was running away from him. That's why I jumped you for supplies. They'd just send me back."

After a long, tension-filled moment, the man released his arm. Lee curled around the injured limb, gasping as renewed blood flow made everything from his elbow to his fingertips ache.

"Get up. I will give you one chance to prove your words are true. If you do, then I'll forget I ever saw you or that you tried to rob me. If you do not…" His smile was a shark's smile, sharp and predatory.

"I'm toast. I got it." Lee stumbled to his feet. "I know the rules, sir."

"Oh, don't call me sir. It sounds too much like an officer." The last word was said with a hint of a sneer.

"What should I call you then, s—mister?"

"Mister will suffice, but if there is any reason for another form of address…" The man paused for a moment. "Your name first, I think."

"I'm Lee. Lee Jones."

The man smiled in satisfaction. "My name is Andre, and you will call me that, or Mister Atkinson."

Lee nodded. "You got it, Mister Atkinson."

Andre shifted the bag on his shoulder. "Lead the way, Lee."

Lee nodded and stepped forward, holding his bruised and aching arm against his still-empty belly and cursing his luck all the way.

4

KIM NAKAMURA

K im stared down the barrel of the shotgun, fighting the paralyzing fear running through her. She held up her hands at shoulder height. "Please, don't shoot. I'm just passing through, I promise. I don't mean anyone any harm."

"I'm sure you don't, but I saw you and your friend looting the strip mall, and that sure isn't law-abiding behavior."

The gun didn't waver, and Kim wished she had the nerve to scream for Dennis. "I'm sorry. We were just looking for supplies for the road. That's all. We didn't realize..." Kim trailed off. What was she supposed to say? That they hadn't thought anyone would notice or care? That they hadn't realized anyone was still defending stores like this?

National disaster or not, these stores still belonged to someone, and it made sense that people would defend what they had if they were in a position to do so. But Dennis was so focused on his search, and she'd been so focused on her impatience with him, she hadn't thought about it. And neither had he.

She swallowed her fear and the urge to scream or curse at Dennis in her head. "Look, maybe we can make a trade or something."

"I don't think so, young lady. We don't need any looters and thieves in this town. I think it's a good idea if you and your friend leave town as quick as you can. Now would be best."

Kim gulped. She was more than willing to leave as soon as they could get out of town, but she knew Dennis was tired and in need of a rest. "We didn't mean any harm, and we won't touch anything else. If you could just—"

"Let me be clear. You can leave of your own volition now, as fast as your feet will take you, or I can handle your thieving in a more permanent fashion." His hand tightened on the gun.

From around the corner of the strip mall, Dennis came stumping along, Mutt plodding along at his side. One hand was depositing a bottle into his pocket. An hour ago, Kim would have been offended by the sight. Now all she could think was how grateful she was that Dennis was there.

Dennis spotted the man—and the gun. His face changed, and the hand not occupied with his makeshift crutch shot to his hip. It came up holding one of the pistols he was carrying. Beside him, Mutt went tense, a growl beginning to rumble in her throat as she shifted her weight into a threatening stance. "Drop that shotgun, nice and slow, or I'll put a round in your shoulder."

"You do that, and my finger will slip on the trigger, and your girl's full of pellet shot," the stranger retorted. "How about you drop the gun?"

Dennis scowled. "Not a chance." He stumped closer, and the man turned to face him.

Dennis froze, staring at the man's face. Then his hand dropped as his eyes widened. "Sergeant Danville? Sergeant Lewis Danville?"

The man frowned, confused. "I know you?"

"Dennis Sullivan, Fighting Fifth Marines."

The man's gun dropped. "Dennis Sullivan? Super Soldier Sullivan?" He took a step closer, then dropped his shotgun entirely to embrace Dennis. "Dennis Sullivan, by the grace of God! Man, you look like you went twelve rounds with the entire regiment! What the heck happened to you?"

"Been a rough road, Sergeant." Dennis returned the embrace with his free arm, thumping the other man on the back before reaching down to soothe Mutt with an absentminded gesture. "Been a heck of a rough road, and I'd love to tell you all about it, but the girl you were threatening is my responsibility."

"Well, shoot, if I'd known it was you and that she was with you, I wouldn't have threatened her." The older man made a face as he turned to look at her. "Why didn't you tell me you knew Dennis Sullivan?"

Kim swallowed her anger. "I didn't know it would make any difference. Dennis didn't tell me he knew anyone in Humboldt."

Dennis frowned. "I knew Sergeant Danville—"

"Lewis. You can call me Lewis. It's been a long time since I was anyone's sergeant." He cracked a grin.

Dennis nodded and corrected himself. "I knew Lewis here had moved to Humboldt some time ago, but I didn't know if he was still here. I thought there was a longshot chance he might still be in the area and might be willing to give us a place to sleep for the night, out of the wind and weather."

It was on the tip of her tongue to point out they had plenty of daylight left and they could make it a few more miles. The idea of an actual bed, or even just someone's couch rather than the uneven ground she'd slept on for the past several nights, however, stopped her from speaking. A bed, and maybe a bath, sounded like heaven.

She couldn't help feeling angry, though, that Dennis had been planning something like that and hadn't told her. He'd insisted on coming to Humboldt but hadn't told her the real reason. Then he'd loitered, searching for drugs in the shops, to the point where she'd nearly been shot by the friend he was looking to contact. If he'd just told her, shared some information with her, then she wouldn't have had to stand there, terrified she was about to get shot. But, of course, it had probably slipped his mind in his growing obsession with his next dose of pills.

She forced her attention back to Dennis and Lewis.

"Of course you can have a place to rest for the night," Lewis was saying, "and for a couple days longer if you'd like to take some time to let those injuries heal."

"I could use some time off my feet." Dennis shifted his weight. "Knee was tanked in a bad wreck a few days back."

"We can let my wife Joan take a look at it if you want to come by the house for a bit." Lewis Danville turned to Kim and offered her a large, callused hand and a shamefaced grin. "I'm sorry for giving you a fright."

"This is Kim Nakamura. I'm escorting her to meet her family in Memphis," Dennis said. "Kim, this is my old sergeant, Lewis Danville."

"As I said, Kim, sorry for giving you a scare. It's just that the citizens of Humboldt have organized in the wake of this disaster, and I'm the head of the militia keeping peace and preventing crime in this town.

Stopping looters and fending off potential miscreants is just a part of that." He extended his hand a little further in her direction. "No hard feelings, I hope."

She reached out and shook his hand, glad her own didn't shake as much as she was expecting it to after the fright she'd had. "No hard feelings. You're just doing your job."

And if Dennis had been doing his, maybe this could have been avoided.

She suppressed the desire to say the words aloud, though, because the truth was that without Dennis, she'd probably be dead right now. In that sense, he really was protecting her. She hitched her pack a little higher up on her shoulder. "So..."

"So now, why don't you and Dennis come by my house, and I'll have Joan take a look at that knee of his. We'll give you a proper home-cooked meal and a place to rest for the night."

She would have rather kept going, but maybe a brief rest wouldn't be a bad thing. She looked at Dennis. "Okay."

Dennis smiled gratefully. "Thanks, Lewis. Lead the way."

5

BILL WHEELER

Bill regained consciousness with a headache, a sore shoulder, and a dry throat. He was also still held in place by the lap strap of his seat belt and mostly upright. That had to be a good thing. He levered himself into a sitting position and looked around.

The truck had gone off the road into a ditch and continued plowing on until the wheels got stuck against a rock outcropping. The engine was still running. Bill unclipped his belt, then reached out and turned the key to cut the power. No sense wasting the battery or the fuel. Then he checked on Shannon.

Shannon was pale, unconscious, sweat beading her face as she shivered. Her skin was hot to the touch, and none of Bill's tentative attempts to rouse her made any difference. Her pulse, when he found it, was fast—too fast.

He unsnapped the seat belt and laid her down across the seat. He pulled free the jacket and shirt to look at the bandages covering Shannon's shoulder. The sight made him wince. The bandages were stained reddish and yellow-green, and sticky with pus that sent a vile odor into the air. Red streaks crawled away from the wound under the skin.

He'd seen marks like that once before: blood poisoning. If Shannon wasn't already septic, she would be soon, and gangrene would set in. Once that happened, the poisons would kill her—if nothing else did. The wound was positioned so that amputation wasn't an option. If he didn't drain the infection and find some antibiotics, Shannon wasn't going to last long.

They were in the middle of nowhere, and he already knew there were no supplies in the truck that could possibly help. He needed to get Shannon into a stable location, one with medical supplies that would help him treat Shannon's wounds. That meant getting to a town, preferably with a clinic.

He went around to the front of the truck. It was dented and scraped, but it would still run. They weren't that far off the road either. It wouldn't be the easiest drive to get back to the road from where they were, but he could do it.

Bill picked up Shannon and gently carried her around to the passenger side. He set her in the seat with a grunt, then hauled himself up until he could reach around and buckle her in. He reclined the seat a little bit and strapped her in as securely as he could, with a blanket from behind the seat as padding for the damaged shoulder.

Shannon moaned, shivering and twisting a little in his grip. "No... don't want to...Andre...don't!"

"Shh. Andre ain't here." He smoothed a hand over her damp hair. "You're safe right now, Shannon."

After a moment, she became a little more lucid, her eyes focusing on his. "Shannon?"

"Bill? What happened?"

"You're sick. We need to find you some medicine."

She closed her eyes and groaned. "We need to go home," she mumbled. "The Black Rats can help us." She fell unconscious once more. Bill soothed her for a moment longer.

Then he went around to the other side of the truck cab and stepped up into the driver's seat—after he'd adjusted it for his greater height. He buckled himself in, adjusted the mirrors to suit himself, then turned the truck on and set both hands on the steering wheel. "I can do this. I can do this."

First step, back the truck up carefully. He put the rig into reverse and applied a little bit of gas, watching the trailer in the mirrors to make sure it didn't swing off at an angle he didn't expect. Shannon had taught him that rule an hour onto the road that first day.

Rule number one: Always watch the trailer. It swings wide and it follows you, but it's got its own trajectory, swinging around the midpoint, and you've got to be aware of it.

The truck rumbled backward, jolting a little over the uneven ground. Bill kept one eye on the front end and one eye on the mirror.

Rule number two: Give yourself plenty of room. As much as you think you need then a couple feet more, just to be sure, until you're used to the rig.

He backed up a few yards, then set it in first gear and turned the wheel slightly toward the road. The truck rumbled forward, and Bill breathed a sigh of relief. Going forward he was certain he could do, even if it was a lot slower than Shannon would drive.

Five minutes later, the wheels cleared the road with a bump and the brief, rumbling sound of wheels going over the wake strips that ran on both sides of the road. Less than a minute later, the back tires crossed over, and they were back on asphalt. Bill took a deep breath and increased the speed.

The best bet would be to continue on as they'd been going, to the junction of Route 152 and Highway 165, and then on up into Stuttgart. It wasn't the biggest town, but hopefully it would be big enough to have a small clinic, or even a veterinary office, where he could try to save Shannon's life.

The winding road wasn't as choked with cars as others they'd passed, but it was still treacherous going. He guided the truck along the worn and broken asphalt, and more than once he found himself having to fumble for the gear shift as the whining, grinding sound Shannon had warned him about came from inside the engine. Once he put it into the wrong gear, and the truck lurched and jerked alarmingly. Shannon jolted in her seat, moaning in pain. Bill put the truck into park and moved to check on her.

Her face was pale, and she was still sweating. Bill grabbed a bottle of water and spent several minutes trying to pour a little water down her throat. Shannon shivered and coughed, but he hoped she'd managed to drink a bit of it. That done, he drank some water himself, got a snack bar from the opened pallet in back, and went back to driving.

The miles slid by with painful slowness. Shannon occasionally twisted and turned in fevered ravings. He caught scattered words here and there, though her voice was too rough and broken for him to make out anything intelligible. Sometimes he heard names. "Kimmy" was the word she said most often. Other times, she seemed to be in the grip of nightmares, and names like "Andre" or "Langmaid" escaped her. The only Andre he knew of was her ex-husband, the man whose murder of a bystander had led to her being in Witness Protection, but the reference to Langmaid was clearly a reliving of the event that now left her far too close to death's door.

He wanted to comfort her, to soothe away the nightmares, but he couldn't stop driving if he wanted to get her someplace where her wound could be treated. He settled for singing, soft and low, the way he'd done to ease his wife when the pain and sickness from the cancer treatments got too bad. "Country roads, take me home..." He sang whatever came into his head. Country songs and church hymns, old-time rock-and-roll songs like the ones he'd listened to in his younger days and still listened to for nostalgia's sake sometimes. He sang until his throat was sore and his voice was hoarse.

He reached the junction and swung the truck up onto Highway 165. This road was wider and a little bit smoother, and he was able to pick up speed to a respectable thirty to forty miles per hour.

By the time he reached Stuttgart, his stomach was twisting into knots. Shannon was getting worse by the minute, and the red lines of blood poisoning were extending further across her shoulder, down her arm, and up across her neck. Her breathing was getting more labored, and for the first time, he wondered what would happen if blood poisoning extended into her lungs or her heart.

Would it kill her immediately? Would her lungs fill with fluid? Would it still be treatable?

He shook his head and spoke aloud to reassure himself. "Now Bill, you just get Shannon to a clinic and take care of her, and everything will turn out all right. Step one, just find a place to take her." He focused on the side of the road, scanning signs as the truck rolled down the street.

A little over halfway through town, he spotted a sign for an urgent care medical facility. Bill turned the truck in that direction, hoping against hope there would be someone in attendance. Ten minutes later, he brought the truck to an unsteady stop near the emergency entrance.

The care center was abandoned, the doors locked. Bill studied the lock for a moment, then went to the back of the truck to grab the tools he and Shannon had collected for truck maintenance on the road. He picked the ones he needed and went back to the door.

In over forty years in various mechanical trades and more than twenty as an auto mechanic, he'd encountered plenty of locked doors that needed to be opened. He might not be the best at picking a lock, but he knew the basics of getting into and out of places when he needed to without breaking in windows or knocking down doors.

Ten minutes later, he was in. He shoved the door open and propped it in place, then went looking for a wheelchair or a gurney. The emergency bay had several rolling beds, so he grabbed one and dragged it outside.

Shannon was fully delirious, and had she been in better shape, he might have had trouble lifting her down. She was shivering and fighting invisible demons in her mind. Bill tugged her out of the truck cab as gently as he could, then set her on the bed. He reluctantly strapped her down to keep her from rolling off the bed and falling to the ground. He closed up the truck and rolled her inside.

There was no power, no way to use any of the high-tech tools in the urgent care clinic. But there was a procedure room for emergency care, and there were scalpels, needles, tweezers, and various other types of tools. A quick search revealed rolls of gauze and bottles of antiseptics and antibiotic ointments. There were also boxes of gloves, including some sized extra-large, and masks. There wasn't much in terms of pain pills, but he could work with what he had.

He grabbed everything he could carry and made his way back to Shannon's side. Working quickly and gently, he removed the jacket and the sling. He used a pair of scissors to cut away the dirty t-shirt and bandages underneath.

Bill gagged once when he uncovered the festering, fetid wound, then swallowed hard and probed at the wound.

His wife had been immune-compromised when the cancer got advanced. He'd had to drain a few wounds that threatened to get infected, though they'd been much smaller and less far along in terms of infection. But he knew the basics of what to do.

Open the wound, drain it until it couldn't be drained any more, and apply antibiotics and antiseptics in both topical and oral forms. That was what the doctor had said the first time he'd had to do this for Edith. He washed his hands with sanitizing solution and donned a pair of gloves, which he doused with more solution.

The doctor's first rule: Clean everything and sanitize it. Twice if you weren't sure. Bill worked methodically to pour rubbing alcohol and sanitizing solution over all the tools. Only when he was sure he'd cleaned everything did he go back to Shannon.

Using the scalpel, he cut open the largest bulge of infected fluids. Pus and blood oozed forth, and Bill set the scalpel to the side and coughed as the smell increased.

Breathe deep through your mouth. That was something else the doctors had told him. And wear a mask. He suited words to actions, sliding a mask over his face before he bent to the task of draining the wound.

Draining an infected wound was a nasty business. Draining one that was clearly septic, on the verge of gangrene, was far worse. Bill pressed and squeezed, cutting the wound wider as needed and using the paper towels he'd found to wipe the gunk away. Shannon cried out and tried to escape, but he held her still, using the straps to keep her from falling as he continued to work.

When he'd drained all he could from the front of her shoulder, he poured antiseptic into the wound and packed it with gauze. Then he gently rolled her over and started the process all over again on the back side of the shoulder. More blood and infection had to be drained out from that side as well if he was going to have any chance of cleaning the infection from her blood.

Finally, the back of her shoulder was as well-drained as he could get it. Bill poured in more antiseptic, wrapped the shoulder in clean gauze, and found a needle of antibiotic he'd gathered from the supplies. He injected it into Shannon's uninjured shoulder, then moved her to a new bed to avoid any possible contamination. Once that was done, he covered her with a lightweight sheet, wrapped a restraint around her waist to keep her safe, and sat back on the edge of the table he'd worked on with a sigh.

He felt bone weary, and he was fairly certain he'd have to repeat the process at least once if not multiple times. An infection this bad wasn't going to disappear so easily. At least he'd managed this much, and Shannon might have a fighting chance.

He'd need to give the antibiotics a little more time. In the meantime, he needed food, and he and Shannon both needed water. Once he'd gotten things squared away on that front, he'd have to decide what to do next.

With a groan, he hauled himself to his feet and added another item to his to-do list. He'd need to clean up the mess he'd made. No sense in leaving it to fester and stink up the place.

He'd also need to set up accommodations for himself. There wasn't any chance they could travel on until Shannon regained consciousness, if she ever did. That was bound to take a while, a couple days at least.

Accommodations. Food. Water. And more medical supplies. He needed to get their makeshift shelter in order.

He grunted, stretched, and looked at the slender figure sleeping uneasily on the hospital bed. "Looks like we're gonna be here a while, Shannon. I'd best get started with settling in."

6

LEE KINGSTON JONES

Traveling with Andre wasn't easy, but once he got over being terrified the guy was going to break his bones and leave him dead on the side of the highway, it was actually not that bad. Sure, Andre was huge and intimidating, but that meant if anyone else saw them, they didn't bother them. Granted, there was still a decent chance Andre would kill him, but he wasn't walking on as many eggshells about it anymore.

Under Andre's supervision, Lee guided him back to the little-used path he himself had used to get out of town and head south. When that ended up closer to a main road, he showed Andre another pathway, one of the old hunting trails he was familiar with. The hunting trail connected to a back road that meandered along part of the west side of town and connected to some other back roads that would go around about a quarter of the town.

Twenty minutes into their hike, Andre broke the uneasy silence. "Your father is a cop."

Lee swallowed hard. He couldn't tell from Andre's tone what the best answer would be. He already knew Andre hated cops, and maybe just being associated with one would be enough to push Andre over the edge into killing Lee. So he said the least he could possibly get away with. "He's an ex-cop, but he's still got friends on the job." It seemed the safest way to answer, and it was the truth, anyway.

"You said you know something of the police activity in the area." Andre gave him that cool shark's smile. "You knew about the barricades. I want to know what else you can tell me."

Talking was better than being threatened, and maybe if he gave the guy enough information, Lee would come out of this mess intact. Heck, if he was really lucky, Mr. Atkinson might throw him a bone or something. Lee swallowed to clear the dryness out of his throat. "I don't know everything. A lot of it is what my old man was guessing happened. I could be wrong."

"Nonetheless. What were your father's thoughts on the matter, as a former cop?"

It took Lee a moment to realize the "matter" Andre mentioned was this whole mess the world had fallen into.

"He figures that the military ditched," Lee said. "Left everyone to survive or fall apart as they could. He doesn't think there's anybody in any of the major cities doing relief efforts or that there's anybody coming either."

"A reasonable assumption, I suppose. And not inaccurate, based on my own observations. What else?"

Lee thought through what his father had said the few times he'd been sober and coherent enough to be worth listening to. "He figured all the towns were left to fend for themselves, and they either fell under martial law, led by someone local, or they just fell apart. Total anarchy. Being a cop, he figures most of them went with martial law or some form of gated community."

Andre hummed. "And your own town?"

"Martial law, with the police force in control mostly. At least, that's the case to hear my old man talk about it." Lee shrugged, then immediately tensed. He didn't want the big man to think he was rude. "I haven't seen any sign that he's lying, but I don't get out much."

"Is that so?" Andre followed him as he switched to a road he knew went more northerly and would start a winding loop toward the north edge of town. "You do seem remarkably well versed in back roads for a young man who does not get out much."

"Hunting." Lee risked another shrug. He wasn't sure if it was the air of expectant silence or the desire to keep talking, to keep Andre Atkinson occupied with any thoughts that might prevent Lee from ending up dead or broken in a ditch that made him continue a moment later. "Well, I say hunting, but..." He hunched his shoulders.

"Yes?"

The simple question was like the last straw to burst a dam. "You saw what my old man did to my face." He gestured to the bruises then stuffed his hand back in his pocket. "Believe it or not, that was a good night at my house. He was always using me as a punching bag— because he was having a bad day at work, or he was drunk, or just whenever." He grimaced. "I've been planning on getting out of there for a while now. That's why I was out on that road trying to score food."

"One does what one must to escape an abusive, temperamental lout."

"Yeah? You have some experience that way?" Lee eyed his companion. "No offense, but you don't look like the type who ever had to worry about getting beat up." Perhaps it was unwise to ask questions, but he figured he couldn't lose anything by it. And if he could get the guy's sympathy, then maybe he'd be a little safer.

Andre made a sound of amusement. "You're smart enough to know I wasn't born at my current size. I was a child once, a long time ago, with an…unfortunate father." Andre gave him a sideways look. "Of course, once I grew a bit taller than the old man, things changed."

"Yeah, well, I ain't taller, and my life hasn't really changed. That's why I was trying to run."

"When one cannot fight, it is best if one retreats and regroups to find another plan of action." Andre smirked at him. "It's a common strategy."

"Sure."

They were out past the north edge of town, and the road was curving back toward the highway. Lee was about to ask if Andre wanted to get back on the highway or stay out of sight for a little while longer when a shout made him look up.

Andre was still mostly in shadow, but Lee had wandered closer to the road—close enough to be spotted by someone on the highway. Just his luck, they'd emerged near a checkpoint as the cops stepped out to do their rounds. And they'd seen him.

Lee looked around, but Andre had vanished back into the under-growth or down the path. Lee was apparently alone. He started to turn to run, but one of the men let out a shout. "Stop right there, or we'll shoot."

Lee froze, cursing his luck for the second time that day.

He stood there feeling wretched and sick to his stomach as the men approached, guns drawn and movements wary. Then one of the men squinted and bit back a startled curse. "Hey, I know you."

Lee gulped. "I don't think so."

"No. I do." The cop huffed. "You're Max Jones's kid. Lee, right?" Both men holstered their guns. "What are you doing out here, kid? Didn't your old man tell you there's escaped convicts running around?"

"I heard, but I was thinking about going hunting." Lee scuffed his shoe on the pavement. "Maybe see if I could get some supplies from one of the abandoned buildings." He tried for a shamefaced expression. "I know it ain't totally legal, but I was hoping you'd look the other way."

"Yeah, sure, kid. We'll think about it. In the meantime, you're going back to your old man, and you need to stay there. It's too dangerous for a kid to be wandering around right now."

Lee grimaced. "Ah, come on, I'm eighteen. I can handle myself. You don't need to take me back. I'll be fine out here."

"Not a chance. Max Jones would blow a gasket if he found out we let you run around out here with a bunch of escapees on the loose." The older of the two cops, wearing a badge that said "Corvelle," sighed and dropped a hand to his belt. "I'll give you a choice, Lee. You can come quietly and under your own power, or we'll have to restrain you and escort you back by force. And I can promise you, you won't like the second option at all."

"Look, Officer Corvelle, there's really no need for that." Lee held up his hands. "I promise, I'll...I'll be fine. Just don't—"

"Last chance, Lee."

Lee tensed, ready to try his luck running, when a flash of movement behind both men caught his eye. He looked just as Andre came hammering out from the tree line and the provisional barricade set up on the road.

Corvelle's partner barely had a chance to turn before Andre was on him. One large hand caught the man's gun hand and twisted brutally. The officer's wrist broke with an ugly crack, like a snapping branch, and he screamed. The scream died to a gurgle as Andre wrenched the gun away and punched him hard in the face. Blood sprayed as the man's jaw shattered with a loud popping sound. The officer dropped.

Officer Corvelle stumbled backward, but it was too little, too late. Andre whipped his partner's pistol around and shot him twice in the chest then once in the face. Corvelle fell without a sound.

It was over in a matter of moments. Lee found himself standing dazed and staring at the corpses of the two men who, moments ago, he'd been talking to.

Two cops. Trained law enforcement officers. Andre Atkinson had obliterated them both in a matter of moments.

Andre bent and wiped the gun clean on Corvelle's pant leg. He calmly collected the officer's spare ammunition clips, humming as he did so. Once he'd taken everything of value, he rose and looked at Lee for the first time. "We should be leaving."

Lee swallowed hard. "I…I mean…they're…"

"Dead. Yes." Andre shifted and went back to the edge of the road. He returned a few moments later with his bag. "Let's go, Lee."

For a moment, he wanted to run in any direction other than the one Andre Atkinson was traveling in. Then his brain caught up with him.

If he ran, Andre might shoot him as a witness. He didn't seem like the type to let witnesses just run off on him.

Aside from that, whether it was intentional or not, Andre had saved him from being hauled back to his father. If he ran—and he survived—he might get caught by someone else at a later date, and he'd just be dragged back to his old life. But if he stayed with Andre, he'd be safe from that at least. It wasn't much in terms of safety, but it was something. Who knew, Andre might be a better guy than Max Jones.

"Lee."

Lee squared his shoulders and jogged to catch up with the imposing figure standing impatiently in the road. "Coming, Mr. Atkinson."

7

KIM NAKAMURA

L ewis Danville had an old, slightly battered green truck parked a short distance away from the strip mall. Kim wondered why he hadn't simply driven up to them, then dismissed the matter. It was hardly the most important issue on her mind. Although, if they could bargain for a vehicle to take them the rest of the way to Memphis, it would make the rest of their journey a lot easier.

That was something to think about later. For now, Kim was content to toss her pack into the back with Dennis's and clamber up into the seat. She found herself squashed between Dennis and Lewis, while Mutt bounded up into the truck bed and flopped down as if she was as tired as Kim. Sitting between the two old soldiers wasn't the most comfortable position, especially being shoulder to shoulder with a man who'd threatened to shoot her a few minutes ago.

On the other hand, her feet were more than happy to take a break, so she felt the trade-off might be worth it. She sat back as Lewis cranked the engine. The truck rumbled in a slow circle and headed for a different section of town.

Dennis was the one to break the silence. "So, Lewis, what are you doing these days?" He shifted the crutch to a new position, and Kim winced as it nearly whacked her on the shoulder. Dennis grimaced apologetically then looked across her as Lewis answered.

"Just trying to survive, same as everyone else." Lewis turned the truck down a side street, away from the highway. "After the power went out, a lot of folks holed up in their houses for a couple days. Then, when we all realized the power wasn't coming back, we had a kind of town meeting to decide what to do next."

"Yeah? How'd that work out? I was on the road before things got to that point in my town." Dennis sounded genuinely interested, and Kim was content to let the two men talk while she listened.

"One of our ham radio enthusiasts picked up an emergency service announcement on one of the military frequencies saying that power was out all across the country and we were on our own, pretty much." Lewis grimaced. "Town kind of split after that. Most people wanted to get on the road, check on family in other places. The rest of us were all for staying put and rebuilding the community. In the end, we let those who wanted to leave go ahead and leave, and then we started working with what was left."

They turned down another street and drove past a small, makeshift barricade. On either side of the road, two young men stood, wearing jeans and dark shirts and heavy vests, both holding rifles. One of them saluted Lewis as he drove past, and Lewis saluted back with an absent wave of his hand.

"Looks like you've got things organized." Dennis sounded approving, and Kim folded her arms, eyeing the rifles with distrust.

"More or less." Lewis nodded at another person who was walking along the road on some errand or another. "We set up a town militia and consolidated the residential area so it would be easier to keep people safe. Moved the folks who stayed into a couple of neighborhoods here."

Kim frowned. "What about people who didn't want to leave their homes?"

"Most people didn't really want to move, but the fact of the matter is, it's just good sense to have everyone living closer together. We only have a limited resources, and once we set up the militia and—well, I guess you could call it martial law—we pooled them so we could make sure no one was starving. Now we have everything in a central food bank, and everyone picks up their daily supplies in the morning."

"What sort of supplies?" Dennis asked.

"Whatever they need, according to the household. Enough food for two to three meals a day. Medicine and medical supplies as needed, though we're doing a bit of guesswork there, since we don't have a proper doctor at the moment. Closest thing we've got is my wife, and she's a veterinary doctor, not a regular one. But Joan does as well as she can."

Kim sat up straight from her slouched position. This was something she could help with, and more importantly, something she might be able to barter with. "I've got some training. I was doing pre-med studies at the university. I was supposed to decide between full-time medical school and nursing school at the end of the year. I could help out while we're here."

"Really? That would be great." Lewis gave her a quick smile before returning his attention to the road. "We could use another set of hands to help with treating medical conditions and day-to-day injuries. We've got a lot of people doing jobs they aren't accustomed to, I'm afraid."

"You have people working? You've organized that well?" Dennis looked out the window. "Are you doing a barter system or a community support system? How do you determine who does what?"

They were all smart questions from Dennis, and Kim was impressed with Dennis's clear understanding of what it took to run a whole community after what happened to the country. She wasn't sure she would have picked up on those details as quickly. She gave him a small glance. Sometimes her irritation at his addiction made it hard for her to remember how helpful and useful he could actually be.

"It's a mutually beneficial arrangement for everyone," Lewis answered, nodding a greeting at another person walking down the street. "After the town meeting, we divided up jobs based on skills and experience. We've got some of the mothers watching the younger kids over in the church, and some of the older ladies and men doing a little schooling for the older kids, when the teens aren't doing chores." Lewis tipped his head at a few men and women in a park. "We've all taken a turn preparing open areas for growing different crops, and we've got others foraging in the nearby areas and scavenging the deserted areas of the town."

Kim felt a brief surge of anger. He'd threatened to shoot her and Dennis for "looting," as he called it, but they were "scavenging"? How was that any different, beyond the fact that the people doing the gathering in the latter case were residents of the town?

She held her questions, knowing there was no point in picking a fight with Lewis, at least not over something as simple as that. Then she spotted something that made her forget the anger entirely. A woman was coming out of what looked like a greenhouse, or an indoor garden at least, with a dripping hose.

"You have running water?" She stared at the woman as they drove past. "How? I thought—"

"People didn't always have electrical pumps for everything, though I guess you're too young to know about that." Lewis gave her a faintly condescending grin. "We got a couple of our mechanics out to the water plant to put in some mechanical pumps, and we keep a couple fellows out there on a rotating basis to make sure they keep running. We also have generators to provide limited amounts of power in key areas and after dark. We have to ration the gasoline and batteries for it, of course, but it does help keep things civil."

"Any chance of a shower?" Dennis gave him a raised eyebrow. "Or a homecooked meal?"

"Sure." Lewis turned his truck into a little rural neighborhood on the edge of the town. "We've got to conserve the water, and I can't promise hot water will be available, but we've got the basic amenities in each house. As for the meal, if you want to come by my place for a visit, I'm sure Joan won't mind two more at the table. She makes some good food, though I'll warn you meat's a little scarce just now."

"If it's not MREs, beans, or jerky, then I don't care what it is." Kim shared a glance with Dennis and offered a little smile. "We've been eating trail rations for the past week."

"A week's not so bad, but I hear you. Looking back at my Army days, it's a wonder we all survived, eating that stuff for weeks on end." Lewis laughed lightly. "I don't know what Joan'll have on the stove— we've got an outdoor cook station, works great —but it'll be tasty and filling."

"Sounds perfect." Kim swallowed a mouthful of saliva at the idea of a real meal.

"We've even got a little beer and wine to go with it, provided you're of age."

"Sure. I'm twenty-three. Dennis can vouch for me." Kim was distracted by a small neighborhood supermarket. There was a line of people of various ages waiting. At the doors to the supermarket, two more of the young men with dark shirts, vests, and rifles stood to either side, while two more individuals handed out packages and a third made notations on a clipboard. Kim frowned. "What's that?"

"Evening collection. Some people need evening meds, and they trade in their foraging and scavenging efforts. Some people don't really have the means to cook in their houses, so we have some of the citizens make simple meals for those who need the assistance on that front." Lewis said. "We also have arrangements to give out new clothing as needed."

"Sounds great, but what's with the guns? I mean, do you really need them?" Kim made a face. "It seems kind of barbaric."

"I'm sure it does to a young lady like you, but unfortunately, it's a necessary peacekeeping measure." Lewis's voice was low and quiet. "Keeping the peace is one of the highest priorities in Humboldt. Community cooperation is essential, and we can't afford to have a lot of unrest or infighting. The militia keeps peace and order, and guns are a part of the necessary precautions."

She wasn't so sure of that, but again, she held her peace. There wasn't much point in arguing. It wasn't like she had any plans to stay here long term. She sat back and watched as Lewis drove a short distance, turned onto a small road just barely more than one lane wide, then rolled into a wide circular gravel driveway. He brought the truck to a stop and shut off the engine. He opened the door just as a woman came around the side of the neat little two-story house.

She was medium height, an inch or so taller than Kim herself, her light-brown hair liberally streaked with gray and bound into a neat braid, though a few strands had escaped to frame her face. Her skin was tanned, her eyes a deep oak brown, and she was dressed in a simple blouse, sturdy jeans, sensible shoes, and an apron. "Good evening, Lewis."

43

"Hi, Joan. Did you have a good day?" Lewis swung out of the truck and greeted the woman with a kiss to the cheek. Kim listened to them talk as she helped Dennis out and grabbed their packs from the back of the truck.

"I did. It was quite productive. I delivered two calves and a litter of kittens, and those three boys with the colds are almost completely well, though they might need a day or two more on the cold medication, just to be safe. Mark Cardney twisted his ankle, but it wasn't bad, and he'll be back at work tomorrow. Oh, and Jackie Garnen says they'll be ready for planting in field three within the next two days."

"Sounds good." Lewis smiled at her. "I had some luck training the new militia boys, and I got a welcome surprise on patrol." He waved Kim and Dennis over. "I brought home some guests for dinner."

"A pleasure to meet you." The woman extended her hand, and Dennis and Kim both shook it. "I'm Lewis's wife, Joan." Her voice was polite, if reserved, and Kim was reminded of one of her professors, a no-nonsense and straightforward older woman who had taught Anatomy 101.

"Kim Nakamura."

"Dennis Sullivan."

Joan's eyes widened. "Dennis Sullivan? Not…" She trailed off with a sidelong glance at her husband.

"The very same Dennis Sullivan I told you all those stories about, hon." Lewis chuckled and clapped Dennis on the shoulder, ignoring the way Dennis grimaced. "Came wandering up the road looking like a wreck and stubborn as a mule. Picked them both up at the old strip mall on the far side of town."

"I'm sure there's a story behind that." Joan smiled pleasantly. "Well, if we're going to have guests for dinner, I'll need to gather

44

some extra food from the garden. Fortunately, I hadn't quite got around to starting the meal, so two more portions won't be any trouble."

"Sounds good. Dennis and I will just head inside then, let this old warrior rest." Lewis reached out and shouldered the bags Kim had set on the gravel pathway. "Kim, I hate to ask you to do anything when you're a guest, but maybe you could help Joan."

"Sure." Kim stretched and rolled her shoulders, tight from carrying a backpack and sitting stiffly in the poorly padded truck seat. "Just show me where to go and what to grab."

Dennis and Mutt followed Lewis into the house. Dennis was limping heavily, and Kim frowned after him for a moment. That was the problem with his need for the pills. He actually *was* hurt and could use some pain relief, she was sure. But it was hard to tell how many of the pills he wanted were to treat the pain versus to feed his addiction. Sometimes, she wondered what she'd gotten herself into, partnering up with Dennis.

She turned back to Joan. "Where do we go?"

"This way." Joan turned and led the way around to the back of the house. A small garden formed neat rows along one side of the large yard. The other side was filled with a moderate greenhouse, and in between them was a riot of what looked like wildflowers, though they were planted in patches, in some sort of order Kim couldn't readily identify. Joan picked up a medium-sized basket off the back porch and made her way toward the greenhouse. "Can you start picking some more dandelion flowers?"

"Dandelion flowers?" Kim blinked but moved toward the nearby plants. She knew what dandelions looked like, and there were plenty of them growing in the wildflower patch, but she couldn't imagine what Joan might want them for.

"Yes. We're having fried dandelion heads for dinner, among other things. We try to eat predominately vegetables, Lewis and I, and we prefer to be self-sustaining." Joan glanced at her. "Pick the unopened flowers, dear."

Kim set aside the open yellow flowers she'd gathered and began again, her mind sorting out what Joan had said and what she thought it meant as she worked. "I thought Lewis said all the food was gathered into a central location?"

"The majority of it is, of course, but everyone has a few things here and there, especially when it comes to foraging and growing crops. I'm planning to take a basket or two over to the central depot in the next day or so myself." Joan shook back a sleeve to open the greenhouse.

Kim froze. The older woman's arms were marked with bruises in a pattern that sparked old and unwanted memories. "What happened to you?"

"Hmm?" Joan looked up from where she was putting kale into her basket. "What do you mean?"

Kim tipped her head to indicate what she was looking at. "Your arm. Those bruises. What happened?"

Joan looked down, and Kim thought she saw a flash of uneasiness, even fear, in her eyes. It disappeared too fast for her to be sure, and Joan looked up at her with a wry smile. "Oh, who knows what happened? Life's been so hectic since the power went down, it's impossible to say. I probably banged up my arm while helping deliver those calves today. Or maybe the day before, when I was helping with the salvage work." She flicked her wrist to drop the sleeve back down and grabbed another bundle of kale. "Let me just pick some of these herbs for the batter. I've got some lovely chives and garlic. You grab those dandelion heads, and we'll go see if there's some more eggs in the free range down that path." Joan tipped her chin toward a track that Kim hadn't noticed earlier. "Then we'll go back to the house and get some dinner going."

Kim deposited the dandelion heads into Joan's basket and followed the older woman down the track. Her stomach was growling, but her mind was troubled.

Militia, guns, and now a town leader's wife with suspicious bruises? Maybe she was being paranoid or looking for problems because she and Lewis had started off on the wrong foot, but something didn't feel right, and she generally tried to trust her gut.

A rest sounded good in some ways, but the urge to find her family wasn't the only reason she wanted to leave Humboldt behind.

8

KIM NAKAMURA

Dinner was a simple affair. Kim and Joan brought in the vegetables along with three eggs they'd found in the free-range chicken coop. Joan mixed up a batter of flour, chopped herbs, salt, and pepper, then coated the dandelion heads in a mix of eggs and milk— thick, creamy milk with a scent Kim hadn't smelled before. She coated the dandelion heads in the batter and passed them to Lewis.

Lewis put the dandelions into a skillet with some butter and started frying eggs in a second skillet while Joan made a salad with the kale and a few other ingredients. Kim helped set the table, including water for herself and Dennis, tea for Joan, and beer for Lewis. Dennis sat at the table, hands tapping on the surface in aimless patterns as he watched everyone else work.

After the dandelions were cooked, Lewis put the empty batter bowl and pans on the floor close to the back door. "Here you go, Mutt." The big dog made a soft sound and buried her head in the bowl.

Kim was dubious about eating dandelions, but fresh food was better than MREs or canned nutrition. It turned out that fried dandelions with eggs and kale were delicious. Kim ate the whole plate with relish and found herself wishing for seconds, though she wasn't going to ask, given the situation. "That's really good."

"Joan is a good cook." Lewis took a swig of his beer. "So, Kim, where are you traveling from?"

"Murray. We're headed to Memphis to find my great-aunt, and maybe my mom."

"Murray to Memphis? That's what, a hundred and sixty miles? You've got about eighty more to go by my reckoning. That's a long way to travel on foot." Lewis shook his head. "I'm sure you've realized it's a dangerous world out there."

Kim shifted in her seat. "I mean, it's a little bit crazy, but—"

"A little bit crazy? It's absolute madness out there. Total anarchy." Lewis gestured expansively. "Without government, there's gangs, looters, thieves, brigands—all manner of people wandering around, like a real-life version of a crazy movie. Even people you wouldn't expect to be dangerous under normal circumstances are out there doing the most appalling things. It's even worse because no one's keeping the criminals off the streets, and who knows what those insane animals are doing."

Kim wondered how he knew all of this if, according to his earlier story, he hadn't left his town since everything had fallen apart.

Lewis gave Kim a concerned look. "With everyone fighting for resources and panicked over the loss of power and amenities, I can't imagine it's at all safe to be on the road, especially for a young lady like you. I'm surprised you weren't attacked and robbed a dozen times over, or worse. Although," he took another swallow of his beer, "I'm sure you were safer than most, what with Super Soldier Sullivan here traveling beside you."

"Super Soldier Sullivan? You called him that before." Kim sat forward. "Why?"

"You don't know?" Lewis raised an eyebrow. "Dennis here was a heck of a soldier in his Marine days. A little wild, and a bit unpredictable, but all the best ones are, you know?"

"No, I don't." Kim gave Dennis a studied look. "Dennis was keeping an eye on me for my mom, but we don't talk much, and he's never said anything about his time in the military."

"Hasn't he? Well, that's a shame. I mean, Dennis, you should have at least told her about how you won your first medal." Lewis gave Dennis a look. "You remember it, right? You were on night watch, and you spotted those insurgents sneaking up on the camp from the hills."

Dennis shifted uncomfortably in his chair, a dull flush rising up his neck. "It wasn't much, really."

"Not much!" Lewis turned to Kim. "Don't you let him fool you. He not only sounded the alarm, he held back the first wave of the fighters while the rest of his platoon were rolling out of their sleeping bags. Then, when the rest of the attackers were repelled, everyone else was ready to go back to bed, but not Sullivan. No, he wanted to know how the attack started, and he wasn't going to rest until he was sure everything was safe. Helped us find three locals who were working with the insurgents. Brought in two of them himself, even with a beat-up arm and a thumped skull."

"That's pretty impressive." Kim shot a sideways look at Dennis, reluctant admiration warring with her thoughts from earlier in the day. It was true that she had seen little of that Dennis and mostly only injured, pill-addicted Dennis. He looked away from her gaze and tried to sink into his seat. His hands clenched the chair arms as he hunched his shoulders. Kim looked back at Lewis. "Did he do a lot of stuff like that?"

"Sullivan? Well, I won't say every day was the stuff heroes are made of, but there's no question he was one of the toughest soldiers out there. First on the line every morning, last to retire every night. Ran the obstacle course in one of the fastest times, and he could carry two men on his back across a hundred yards, barely breathing hard." Lewis nodded. "He was a survivor, and he was bound and determined to see that everyone else in his unit stayed alive right alongside him."

"Survivor? How do you mean?" Kim sat forward, ignoring both Joan, who was clearing the dishes, and Dennis, who was trying to wave Lewis into silence and having no luck. The former marshal looked mortified, and Kim felt a petty satisfaction at his evident discomfort.

Lewis, on the other hand, was having fun. "Dennis was one heck of a hunter. Hot-blooded when he was in the middle of a fight, but he could sit and wait for game with the best of them. He had a canny sense of when to dig in and when to move on. I remember this one time, we got caught in a thunderstorm. Well, our platoon leader was all for digging in, as per the military recommendations, but Dennis was adamant that we move on. Said he didn't care if he got demoted for insubordination, but we needed to move."

"Yeah? So what happened?" Kim was enthralled in spite of herself.

"He was right. Turns out we were in a dangerous area. Dennis had figured out our orientation and location, and he knew we were in a place where we were at high risk of getting hit with flash flooding or a secondary dust storm. We could have been in trouble if he hadn't insisted the unit push forward."

"You mean everyone else in the platoon went ahead and did what he said? Even though he was risking insubordination? Wasn't that, like, treason or something?" Kim's brow furrowed in confusion.

"No one reported it, not after we figured out what he knew." Lewis shook his head. "Not that we would have, in any case. We all knew that when Super Soldier Sullivan said something, he meant it, and if he was going against orders, he had a good reason."

"You all trusted him that much?" Kim asked. She had trouble imagining trusting anyone so much she'd risk getting jailed or worse for them. Though she supposed the same couldn't be said about her mom.

"Of course. Some units have their lucky man or their eagle eye; we had Sullivan. The superman with the mind like a steel trap and the skills to match." Lewis smirked. "One of the best soldiers in the Corps." He finished his beer and glanced at his fellow veteran. "I'm a little surprised you ever left."

Dennis flushed. "Shrapnel shredded my hip, and they discharged me."

"And you went right into the marshals. That's just like you." Lewis toasted Dennis with his empty bottle. "You might be a little bit older, a lot balder, and carrying a few more scars, but I bet you're still just as tough."

Kim suppressed a snort, but Dennis must have read her disbelief of Lewis's tales in her expression, because he winced and looked away quickly. His face was red with distress, and one hand moved to clench on his crutch as if he wanted to escape.

She knew addiction was a disease and, especially from her studies, how easy it was to get swept into an addiction when one suffered a painful and devastating injury like Dennis had. But it was hard for Kim to set aside the promise he'd given her about getting off the pills —the promise he'd yet to live up to.

Lewis didn't notice as he finished his beer and accepted another one from Joan. He turned back to Kim. "Has he showed you all his little survival tricks yet? We used to joke that he had a whole guide in his head. He had these rules—how many were there, Dennis?"

Dennis shook his head. "I don't remember." He hauled himself to his feet, shifting his crutch under one arm. "I'd like to keep talking, but I need to get Mutt outside to have her evening run and do her business." He stumped around the chair and tapped his leg. "Come on, Mutt." The dog huffed and clambered to her feet from where she was lying by the back door. She shook herself, then ambled after Dennis as he moved toward the front of the house.

Lewis waited until they heard the front door shut behind Dennis before he turned to Kim. All the levity had disappeared from the militia leader's face. "Now that Dennis has gone out, perhaps you can answer a question for me, Kim."

Kim shifted, caught off guard by the abrupt change in both tone and topic. "Maybe. But if it's about Dennis, I really don't know all that much about him."

"Even so, it's a simple question: How long has he been addicted to pain meds?" Lewis's voice was low and stern, heavy with disapproval.

Kim winced internally. She might despise Dennis's addiction, but telling someone Dennis obviously respected didn't sit well with her. "I only know that he's been taking meds for his hip and knee. He was pretty beat up when he turned up at my dorm room."

"I appreciate your loyalty to Dennis." Lewis leaned forward. "I really do appreciate it, and I know he would as well, but there's no reason to try and protect him by prevaricating. I've seen plenty of men who were addicts. I know the signs."

Kim swallowed hard. Even when it was obvious the secret wasn't really that much of a secret, it felt wrong to talk about it. But then, if Dennis respected Lewis, he might listen to him the way he hadn't listened to any of Kim's protests. "He's...I don't know how long he's been addicted. If he even is addicted." She added this last bit, even though it was a lie, because she didn't like the idea of completely throwing Dennis under the bus. Lewis may have been his friend, but she and Dennis were in a partnership. That felt like it was worth something, even if that something was just a white lie.

"He is addicted," Lewis said. "I've seen the symptoms. The fidgeting with his pocket, where I would guess he has a stash of pills, the sweating, the restlessness. It's clear he's suffering from an opioid addiction. I'm just trying to gauge how far he's fallen under the influence." Lewis shook his head, a grim expression on his face. "It's a sad thing when a man like Dennis suffers from something like this."

She considered his words and finally offered him the only information she had. "He said he was in a bad accident a year ago, and he's been on meds since then. But I don't know if he ever stopped taking them after the accident that got him transferred to the marshals."

"He probably did, or someone would have noticed the problem before this. But no doubt that made it easier for him to fall under the influence and develop an addiction after his more recent injury," Lewis said.

"I guess." Kim shrugged. "I mean, I don't know that much about it." She felt a brief surge of bitterness. "I sure don't know what to do for him."

"Well, you can't do much for him unless he's willing to help himself. But I'll tell you what." Lewis folded his arms and leaned toward her across the table. "Did he tell you he can't stop because you two are on the road and he needs the meds to keep going?"

She blinked at him, startled. "How did you know?"

"Because it's the kind of thing an old soldier like Dennis would say. He'll excuse weakness in the name of duty, foolish as it is. Here's what I propose. You two settle in for a little bit, and you try and convince Dennis to go ahead and come clean. We've got the resources to keep you fed and a roof over your head while he gets his head on straight."

Kim bit her lip, trying to weigh the pros and cons in her mind. "I don't know."

"That's fine. You just think about it for a night if you like. I do think it could help you, and it would be best for you and Dennis. But the choice is yours." Lewis rose from his seat. "Either way, I'd best get someone to open up a house for you so you two can rest."

"Thanks." Kim rose and stretched. "I'll think about what you've said."

"That's all I ask." Lewis smiled and left the room. Kim watched him go, conflicted.

It would be easier to travel with Dennis if he was free of his addiction, but she wasn't sure she wanted to stick around Humboldt long enough for him to detox and recover.

9

BILL WHEELER

Cleaning up the mess of rags, towels, stained bandages, and other remnants of the work he'd done was exhausting. Bill was about ready to drop. He managed to find a large scrub shirt to replace his stained one, which was a relief. Then he found a hospital bed for himself and dragged it into the room where Shannon slept.

He was too tired and too nauseated from cleaning out Shannon's shoulder to care about getting any food. He knew he needed water and nutrition, but that could wait. His mind was working through what needed to be done.

He'd have to drain Shannon's wound again, most likely. He wasn't expert enough to have cleaned it out completely on the first pass. He'd thought about cauterizing the wound as he finished but had discarded the idea. Closing and sealing the wound would only lock any remaining poisons into her blood. Antibiotics would help, but she was already so close to sepsis and gangrene. He needed to do more—if he just knew what to do.

While he was thinking and worrying, he fell into an exhausted, restless sleep, scrunched up on the small bed.

He woke to the sound of distant thumping, the kind of thing that most people might not notice. But he was a mechanic, had been one for the better part of half a century, and he was used to paying attention to muffled noises that might mean something was wrong. Now his ears were telling him something was happening outside.

He slid out of the bed, wincing at sore and cramped muscles, and looked at Shannon. She was still unconscious, sweat beading her brow and disconcerting splotches on the previously clean bandages. He brushed a hand over her forehead and grimaced at the heat emanating from her brow.

Another series of muffled thumps came from beyond the door. It sounded like it might be coming from outside. Bill tensed as he identified the direction the noises were coming from. It sounded like someone might be messing with the truck.

He'd closed the truck down, and he had the keys in his pocket, so there wasn't much chance that anyone would be able to steal it. They might be able to break into the back and steal the supplies. But really, what harm could that do? There were pallets full of supplies, a whole truck's worth.

If word got out that there was a truck full of supplies sitting abandoned, though, the whole thing might be looted. The truck itself might be stripped down or have the tank siphoned. He'd heard of such things happening to abandoned cars, even in less desolate times. For that matter, he and Shannon had discussed taking similar measures if they wound up needing fuel or an emergency replacement part.

What if someone came into the urgent care center looking for the keys or additional supplies? Shannon was in no shape to defend herself. It might be safer to warn them off before things got that far.

Bill hesitated, then went to one of the side counters. Among the other belongings he'd removed from Shannon's person were the knives she'd carried. They weren't as formidable looking as the hatchet they'd left buried in Langmaid's skull or the gun they'd left by Connor, but they would do. And he knew the basics of how to hold and use a knife.

He took the long-bladed folding knife and opened it up. He made his way toward the door, eyes open and watching for intruders as he traversed the short distance from the treatment room to the lobby.

The doors were closed, and there was no sign anyone had even realized they could get into the urgent care center. Bill stood a moment, listening, and heard another set of thumping sounds. Someone was definitely messing with the truck, and from the sounds of it, they hadn't given up yet.

Bill popped the lock on the door and pulled it open, shivering a little as the spring breeze sneaked through the thinner fabric of his borrowed scrub shirt. The front of the truck was nearest, and he moved toward it, looking for signs of tampering.

The doors were still locked. The thumping sound was coming from the back end. Someone was trying to break into the back, trying to get at the supplies.

Bill eased his way along the side of the truck, knife in hand and stomach churning with nerves.

He knew how to hold a knife, but he'd never used one in a fight, in self-defense or otherwise. He'd seen TV shows and movies, but he wasn't sure he could wield a blade the way those characters did. Hopefully it wouldn't be necessary.

Two-thirds of the way down the side of the truck, he took a deep breath. "Who's there? Get away from my truck!"

Startled gasps sounded as he lunged around the end of the truck. Several figures scrambled back. Bill raised the knife in warning.

"Get back!" he yelled. One of the figures raised both arms, and Bill caught a glimpse of something black with a familiar shape. A gun.

He dove back around the side of the truck into cover, his heart hammering in his chest. "I warn you, I'm armed!"

"So are we! We found this truck first, and we're not giving it up!" The voice was male, and scared. "Leave now and you won't get hurt!"

The voice was shaky and sounded much the way Bill felt. But it also sounded young. The voice reminded him of Rick, the greeter at the supercenter he and Shannon had been trapped in. Bill swallowed hard and gripped the knife tighter.

They had a gun, but they hadn't started shooting yet. Nor had they run away, by the sound of it. He was in a stalemate. Bill took a moment to steady his nerves and spoke again. "I'm warning you! This truck is mine, so best you leave now!"

"Not a chance! We found it; we're claiming it!" The voice definitely sounded young and nervous. Bill chewed absently on his lower lip for a moment, considering the situation.

He wasn't going to make any progress shouting back and forth around the end of the trailer. He might as well go face-to-face with the others and see if he could get them to leave. He made sure his grip on the knife was firm, then stepped away from the side of the truck and came around the back end.

Three young men jerked away from where they'd been trying to pull the door of the truck open. The one standing farthest from the truck whipped around and leveled the gun at him. "Go away!"

"Not gonna happen, young man. That's my truck, and I've got the keys to prove it." Bill frowned at them.

"Hand 'em over, or I'll shoot." The gun and the youth's voice both wavered.

Bill looked at his nervous face and made a quick decision. "That's not gonna happen either." He took a single long, slow step toward the three boys, making use of every inch of his muscular frame as he gave them a stern look. "You want the keys, you're going to have to take them."

The boy's hands trembled, and Bill sighed. "Look, I don't think you boys really want to do this."

One of the boys—the one who was closest to him, and who had been trying to work the latch of the trailer—gave a wild yell and lunged at him, fists swinging. Bill blocked, just barely remembering to keep the knife blade away from the youngster, then pushed him back.

The kid stumbled and recovered his balance, then all three of them were charging, an uncoordinated little mob of flailing limbs and desperate, childish faces. Bill stepped out of the way of one wild swing and winced as another fist caught him in the side. It wasn't hard enough to hurt, not against the muscles of a mechanic, but it was enough to make him jerk his elbow out to reflexively swat the boy away. Bill dodged sideways, closer to the truck trailer.

The next few moments were a scrambling, weak imitation of a brawl he'd had the misfortune to sit through once. The mechanics from his shop had gone out for a drink, and one of them had upset the wrong fellow. Bill avoided or blocked blows from the boys and tried to keep from losing the knife or the keys in the scuffle.

One kid tried to tackle him low, and Bill swiped at him, realizing a second too late that he'd used the hand holding the knife. He tried to pull the blow even as the kid stumbled and tried to stop, but the tip of the blade scored a long line of red down the youngster's arm. He fell back with a cry of pain.

Everything stopped. Bill dropped back against the trailer, breathing heavily, while the three boys huddled together. One of them looked at him with shock in his eyes.

"You cut Mitch."

"You threatened to shoot me." It was the only thing he could think of to say while his stomach twisted in guilt.

The kid looked up at him with anguished eyes. "Wasn't like the gun was loaded! We were just gonna use it to scare anyone who tried to take what was ours."

Bill sighed. The fear and adrenaline were draining away, and he felt bone weary and sick of the whole thing. He crouched down. "You can't go around threatening people like that, not with everything going on. But I guess you've learned that. So why don't you let me see that cut and patch you up, and we'll talk about what the heck you were doing, trying to break into my truck and threatening people with an empty gun."

The youth with the cut arm started to pull back, but Bill caught his arm and started to examine the wound. All three of the boys settled into tense stillness.

The cut was shallow and looked worse than it was. Bill checked it with gentle hands. "This isn't too bad. Should heal in no time." He addressed the other two boys. "Either of you got a handkerchief?"

"No." The one to the right shook his head, his motion echoed by his companions.

"All right." Bill considered his options, then pulled at the pocket of his borrowed scrub top. After a minute, he managed to rip it free. He folded it once lengthwise and pressed it against the shallow cut on Mitch's arm. "Here we go. Hold that in place, and the bleeding will stop soon enough."

Mitch nodded and slid a hand over his arm. All three boys scrambled to their feet as Bill rose, his knees cracking. The boys started to back away, but Bill held up a hand. "Wait up a moment." All three froze.

Bill studied the three of them. Their clothing was grubby, and their expressions were wide-eyed and hungry. There was an air of desperation and despair about them, and Bill's heart ached.

It'd been two weeks since the power went out. Not everyone would have enough food and supplies to last that long. He sighed. "All right. Come on, boys."

"What? What are you gonna do?" the boy with the gun said.

Bill gave him a smile. "I might come to regret this later, but I told you boys this was my truck." He pulled the keys from his pocket. "And as it happens, I've got some food to spare."

He unlocked the door to the trailer, unlatched it, and shoved the metal sliding door upward to reveal the pallets of dried goods. He heard a series of gasps as he ran out the ramp up to the tailgate. He tromped up the ramp then turned to look at the young men. "Come on, let's see what we can get you. I reckon you can each carry enough for a good few meals, at least."

Mitch was the first up the ramp, eyes wide as he took in the boxes of cereal, soup, and other dry goods. "Whoa." He looked up at Bill with a thunderstruck expression. "You're gonna let us have some of this?"

"As much as you each can carry." The amount three boys could carry would barely make a dent in the supplies the truck was holding.

By that time, Mitch's two friends were close behind him, staring at the bounty inside the vehicle. Bill turned and worked the torn plastic around the nearest pallet open wider, then began handing over boxes. It took some work and shuffling of the various boxes and containers, but he managed to get a box of cereal for Mitch, and box of soup for his friend with the gun, and another box that looked like it had pasta or something else in it for the third youth.

He also pulled a box of canned chili for himself, wanting the meat and the beans for the energy, even if he had to eat it cold.

"There you go. You share that out among you, and you'll have some varied meals for a couple of days."

Mitch looked up at him with damp eyes. "Thanks, sir. You've got no idea how much we needed this."

"Yeah." One of the others nodded. "Kenny's got two sisters, and Mitch's mom is sick."

"Lowell's helping his family out too." Kenny gave him a shamefaced look. "We didn't plan on stealing, honest, but we thought the truck was abandoned, like out of gas or something, and we were thinking maybe we could salvage something."

"I understand." Bill hopped down from the truck and pulled the door down to latch it into place. "Well, no harm done. But it might be best if you boys get on home and get some food in your stomachs."

All three nodded jerkily around the boxes in their arms, then began making their way back up the street. Bill wondered how far they had to go but dismissed the matter from his mind. He was confident they'd make it home.

In the meantime, he felt exhausted in the aftermath of the excitement. His side and his arms ached from where he'd been hit, and his hands were shaking lightly from how close he'd come to seriously hurting one of the boys.

He couldn't make himself believe this would be the last time he'd have to protect the truck. There was no telling how long it would be before Shannon either recovered or succumbed to her wounds. In the meantime, he'd need to protect both her and their resources, and he couldn't trust either would be easy.

Bill groaned and leaned against the truck for a moment. Then he rose, picked up the box of food, and made his way back to the urgent care doors. The knife was heavy in his pocket, and a fresh breeze made him shiver as it dried the sweat on his arms and face.

He slipped inside after a quick check to make sure there was no one watching, then locked the doors and stood there thinking.

He didn't want to move Shannon too much or leave her somewhere like the entryway, where someone might see her and realize she was vulnerable. But if he stayed in the treatment room with her all the time, he might not hear the next attempt to loot or steal the vehicle, and they couldn't afford to lose it. By his judgment, they were still close to a hundred miles from Memphis.

He'd have to divide his efforts and set up a camp between the two. Bill grimaced. "I'm getting too old for this."

If he could trust the clock on the wall and the sunlight coming through the windows, he'd been asleep and then occupied with the boys for about six hours. He needed to eat. Then he needed to check on Shannon, see if he could get a little water or food into her so she didn't suffer too much from dehydration or lack of nutrients. It might be best if he moved himself out to the emergency entrance where he could keep an ear out for Shannon and an eye on the truck as well.

Bill went to set the food in the treatment room and eyed the mattress of the bed he'd been using. It was small and cramped, but it was also removable. He could pull two or three of them—assuming he could find that many beds—and make himself a pallet in the entrance area. It wouldn't be perfect, but it would at least serve the purpose, and it might be marginally more comfortable.

First Shannon. Then he'd see about his own comfort. Bill moved to her bedside.

The stains hadn't gotten any larger on the bandages, and the fever didn't feel much worse, though her skin was getting a little dry, a sign she probably needed fluids. At his touch, she moaned and shifted a little. Bill brushed her oily hair away from her face and went to get some water and the remains of the drinks Shannon had carried from the supercenter. If nothing else, they'd have electrolytes.

There was no sign of anyone in the parking lot or on the road when he went out. He moved as quickly as he could to grab Shannon's bag and his own supplies. Before he went back inside, he looked at the truck. At some point, he might want to try and figure out what all was in the trailer. He knew Shannon had an inventory, but as far as he knew, that had been left in the supercenter, in the office of Noah Mochire, who'd died there.

On the other hand, opening the trailer might invite more attacks. Bill stood for a moment, then shook his head and shouldered the bag. "I'm getting distracted. Gotta take care of first things first."

Inside, he coaxed a little bit of an energy drink down Shannon's throat. Not as much as he would have liked, but it was at least something. Then he opened the box of chili and fished out a can. Practical experience allowed him to pry the can open with the edge of a sharp single-bladed screwdriver and some leverage. As he ate, he considered the benefits of cobbling together a can opener or multipurpose tool while he waited for Shannon's condition to change. It would at least help him pass the time.

Cold chili and water wasn't much of meal, but it filled his belly and eased some of the shakiness in his limbs. He was still bone tired and worried—for Shannon and for himself—but he felt better. He finished the chili, cleaned his utensils, and rose from his seat.

There were probably more hospital beds in nearby rooms, and possibly sheets. He hadn't bothered looking earlier, but if he was going to set up a sort of camp here, then sheets would be welcome. There wasn't much to do besides make himself comfortable and hope he could handle whatever happened next.

10

KIM NAKAMURA

About an hour after dinner was finished, Lewis returned. "All right. Got you set up in a house a few streets over. It's a two-story, which I hope you won't mind, but it's comfortable and it's got rooms for both of you."

"Two-story is fine." Dennis heaved himself out of the seat he'd resumed after he returned from Mutt's evening walk. Kim followed his lead. "As long as it's got a roof and something like a bed, then it'll work perfectly."

"All right, I'll take you over there." Lewis turned, then hesitated. "I hope you don't mind walking. I know it's not ideal, with your condition, but we've got to preserve gasoline."

"I'll manage." Dennis slid his bag over his shoulders and balanced himself. "I've plowed my way through worse."

"I'm sure you have." Lewis smiled and led them out into the waning light of evening. Kim grabbed her bag and followed.

Lewis led them through the neighborhood, back toward the main part of the community. They left behind the more rural housing Lewis and his wife lived in and crossed into another neighborhood, more like what Kim was used to seeing. Houses, worn but in good condition, set along the edges of two-lane streets with neatly marked lawns.

After a few minutes, Lewis led them up a battered sidewalk and three steps to the door of a small house with a lantern on the front step. Lewis bent and lit it with practiced motions. "Sorry, no electricity here at the moment. We'll have to deal with that in the morning if you decide to stay in Humboldt for very long. For tonight, you'll have to make do with the lantern."

"Not a problem." Dennis limped up the steps and took it from Lewis's hand. "You got a key?"

"Right here." Lewis produced a key on a simple key chain. He unlatched the front door. "Should be fresh sheets and whatnot inside: some drinking water, basic cooking supplies, and towels." His eyes slid over their appearances. "If you want, you can stop by the store tomorrow, pick up some fresh clothes, as well as supplies for a wash. If you don't mind my saying, you look like you could use it."

Kim couldn't argue with that assessment as she followed Lewis and Dennis inside. The interior of the house was spartan but comfortable, with worn chairs and a spacious kitchen. Stairs next to the door rose in a fairly gentle angle up to the second floor. It looked a little dusty, but otherwise as if the family had just stepped out. "What happened to the people who lived here?"

"Left. Headed out to try and find family in another town." Lewis shook his head. "I did tell them it was dangerous, but they insisted. They left a couple days after the power went out."

Dennis nodded. "It happens. I headed out on the second day myself." He studied the room, then dropped his bag by the staircase and stumped across to drop into a recliner. Mutt followed and flopped down at his side, leaning her head into his knee. "Thank you for the accommodations, Lewis."

"Not a problem. If you decide to stay longer than tonight or a day or two, just let me know." Lewis gave them both a friendly nod. "I'd stay to chat, but I've got final rounds to do, and then I need to get home to Joan."

"Yeah, sure. You go ahead." Dennis waved a hand. Lewis returned the wave then started walking home.

Kim heaved a sigh of relief and shut the door behind him. She dropped her bag and flopped into the couch, reveling in the soft cushions and the comfortable seat. "Man, this is like heaven."

"It's nice enough." Dennis leaned back in the chair and scratched Mutt's ears. "I'm glad to be getting off my feet, I admit."

"Yeah." Kim kicked her feet up onto the other cushion and leaned back herself. She watched Dennis for a few moments. "Hey, can I ask you something?"

"Sure." Dennis nodded, his eyes half-lidded with contentment. Kim suspected he'd taken his pills, either when he went out for his walk or on the trip over to their current abode. His hand was scratching slow, easy circles between Mutt's ears.

"Those stories Lewis told, were they real? True, I mean?" Dennis's shoulders tensed up. "It sounds pretty incredible."

Dennis took a deep breath and scowled absently at the far wall. "Lewis has a big mouth, and he's prone to exaggeration."

"So he lied?"

Dennis shot a glance at her. Then he shook his head slowly. "Not exactly. He might have made me sound better than I was, but the incidents themselves did happen. A lot of things happened while I was part of the Marines."

"So you really fought off a bunch of insurgents, and tracked down spies that were reporting Marine movements, and managed to keep your whole troop from getting caught in a flash flood or something?" Kim stared at him. "All of that?"

"It was over a period of several years. I had a lot of days where I was just another grunt in the line, doing my PT and trying to stay out of trouble." Dennis made a dismissive motion. "It was a long time ago."

"Too bad. We could use the super soldier." Kim huffed the words under her breath, but Dennis apparently had sharper hearing than she'd given him credit for.

Dennis sat up straighter in his chair and gave her a sharp look. "What's that supposed to mean?"

She hadn't intended to bring up Lewis's suggestion in exactly that manner, but she wasn't going to let the opening pass her by. Kim sat up and met his scowl with one of her own. "Simple. This whole trip would be a lot easier if you were even half the man you used to be."

Dennis scowled. "I can't help being injured."

"I'm not talking about that." Kim shook her head. "I'm talking about the fact that you're a drug-addicted, strung-out mess." Dennis opened his mouth, and she cut him off with an impatient motion. Then she sighed and lightened her tone. "You can barely walk, and it has less to do with your injuries than it does with the amount of meds you're taking. I've studied enough medicine, and seen enough real-life examples before that, to know the signs. It may seem like those pills are helping, but they're not. Not in the long run."

Dennis gave her a dirty look. She stared back at him, waiting to see if he'd deny it. He flushed and looked away.

After what seemed like a hundred years, Dennis heaved a sigh, and his shoulders slumped. Shame crossed his face. "I know I'm out of shape and not operating at my best, physically or mentally. I should cut back on my meds."

"No. You should stop taking them period. It'd be better to move slow because you're hurting than because you're too stoned to travel." Kim gave him a stern look, trying to copy the expression her great-aunt had sometimes used when she was really angry.

Dennis winced under her glare but rallied enough to offer a feeble response. "Kim, I have a chronic condition."

"I know. Which means it's something you have to live with." Kim swung her feet down and sat forward, resting her elbows on her knees. "Look, I know. Your hip's a problem, and you've probably got chronic pain issues that will have to be managed. But the fact is, they aren't going to go away. The way you're dealing with them, trying to numb them and pretend they aren't a problem—that's not healthy. Any pre-med student could tell you that."

"I don't know what else I'm supposed to do." Dennis shook his head.

"Surely you had therapy exercises you were supposed to do after the first accident."

"I did." He nodded. "And I did them."

"After the second accident as well?" She raised an eyebrow, and Dennis flushed and looked away again.

Kim sighed. "Look, there are pain management exercises, and there are exercises to help heal the muscles and get them working. It isn't easy, and it isn't fun, and I can get why you wouldn't want to deal with it right now, but there's a trade-off."

"Trade-off?" Dennis looked at her.

"Clearer head. You'll be able to get stronger. And your hip might actually heal if you stop pushing too far because you've numbed it so much you can't tell when you're doing more damage. Plus, you'll feel better overall. More like yourself." Kim shrugged. "That's what I think, at least." She met his gaze. "What could it hurt?"

Dennis made a face. "Kim, it's not that easy." He sighed again and leaned his head back. "It's just not. What you're talking about takes a long time. Months, years even."

"Sure it does. But you can take it one step at a time. That's how most people do it. Anyway, before this whole apocalypse thing happened, there were thousands of people living with chronic injuries and getting by without narcotics. If other people can do it, then a guy who used to be called 'Super Soldier Sullivan' ought to be able to." She gave him a challenging look. "Even in these circumstances. Anyway, those pills won't last forever. Sooner or later, you won't be able to scavenge for any more, and then your decision will be made for you."

Dennis sat quiet for a moment, scowling at the far wall as if it had offended him. Then he shook his head. "Even if you're right, what am I supposed to do? I promised I'd get you to Memphis, and I won't be able to do both things at once. Treating chronic pain and traveling at the same time would be difficult."

Kim bit her lip then met his eyes. "I know. But Lewis—Lewis knows about your meds. And your addiction." She saw Dennis flinch and continued speaking before he could say anything. "He mentioned it when you went for your breath of fresh air after dinner."

"And?"

"And he said that if you wanted to come clean, get your head on straight, he'd let us stay here in Humboldt while you recovered and got your feet under you. I could help out around the community, so it wouldn't be like we were freeloading or anything." Kim folded her arms around herself. Her desire to continue to Memphis was warring with the hope that a little patience might result in a better companion for the road—and a better protector.

Dennis frowned at her, but he didn't look angry. "What about getting to Memphis? You were pretty set on getting there as soon as possible."

Kim swallowed hard. This was it. She had to make a choice. She took a deep breath. "I know. But if you decide you want to get clean, if you want to stay and detox and recover from your addiction as well as maybe start healing your hip for real, then…then I'm okay with that." A clean Dennis would probably be the asset she'd thought he'd be from the beginning. A clean Dennis would be worth waiting for. She hoped, anyway.

Dennis startled. "I thought—"

"I know what you think, and I know what I told you. But after watching you for the past week, I think this might be more important." Kim scowled. "The way you've been going, I'm not sure you'd even make it to Memphis."

Dennis winced at the candid observation, and his jaw clenched. "I made it this far."

"Yeah, barely. You really think you can keep looting stores and stumbling along, all the way to Memphis? Even if you could, you know what my great-aunt and her husband are like. You really want to deal with them in that state?" Kim smirked.

Dennis grimaced. She knew he was imagining how Carol would handle him if he came staggering in, addicted and stoned while he was supposed to be taking care of her family. Great-Aunt Carol didn't like cops at the best of times, but she wouldn't tolerate a drug addict former cop in her home or on her land. That went double for Dennis, whom she despised.

Carol might accept him, grudgingly, if he was useful as a fighter or in another capacity. But if he showed up strung out and stumbling the way he had been? Not a chance.

He was wavering, she could see it. "Dennis, you wanted to stay in Murray, and you agreed to come this far because I demanded that you do so. But now I'm asking you to consider accepting Lewis Danville's offer. I'm really okay with staying here long enough for you to get clean and heal if it means you'll be stronger and more alert when we get on the road again."

Dennis nodded, though his eyes were distant. She wasn't sure he was actually looking at her. Kim sat back and watched him. She'd said all she could say and had made her argument the best way she knew how.

After several minutes, Dennis looked at her, shadows in his eyes. "It won't be easy, Kim. Detox and recovery never is."

"I know that."

Dennis shook his head. "I don't think you do. Everyone thinks they know what it's like, but trust me, you don't know unless you've been there and gone through it, or helped someone close to you through it. That's just the truth."

He looked her in the eyes, and she saw emotions she didn't really have a good name for in his face, despite his attempt at a stoic demeanor. "It's ugly, Kim. Once the detox and recovery is over, there's still the issue of the chronic pain to be managed. It's a never-ending battle. Good days can be close to normal, but bad days bad days are hell."

"Worse than trying to hobble down a road in the middle of a disaster when you're so drugged you can't think straight?"

Dennis looked at her for several minutes. She matched his gaze, aware he was searching for something, and hoped she could help him find it.

Finally, he gave her a wry twist of something that might be a smile. "You might be right."

"So you'll think about it? About getting clean?"

"Yeah. I'll think about it." He shoved himself to his feet. "I'm gonna take a walk with Mutt while I do."

"I can take her out."

Dennis shook his head and grabbed his crutch. "No. I need the fresh air and the movement. It'll be good for me." He gave her another of his wry, twisted smiles. "You just rest and relax while you have the chance. I won't be long."

She was tempted, but she was concerned about him. "I could come with you."

He shook his head again. "No, I don't think so. I do my best thinking alone, and I'd just as soon take the time to breathe and sort out my thoughts."

She was still reluctant, but she was also tired, and her blisters hadn't fully healed. She slumped back against the sofa. "Okay. If you say so." She rolled her head back. "Maybe I'll try to get a shower and a change of clothes while you're out."

"You should." Dennis nodded, then tapped his leg. "Come on, Mutt." The large dog stood up and came to his side, and the two of them left the room. Less than a minute later, she heard the front door close.

She kicked off her shoes and slouched against the sofa, enjoying the softness against her back and the comfort of being in a house with a roof over her head, real furniture, and the possibility of real meals— even a chance of a shower.

After a few minutes, she sat up and shoved herself free of the sofa. A shower and a change of clothing were just too tempting to pass up. She grabbed her pack and heaved it over one shoulder, then climbed the stairs to the second floor.

There were two bedrooms, and the second one had a full bathroom attached. Kim dove into it and dropped her pack on the floor. She went to the bathroom and poked the toilet, then twisted the handle of the faucet. The pipes spluttered and spat, then released a stream of almost clear water. Lewis must have had someone connect them to the water while he was prepping the house.

She didn't like the man, and she wasn't sure she ever would, but that water coming out of the shower head made her want to give him a hug. She grinned and darted into the other room to dig a change of clothes free of her backpack.

Thirty minutes later, she felt somewhat cleaner and a hundred times better. The water hadn't been warm, but at least it was clean. There hadn't been any soap or shampoo, but thanks to Dennis insisting that she take a washcloth and small towel, she had what she needed to at least scrub a few layers of grime off her skin and out of her hair. The clean clothes against her skin felt like a small slice of heaven.

She padded out into the bedroom, wet hair soaking her shoulders as she went. She found the small hair tie she'd used to keep her hair out of her face and wound it absently around the damp locks. The air was chilly, with no central heating or small portable heaters, and she shivered a little as she looked around.

There were sheets on the bed. And pillows. She wondered if they'd been there all along or been brought in when the water was turned on. Not that it mattered. They were still soft and comfortable when she flopped into them, and she gave a soft moan of pleasure at the sensation on her skin.

After a moment, she rolled over, looking at the ceiling. She was glad to be safe and comfortable, but she was also confused. She was curious.

What kind of people had lived in this house before? Was it really okay for them to just take over someone's home?

Did she really want to stay in Humboldt long enough for Dennis to go through detox and whatever recovery he needed to go through to be in decent shape? She wasn't sure. On one hand, it could only help if he was in better condition. On the other, it would take days, perhaps even a week or two, for him to be close to functional. At least, that was the case if what she remembered from her studies in addiction and its consequences was accurate. Even once he was clean, he would still be in terrible pain.

With a groan, she shoved herself into a sitting position. She was so tired and so frustrated, there was no sense letting her thoughts run in circles.

She was too restless to sleep, so she rose from the bed and padded out into the hall to explore the house. There was a typical hallway with white plaster walls and pictures on either side. The photos gave her a good idea of what the family looked like. Two men and two women were in most of the photos, slowly changing ages as the images progressed. A family of four, though there was no telling if they'd all been here when the EMP went off.

Two bedrooms, one small study that looked like it might have been a bedroom in the past, and a small craft room occupied the upper floor. Downstairs, she found a kitchen and the sitting room, and another large room that she wasn't sure what it was for.

The kitchen had some basic pots, pans, and utensils, equipment she knew how to use but nothing too fancy. Looking in the defunct fridge was probably pointless, so she didn't bother, but she did check the pantry. There was nothing there, not that she'd expected there to be, given what Lewis had told them earlier.

She shut the door with a scowl. "Would have been nice if he'd given us a few basics in case we get hungry later."

She moved back into the living room and flopped into the sofa again. She felt restless for more than one reason. Dennis had been gone a long time.

She wanted to believe it was nothing. That he was just out for a walk and taking his time with his injuries. Or maybe he'd stopped to take a breath, really think things over. There was no reason to worry about Dennis.

Besides, Lewis Danville said they had a militia on guard, so it wasn't like Dennis was going to get jumped in the street or robbed in a back alley. That would have been reassuring if she trusted Lewis Danville, or the militia in general. The problem was, she didn't trust either of them. And she couldn't get rid of the nagging feeling that something was wrong.

She tried to distract herself by looking around the room again, but there wasn't much to see besides the books on some of the shelves. The sun had almost set, and there wasn't enough light for her to read by, so Kim ignored the books for the moment.

She tried to relax enough to sleep, but it was impossible when she was alone and worried about where Dennis was. What if he'd fallen over and couldn't get up without help? What if he'd taken his pills and finally taken too many? What if he'd passed out during his walk and collapsed in some dark place that meant no one would find him for hours?

With a growl of frustration, Kim rose and grabbed her shoes along with two clean pairs of socks. She might as well go look for him, given that she'd do nothing but worry uselessly otherwise.

She put her shoes on, went up and got her jacket and a flashlight, and went to the door. Dennis had left her the key, so she locked the door behind her. She clicked the light on and glanced down the street both ways, hoping to see Dennis coming up the road. But there was no sign of him. With a sigh, she picked a direction and started walking, looking for any sign of man or dog.

One block, then two, then three. Kim felt her jaw clenching.

How far can he go? I thought he was only out for a short walk!

She turned up another street, wondering if his addiction had driven him to seek more opioids in the town.

She was crossing the street and heading for where she thought she'd seen the small supermarket when she heard a shout. "Hey you! Stop right there!"

She twisted in the direction of the voice and made out two figures walking toward her, carrying guns and flashlights. She grimaced. Members of the militia. She stayed where she was, not bothering to try and escape. She didn't want to risk getting shot at by some guy with a rifle and an itchy trigger finger.

The two men stalked up to her, and one of them leveled his rifle in her face. "Identify yourself."

"Kim Nakamura. I came in with Lewis Danville this afternoon." She held her hands up.

"What are you doing out after curfew?" The words snarled out, the tone a match to the suspicious scowl on his face.

"I was looking for my friend Dennis. He's an older guy, with a dog."

"What's he doing out after curfew?" The gun shifted as if the man might shoot her, and Kim's shoulders stiffened in anger and fear.

"We didn't know there was a curfew." She swallowed. "Lewis never told us."

"Militia Leader Danville would never forget to explain the rules. I think you're lying."

She winced. "I promise I'm not. Look, you can take me to Militia Leader Danville's house if you don't believe me."

That earned her another scowl, and the two men exchanged a long look full of suspicion and anger. Then the man standing behind her prodded her with the barrel of his gun. "All right. Get moving. And no sudden moves or stupid tricks, or we'll put a hole through you."

"Not planning on it." Kim stepped forward and winced as the second man seized her arm and dragged her around, back down the road.

The two men marched her down the road, one holding her arm in a bruising grip, the other prodding her with the barrel of his gun with every few steps. She half hoped she'd see Dennis as they marched past the house, but of course there was no sign of him. Her mouth twisted in a surge of bitter anger.

Of course he's not around when I need him. He never is.

She kept walking, alone.

11

LEE KINGSTON JONES

Traveling with Andre—Mr. Atkinson, Lee had to remind himself —wasn't so bad once he got used to it. Mr. Atkinson was content to walk along at a brisk place and let Lee follow as he wanted. Sometimes he would ask a question about the surrounding area or about possible police presence. Other times, he would hum quietly to himself as he strolled along.

Lee trotted along behind him, stopping now and then to gather a little bit of food or get himself a drink of water. There wasn't much food to find, but it was something, and he'd made do with less. He wasn't sure why he was following Mr. Atkinson when he was aware the large man was dangerous.

Maybe it was because the guy had listened when he talked. Sure, he'd nearly broken Lee's arm, but then, Lee had started that confrontation. His father Max Jones probably would have gone ahead and snapped the bone to teach him a lesson.

And the guy had dealt with the police officers instead of just waiting until they hauled Lee away and then going about his business. Granted, he'd killed them, but in a strange and terrifying way, he'd sort of saved Lee. That was worth spending some time looking into, wasn't it? Plus, Atkinson was a big man, the type of man who could intimidate others easily. If he let Lee tag along with him, then he could keep Lee safe.

Safe wasn't a concept Lee had much experience with, but if there was any chance of even a margin of safety to be had by following Mr. Atkinson, then he was going to follow until the big man drove him away.

They walked all day, stopping only now and then for Andre to eat. Lee's feet were sore, but he didn't bother to complain. Mr. Atkinson probably wouldn't want him around if he whined like a little kid. So he sucked it up and kept walking, putting one foot in front of the other with dogged determination.

As the sun dropped low in the sky, Andre turned off the road and headed up into the woods. He walked a little way through the trees until they were no longer visible from the road. Lee scrambled along in Atkinson's wake.

Finally, the man stopped in a clearing. He looked around, made a satisfied noise, and dropped his bag with a thump. "Lee."

Lee jumped when the man addressed him, startled at having his name spoken for the first time in hours. "Yes, Mr. Atkinson?"

"I assume a young hunter, as you proclaim yourself to be, would know how to build a fire." Andre turned to him.

"Yeah. Sure." Lee bobbed his head. "I know how. Do you have any matches, or a lighter? I can do it without, but that's easiest and fastest."

"I have matches in my bag." The older man bent over his bag, opened it, and extracted a small, flat package, which he tossed Lee's direction. Lee caught it with fumbling hands.

"Okay. Be just a minute, Mr. Atkinson."

"Andre." The big man sniffed in his direction as he gave Lee an enig-matic look. "I prefer Andre. Mr. Atkinson is so formal, and we have been traveling together for the day." He gave Lee a smile that might have been pleasant if Lee hadn't been aware of what the man was. Instead, it sent a small shiver along his spine.

"Sure. Andre." Lee nodded, then bent to the process of scraping out a fire pit and ringing it with stones he found nearby. He added some small twigs and dried leaves and lit a match. The first one didn't catch. He lit another, pressing it to the leaves with shaking fingers.

The second one spluttered. Lee lit and added another one, then pock-eted the matchbook and bent to breathe on the embers and the small flames, coaxing them to grow larger and consume the available fuel. When it was big enough, he added more twigs and then larger branches until the blaze was a modest one, flickering among arm-sized limbs. Only when he was sure the fire would keep did he sit back.

Andre watched him from a seat near the trees, one eyebrow raised over his chiseled face. "Well done, Lee."

Lee flushed at the unexpected praise. "It's just a little fire. My old man taught me how to build these when I was, like, six."

"Still." Andre tipped his head to one side. "Students learn lessons best with positive reinforcement, or so I've read."

"Yeah, well, it's not a big deal." Lee shrugged and dropped to the ground, glad to be off his feet.

"As you will." Andre reached into his bag and grabbed something else, which he tossed over the fire toward Lee. Lee caught it and found himself staring at a can of chili. "For your work and your services in avoiding unwanted trouble."

"Thanks." Lee popped the top of the can, then looked around, wondering how he was going to heat it. He watched as Andre pulled another can from the bag and opened it, then set it near the coals. Lee copied the movement. If it worked for Andre, it was good enough for him.

He watched the chili heat, the light dancing off the brown liquid and the chunks of meat and beans. It looked a bit like Corvelle's partner's chest after Andre had shot him. Lee swallowed hard, nauseated. He wasn't going to turn down food, but he couldn't deny that his stomach was twisting up a little and threatening to expel the food he'd eaten. He swallowed a bit of chili with a grimace.

Andre gave him a disinterested look. "Food disagree with you?"

"Not at all." Lee forced himself to swallow another bite of chili. "I was just thinking. I mean, the way you handled those cops. Seemed like you'd done that sort of thing before."

"I have." Andre's candid admission made Lee choke. "When the occasion warranted."

"Seriously? What kind of occasion…" He stifled the question and ducked his head. "Sorry. I know it's none of my business."

Andre shrugged. "If you wish to follow me, you might as well know a few things." Andre rolled his shoulders and finished his chili before leaning against the tree. "If you're interested."

"Um, well, I guess I wouldn't mind knowing where you're going, and," Lee gulped, "why you killed someone."

"A reasonable ask. Appropriate for a young man in your situation." Andre nodded cordially.

Lee wasn't sure what was happening, but he knew enough to go along with it. "Okay, so where are we going?"

"We are going to Memphis, where I will contact the members of a motorcycle club known as the Black Rats. I used to work for them."

"Okay." Lee nodded. "You were, like, an enforcer or something?"

Andre's expression turned amused. "No. I carried heroin between different motorcycle clubs and gangs. A lucrative and comfortable business—one I excelled at and enjoyed."

Lee nodded. "And you got caught?"

"No. One of my men tried to double-cross me, and I shot him." Andre scowled. "That should have been the end of the matter."

Lee winced. "Something went wrong?"

Andre's scowl deepened. "My wife ratted me out to the police. She testified against me and proceeded to tell the police about the shooting —which I might have passed off as self-defense—and other activities of mine. She convinced them I was a criminal and a monster."

"Oh." Lee took a deep breath, weighing his words. "She sounds like kind of a...a real piece of work."

"She is. And she'll pay for what she did. I've had quite a long time to consider what kind of punishment would be appropriate." Andre's cool, level voice made the hairs on the back of Lee's neck stand up. The firelight flickered on his face, sharpening his features, and the more Lee looked at him, the less human he seemed. Lee gulped.

He had a good idea of what kinds of things Andre would consider an appropriate punishment for a traitor. He hoped he never made Andre angry enough to consider using those punishments on him.

"Are you armed?"

The words took Lee by surprise. He blinked across the fire. "What?"

"Do you have a weapon? You didn't use one when the police stopped you."

Lee flinched. "No. I lost my knife when we…when we met." That was better than reminding Andre that he'd jumped him and nearly gotten himself killed. "I didn't stop to try and find it after we talked."

"Ah. Well, in that case." Andre bent over toward his bag and rummaged around in it for a moment. Then he pulled something out and held it toward Lee. "Here."

Lee rose and came around the fire to take the object. It turned out to be a large bowie knife in a utilitarian sheath. "A knife?"

"I assume as a hunter you know how to use one."

"Sure I do." Lee pulled it free and studied the edge, gleaming in the firelight. It looked sharp. He slid it back into its sheath. "Thanks."

Andre gave him a distracted wave and tipped his head back, clearly done with the conversation. He looked to be settling against the tree to sleep. Lee stumbled his way around the fire and back to his previous seat. After a moment, he lowered himself carefully to the leafy ground and did his best to make himself comfortable.

It wasn't the most comfortable place to sleep, but at least it wasn't anywhere near his father, and Andre wasn't trying to beat him up over little things. Yet, anyway.

He tucked the knife in its sheath close to his chest and closed his eyes. He couldn't help remembering the way Andre had hit the first officer and the crunch of his jaw as it shattered. He also couldn't stop thinking of how the gun had sounded, the squishing of the bullets thumping into Corvelle's chest.

The memory made him queasy, but he swallowed the feeling.

The sounds had been scary, sure, and a little nauseating, but it wasn't that much different from all the times Max had thudded his fists into him, was it? And no one had ever stopped Max, not when he was on the force or after he retired. So why should Lee care if someone else was on the receiving end?

Killing was harsh, but then, was it any worse than beating up a kid just because you were out of beer? He was betting Andre didn't think so. Lee also didn't think Andre would beat him up if he was kept happy. And it might be easier to keep Andre happy than it had been to placate his old man.

Lee scooted a little closer to the fading heat of the fire and exhaled, forcing his muscles to relax.

Andre might be a remorseless killer and a psychopath, but at least he wasn't Max Jones. That was good enough for now.

12

KIM NAKAMURA

B y the time the Danville house came into sight, Kim's hand was numb with the lack of blood flow to her fingertips, and she was sure she had a bruise on her back from the pressure of the gun. She grimaced as the two men hustled her up the two stairs onto the front porch. The one holding her arm knocked on the door. "Militia Leader!"

"Come in."

Joan opened the door, and the two men marched Kim inside. The three of them came to a stop in the dining area, and Kim fought the urge to snarl in frustration.

Dennis was sitting there with Lewis at the table, Mutt beside him on the linoleum floor. The two men looked up from their conversation as they entered, and Mutt huffed and surged to her feet, reacting to Kim's expression.

Lewis was on his feet a moment later. "What's all this?"

The man holding her spoke first. "We caught her out on the street after curfew. She said she was looking for someone."

Lewis waved a hand, and the man released her arm. Kim grimaced and tried to rub the feeling back into her arm.

"I'm sure there's a good reason for Kim being out after dark," Lewis said.

Kim nodded. "I was worried because Dennis hadn't come home. I was afraid he might have fallen or something."

"There you go. Perfectly reasonable explanation." Lewis smiled. "That'll be all, boys. In the future, be sure you treat our treasured guests with more care. You can't go around manhandling Miss Nakamura like she's a criminal."

The hypocrisy of that statement, coming from him, was enough to make Kim snort. She turned it into a quick cough as everyone looked at her. "Sorry. Just a little winded."

"You boys need to be more careful." Lewis gestured again. "Now go on, get out of here, and pass the word along to the rest of the militia."

"Yes sir." Both young men saluted and left.

Kim scowled after them, then turned back to the table.

Lewis waved her to a seat. "Sorry about that, Kim. We have a curfew here in Humboldt to help keep things safe at night. Unfortunately, some of the young men who work as guards can be a little overenthusiastic about enforcing it."

Kim slid into the seat reluctantly. "Why didn't you tell us about the curfew?"

"I didn't think of it, I guess. I didn't think it would be an issue. Of course, I'll have to tell you all the rules we have now." Lewis offered her an apologetic smile.

That was distracting enough to take her mind off her aching arm. "What? Why?"

Dennis answered her. "Because I've decided to take Lewis's offer, and your suggestion." He pulled a bottle out of his pocket and set it on the table. "We'll be staying in Humboldt while I get clean and get my head on straight."

Astonishment shot through her. She sat forward. "Really?"

"Yes. I came over here to give Lewis my pills and tell him what we planned." Dennis looked at her as if asking for approval. "I know it'll delay us getting to Memphis, but I thought the benefits might outweigh the delay."

"I agree." Kim nodded.

Lewis leaned across and took the bottle of pills. "We'll put these in the pharmacy. I'm sure they'll be put to good use."

"I don't doubt it." Dennis nodded. His face already looked a little pale and drawn. Of course, if he hadn't had his meds in a while, that was to be expected. He levered himself to his feet. "But if there's a curfew, I expect we ought to get back to our house."

"Oh, that's probably true. Don't want to make too many exceptions or order will fall apart." Lewis rose as well, and Kim followed suit. "I have to say, Dennis, I'm real proud of you. I know it's a hard thing you're doing now, a really hard thing. But I always knew you were a brave fellow."

"I don't know about that." Dennis shook his head.

"Nonsense. It takes a brave man to face up to his problems and try to correct them. You're a real hero, Dennis, and don't you forget it. A real American hero. You'll know that, too, once you've come out the other side of this." Lewis shook Dennis's hand and took up a lantern. "I'll walk you back to your house so you don't have to worry about the guards getting all up in arms again."

"Thanks." Kim followed Lewis outside, then fell back to walk beside Dennis as he and Mutt made their way up the street.

The trip was made in silence. Kim used the time to study the man who limped along gamely beside her. She hadn't really expected him to take her up on her suggestion. She hadn't really expected him to take the chance. All the times they'd talked about it before, he'd shown no inclination to listen.

Dennis stumbled and caught himself on Mutt's shoulder. The large dog huffed and tilted her head up, as if encouraging him. Kim started to offer him her arm, but Dennis was moving again before she had a chance, hobbling along with one hand gripping his crutch and one hand close to Mutt, as if the dog was an extra support.

She hadn't liked his addiction or the way he acted under the influence of his pills, but she had to admit Dennis was tough. Stubborn. Determined. Now that he was actually making an effort instead of excuses, she could feel a kernel of admiration for him sprouting within her. He wasn't perfect, but he was making an effort, and she could respect that.

She wasn't sure which impressed her more—that he was listening to her and Lewis and taking their advice, or the fact that he'd actually given his pills to Lewis. There was no turning back now. He was really going to try and get clean. She didn't know exactly how hard that was for an addict, but even so, he was going to do it. And Dennis was stubborn enough to go through with it.

They arrived at the house without incident, and Lewis watched them from the street as they made their way inside. Kim opened the door and helped Dennis through, then closed and locked it behind her.

In the light of the lantern, Dennis looked visibly worse. He was pale and sweating, and his hand by his side was shaking slightly. His eyes were glassy with pain and the first stages of the detox. Kim grimaced. "You should get upstairs and try to get some sleep."

"Yeah. What little I can before the worst of it comes." Dennis sighed and scrubbed his free hand down his face. "This isn't going to be pretty, I'm afraid. We're gonna be stuck here for a while."

"I know. That's okay." Kim smiled at Dennis, almost laughing at the startled expression on his face. "I told you I'd be willing to stick around for a while if you wanted to take the chance to kick your habit."

"I know, but—" Dennis broke off as she gave him a quick hug.

"It's okay. Really." She grinned and leaned back against the door. "I know how hard kicking a habit is. So," she swallowed an unfamiliar lump in her throat, "I'm proud of you. For deciding to finally deal with your problem."

Dennis stood still for a long moment, and she thought she saw the sheen of moisture in his eyes. Then he cleared his throat and nodded his head once. "Thank you, Kim."

"You're welcome. Get some rest." Kim turned and darted up the stairs before either of them could say anything else. She didn't want to indulge in too much sappiness.

She was proud of Dennis for taking the first step to reclaiming his life, but she couldn't help being worried about the place they'd found shelter. The aching bruise on her arm reminded her that everything wasn't perfect.

Dennis might be on the road to getting better, but she couldn't quite shake the feeling that they might have chosen to make their bed in a minefield of unseen dangers—ones she wasn't sure she was ready to handle with Dennis incapacitated and unable to assist her.

13

LEE KINGSTON JONES

S *nap.*

The loud, sharp sound shocked Lee out of slumber. He was up and halfway to his feet before he realized where he was and what he'd heard.

It wasn't his father breaking open a beer bottle. It was Andre cracking open another can of chili and sticking it into the coals of the newly rebuilt fire. Lee sat up and eyed the man warily. "Sorry, Andre. Didn't mean to sleep so late."

"It's fine." Andre fished another can out of the bag and tossed it to him. "I'm not on a schedule, and if I wanted you awake, I would have awakened you."

Lee felt the cold length of the knife he was still clutching close to his ribs and resolved to make sure he woke up early every morning so Andre would never consider it necessary to wake him. Andre might wake him with a boot to the ribs or something equally unpleasant.

He opened the tin of chili and wrinkled his nose. "Mr. Atkinson— Andre—do you really like chili?"

"It's food, and it's better than prison fare." Andre looked at him with a bland expression and a raised eyebrow. "Do you have some objection to it, Lee?"

Lee flushed. "Not really. I was just wondering if you might want something different."

"What are you suggesting?" Andre was still giving him that look, but at least he wasn't getting angry, the way Lee's father would if he were questioned. Lee took it as a good sign.

He gestured to the surrounding woodlands. "I mean, there's turkeys in these woods. I could hunt one if you wanted."

"You think you could manage to hunt a turkey?" Andre looked at him.

Lee looked around. The woods were pretty much the same as the ones he'd grown up in. "Yeah. Sure. I can probably get a turkey. Just need a gun and something about the size of a pill bottle for a turkey call."

Andre gave him a bemused look, but reached into his belt and produced the gun he'd taken from the cops the day before. He then rummaged in his bag and found a small pill bottle that looked like it held generic painkillers. He held out both. "Please, do demonstrate."

"Sure." Lee reached out and took both. He usually hunted turkeys with a rifle, but he could make do with a pistol. He'd just have to let the turkey get a little closer before he fired.

He pulled out the knife and carefully dug a line around the edge of the pill bottle top in a half circle. He cracked it out, then cut the bottom off the bottle. He just needed a little bit of something for the latex. He dug in his pockets, but he couldn't find anything. He thought about asking Andre if maybe he had something, but he wanted to prove he could do this without help.

Well, he'd have to improvise. He knew how to make a leaf whistle. Or maybe he could use some of the paper from the chili can. He ripped it

94

off and tested it. It wasn't perfect, but he could make it work, and turkeys weren't the brightest game in the world. All he needed to do was get a turkey to answer him or react to his presence.

Andre watched him work. "What are you making?"

Lee glanced up. "Turkey call. It'll make a noise that will encourage turkeys to respond. Once they give away their positions, you can chase them into the open and shoot one."

"That sounds promising." Andre sat back and watched as Lee finished making his preparations for the impromptu hunting trip. "I'm interested to see your results."

Lee nodded. "Give me an hour or so." He tucked the gun close and the knife into his belt then clambered to his feet. "I'll be back."

Andre leaned back against the tree. "I'll keep the fire going."

Lee took that as a dismissal and wandered off into the trees.

It took a little time to get far enough away from the camp that the turkeys wouldn't be spooked. Fortunately, there wasn't a lot of wind, and it was still early enough in the day that the turkeys would be active. As long as no breezes picked up to put him upwind, and he kept himself quiet enough, it wouldn't be too hard to get a bird.

He settled into a position across from a likely stand of trees. The underbrush was thick enough to provide a good hiding place for nests, and he'd seen a few feathers in the nearby undergrowth. That meant turkeys moved in and out of the area.

He set the turkey call to his lips and blew. No response, but he hadn't expected one on the first attempt. He waited for a few minutes. Then he repeated it.

He shifted position after the second attempt and made an effort to blend into the forest. After several minutes, he blew the turkey call again.

This time, he got a response. The sharp noise of a tom turkey. Lee pointed his gun in that direction and fired.

Turkeys bolted from the undergrowth, none seeming to be wounded. Lee sighted the gun on one particular specimen and fired again. He missed with his second shot, growled in frustration, and fired a third time.

The turkey fell over with a squawk, but then got up and started running.

Lee swore and got up, racing after the bird. It flapped its wings uselessly. Still, it wouldn't take much for the bird to get away from him. He had to catch it. He didn't want to have to tell Andre he'd wasted three bullets.

Lee lunged for the bird as it jerked left, just out of his grasp. Lee's foot caught on a stick, and he tumbled, falling forward onto his chest with a breath-stealing slam. His chin hit the forest floor and slammed his teeth together.

It took a second for the air to rush back into his lungs, and when it did, he gasped greedily before pushing himself to his feet once more. The turkey was getting away.

Go, Lee!

He stumbled after the bird, regained his stride, and was off once more. This time he waited until he was closer before dashing for the bird. It squawked loudly as he grabbed it. The turkey flapped its wings, batting at him painfully, but he managed to grab its neck before jerking the bird sharply and ending its struggles.

Lee panted, the turkey in his hands. He dabbed at his chin with the back of his hand, and it came back with some blood, but not too much. Probably just a small scrape. But he'd done it. He'd caught the bird.

Lee grinned. The turkey was moderate-sized, probably not that old, but more than big enough to feed two people. It was also small enough that he'd have no trouble carrying it back to the campsite.

He transferred his grip to the bird's feet, avoiding the sharp spurs, and hauled it up. Then he began the trek back to the camp, trying to ignore the smell of the bird's loosened bowels and the tinge of blood from his chin and where he'd shot and wounded the bird.

Andre looked up in surprise as he came stumbling back through the trees. "I didn't expect you back so soon."

"Well, morning's prime hunting time, and I got lucky. There was a flock only about a hundred yards or so up that way." Lee dropped the turkey and stretched his shoulders to pop them. He flexed his arms and rolled his wrists.

"Impressive. And you managed with a pistol and a modified pill bottle. Well done." Andre's voice was warm, genuinely pleased in a way his old man had never sounded, not even on his best days. Lee flushed at the praise. "Do you know how to prepare the turkey?"

"I just have to field dress it." Lee drew the knife Andre had given him and crouched at the turkey's feet. He reached up and began prodding the feathers until he found the breastbone and then its tip. He carefully inserted his knife there and began to cut down to the tail. He reached in and pulled out the guts. It was a nasty job and got him smeared with gore, reminding him uncomfortably of the policemen the day before. He brushed the thought aside, telling himself that turkey was delicious, and he'd enjoy eating it. The blood was just a part of every hunter's work.

He looked up at Andre. "You want the giblets?"

"I've never found them particularly appetizing." Andre was watching him work with an interested expression that made Lee slightly proud.

Guts were dispensed with, and he began the process of plucking the bird. It would have been easier with a hot water bath, but he was used to doing it the hard way. He started at the head, cut it off, then began working his way down the body, removing every feather with methodical efficiency. When the last feather was gone, Lee bent his effort to removing the feet.

"Here. Let me try." Andre moved closer. "A little judicious use of force sometimes goes a long way."

Lee sat back as Andre severed the legs at the lowest joint with two brutal jerks of the knife. He couldn't help admiring the smooth motion and the ease of Andre's work. "Nice."

Andre handed the knife back to him. "I assume you know how to butcher as well?"

Lee smiled and took the knife. "Yep. I know how to butcher as well."

"I'll make preparations to cook the turkey then." Andre rose to his feet and moved off into the trees, where he broke off branches for makeshift skewers.

By the time Lee had finished cutting the bird apart, some time later, Andre had produced a half-dozen skewers for the meat. He passed half the skewers to Lee and joined him in sticking the meat onto the sticks and into the fire.

Lee jumped as Andre pulled out a water bottle from his bag and handed it to him. "Here. Clean up."

"Thanks." Lee lifted himself to his feet and moved a little ways away so he could wash his arms without splashing the fire. He washed the blood off his face and hands, then took a hefty swallow of what was left in the bottle. He couldn't do much about his clothing, but he was a neat butcher, so his clothes weren't too badly splattered.

He came back to the fire to find Andre testing the turkey. He crouched on the other side of the fire. Andre offered him a smile. "You've provided quite a feast for us, Lee. Well done."

Lee flushed. "I just figured, you know, some fresh food would be welcome."

"It's quite welcome." Andre lifted one of the smaller pieces of turkey away from the fire. "This looks about done." Then to Lee's surprise, he offered the skewer to him. "Here, you should eat."

Lee stared at him. "I thought you'd want the first bite?"

Andre shook his head. "You hunted the bird and did most of the cleaning. Of course you deserve to be the first to eat."

It was so unlike anything his father would have done that it took Lee a few moments of dumbfounded staring before he managed to reach up and take the skewer. "Umm, thanks."

"You're welcome."

Lee nibbled on the turkey and watched as Andre picked up another piece and began to eat it. "You know, no one ever said anything like that to me before."

"That's a shame. Skills such as yours should be nurtured." Andre shrugged his massive shoulders. "I don't believe in wasting valuable skills such as your talent for hunting and preparing game."

Lee ducked his head to hide his smile and the blush that stole across his cheeks.

Andre was dangerous, but maybe…maybe he wasn't too bad. How could he be, when he was willing to acknowledge Lee's skills and abilities? It was more than anyone else had ever done.

Maybe Andre's being dangerous was better than he'd previously thought.

14

KIM NAKAMURA

The sound of someone gagging and heaving directly outside her window was not something Kim wanted to hear first thing in the morning. Unfortunately, that was the first thing she heard when she pried herself out of a deep slumber the morning after their arrival in Humboldt.

She grimaced and stumbled out of bed to the window. She blinked, scrubbed gunk out of her eyes, and looked down.

Dennis was leaning against a small shed in the backyard, bent over and gagging. Kim had cracked a window to get some fresh air the night before, and the faint smell of sickness came wafting up and made her wrinkle her nose. She frowned, then shut the window and turned away to get dressed.

She pulled on her jeans, socks, and shoes, tied her hair up, and made her way downstairs and outside. She picked her way through the high grass to Dennis's side. "Are you okay?"

Mutt barked. Dennis groaned, gagged, and threw up again. The sharp smell of bile made Kim wince. "Dennis?"

He coughed, then finally managed to turn around and give her a pained look as he leaned against the side of the small shed. "Kim. Did I wake you?"

He had, but she was willing to lie. "Not really. What's going on?"

Dennis made a face and swiped his arm across his mouth. "It's detox. It's a nasty business, and this is one of the nastiest parts of it." He swallowed hard and tried to stifle a groan.

"Why not use the bathroom?"

"Don't want to clog the pipes. Not sure how good the water purification is." Dennis groaned and twisted around to heave into the dirt again.

Kim watched with sympathy. She couldn't help feeling bad for him, but she was also proud he was willing to go through the ordeal. He wasn't yet asking her to give him a fix, the way she'd heard some addicts trying to kick the habit did.

She patted his back as he retched and heaved a few more times, then stepped back as he staggered away from the place where he'd been throwing up. "You done?"

"Think so." Dennis grimaced. "A little sore, but I think I'm finished for a while."

"Want to eat or drink something?"

"Not on your life." Dennis swayed, and Kim moved around to take his weight on his unsupported side. "I'd rather try breakdancing."

"I don't think you're ready for that."

"You're right." Dennis coughed a few times.

Kim laughed lightly as she helped him back into the house and up the stairs. She guided him into the second bedroom and helped him sit on the bed. She would have helped him with his shoes, but Dennis waved her away. "No need for that. I'll manage well enough."

Kim nodded, respecting his need for as much independence as he could manage to sustain. "Sure. I was thinking of going into town, helping out a bit with medical stuff, or whatever they need me to do. You think you'll be okay?"

Dennis nodded. "You go ahead and do whatever you feel like doing. Better than being stuck here with a sick old soldier like me."

Kim hesitated. "Do you want me to bring you anything?"

"Not right now." Dennis shook his head and dropped back onto his pillow.

Kim took the hint and ducked back out of the room. She headed for the front door.

Once outside, it took her a few moments to decide where she wanted to go. She set out toward the Danville residence. It was the best place to go, since she didn't know anyone else in the town.

Lewis's truck was still in the driveway, and she didn't know if Joan even had a car available to her. Kim hesitated at the door, then stepped up and knocked. Seconds later, Joan opened the door.

Kim smiled and offered an awkward smile. "Hi. Is this a bad time?"

"Not at all." Joan swung the door open. "We're happy to have guests. Have you had breakfast yet?"

Kim shook her head. "No. We don't have any food in the house yet, and even if we did, Dennis isn't really up to eating anything."

"I imagine not." Lewis appeared from the living room. "He's probably feeling pretty wretched at the moment."

"That about sums it up." Kim accepted a bowl of oatmeal from Joan and ate a spoonful gratefully. "Thanks."

"Not a problem. We had a little left over." Joan smiled. "So, what brings you by our house?"

Kim ate a few more bites. "Dennis suggested I get out, leave him be while he's feeling like death warmed over. I remember you mentioned you could use someone with medical training, and I thought I could offer to help out while we're here."

Lewis smiled broadly. "That sounds like an excellent idea. You were planning to make rounds after breakfast, weren't you, Joan?"

"Certainly." Joan wiped her hands on a towel. "I'd appreciate any assistance you could give me, Kim."

"I'm glad to do whatever I can." Kim finished her oatmeal and put the dishes in the sink under Joan's direction. "So, what do we do?"

"We'll go to the houses of a few people who need regular care, out to the farms where we might need to help deliver livestock, and then to a small clinic near the supermarket. People know they can find me there if they need something."

"Sounds good. You'll have to tell me what to do with the livestock though."

Joan smiled. "It's not much different from dealing with human wounds. Well, some of it isn't. Some of it is. I'm sure you'll pick it up in no time."

Kim nodded. "Do you have any supplies?"

"I've got an emergency care bag that I refill at the clinic every day." Joan vanished into another room and came back with a large satchel. "We can set up a bag for you as well, if you feel it would be beneficial."

"It probably would help. I don't really have anything of my own. Dennis has a first aid kit, but I wasn't thinking and left it at the house."

"That's fine. I dare say he could make use of the supplies." Joan clicked her tongue. "Addiction is a nasty business, and unfortunately the recovery isn't much better."

"Yeah." Kim followed Joan out the door with a brief shout to tell Lewis they were leaving. They walked down the driveway. "How many patients do you have on your regular visit list?"

"Half a dozen or so. And five different farms. Also, we'll need to check on Mark Cardney."

Kim frowned, trying to remember why the name sounded familiar. "That's the guy who twisted his ankle, right?"

"Exactly." Joan set off down the road. "Best we get started." Kim shrugged and trotted along behind her.

The first house held an older woman. "Mrs. Morgan. Has a heart condition I try to monitor," Joan explained in an undertone as they walked inside. "She's taking medicine for hypertension, but I don't know much more than that."

They went into a living room, and Joan said to Mrs. Morgan, "This is Kim. She's helping me with medical care. Will you allow her to examine you?"

Mrs. Morgan nodded, and Kim approached, trying frantically to remember everything she'd ever learned about conducting a physical examination. Check the temperature, the breathing, the heart rate, and the blood pressure. Maybe check for any inflammation that might be a cold or something else. Ask the patient if anything felt wrong.

She couldn't remember any more. "Do you have a thermometer?"

Joan handed her one. She held it out, and Mrs. Morgan took it in her mouth.

"Normal temperature." Kim returned the thermometer to Joan and took a blood pressure cuff. It took her a little bit of effort and two tries to get a sense of the older woman's blood pressure, but eventually she felt confident enough to remove the cuff and look up at Joan. "Looks pretty normal."

She used a stethoscope to check the woman's lungs, which sounded regular as well. She moved closer. "Can I check your lymph nodes?" She gestured to her own neck.

Mrs. Morgan nodded, and she ran her hands up and down the patient's neck with gentle pressure. "Everything feels normal to me." She sat back. "Mrs. Morgan, is there anything you'd like to tell me about? Anything that doesn't feel well? Headaches, chest pains, stiffness in your shoulder, or tingling in your limbs?"

"None of that, dear. I feel fit as a fiddle." Mrs. Morgan smiled at her.

Kim rose to her feet and dusted her hands off. "In that case, I'd say just keep doing what you're doing, and you should be fine, for a while at least."

Joan and Mrs. Morgan said their goodbyes, and Joan led the way out of the house. Once they were in the road, she spoke. "That was quite well done. You have a touch."

"I was just trying to follow the procedures I remembered from my doctor's visits as a kid." Kim shrugged. "It's not too difficult."

"If you say so." Joan shook her head. "I'm better with animals. I know how to check the temperature of a sheep or the temper of a horse, and I can tell you if a cow is pregnant or has a bloating problem, but I haven't studied human ailments so much."

"There's some overlap, or so I've heard." Kim followed the woman to the next house.

The second person was a man recovering from a concussion caused by an accident on the day of the EMP. His head was still aching, according to him, but his eyes reacted properly to the small penlight Kim borrowed from Joan, and the bruises were healing in what looked like good time. Kim recommended aspirin and rest until he stopped being light sensitive.

The third person was more difficult. "Mr. Craig is diabetic. He hasn't been doing well." Joan led her inside after a polite knock. "We haven't been able to keep any insulin refrigerated."

Kim swallowed hard. "Is he type 1 or type 2?"

"Type 2. Why?" Joan asked.

"Because type 2 is more manageable. We might be able to help him a little." Kim moved to talk to Mr. Craig. "Sir, what do you usually eat?"

Mr. Craig shifted in his seat as she ran him through the standard tests. "Fruit and vegetables, bread and dairy, just like everyone else."

Kim nodded. "Okay. I'd like you to try something, if Joan agrees." She looked at Joan.

"Of course." Joan gestured encouragingly. "If you have an idea, I'd be happy to hear it."

"Try high-protein foods, like meat and peanut butter and other things like that. I'd have to look for a list of what all I'd recommend. If you eat fruit or bread, drink some extra water. If you start noticing the symptoms of low blood sugar, eat a little fruit. If you start feeling like you have high blood sugar, drink more water. And if you can, keep a journal of what you eat and what you feel, and when. We might be able to set up a dietary plan to manage your symptoms." She flushed and looked up at Joan. "I mean, if circumstances allow us to do that?" She hated how her voice wavered uncertainly, but neither of the others seemed to notice.

"I can tell the boys at the supermarket to adjust your rations list." Joan said. She frowned thoughtfully. "Of course, I'll have to discuss it with Lewis and the others in charge of rationing first, and I'm not sure if it's a sustainable long-term plan, but it might be a short-term option."

"Do you think it will be approved?" Mr. Craig asked. "If it helps, would I be able to work some as well?" Mr. Craig looked from one woman to the other. "I could do record keeping, or simple work, like cleaning or sorting."

Joan patted his hand. "Let's see what we can do for you, and then we'll talk about work later," Joan answered. "Come by the pharmacy, and Kim and I will try to have a list for you, and a notebook for you to keep a food diary."

Mr. Craig looked downtrodden, but he nodded. Kim supposed it must be hard to manage a chronic illness with the world the way it was. Still, he'd seemed so worried—but not really about his health. More about rations and working.

And so it went, with Kim trailing along behind Joan, offering what tips and tricks she could dredge up out of her memory. At the farms, she offered her hands instead of her advice. She listened as Joan explained the finer points of checking a cow's pregnancy and a horse's legs for strain, or their mouths for health problems.

Their last stop of the day was the house of Mark Cardney. He greeted them at the door with a set of crutches and a pained smile. "Hey, Doc. Thanks for coming by." He turned his gaze to Kim. "And who's this?"

"This is Kim. She and her friend came into town last night, and she'll be helping me while they're here." Joan herded the man to a seat.

"She has some experience with medicine, so I wanted her to check your ankle."

"I thought it was just a sprain. Be healed in a couple days." Mark shifted in his seat. "It doesn't even hurt that—*ow!*"

Kim looked at him. "It doesn't hurt that bad, right? All I did was touch the bandage."

"I just wasn't expecting it."

"That was the point." Kim began to unwrap the bandage. The limb underneath was swollen, reddish-purple, and painful looking. Kim prodded it, ignoring the hissing and muffled yelps from the limb's owner. "Can you move it?"

There was a twitch and another hissing sound of pain. Kim took the foot firmly and shifted it in a slow circle.

Mark's pained noises escalated into a shriek. "*Owowowowow!* Jeez, that hurts worse than dropping bricks on my hand. What are you doing?"

"Checking to see if you can move the ankle and if the tendons and ligaments are intact, or if there's something broken or torn." Kim manipulated the limb a little more. "I think you might have torn a tendon. Maybe the Achilles? It's hard to say."

She was pretty sure something was torn, but she couldn't identify exactly what. How could anyone diagnose that without an imaging device, like an x-ray, ultrasound, or MRI machine? If there was a way, it wasn't one she'd studied. Which brought her to the next question: how was she supposed to treat the injury?

The normal regimen was twenty-minute intervals of ice and a cast to keep the limb immobile, along with painkillers and keeping the ankle elevated. But there weren't any ready sources of ice that Kim knew of, and she wasn't certain what sort of painkiller supply Humboldt had.

"Are there any sources of cold packs or ice around?" she asked Joan.

Joan frowned. "Not that I know of, but I'd have to check. I wouldn't count on it though."

That was about what she'd expected. "Do you have access to a medical boot?"

"Oh, yes. That's easy enough to come by. They'll have them in the marketplace or the old doctor's clinic." Joan made a note. "Is there anything else you think he needs?"

"Anti-inflammatory medication. Two weeks' supply of pills." She wracked her brain. "Or two, maybe three, injections of corticosteroids, spaced over the same amount of time? Whichever works better with the current supplies. Then we'll probably need to reevaluate."

"I'll double-check the supplies on that front as well." Joan made another note. "I can easily bring everything by later."

Kim nodded and rewrapped the ankle, glad she'd taken first aid training in the past. Once she was done, she rose. "Okay. Until Joan gets you that boot, you'll want to keep that foot elevated as much as possible. If you find something cold to help bring the swelling down, great. If not, just wait for the medicine. But don't walk on it, or you could make the injury worse."

Mark grimaced but nodded in resignation. "How long will I be out, do you think?"

Kim thought hard, trying to remember what she'd learned about that sort of injury. A bad sprain could take two to three weeks to heal, but a torn tendon or ligament was worse. "You'll have to wait until the pain and swelling have subsided before you can even start using that ankle again. I'd say three weeks to a month minimum before you can do any sort of long or strenuous standing work, maybe longer, depending on how bad the injury is and any possible complications."

"Three weeks to a month or *more*?" Mark's eyebrow shot up, and his voice rose. "I can't be out that long. I've got responsibilities! Plus, you said I'll have a boot! Surely that means I can work, right?" Mark looked between the two of them, his expression pleading.

"Now, Mark." Joan waved a placating hand. "Kim's a smart girl. If she says a month, then a month is what it'll take. I'm sure we can work out something you can do. Maybe helping at the store with passing out rations or something else that won't take much standing. I'll talk to Lewis and the others about it."

After a moment, Mark nodded, but his expression was unhappy as he turned to Kim again. "Isn't there some way to make it heal faster? Like maybe surgery so I can get back to work?"

"There might be, but that's not something I know how to do." Kim hunched her shoulders against the disappointment in his gaze, wishing she could do more. "I wouldn't know the first thing about trying to patch a torn tendon or ligament, and certainly not under conditions with minimal equipment."

"All right. I guess I'll just have to tough it out then." Mark sighed, then gave her a forced smile that was worse than his pained expression moments before had been. "Thanks for the help and the advice, Kim. Joan. I won't keep you any longer."

Kim recognized the dismissal for what it was and stepped back, content to be ignored as Joan said her goodbyes and packed up her kit. She followed the older woman out into the crisp spring sunshine.

Helping Mark left Kim feeling down when she'd expected the opposite. She thought helping him would make her feel accomplished, but he'd been so worried, almost the same way Mr. Craig had been. They both wanted so much to work and help the community.

Kim shook her head and thought about the surgery Mark would have probably needed in the past. Mark's question had only reminded her of the vast gulf between the skills a real doctor possessed and her own limited training. She wanted to help, but she was barely even starting her medical education. She only qualified as a first responder or a lifeguard, really. She'd taken about half the classes to be a registered nurse, and that was it.

It stung, but the truth was that she had limited skills. She wanted to help, but if she wasn't careful, her own lack of training meant she might do more harm than good.

Even if she could help, she didn't plan to linger any longer than it took Dennis to recover from his detox. She could talk all she liked about reevaluations, but the truth was she intended to be long gone by the time Mark needed one.

"You're pretty quiet. Are you all right?" Joan's voice broke through her thoughts.

Kim nodded. "Yeah. I was just thinking." She waved hand at the community around them. "I don't really—I mean, I've got some pre-med classes under my belt, and first responder and CPR training, but I'm not exactly a fully qualified medic. Not a doctor, or even a nurse."

"You're doing just fine, dear. Your help today with Mr. Craig and Mark was exactly the sort of help I need." Joan smiled at her.

"Maybe. But I'm really not qualified. You guys should probably have a real doctor check my work."

Joan's smile was strained as she answered. "That might be true, but I'm afraid you and I are the best Humboldt has at the moment."

"Yeah. I'm kind of surprised by that, honestly," she said. "A town this size usually has one general practitioner in it if not more. Surely, they didn't all pick up and leave town, right?"

Kim was sure she saw Joan's shoulders tense up. "I wouldn't know. It was a pretty chaotic time, those first few days. Anything might have happened."

That might be true, but Kim wasn't so sure she believed what Joan was trying to imply. She'd spent years trusting her instincts, and those instincts said there was more to the story. Joan was hiding something, and usually when people hid something, it was because it was important.

It was also going to take some work to uncover the truth, if Joan's response was anything to go by. She couldn't push too hard for answers, or she'd spook the older woman. Kim adopted a nonchalant attitude instead. "I guess you're right. Still, it seems weird you don't have a doctor in the town. I mean, didn't anyone need medical assistance in the first couple days?"

"Of course. There were all sorts of accidents."

"You mentioned a clinic before, so someone was probably helping with all those accidents. Why didn't Lewis make sure they stuck around? He seems very community oriented."

"Good grief, girl, you do ask a lot of questions." The sharpness in Joan's voice was surprising. "As if it matters why there isn't a doctor in the town right now. There's no point in stirring up folks with all sorts of pointless inquiries when we've enough to do with getting by."

Kim was surprised by Joan's vehemence. She was about to ask another question, but Joan shushed her impatiently. Kim saw her eyes flick toward the two militia members on patrol who had just appeared on the street. The older woman stepped out of their way and pulled

Kim to the side, smiling warmly at both men as they passed. The older of the two tipped his hand to her in a sort of halfhearted salute.

Once they were gone, Joan turned back to Kim. Her eyes were dark, her face lined with worry and a barely concealed fear under a smile as false as a Halloween mask. "I know you're a curious girl, Kim. It's only natural. But asking questions without good answers in Humboldt —well, it's just not the smartest thing you could do. That's all I'll say on the matter. I think you're smart enough to take a hint."

Kim nodded, unwilling to press her further. She'd seen the signs before, heard words like that before. She'd grown up with subtle glances and strained expressions like the one Joan Danville wore. "You're right. Maybe I'm a little tired, not thinking straight."

She saw Joan's shoulders relax. "That's not surprising, fresh off the road as you are. I should have thought of that." Joan shifted her kit in her arm. "We've finished the rounds for the day anyway, so why don't we head on back to the house? I'll get you a drink and some food, and then you can head back to where you and Dennis are staying and get some rest."

Kim managed a weak smile of her own. "Thanks. That sounds like a good idea." She fell into step at Joan's side as the older woman started walking toward the neighborhood she and Lewis lived in. Kim kept her steps light, her shoulders slumped as if she was tired and lacking energy, but her mind was far from calm.

She knew the signs of secrets and shadows no one liked to think about or talk about. She knew when something wasn't right. She'd grown up in an environment of dangerous secrets and avoided truths when she and her mom had still been with Andre, still linked to the darker elements of the Black Rats.

Something wasn't right in Humboldt, and she wasn't sure whether she wanted to find the answer or get out of town before it blew up in their faces.

15

KIM NAKAMURA

L ewis met Kim and Joan at the Danville household and joined them for the meal, a simple affair of fried eggs and a spring salad mix. Afterward, he offered Kim a ride to the distribution center and then back to the house. They picked up some basic supplies from the provision center, including soup stock and crackers for Dennis, drinks, and assorted easy-to-prepare foods, then headed for Kim and Dennis's house.

Lewis was the first to break the silence between them as they drove. "I heard from Joan that you did good work today, doing rounds with her. She said you had real skill."

Kim shrugged. "I don't know about that. I'm not a fully trained doctor, or even a nurse. I was kind of bluffing my way through some of it."

"That's not as bad as you think it is." Lewis gave her a jovial smile. "Most real education happens with hands-on experience. I'm sure that with a few reference books and some practice, you'd make a fine doctor."

Kim shook her head. "That might be true, but trying to learn it all on my own, I'd do more harm than good while I was getting a handle on things. I'm not sure I could live with doing that kind of damage, especially these days."

"I think you're harder on yourself than you need to be. Joan can probably help you out with a few things."

She wasn't in the mood to argue with him. They were also pulling up to the house. Kim gave him a strained smile. "Maybe. But right now, I gotta get this put away." She hefted the sacks of groceries from the seat of the truck and into her arms. "Thanks for the ride."

She opened the door and dropped to the ground, only to pause with a frown. Outside the truck with the diesel engine shut off, she could clearly hear loud barking coming from the backyard. Mutt's deep, resonant voice was loud enough that if they'd had any neighbors, they'd probably be complaining by now.

There was no sound of Dennis responding to the dog either. That was what really troubled her. Kim hurried to the door and opened it, then set the bags down and made a beeline for the back door and out into the garden.

Mutt was by the shed. She could hear the distress in the large dog's barking. Kim moved forward, her heart in her throat.

Dennis lay crumpled on the ground only inches from a puddle of bile and other liquids that made Kim shudder. The smell was pungent and made her nose wrinkle. She couldn't imagine how Dennis could stand to be that close to the mess.

He wasn't moving, but she could hear slow, rasping breaths and see the grimace on his face. There was more vomit on his shirt, along with dirt, spittle, and dark streaks she hoped were only sweat. Kim stood there, torn between pity and disgust.

"Skies above, man, but you look like horse crap that's been wrung through a few toilet bowls before being stomped through a compost heap."

Kim jumped. She hadn't realized Lewis Danville had followed her.

Dennis groaned and cracked his bloodshot eyes. His expression twisted with shame and despair, and he turned his face away. A hoarse, barely audible whisper reached them a moment later. "Go 'way. Leave me alone." The words were slurred with exhaustion and pain.

"That's not happening." Kim was still frozen with indecision, but Lewis apparently had no such problems and no issue with the smell either. He stalked forward, got his hands under Dennis's shoulders, and heaved him into a sitting position. Dennis gagged, and Lewis helped him twist to puke on the ground. Once he was done, the militia leader grimaced, dragged him the rest of the way to his feet, and hooked one of Dennis's arms over his shoulders. "You're a mess, soldier."

"Not a soldier." Dennis scowled blearily at his old friend. "Just a sick, drug-addled, broken old man."

"For the love of Pete, I thought you had more spine than that! And I thought you knew, Sullivan—once a Marine, always a Marine." Lewis's voice was sharp, equal parts sympathetic and abrasive. "You don't have time to be lying around on the ground. You've got a civilian to watch out for."

Kim bristled at the description of herself as a civilian, as if he and Dennis were something different. She kept her silence as Dennis growled some response and began to stagger back toward the house with Lewis's help.

She followed the two men inside. Lewis paused for a moment with Dennis at the foot of the stairs and looked back at her. "Stove's gas and should be working just fine. Why don't you heat up some of that broth and soup for Dennis while I get him cleaned up? He needs something in his system."

Kim nodded. Both of them ignored Dennis's growls about not needing to be "mother-henned." Lewis began the process of guiding the sick man up the stairs, and Kim went to grab the groceries from where she'd left them.

She heard the pipes start up, running water for a shower, as she dug around for a pot. She listened with half an ear as she found the necessary utensils and lit the stove top. She wasn't as practiced with gas stoves as she was with electric, but the mechanism was fairly simple. It only took her three tries to get the burner lit and a steady medium-heat flame going. She set the pot on the stove top, poured in a can of soup and some of the chicken broth, and started heating it.

By the time Dennis staggered back downstairs with Lewis's help, the soup was hot, and Dennis looked a little more alert. His face was haggard and his clothing rumpled, but both were clean. His eyes were still bloodshot with lines of pain marking the corners but no longer so glassy they resembled a sleepwalker's. Lewis helped him settle into a recliner.

Kim brought him a mug of soup and his crutch. "Here you go."

"Thank you." He didn't look at her. His hands were shaking slightly as he took the cup. Fortunately, she'd remembered that people going through detox and withdrawal often had the shakes, and she'd only filled the mug about halfway.

Dennis scowled at it, but he took a cautious sip and cursed. "That's hot."

"It's soup." Kim scowled back. "It's good for you."

"Yeah, yeah." He sipped again. "Sorry about earlier. I just—I got sick, and I stumbled down to the shed. Then I tripped, and I couldn't get back to my feet after it passed." His voice was a rough, cracking growl of mingled anger and shame.

"You mean you didn't try hard enough to get up." Lewis spoke with a disapproving voice before she could respond. "Come on, Dennis. I know you better than that."

Dennis glared at his friend. "You *knew* me better than that. It's been a long time."

"You're still a soldier at heart, or you wouldn't have gone to the lengths you did trying to protect this girl." Lewis shook his head. "But that's just the problem. You're not in any shape to actually take care of her, or protect her, or whatever it is you were trying to do."

Dennis jerked his head up. "You think I don't know that?"

"I think you've deluded yourself into thinking this pussyfooting, weak excuse of an effort is your best. But the Dennis Sullivan I knew was tougher than to let a little vomiting leave him on the ground. And he'd be embarrassed to be caught lying around like you were."

"You know what's going on." Dennis looked ashamed, but his response was stronger, less hoarse. "This thrice-blasted detox takes it out of a man."

"That's as may be, and I do sympathize. Addiction's a nasty illness." Lewis leaned forward to rest his forearms on his knees. "Even so, you're better than this, Dennis. I don't know when you forgot that fact, but you need to remember it if you want to be any help to anyone, especially Kim."

Dennis gave him a dirty look as he sipped more of his soup. His face was drawn, but there was some more color to it. Kim went to put a lid on the remainder of the soup and tried to pretend she wasn't listening to the conversation. She cared about the results, but she also didn't want to interrupt. It seemed better, somehow, for Lewis to be the one confronting Dennis.

Her thoughts were interrupted by a muffled *thunk,* and she stuck her head into the living room to see Dennis had set his mug on a side table and was working to lever himself to his feet. Lewis started to rise, but Dennis shook his head.

"Let me be. If you're right, then I ought to at least be able to get myself out of a chair and upstairs." He managed to get upright, and his gaze found Kim where she lingered in the doorway. "Thank you for the soup, Kim. I appreciate it, but I think I need to go get some rest." He gave her a wan smile. "I didn't sleep very well last night."

She could just imagine. "Yeah. Okay." She tilted her shoulder to lean against the doorway. "There's some more soup if you want it later."

Dennis shook his head. "I'm not likely to be hungry again for a while. You should eat it whenever you want something." Then he turned and stumped away. A second later, she heard his uneven footsteps ascending the stairs.

Lewis sighed and met her eyes with a commiserating look. "I'm sorry to see that man in such bad shape. Still, he's taking the right steps."

Kim nodded and took a seat in the chair Dennis had recently vacated. "I just wish he'd taken them sooner. We'd all be in a lot better shape if he'd kicked the habit before everything happened."

"That's true, but there's no point in fussing about it now." Lewis offered her a smile she thought was meant to be encouraging. "You give it a few more days, and Dennis will get himself back on his feet. Then you'll see more of the man you and I both know he can be."

Kim wasn't nearly as sure as he was, but she wasn't about to argue the point. She was more interested in trying to find a polite way to convince Lewis to leave so she could wash her face and seek her pillow for a nap. Or maybe she'd read a book.

She wasn't sure what Lewis saw in her expression, but he chuckled. "You look a little skeptical, Kim, but you'll see. Give it two weeks or so, and you and Dennis will both be solid citizens of Humboldt, working to keep the community going."

Kim frowned. "What do you mean?"

Lewis waved a hand in a vague gesture. "You're already doing good work helping Joan with medical problems people have. Dennis, once he gets on his feet, can do well in a number of roles. He could be a hunter to bring in game or a member of the militia. Or he could even train some of our younger members, teach them woodcraft and the tricks of being a proper soldier and survivor."

"Yeah, no, I understand all that." Kim shook her head. "But didn't Dennis tell you? As soon as he recovers, we're going on to Memphis. I need to reach my aunt and find out if my mom made contact." Carol was her great-aunt, but she wasn't going to get into all of the complicated relationships in her family.

Lewis frowned, all the good humor gone from his face. "I understand that you were headed to Memphis when you stopped here, but I thought you might be staying a while."

"Just until Dennis recovers from the withdrawal symptoms and gets back on his feet. After that, we'll be on our way." She tucked her hands into her lap and tried not to clench them into fists as irritation swept over her.

Was Lewis making baseless assumptions, or was it another one of those things Dennis had been thinking about and simply hadn't bothered to discuss with her? She didn't know, and she couldn't go ask Dennis right then.

Lewis was still frowning, but there was an edge of concern and something else—something she couldn't readily identify—in his expression. "I realize family is important, Kim, but Dennis was talking to me a bit about your situation. He said your mother was in Texas or Oklahoma."

"Well, she was, but with everything that's going on, I can't imagine she wouldn't want to check on Aunt Carol. I really think she'd try to get to Memphis if she could."

"If she could—that's the key phrase. It's a long way from Texas to Memphis. And anyway, are you sure your aunt would have stayed in town? A lot of people took to the road after the disaster happened."

Kim swallowed hard. She knew he was making a good point—a lot of good points, actually. Aunt Carol and Uncle Bruno were both longstanding members and leaders of the Black Rats MC. Nothing would stop the gang from getting on the road and heading out if they thought it was in their best interests.

Still, she couldn't see Carol abandoning her completely. She was sure her aunt would have tried to detour through Murray to find her if they were going on the road. Either that, or Carol would leave a message at their home base for Kim or any Black Rat who might come looking.

She took a deep breath. "You might be right. But I have to find out for certain. I need to go to Memphis to make sure everyone is okay. Even if it turns out to be pointless, I have to try."

Lewis sighed. "Well, I understand if you're determined to be sure. Even so, I'd like you to think about it while Dennis is finishing his recovery." He shoved himself to his feet. "To be sure you make an informed decision, I'd like you to come with me."

Kim hesitated, and Lewis gave her a smile. "Don't worry. I know you're tired, and I won't keep you long. I just want to show you what kind of resources you'd have to work with if you decided to stay in Humboldt as our doctor, or doctor-in-training, if you prefer."

She wasn't interested in seeing anything, but she felt it was better to humor him. "All right. Let me just go tell Dennis where we're going."

Dennis was half-asleep but managed to offer an approximation of a wave in her direction. Kim decided that was as good as she was going to get and left, tucking the key deep into a pocket where she didn't think she'd lose it.

The drive across the town was quiet. The sun was setting, scattered lights of different types coming to life as people headed home for the day. Kim watched the streets go by, adding to the map in her mind as they wound their way back toward the former town center.

On the edge of the occupied area, Lewis pulled the truck up at a moderately sized building with a neatly lettered sign by the front door that read "Dr. Benjamin Kennedy, Gen. Practitioner."

Lewis led her up the two wide steps to the building then dug out a key ring, selected a key, and twisted the mechanism. He pushed the door open and held it. "Go ahead and have a look inside."

Kim moved inside. There was a nice, if slightly old-fashioned, waiting room, and beyond that were a set of examination rooms, six in total. There was also a filing room, still full of folders. Lewis coughed. "Of course, a lot of these people are gone, but you could probably find files for most of our current residents in here somewhere."

Kim looked through the drawers. They were filed neatly in alphabetical order. "Hmm." She moved on.

There was a room full of cabinets, each one marked with neat labels that indicated a type of medication. The labels looked newer, like they might be a recent addition. She recalled Joan mentioning that she'd stop by the clinic. Presumably medical supplies were stored here, or at the veterinary clinic, or possibly divided between those locations and a pharmacy in the dispensing center.

In the back was an office with two small filing cabinets, a large oak desk in front of a comfortable-looking chair, and a wall full of awards, certifications, and photos. The central photo drew Kim's attention at once. The picture was of an older gentleman, his gray hair cut neatly and styled. He wore a white doctor's coat over a crisp dress shirt and trousers, and a pair of old-fashioned glasses with thin, gold rectangular rims. Her grandfather had worn glasses with a similar shape; she'd seen him in photo albums when she was a tiny kid. Kim studied the man's face. It was broad and friendly, with warm brown eyes over a strong, confident smile. He looked like the kind of man who knew what he was doing and who people would trust.

"That's Doc Kennedy." She turned to see Lewis looking at the picture, his expression solemn.

"What happened to him?" She hadn't meant to ask, but the question popped out before she could think to stop it.

Lewis sighed. "Hopefully nothing, but I wouldn't know for certain." His mouth twisted in a wry smile. "Ben Kennedy was a fine doctor, and no mistake, but he was a touch hardheaded. And much as I hate to say it, he and I never quite saw eye-to-eye on most things, including how Humboldt should be run after the power went down."

It sounded like Dr. Kennedy was a man Kim could agree with. She kept her eyes on the picture and her thoughts to herself as Lewis continued speaking.

"After the militia formed, Doc Kennedy decided he'd rather take his chances elsewhere, so he headed out toward Jackson to be with his daughter. I offered to take him, but he wouldn't hear of it, said he'd make his own way. Haven't heard a word since, though that's not really a surprise."

"Sounds rough." Kim said. She wasn't sure whether she was referring to the doctor's possible situation or to the lack of medical expertise in Humboldt. She simply said the first thing she could think of to say.

"It is." Lewis shook his head. "I tried to get the doc to stay, but he wouldn't hear of it. It's a shame, because we could really use a doctor around here."

"Yeah. It's a shame." Kim muttered the words, a lump in her throat. She understood Dr. Benjamin Kennedy's feelings all too well, but she couldn't help wishing he'd made a different decision.

She also couldn't help noticing the similarities between her own situation and the previous doctor's. It should have reassured her that he'd apparently left without any struggle, but it didn't. She couldn't help feeling like there was more to the story.

She followed Lewis back out to the truck, thinking hard.

The doctor's office was nice, eerily like the kind of place she'd once dreamed of owning and working in as a kid. It had been her final goal, her hope for where she'd wind up after she'd finished her studies and built up her experience and reputation. It was tempting, but it wasn't enough to make her want to stay in Humboldt.

And it certainly wasn't enough to allay her suspicions that there was something wrong underneath the surface of the supposedly quiet and well-ordered little town.

16

LEE KINGSTON JONES

Lee woke to cold and silence. He groaned, then sat up, stretching against the aches that came with sleeping on the ground. "Andre?"

There was no answer. Lee blinked, then scrubbed the sleep out of his eyes, his heart falling as he looked around the clearing where they'd settled down to rest for the night.

After eating as much of the turkey as they could stomach, then cooking and bundling the rest into Andre's bag, they'd spent the rest of the day hiking. Andre had set the basic route up toward Memphis, and Lee had helped him scout different paths for signs of more police roadblocks. It had been a long day. Lee had been exhausted by the time they stopped for the evening, about five miles outside Memphis. He'd had just enough energy to build the fire and eat some turkey before he'd passed out.

Now he was alone, and there was no sign of Andre. No sign that he might have just gone to take a leak or get more firewood. Nor was there any indication he'd made a place to sleep.

Lee bit the inside of his cheek, disappointed and a little hurt, an ache in his chest. It looked like Andre had decided their association was over. He'd left a little of the turkey by the remains of the fire, but that was all.

Lee swallowed a lump in his throat and reached for the bag he'd acquired during their walk yesterday. Andre hadn't taken it nor the bottles of water and soda inside. He'd also left the knife he'd given Lee the night before last. Lee zipped the bag shut and stuffed the knife into his belt. "Better than nothing, I guess."

He ate half the turkey cold and packed the rest up for later. Who knew when and where he'd find more food. He was scuffing around the remains of the fire to make sure it was completely out when he heard footsteps coming close. Lee settled himself into a crouch, knife in hand.

Seconds later, a large figure pushed through the trees. Lee relaxed as he recognized Andre. He sheathed the knife.

"Andre."

The older man glanced at him. "Ah, you're awake. Did you find the turkey I left for you?"

"Yeah. Sure." Lee's eyes widened as he stared at Andre's hands and forearms. Both arms were liberally stained red and drying in tacky streaks in shades from bright crimson to a dull rust color. A familiar iron smell hit Lee's nose. "Andre, is that yours?"

Andre followed his gaze to his arms. He frowned. "Some of it, I suppose." He turned his arm over to reveal a series of jagged cuts. "I encountered an individual who came after me with a broken bottle."

"Jeez. That looks like it hurts." Lee shoved the knife into his belt and moved closer. "You really need to get that cleaned out and looked at."

Andre frowned. "I can hardly go to a doctor's office, even if one happened to be open."

"I get that, but..." Lee shifted his feet. "Here, can I take a look?"

"Fine." Andre held out his arms.

Lee unzipped his bag and yanked out a bottle of water. He cracked the cap and poured it over Andre's arms, rinsing away the blood to reveal several irregular gashes of varying size and depth. "Dude. It looks like you got into a fight with a weedwhacker or something."

"He was about as violent and smart as one." Andre's voice was oddly amused.

"Okay." Lee scowled. "You got some spare cloth or anything?"

Andre clicked his tongue. "I have the clothing from the prison." He tipped his head toward the roots of a tree.

Lee scrambled toward it. There, under a thin covering of leaves, was Andre's bag. Lee scooped it up, feeling a little foolish that he hadn't noticed it before. He hadn't even really looked for it. If he had, he would have known that Andre hadn't abandoned him after all. He shoved the thoughts aside and opened the bag, rooting around until he found a prison uniform. It was green, as opposed to the orange he kind of expected from watching movies, with a patch labeling it as the property of Mississippi State Penitentiary. He dragged it out, along with a bottle of beer, closed the bag back up, and went back to Andre.

He dried both Andre's arms and held up the bottle. "Is it okay if I use this? Alcohol is supposed to clean out wounds."

"You might as well." Andre said.

It took some work to pop the top, but he managed. "Right, so, I'm just gonna pour this over these cuts. Might sting a bit."

"I'm sure I've had worse." Andre shifted, an expression of impatience crossing his face. Lee took that as a warning and got to work.

Beer didn't bubble the way peroxide did, so he couldn't say if it was really cleaning anything out, but he figured it was the thought that counted. He used the knife to cut strips of cloth from the prison shirt to use as bandages. He used more water to clean away the sugar and flavorings from the beer. He checked to be sure the bleeding had stopped, then bandaged the wounds and tied off the cloths. It was easier than he expected—none of the awkward angles he was used to dealing with when he bandaged his own injuries after Max beat him up.

Andre studied the bandages after he finished, flexing his arms against the cloth. "Well done. You have some skill with this."

Lee scuffed his toe against the ground. "Just a lot of practice." He glanced up at Andre. The older man looked pretty calm, like maybe he would be okay with a question. Lee thought he might as well risk it. "So, uh, what happened? I mean, how'd you get so cut up? I know you said you got attacked, but it kind of seemed like there was more to the story. If you want to tell me, that is."

Andre smiled at him, though once again it was an expression that didn't reach his eyes. Even when Andre was being kind to him—well, his version of kind—there was always an undercurrent of menace. Andre took his bag and rummaged around to get another bottle of beer. "I couldn't sleep, so I decided I might as well fill the evening hours with something useful. I took a knife and walked the rest of the way to Memphis to gather some information."

"Oh. Makes sense."

"Indeed." Andre took a swallow of beer and made a face. Lee wasn't sure if his expression was in response to the flavor of the beer or the explanation. "I found someone I knew. He was not pleased to see me.

We fought, and I disarmed him. I then proceeded to ask him for any information he had on the status of my old gang, the Black Rats. He didn't want to share, so I persuaded him."

"Like, talked to him?" Lee wasn't sure why it mattered, but he was curious. From the look of the wounds, not all the blood on Andre's arms and hands had been his.

"At first. Then, well, when words fail, sometimes people need a bit more encouragement."

Andre's eyes looked dead when he said this, like he had no feelings at all inside him. It made Lee's whole body want to shudder, but he suppressed the impulse.

"That worked?" Lee asked.

"It always does."

Lee gulped. Andre spoke so casually about what he'd done, but Lee couldn't help thinking of blood splattered on the pavement, intermingled with moans of pain abruptly silenced with a single, merciless strike, like the officers outside Tunica. At least Officer Corvelle and his partner had died quickly. Whoever Andre had talked to last night hadn't been so lucky.

Andre cocked his head. "Does that bother you?"

Lee shook his head. There was no sense showing fear or disgust. Besides, the guy had cut Andre up, so he hadn't been defenseless. Even if Andre had beaten him up, hurt him—well, he could have chosen to avoid the pain by talking.

Lee couldn't help thinking of all the times he'd gotten battered by his father, when he would have given anything to make it stop. He shook his head again. "Nah. If he's dumb enough not to take advantage of a way out, that's his problem." He took a breath to settle the faint churning of unease in his stomach. "So, what did he tell you?"

"The Black Rats are still in Memphis and still an active motorcycle gang. They are based in the old scrapyard owned by relatives of my former wife, Sarah." His eyes dropped to half-mast. It didn't make him look sleepy. In fact, Lee was reminded of a predator lazily contemplating prey. "Sarah will likely make her way there if she hasn't already done so."

"Okay. What's the plan?"

Andre shrugged. "I don't have one yet. Besides, I'll need rest to be at my best. You too."

"Should I build the fire again?"

"If you wish. I'll rest for a while, and you can do whatever you like. Hunt, sleep some more, find yourself some fresh clothing—whatever you choose."

"Sure." Lee shifted. "I might take some time to look around. Anything I should look for?"

"Anything you find useful." Andre studied his face, and Lee got the distinct impression that Andre was sizing him up, measuring how useful he found Lee to be. After a moment, he looked away. Lee felt like he had passed some sort of test. This time.

Lee swallowed. A part of him wanted to run screaming in the other direction, to head for the woods and never come back as soon as Andre was asleep. But Andre had been kind to him—better than his old man Max Jones, at least—and Lee was reluctant to leave the protection and leadership Andre offered.

There were worse things in the world to commit to than Andre. "Whatever you need, Andre. I'll do whatever you want me to do as long as it's something I'm capable of."

"That's fine." Andre smiled with his dead eyes. "I trust you'll be here when I wake?"

132

"Yessir." Lee bobbed his head. "Or I'll be back soon, if I'm not right here."

"Good. I trust you, Lee, and I'm glad to have you with me." Andre gave him a last look of approval, drained the remainder of the beer from the bottle, then closed his eyes. Soon after, his breathing slowed and evened out. If he wasn't asleep, he was doing an awfully good imitation of it.

Lee sat for a long time, staring at him.

Andre had said he was proud of him and that he trusted him. That was more than he'd ever had from his actual father. Despite all he knew about Andre and all he feared, he couldn't help feeling prouder and happier than he could remember being in a very long time.

Andre was a tough guy. Strong and smart and able to defend himself. Having his approval and his trust not only made Lee feel safe, but for the first time, he finally felt like he might someday be able to be tough and capable. Like he might be worth something and have some valuable skills and strengths.

Andre had taught him that. Andre respected his abilities.

He knew, despite the fear that drifted in the back of his mind, that he'd do whatever it took to be sure he never let Andre down.

17

KIM NAKAMURA

K im woke the next morning to the familiar sound of retching, but this time it was down the hall as opposed to outside. She lay in bed for a moment, thinking about everything that had happened the day before—and that evening.

Lewis had been cordial enough when he'd brought her back to the house and dropped her off, but she wasn't sure she trusted his good mood. He seemed a little too determined to keep them in Humboldt for as long as possible and a little too used to getting his way.

She hadn't missed the way Joan watched the militia members the previous day. Or the fact that the town was essentially under martial law and Lewis Danville was very much the man in charge. She couldn't forget the desperate pleas of Mark and Mr. Craig, nor the bruises on Joan's arms. Lewis, for all that he might put on a friendly face and reasonable demeanor, was dangerous. That was the only explanation for a man being in charge of so many people who were cowed by militia members with guns. Lewis reminded her of her father. Maybe not as bad as Andre had been, but there were similarities she just couldn't bring herself to dismiss. It left a heavy weight in her stomach that she couldn't get rid of.

The sounds of puking stopped. A few minutes later, she heard running water and a toilet flushing. It sounded like Dennis was finished being sick. Kim sighed and rolled herself out of bed to find the cleanest set of clothes she had.

She wanted to talk to Dennis to air her concerns and observations. She felt out of her depth, dealing with all the undercurrents and hidden pitfalls of Humboldt. Dennis might not be at his best, but he was still a smart man. She just needed to find a time and place when she could be sure Lewis and his militia weren't listening or likely to walk in at any moment.

Dennis was back in his room by the time Kim left hers, but she could hear him shuffling around and the soft, mumbled words that probably meant he was talking to Mutt. She considered knocking, then decided to wait for him downstairs. Things were tense enough without invading each other's space. Once they got back on the road, privacy would be a rare commodity, so they both might as well enjoy it as long as they had it.

She went to the kitchen and dragged out some oatmeal. It was easy enough to make, easy to flavor to individual tastes, and bland enough that it shouldn't upset Dennis's stomach. Joan had also suggested lemon-ginger tea during their rounds the previous day, and Kim figured it couldn't hurt. Lewis had authorized that as part of their rations, and at the very least, the taste would help wake both of them up.

The water was near boiling by the time Dennis came stumping down-stairs and thumped his way into the kitchen. He gave her a brief glance then went through to the back door, where he released Mutt into the yard. The dog bounded away, huffing softly as she dashed through the overgrown grass to stretch her muscles and take care of business. Dennis watched her for a moment then left the main door open and the screen door shut as he turned and made his way back to the table.

"Morning."

"Good morning." Kim indicated the bowls she'd already put out and the two mugs. "I'm making oatmeal with some of the dried fruit we were given, and a bit of honey if you want, and some lemon-ginger tea."

"Lemon-ginger tea?" Dennis wrinkled his nose. "What's wrong with regular tea, or coffee?"

"Nothing. But we don't have any of that right now. Anyway, lemon and ginger are both supposed to be good for settling an upset stomach." She gave him a pointed look.

Dennis grimaced but nodded. "Guess it can't hurt to try it."

"Great. Can you get the spoons, please? One for each of the bowls and one to stir the tea." Lewis had made sure they had four of each utensil, along with basic utensils and cookware.

Dennis grunted, but he pushed himself to his feet and went to rummage in the drawers for the proper items. After a moment, he brought back the spoons, and Kim turned her attention to dishing out the oatmeal and straining the tea bags. She would have preferred loose-leaf green, a preference she'd developed in college, but the lemon-ginger tea smelled good and hauntingly familiar.

It took a moment to place the memory. When she did, she had to bite back a lump in her throat and a sudden burst of emotion. *Mom loves ginger. She always liked to chew candied ginger, said it was better than coffee for a pick-me-up and way less addicting.* She took a deep breath and forced the feelings, and the memory, away. Now wasn't the time to stand around reminiscing.

"You okay?" Dennis frowned as she set the bowl in front of him.

"Just thinking." She plopped into her seat and added fruit and honey to her bowl. "I ought to be asking you that. You're the one who's been under the weather."

Dennis gave her a gruff smile. "You can say it. I've been detoxing, and there's no point in pussyfooting around the terminology. As for how I'm feeling," he considered a moment, "I won't say I feel great, and I sure don't have much of an appetite, but I feel a bit better than I did yesterday. Less like death warmed over and more like the day after a bender."

"I guess that's an improvement." Kim took a few bites of her oatmeal. "You know, we were so busy trying to cover the miles before we stopped in Humboldt that I never took the chance to ask you for those survival tricks Lewis was talking about."

"That's true. Was there something in particular you were thinking of?" Dennis looked like he was playing with his food more than eating it. She raised an eyebrow, and he made a face back at her. Then he stuffed another spoonful in his mouth.

What could they do that would get them out from under the eyes of Lewis and his militia? Kim said the first thing that came to mind. "What about hunting? It might be a good idea for me to know how to get my own food when we get on the road again."

Dennis's brow furrowed, but after a moment, he nodded. "That's not a bad idea. It'll take some doing to get out to a good spot, but if we head toward Humboldt Lake, we'd have a better chance of spotting game."

"Sounds good. If you're feeling up to it, of course." Kim kept her tone light and casual.

Dennis sipped his tea, looking thoughtful. Finally, he set the mug down and pushed himself to his feet. "If we're going out hunting, I'll need to get my boots on and get my gear. You should see about prepping some water bottles for the two of us, and maybe something to eat. It's a bit early for good foraging—at least for anything I could be sure was edible." He gave her a rueful half-smile. "I'm a little rusty when it comes to edible plants in early spring Tennessee."

Kim grinned back. "That's okay. I got a decent look at Joan's garden." She waved a hand at him. "Go ahead and get dressed. I'll clean up here." A low whuff came from the door, and she rose to let Mutt in. The dog was covered in bits of grass, but she didn't hesitate when Kim set the bowls on the floor.

Oatmeal probably wasn't proper dog food, but she figured it would be filling enough for now. With any luck, they'd catch some meat to share between all three of them.

Half an hour later, they'd consulted a map and were headed west out of town. No one stopped them, but Kim breathed easier when they passed the edge of town and started down a little-used road toward the lake. On the way out, she'd thought about telling Joan where they were going, but the house had been empty. Kim assumed Joan was out tending to someone's horse, maybe. It was fine. She could use a break from Joan and the strange heavy tension the woman brought with her.

Without the pressure of trying to make good time, they were able to set a more leisurely pace, and Kim got a chance to enjoy the scenery. The time was somewhere between early and mid-morning, the air crisp with the scent of dew and damp grass. It was starting to warm up as the sun rose above the horizon. They'd left everything but the essential supplies they needed for hunting at the house, so the packs were lighter and easier to carry.

An hour or so of hiking brought them to the bank of a small river. Dennis motioned to the trees close to the river. "Here's a good spot.

Animals will come to the water. If we're quiet, we'll be able to get them before they even realize we're here."

Kim nodded and set her pack down. "What kind of animals? Deer?"

"Not likely to be deer at this time of day, not unless they've had a really lean winter. We're more likely to see small game, like squirrel or rabbits." Dennis was making himself comfortable at the base of a nearby tree where he could watch the riverbank. Mutt bounded down to the river for a drink, then came back up and flopped at his side, her head on her paws.

Kim dropped down beside him. "What about fishing?" She hadn't thought of it before, but fishing would work too. Even better, she didn't think it would require much movement. It might be easier on Dennis.

Dennis considered, then shook his head. "Didn't bring the supplies for it. I had a collapsible pole when I started, but I lost it when I lost the car I was driving."

Kim made a face. He'd told her about the incident with the Moon family, and knowing he'd lost more than a vehicle in the incident made her want to slap someone. Even if she sort of understood where Martin Moon had been coming from.

"You ought to suggest the fishing to Lewis though." Dennis's words made her blink.

"Why?"

"Because he could authorize giving us some fishing gear. If he hasn't already thought of it, he ought to take a crew up to the Humboldt Lake Hatchery. There should be plenty of fish, and it's a good year-round source of meat."

Kim bit her lip. "Okay, but, about Lewis…"

"Don't let him get to you. He's a bit gruff, and he can be difficult, but he's a good man." Dennis shook his head. "Anyway, that's enough chatter. We're here to hunt, not talk."

That wasn't entirely true on her end, but she let him change the subject. "Okay. So what do we do?"

"To start with, you show me how well you can hold this." Dennis shifted his weight, fished a pistol out of its holster, and offered the butt of the gun to her.

Kim jerked back, lip curled as she stared at the weapon. "I don't like guns. Scratch that, I hate guns. I have ever since I was a kid. I don't touch them." She shivered. "I thought we were going to build snares or traps or something."

Dennis shook his head. "Traps and snares are hit-or-miss in hunting, and they require bait and daily monitoring. They're fine if we're going to be staying somewhere long term. But for a quick day trip like this, we need to take a more active approach. That means using a weapon, and the pistol's our best bet."

When he explained it like that, it all made sense to her. It was clear he knew what he was talking about. But that still didn't mean she liked the idea of using the gun. "Okay, so you shoot, and I'll just watch. Or maybe I can take Mutt and chase animals toward you. Or, you know, I could take Mutt and hike the rest of the way to that hatchery you talked about and get us some fish," Kim said.

"No. You don't need to be wandering around on your own. Besides, you wanted me to teach you, didn't you?" Dennis asked.

Kim winced. She'd really just wanted to distract him and get him out of the house for a while, and maybe learn a few little survival tips while she was at it. She hadn't planned on a lesson in firearms. "I did. But guns are—"

"Guns are a tool, just like anything else. It's how you use them that counts. The world's a dangerous place, and your odds are better if you know how to handle a firearm, even if you never have to use the knowledge. You need to know what you're doing for your own safety."

She couldn't argue with him, not with the memory of Lewis's rifle pointed at her and her own helpless fear. She would have felt a lot better if she'd had a way to possibly defend herself. She gave in. "Okay. What do I do?"

"First, you take this." He held the pistol out, grip first. "This is a nine-millimeter. It's a pretty common weapon, so finding or making ammo for it's pretty easy, relatively speaking."

She took it from him and started to lift it, only to have Dennis grab her hand. "Safety first. Anyone hands you a gun, you follow these rules before you ever think about doing anything else. Rule number one is, never point a gun at anything you wouldn't want to hit."

"What if it's not loaded?"

"Always treat a gun like it's loaded, even if you know for certain it isn't." Dennis scowled at her. "Less chance for accidents that way."

"Okay." She pointed it carefully at the ground, the muzzle facing away from them. "What next?"

"Start by keeping your finger off the trigger, outside the trigger guard."

Kim blushed. She hadn't even realized she'd slipped her finger close to the trigger. She'd been trying to hold it the way she'd seen it held in movies. She shifted her grip, and Dennis nodded.

"Next, you check the safety and engage it." He pointed her to a small switch close to the base of the slide. He had her click it on and off a few times. "Okay, now you check to see if it actually is loaded. Pop the magazine with this tab." He indicated the button, and she pressed it. The magazine popped free, and she removed it.

"Now check the chamber. If a gun's loaded, there's usually a bullet in the chamber, and you want to make sure. A lot of people get hurt because they forget to check."

Kim followed his instructions and removed that bullet as well. Dennis showed her how to reload it into the magazine. Then he took her through the basics of handling the weapon:

"Two hands on the grip—you'll need better control and grip strength before you're ready to use it one-handed.

"Line of sight should follow the sights on the front and back end of the slide, there at the top. Use both eyes, none of that one-eyed squinting hotshots and movie stuntmen like to use.

"Finger stays outside the trigger guard until you've got a target and you're ready to fire. Anything else is asking for trouble."

Dennis had her reload the magazine, then he rose and pointed toward a tree some yards away. "We'll start easy. Sight on that tree, and aim for dead center at about eye level. Line up the sights. Let me know when you think you've got it."

She aimed. "Okay. I think I've got it."

"All right. Now disengage the safety. Here's the most important part, once you get past the safety rules." Dennis stepped behind her. "You don't want to pull or jerk the trigger. You want to squeeze, like you're trying to make a fist and the metal just happens to be in the way. Steady pressure, nice and easy. Don't lock your elbows. You want your stance firm, but not stiff. Balance yourself so you can absorb the recoil without falling."

Kim frowned, trying to adjust her position according to his direction.

Dennis continued talking. "When you're ready, take a practice shot at that tree."

She'd rather not. But she'd asked for instruction. She set her feet.

"Bring your top hand down a bit, or you'll get nicked by the slide." She adjusted her grip.

"Whenever you're ready. Remember, nice, even pressure. Squeeze, don't pull or jerk." Dennis paused. "And don't forget to breathe. In and out, nice and easy. Don't tense up."

She tried. But it was hard not to tense as her finger began to tighten on the trigger. She felt the tension, pulled a little harder, and the gun went off with a sharp bang that made her jump and stagger, her balance lost. The bullet thudded into the tree several inches above where she'd been aiming.

"Easy." Dennis helped steady her then turned to appraise her shot. "Not bad for a first time."

Kim shook her head to get rid of the slight ringing. "Shouldn't we have earplugs?"

Dennis shrugged. "Ideally? Sure. But in the real world, you don't always have earplugs. And if you're in a jam, you're not going to have time to put any in, even if you have some with you. You might as well get used to the noise now."

That was a fair point, even if she didn't like it much. "Okay. What about my wrists?" They ached from the recoil.

"You've got to build up strength and tolerance for the recoil. Also, I saw you pull the trigger a bit at the end instead of squeezing. That motion will shift your wrist position and amplify the feeling of the recoil."

Kim scowled at the gun, careful to keep it pointed away from them, muzzle toward the ground at an angle and finger away from the trigger as directed. "Can you show me?"

"Sure." Dennis held out his hand for the gun, and Kim passed it over to him with a soft sigh of relief.

Dennis steadied himself on his crutch and his good leg, then raised the gun and aimed at the same tree he'd pointed her toward. Or rather, he tried to aim. His hands were shaking, and despite his obvious effort, he couldn't keep them steady. The muzzle wavered in a wobbling circle, never still enough for Dennis to pull the trigger.

After a moment, Dennis dropped the gun, his expression twisted in self-disgust. "Looks like I can't show you after all." His voice was brusque, but under the gruff dismissal, Kim heard shame and anger that filled her with sympathy.

Dennis hefted the gun out toward her, and she took it. "Well, that's okay," she said. "I'm sure I'll figure it out."

"I'm sure you will. You're a bright girl, after all." His voice was still thick with negative emotion as he settled back against the tree.

She'd felt anger and disgust toward him for so long, but now all she could feel was regret and sorrow for his predicament, and the difficulties it had created between them. She carefully engaged the safety and shifted the gun to a safe position then crouched beside him. "Dennis, it's okay."

"Not really, if I can't even hold a measly little nine-millimeter well enough to hit a tree trunk." The bitterness was sharp enough to sting.

"Hey, that's not..." She paused. She'd been about to say it wasn't his fault, but she knew he'd see right through that. He'd gotten himself addicted to pain meds, and his refusal to kick the habit sooner was the reason he was having so much trouble now.

She changed her words. "It won't last forever. Only a little while longer. Then you can show me what sort of marksman you are. I bet you're a really good shot." She reached out and put a hand on his shoulder, trying not to wince as she felt the tremors running through the muscles. He might not be puking, but he was far from well. "I really didn't know anything about hunting or using a gun before today, and now look what I know. I couldn't have done that without you." It was true. Just spending this little bit of time with Dennis when he wasn't stuffed full of pills had already made her better prepared to deal with this new world. She'd been right to stick by him.

"Still pretty pathetic to be shaking like this," Dennis said.

"Not pathetic. It stinks that you feel like a marathon runner at the end of a race, yeah, but it's not pathetic. Not many people would try kicking a pill habit like yours cold turkey. You've only been clear for, like, two days, and you're already trying to hunt and teach. That isn't pathetic at all."

Dennis didn't respond, but she could feel him relaxing, and she could tell he was listening, so she continued. "I think what you're doing is great. And it's pretty impressive. I won't say I'm not ticked at how long it took you to realize you had a problem, but the fact that you're working so hard to recover—I'm really proud of you for making the effort and for coming out with me, even though you don't feel so hot. If you keep working as hard as you have been, you'll be back to being Super Soldier Sullivan in no time."

Dennis flushed, color filling his cheeks and displacing the pallor his convalescence had marked him with. Then he coughed and shifted his shoulder out from under her hand. "Sure. If you say so. But now you need to stop talking and sit still if you want any chance of seeing a rabbit or a squirrel before next week."

Kim grinned, recognizing the gruff dismissal for embarrassment rather than unwillingness to listen. She moved a little farther away, taking up a position on the other side of Mutt, and turned her gaze to the river and the surrounding woodlands.

She wasn't sure how she felt about the gun, sitting cold and heavy in her hands, but she was pleased about the progress she and Dennis had made.

They waited quietly for a while before Kim cleared her throat. There was too much weighing on her, and with Dennis more clear-headed than he had been in a while, now seemed as good a time as any.

"Have you noticed anything strange about this place?" she asked, her tone light. It was an intentionally vague question, offering her an easy way out if she needed one.

But Dennis turned a sharp eye in her direction and studied her. She should have known he would see right through the question to her true concerns.

"I've been sick on the couch and by the shed. I haven't seen much of anything. What have you seen?"

She waved a hand, regretting speaking up at all now. "It's nothing."

"It's clearly not. Not if you felt the need to bring it up."

She frowned. Dennis was too astute sometimes. "Just, when I was out with Joan tending to patients, they were all so worried about when they could get back to work. Panicked, almost."

Dennis watched her for a moment before turning back to the trees. "Well, they probably just want to feel like they're contributing to the community."

Kim slapped a mosquito off her arm. "Yeah, but, well, Joan had a bunch of bruises on her arms."

This got his attention once more. "Did you ask her about them?"

Kim nodded. "She said it was dealing with cows or something."

Dennis grunted. "Yeah, I suppose that would do it."

"Lewis wants us to stay. Permanently. He showed me where the old doctor used to work. I think he was trying to woo me or something."

"I'm sure he was. Like he said, you're an asset to this community."

"Yeah, but—"

"Kim," Dennis interrupted her. "Has there been anything that concerned you besides people working hard to keep Humboldt safe and running smoothly for everyone?"

When he said it like that, she couldn't really answer. Finally, she shook her head.

"Okay then. Let's just drop it."

The silence that settled between them was much less comfortable than before. Maybe Dennis was right, and she was seeing shadows and threats where there weren't any. But still, she hadn't gotten this far in life by not trusting her gut.

It was just a shame that Dennis didn't trust it as much as she did.

She had a feeling that convincing Dennis something was wrong in Humboldt might be harder than learning to handle a gun or hunt.

18

LEE KINGSTON JONES

Memphis was both better and worse than Lee had expected a big city to be. He'd been thinking it would be like the movies—creepy and deserted. Maybe a ghost town. Or one of those wild, lawless places with Mad Max-style gangs roaming the streets, looting and looking for innocent civilians to rob, beat up, and possibly enslave.

In reality, it was a lot like Tunica had been, only much larger and with less of a police presence visible in the streets. There were people, but most of them were in their homes or moving about in cautious groups. Here and there were individuals, but they all gave Andre a wide berth. People were wary and hungry-looking, but they didn't seem any more crazed or violent than people anywhere else.

Andre was probably more dangerous than most of the people they encountered. The thought was both unnerving and bracing at the same time.

They passed the outskirts of Memphis and traveled deeper into the city, and Lee had to revise his opinion. Downtown Memphis definitely looked like the sort of devastated shopfront wasteland he'd been picturing.

Windows were broken in various stores, and the wares inside were scattered, as if those places had been ransacked. Trash littered the streets, carried here and there by the light breeze. Some of the buildings looked like someone had made an effort to secure them, either by boarding the windows or creating makeshift barricades. It hadn't worked, though, especially in the supermarket they passed. Even from the street, Lee could see that most of the shelves were empty, and the food aisles had been picked almost clean, except for the perishables rotting in place and sending a faint stench into the air. All it needed was a few zombies, and it would be a scene straight out of *The Walking Dead.*

Lee shivered and hurried to catch up to Andre. "Where are we going, Andre?"

"We're looking for a place to stay before we call on the Black Rats." Andre kept walking.

"Like a hotel?"

"I think we'll do better in a house. There should be an abandoned one in the neighborhood close to the Black Rats scrapyard that will serve our purposes."

"Oh, so like squatting." Lee had never thought about doing that. But then, he supposed he'd never been homeless before—not that he hadn't considered it—or a convict on the run.

"I prefer the term 'repurposing.'"

"Okay." Repurposing seemed like a nicer term, and it made Lee feel a little better about the idea. "What kind of house are we looking for?"

"We'll see what options are available." Andre paused, then detoured to the right, going over four blocks before continuing north for a few blocks before he turned again to the left.

Lee followed, curious. "Are you looking for something?"

"There are signs, if you know where and how to look for them, of different territories. The Black Rats are not the only gang in the area, and I have no interest in running into the others." Andre's voice was offhand, but his shoulders were tense.

Lee swallowed hard. If Andre was concerned, Lee figured he should probably be changing his pants right about now.

Tunica had never been big enough for a serious gang presence. There were guys who ran together and called themselves a gang, but Lee knew from listening to the cops that they were what his old man called "jumped-up wannabe hoodlums who wouldn't last a minute in a real gang neighborhood." Somehow, he didn't think people Andre would detour to avoid were in the same category.

His first impulse was to ask who Andre was avoiding, but he hesitated. Max Jones would have taken that question as a challenge, a subtle hint that he was afraid, acting like a coward. Lee didn't want to make the same mistake with Andre.

He settled on a different question. "Can you show me which signs mark the territories I should stay out of?"

"In time. Finding a house is our first priority." Andre relaxed, and Lee relaxed with him. He still wasn't sure what signs Andre was looking for, but he could guess they'd crossed out of the immediate danger zone.

Andre led him along streets into a neighborhood a lot like the one Lee had grown up in. Most of the houses were neat little one-story boxes with dull red bricks and whitewashed front doors, and screen doors to keep out mosquitoes. Cracked pavement made a dull, time-worn sidewalk along the street with branches up to each house. Most of the yards were beginning to look overgrown—no surprise with the way things were. No one with any sense would waste gasoline on a mower, even if they had one that worked.

All of the houses had that look of middle-class, semi-maintained status: houses that had been built a decade or more ago and were in the process of becoming a little worn down, but where the owners still had enough pride in their homes to paint the trim every five years and wash the windows at least once a month. Lee thought they looked kind of like the house version of people's favorite sneakers, a little beat up but worn in all the right spots and comfortable to be in.

He had no idea what sort of criteria Andre was looking for in a house, and he didn't really care. Let Andre pick a place. It was all the same to him, as long as it had a bed, and maybe some food that wasn't wild turkey or canned chili.

Finally, Andre went up the walk to a house a little newer than its neighbors, or at least more recently tended to. Lee followed behind, wondering how they were going to get into the place and how Andre knew it was abandoned.

Andre prowled around the house, peering in windows and idly testing doorknobs and window frames for any sort of opening. The backyard was surrounded by a seven-foot-high wooden fence, sturdy and well-maintained, but Andre slipped through the gate without a care in the world. Lee closed the gate behind him and followed his mentor to the wide slab of concrete that served as a utilitarian back porch. There was a small grill standing to one side. It looked recently used, which gave Lee hope that there might be food inside.

He was distracted from the thought by Andre making a noise of triumph. "I thought so."

"What's up?" Lee hurried to Andre's side.

In answer, Andre tugged upward on the frame of the window over the sink. The lower pane slid up an inch or so, apparently unlatched.

"How'd you know?"

"It was a guess. Without electricity, many people will leave windows open for air." Andre heaved on the window, clicking his tongue when it stopped three-quarters of the way up. "Of course. No one would consider an opening of this size to be a problem." Andre turned his shoulder. "Come here, Lee. Can you get through this?"

Lee eyed the opening. It wasn't large, but then, he wasn't that big. "I think so. Might need a bit of a boost though, and some support until I can get a good grip."

Andre pulled his belt knife free and jammed it into the wood under the open frame to pin it open.

Lee stepped up and set his hands on the window ledge. Andre grabbed him and heaved him upward and forward. Lee just missed scraping his chin on the brick or cracking his head on the top of the opening as he scrabbled for a grip. He got both hands across the edge of the sink and tugged himself forward, kicking slightly to increase his momentum.

The faucet dug hard into his face. He arched his back and reached forward until he managed to reach the inside ledge of the countertop. He pulled himself forward, ignoring the way the faucet left a trail of bruises across his chest and ribs as he wriggled and twisted his way through the window.

One leg finally came up far enough that he could twist himself sideways across the counter and pull one leg through. After that, it was easier to get the second leg through. His arms shook as he rolled clumsily off the counter. He would have loved to have a seat and a drink of water, but he knew he needed to let Andre in, so he turned and staggered to the back door.

Andre was waiting when he opened the door, a pleased expression on his face. "Well done, Lee."

"Th-thanks." He gulped some air and tried to calm his racing heartbeat. A part of it was exertion, but a part of it was a sort of numb surprise.

He'd just broken into a house. He'd done a lot of questionable things over the past few days, and he'd thought of doing a few more. He'd even watched two men die. But this was the first crime he'd actually committed himself. At the very least, it was the first felony. He wasn't sure how he felt about that.

He was still thinking about it, trying to reconcile himself to the necessity of it, when he heard the front door latch click. Andre stiffened from his position next to the pantry, eyes going dark as he gestured for Lee to step back against the wall. Lee obeyed, his heart hammering as the door opened.

A stocky middle-aged man stepped into the house and shut the door, holding a bag full of supplies he'd probably scavenged from somewhere nearby, perhaps one of the stores Lee and Andre had passed on their way through the neighborhood. His hair was dark brown, only lightly threaded with gray. He wasn't as tall or as heavily muscled as Andre, but he definitely outmatched Lee.

He moved swiftly down the hall from the entry to the kitchen, only to stop short at the sight of Andre leaning carelessly against the counter.

"Who the blazes are you?"

Andre smiled, a slow, predatory expression that made goosebumps rise on Lee's arms. "It doesn't matter. What does matter is I'm staying here, for the time being. You can leave, or I'll see you gone in a far less pleasant fashion."

"That's not happening. This is my house, buddy, and no wannabe gangster is going to chase me out of it. I don't care if you're with Crips, or Bloods, or Rats, or whoever. I'm not shifting, and you can't make me."

He dropped his bag of supplies and reached for something at his waist.

Andre gave him no chance to grab whatever weapon he had. With a snarl, the former convict charged forward. Lee barely got out of the way before the two men crashed into the wall nearby, grappling furiously. Lee heard a grunt from Andre then a pained cry as Andre got a hand on the man's arm, followed by the distinctive crack of a bone breaking.

The house owner screamed. Lee thought he was about to be sick. Andre, on the other hand, didn't seem to notice or care. He jerked the man away from the wall, spun in a quarter circle, and drove the man through the back door and into the yard. The two men hit the concrete with a heavy thud.

There was a brief struggle, then Andre pinned the man to the ground, one hand clenched brutally on his jaw so he couldn't scream any further.

So he can't alert the neighbors.

That was all the thought Lee had time for before Andre twisted his head to give him an impatient look. "Lee. Come help me."

Lee stumbled to the door. "Okay. You want me to find something to tie him up?"

Andre scoffed, his face a mask of disdainful anger. "Permanent solutions are always best." He tipped his head. "The officer's gun is in my bag, and you have your knife. Choose one."

He wants me to...to kill him.

There was a curious rushing noise in his ears, like standing in a wind tunnel. His stomach was churning, and he felt faint—barely able to breathe, barely able to think.

He staggered forward, his hand on his knife, but he was shaking. Maybe the gun would be better.

He went back inside, dug through Andre's bag, grabbed the pistol, and stumbled back out onto the patio, both hands white-knuckled around the grip. He held the gun up, but his hands were still shaking, and he couldn't aim. He couldn't force himself to pull the trigger.

Come on, come on, it's just like a turkey. Andre needs you to finish the guy. You're just helping him out, like you promised. Come on...

The mantra of excuses and validations didn't help. He couldn't get his hands to steady, and he couldn't bring himself to reach for the knife at his waist.

"Hurry up." Andre snapped the words, face darkening with anger in a way Lee was all too familiar with.

He tried. He really tried. But it was no use. He lowered the gun with a heaving breath, already cringing away from the inevitable consequences of his words. "I can't."

"You can't." The flat tone was worse than the anger he was used to from his father. The utter dismissal in that cool voice was like a lash, harsher than even physical blows would have been.

Andre turned away from Lee and raised his fist.

The first blow shattered the man's jaw. The second broke his nose. Then Andre reared back, heaved the man's head and shoulders off the pavement, and slammed him back down with a sickening crack. Blood splattered the concrete, and the man went limp, no longer fighting.

Andre lifted the man and slammed him back down again. Then he let go, wiped his hands disdainfully on the man's shirt, and pushed himself to his feet. He turned to Lee, and Lee shuddered.

Andre's eyes were like ice, cold and cruel and vicious in a way that made his father's temperamental rages toddler tantrums in comparison.

"You can't. And here I would've thought you would've learned such words are for the weak and the childish. Clearly your father had *reason* to be disappointed in his cowardly son."

The barbs hit deep and hurt worse than anything Max Jones had ever said.

Andre moved toward the door to the house. He paused on the threshold. "If you must be useless in anything that matters, I trust you *can* at least dispose of the trash. Do that." He gave Lee a cold, flat look, as if Lee were nothing more than dirt beneath his feet, something to be crushed without thought.

Then he walked into the house. The screen door clacked shut behind him. Lee let out a jagged breath.

He couldn't look away from the man lying on the ground, the red pool under his head, and the splatters on the ground. He knew, even without checking, that the man was dead. The fact shook him almost as much as the fear of how close he'd come to being next.

He knew Andre was dangerous, but he'd never thought his anger would be so cutting, wielding words as mercilessly as blades and more painful than a beating. It was worse by far than anything his father had ever done. What would Andre do if Lee ever *really* angered him?

He didn't want to find out. It was becoming painfully clear what Andre did with people who got in his way.

Lee swallowed against the dryness in his mouth and throat. He set Andre's gun to one side and stepped toward the body.

Andre had said before that Lee had skills. He'd praised him for those skills. Minutes ago, he'd been pleased by the way Lee managed to get through the window to get them into the house. Andre hadn't hurt him because he knew Lee wasn't completely useless, even if that wasn't what he'd said. Lee clung to that thought.

He wasn't useless. He'd proved that before. He just had to work harder to prove to Andre that he was useful and helpful, and to remind him of the skills he did have. And he'd have to get over his weak nerves.

It was him or us. Andre just made sure it wasn't us. I gotta remember that. It's us versus the world, and I can't let him down by not being ready to protect myself or watch his back. He's just mad that my weakness could have got him hurt or killed. That's all it is.

He moved closer to the body and winced as the smell of blood and offal stung his nose. It reminded him of the turkey he'd shot and dressed only a few days prior. He coughed, then clenched his jaw against the nausea that wanted to bring him to his knees.

Just treat it like a turkey. Or a deer.

Lee took a deep breath. Then he bent down and got to work.

19

KIM NAKAMURA

For the first hour or so of hunting, Kim had focused on scanning the area around her, looking for any sign of a wild animal. But as the time ticked past and the sun rose higher, she found her attention starting to wander. It didn't help that Mutt had fallen asleep. The dog was snoring softly next to her knee and drooling on her jeans.

She wanted to talk to Dennis more about Humboldt and about Lewis, but she wasn't sure how to broach the topic, especially as the silence lengthened around them. It didn't help that Dennis was also dozing, exhausted by his ordeal of the past few days. Out of the corner of her eye, she saw him jolt himself awake several times.

How long were they supposed to wait for an animal to come by? Would the practice gunshot from earlier have scared off the game? How long would animals avoid an area before venturing close again? And how could she, or Dennis for that matter, even be sure there would be any animals? Sure, there was the stream—or river, if you were being generous—but why would animals come to this section as opposed to some other location?

Kim knew hunting required patience and silence. That didn't make it any easier to stay where she was as the minutes ticked past.

The sun inched its way toward noon, and Kim started to feel hungry. She ignored it with the patience she'd developed since the EMP blast. She sipped water from the bottle she'd brought and kept her eyes on the woods.

There. A flicker of movement caught her eye. Instantly, she felt wide awake and alert. She shifted carefully to face the source of the movement and flipped the safety off. She cradled the gun lightly in both hands, mindful of what Dennis had told her. Both hands on the grip, both eyes open, finger away from the trigger until she'd lined up a target in the sights.

She kept her breathing light and shallow and settled into her new position, watching and waiting.

Another flicker of movement. Kim waited. She didn't even dare to nudge Dennis or Mutt. She was surprised the dog hadn't woken when she'd moved, but she was grateful for the small favor. Mutt couldn't resist chasing things, but Dennis was of the opinion she'd never been trained for hunting.

Another movement, and this time Kim saw the animal as it popped out of the undergrowth a few yards away. A large, fat rabbit, ears twitching to and fro as it hopped hesitantly toward the stream. Kim kept herself steady, barely even breathing as she slowly lifted the gun into position and aimed at the rabbit.

Head shots were supposed to be the most humane, guaranteed to kill. But could she make a head shot? She'd never tried to target anything smaller than a tree.

A rabbit was small enough that a body shot would probably do the job, even if it wouldn't bring down anything bigger, like a deer.

She lined up the sights on the rabbit as it hopped free of the undergrowth, inches from the water. The wind was light and blowing in a direction that meant the rabbit hadn't smelled her. It hadn't noticed her presence at all.

Her finger slipped inside the trigger guard. The rabbit took another hop forward, and she adjusted her sights accordingly. Her throat felt tight, her stomach clenched. She'd never killed anything before. But it was a rabbit, and it wasn't like she was a vegetarian or a pacifist, even if she did plan to go into medicine.

A rabbit meant food. Food meant survival. That was all she needed to think about. That and making sure she squeezed the trigger as Dennis had instructed her. Squeeze, not jerk or pull. Her finger tightened on the trigger.

She was so focused on the rabbit, on keeping it in her sights, that the gun going off in her hand startled her almost as much as it did the rabbit, Mutt, and Dennis. The loud crack of the weapon firing rang through the trees.

Mutt jolted to her feet, head up and eyes scanning the woods for any potential threat.

Dennis jerked awake with a grunt. "Kim?"

The rabbit jerked and collapsed in a spray of red.

Kim lowered the gun, dazed by the combination of loud noise and apparent success. Then she hauled herself to a standing position and made her way toward the small, crumpled form that had once been a living animal.

By luck, or by dint of Dennis's teaching, she'd hit it in the chest. It looked like she might have hit the heart, though she couldn't be sure. She stared at the red, viscous liquid staining the grass next to the riverbank.

"Kim?" Dennis stumped up beside her. He spotted the rabbit and grinned. "Looks like you got a nice fat one. Well done." He studied it. "I would have aimed for the head, but for a first time, and never having handled a gun before, you did well. Looks like you've got a knack for this."

She wasn't sure that was a good thing. Still, she had been successful. She took a deep breath. It was only then she realized she was still holding the gun, pointed down at the grass. She tapped the safety on, then looked up at Dennis. "What do we do now?"

Dennis looked at the ground then lowered himself to the grass with a grunt and dropped his bag off his shoulder. "Need to field dress the rabbit so we can cook it when we get back to town."

Kim gulped. "Field dress?"

"Skin and butcher, at least the basics, then package it up. I brought some plastic bags along in case we got something."

Kim crouched next to him. "I don't know how to skin a rabbit."

"Didn't expect you to. I'll talk you through it." Dennis gave her a lopsided, encouraging smile. "Do kids still do dissections in biology classes, or did you do something like it in your pre-med courses?"

"A frog. In a lab. Not like this." She felt a little queasy and forced the sensation down. Doctors couldn't afford to get queasy. Even if she'd had the luxury of a weak stomach before, she didn't think she'd survive long if she didn't toughen up a little. "Don't we need a knife or something?"

"Sure." Dennis reached down to his ankle and pulled free a knife in a holster. The blade was about six inches long, and perhaps an inch wide. "I should have given you this before, but I wasn't sure if you'd need it, or use it." He offered it to her handle first. "This is my old military Ka-Bar, and it's pretty sharp, so you need to be careful how you hold it and how you use it. Do you know how to handle a knife?"

"Umm, sort of? I know how to use a scalpel." Kim eyed the knife with trepidation. "I know the obvious stuff, like don't grab the blade and keep the tip pointed away from you. And don't run with a blade in hand. You know, stuff everyone knows."

"Good starting point." Dennis nodded. "Now, a knife is a bit like a gun. Always assume it's dangerous, even if it's supposedly dull or in a sheath. Sheaths can slip, and in the right circumstances, even a dull knife can do a lot of damage. Sometimes they can do more harm than a sharp blade would do."

Kim eyed the blade then wrapped one hand carefully around the handle. She started to pull it toward her, but Dennis shook his head. "Make sure you've got a firm grip, then say 'thank you.'"

"Why?" She couldn't help asking. She understood why she'd need a firm grip, but the sudden demand for courtesy seemed a bit much.

"Easy. 'Thank you,' among people who handle blades, is a shorthand way of telling the other person that you've got control of the blade, and it isn't going to fall and hurt someone when they let go."

"Oh." She tightened her fingers around the handle. "Thank you." Dennis let go, and the weight fell into her hand. It was lighter than she expected, and somehow smaller. The guard pressed against her knuckles as she shifted her grip. She moved her hand, experimenting with different ways to hold the blade until she found one that felt both comfortable and secure.

She looked back down at the rabbit. "So, what now?"

"Start by laying the rabbit out flat and cutting around the neck."

Skinning a rabbit and butchering it turned out to be very different from dissecting a frog. For one thing, the body was still warm, and the fur was soft against her hands, not cold and slick. And the Ka-Bar was larger and harder to use than a scalpel. It didn't fit the movements she knew for dissection. But she managed, with Dennis talking her through the steps.

Cut a ring around the neck, set the rabbit on its back. Cut lightly from throat to pelvis. Remove the pelt, starting with the hind feet, peeling it away from the underlying muscle. Be careful not to nick any internal organs, or they'd contaminate the meat.

She wasn't sure how much that mattered, given that the bullet had done plenty of damage on that front. It had obliterated the heart and lungs. She said as much.

Dennis shook his head. "Part of it's principle. You need to practice doing it right so you don't pick up bad habits later. Besides that, heart and lungs won't foul the meat with toxic stuff. But if you puncture the stomach or intestines, you will."

She filed that away for future reference and continued working under Dennis's guidance. The hide didn't come off neatly, the way she'd thought it would, but eventually that part was done. Then Dennis talked her through cleaning the organs out and removing the feet and head. They rinsed the carcass off in the river, and then Dennis pointed out places to cut for the butchering. Behind the shoulder blades, at the hip, across the ribs—away from the spine, he instructed her—and across the belly.

Everything—except for the remnants of the rabbit crap trapped in the hind end—went into different bags. Kim took mental notes as Dennis laid out what the non-meat portions could be used for.

Hide—gloves or shoe linings.

Guts and the like—bury for fertilizer for the soil, or store as hunting bait for predators or even fishing, instead of worms or artificial bait.

Bones—Mutt could eat some of them, but they could also be used to make stock for a soup or a stew, to add flavor.

Kim passed Mutt a hind leg, and the dog flopped down next to the water and began to gnaw on it, slobbering enthusiastically.

The whole process was a nasty, bloody business, but it was educational. In the end, they had meat for one or two meals, and she felt like she might be a little more competent. A little more ready to survive the world she'd been thrown into with the EMP blast.

Dennis looked satisfied when they finished up. "We might hang around a little while longer, see if we can get another one. Even if we don't, I'd have to say this was a successful day." He smiled. "Lewis will be impressed you got a rabbit on your first try. He's already told me you've got the makings of a fine doctor and a real community asset."

Kim took a deep breath. "Look, I know Lewis is your friend from the military and all, but I don't think he's the great guy you think he is."

Dennis frowned. "Kim, we talked about this."

"We talked about the fact that Humboldt has this militia, this martial law, with one man essentially running it—Lewis Danville. We talked about how it's like a thinly veiled version of a dictatorship, and it's not even that thinly veiled. And that the militia aren't like a real military, just some guys acting like thugs with guns. And believe me, I ought to know. I've seen their type before."

Dennis pinched the bridge of his nose, clearly irritated with her. "Militia keeps order, and Lewis was a good enough sergeant. I'll admit some of his boys are a little rough around the edges, but these are troubled times."

"Where do you draw the line between being rough around the edges and being a bully, or worse? Joan said those bruises were from cows or something, but I know what bruises made by someone grabbing you really hard look like. Those were bruises from human violence, not an accident with a cow. The people in town give the militia a wide berth, too, like they're afraid of them. They don't act like they feel protected." Kim's frustration was mounting, and she fought to keep her tone level and civil. Shouting wouldn't make her point.

Dennis shook his head. "Lewis Danville's a good man. He'd watch out for his people, and he knows better than to let armed troops run wild. People might be a little on edge, but it's been barely two weeks since the world got turned upside-down."

"It's more than that."

Dennis turned a sharp look on her, his own exasperation showing through clearly, even with the haze of pain and weariness that clouded his eyes and carved lines of strain into his face. "Even if you're right, what do you suggest? Humboldt might not be perfect, but it's the place these people call home. And it's a good bit better than a lot of places I've seen. They've got food, they've got shelter, and they've got protection from marauders, looters, and violent gangs. They've even got a limited use of power and vehicles. Compared to all that, martial law—even with curfew and rationing in effect—isn't such a heavy price to pay."

"But what's to stop Lewis Danville from ordering other 'security' measures?" She emphasized the word with a hefty dose of sarcasm. "He's the head of the militia, so he practically runs the town already. He's got curfew and rationing already set up, he decides who gets what food and who has access to weapons and vehicles. What about when he starts restricting water, or who can go where and when?"

"He wouldn't do that without a good reason," Dennis said.

"All tyrants think they have good reasons for oppression."

"He's keeping this town safe, Kim." Dennis was getting angry, and Kim was fine with that. It seemed fair that someone else should feel the frustration she felt. "They lose some liberties for the short term, but right now, Lewis is acting like a commander in a hot zone, and he's not entirely wrong to do so. Once things settle down, and the community is more self-sufficient and better established, he'll ease up on the restrictions."

"Sure he will." She couldn't keep the skepticism out of her voice. She rose to her feet, too restless and irritated to sit still. "It'll take some time for the animals to come back. I'm taking Mutt for a walk."

The dog heaved herself upright from where she'd been dozing once again. Kim sheathed the knife, stuffed the gun Dennis had given her into her belt, and held out a hand. "Come on, Mutt." The dog huffed and bounded over to stand beside her.

Kim gave Dennis one last frustrated look then turned and stalked off, heading south along the bank of the stream. She knew he wouldn't follow her.

How could she make him understand something was wrong? She understood loyalty, and she respected it, but there was a line between that and blind faith. She feared Dennis was on the wrong side of the line in regard to Lewis Danville.

She couldn't help thinking of a quote she'd heard in one of her history classes, one she'd carried with her. She wasn't sure of the exact wording, but the gist, as she remembered it, seemed to sum up Humboldt perfectly: *Those who sacrifice liberty for safety will have neither.*

The first time she'd heard it, she'd been put in mind of her mother, living under the restrictions of WitSec to avoid retribution from her father's more unsavory friends. The quote was a validation of her anger, like confirmation that her mother had made the wrong choice.

Her gut said that the citizens of Humboldt were making the same mistake, but Lewis Danville wasn't Dennis. She didn't trust him to know when to back off and when to tighten his control. She didn't like his attitude, and she didn't trust the way it had changed when he saw Dennis or when he learned she was a doctor.

Was she grateful he'd convinced Dennis to take the first steps in his recovery from addiction? Yes. But she had the feeling that he considered it less an act of friendship and more a way of accruing a debt, which he'd call due when it suited him. Maybe it was uncharitable to think so, but if there was anything she'd learned, it was that sometimes a little unwarranted wariness was the safest way to go.

A soft bark from Mutt distracted her and brought her back to the present. They'd wandered quite a ways from Dennis and their hunting site. From the look of her coat, Mutt had been having a grand time splashing in the water and rolling in the dirt while Kim was lost in her thoughts.

Now the dog was pawing at something in the ground, prodding it with her nose. Kim grinned. "What do you have there, Mutt? Someone else's buried bones? Gopher down a gopher hole?" She walked closer to get a better look.

Something glinted in the dirt. Kim frowned, then crouched down and nudged Mutt to the side so she could get a better look. It was definitely metal. She reached out and began to brush away the dirt, working carefully to unearth the object.

The metal was thin, forming a small frame twisted out of alignment but oddly familiar. She worked the rest of the object free, then moved to the stream and rinsed her find clean.

It was a pair of glasses. Thin rectangular frames with rounded-off corners that made them look more hexagonal. The frames were gold colored, though by the tarnish and appearance, they were probably brass. The lenses were shattered, the frames were twisted, but they were still recognizable.

It took her moment to place them, but when she did, she felt cold. They reminded her of her grandfather's glasses.

Dr. Benjamin Kennedy. The man whose office Lewis had tried to use to tempt her into staying in Humboldt. She'd seen these glasses in his picture.

Lewis said Kennedy'd gone to Jackson to be with his daughter. But then, why were his glasses here? Why had they been hidden in the dirt? She couldn't see him just leaving them behind. And wasn't Jackson in a different direction?

She needed to talk to Dennis. She wiped the excess water off the frames and tucked them into a pocket, then rose from the ground. "Come on, Mutt."

The dog was still digging. Kim didn't like to think of the implications. Dogs were said to have a better sense of smell than humans. What if Mutt really was looking for someone's bones? The dog wouldn't know what finding them meant.

Kim marched forward and grabbed Mutt by the scruff of the neck. "Come on, Mutt." She emphasized the words with a firm tug. This time, Mutt came with her. She grumbled a bit, dog style, but she came, and Kim breathed a sigh of relief.

Dennis was near where she'd left him, though he'd moved back to his spot under the tree.

Kim strode up to him and shoved the frames under his nose. "Take a look at these."

Dennis took them and turned them over. "Broken glasses. What about them?"

"These belong to the previous doctor. Why would they be out here in the middle of nowhere?"

"He probably dropped them and didn't realize he'd lost them." Dennis's brow furrowed. "Why does it matter so much?"

"Because it doesn't make sense! If he'd left town like Lewis said, why wouldn't he have followed the road? Even with all the accidents and everything, it's the easiest path to take. And isn't Jackson in a different direction?" Kim tried not to snarl the words, but she felt like she was arguing with a brick wall. She'd thought he'd be different now that he was detoxing, but apparently it just meant he'd be stubborn as a mule about a different subject.

"I don't recall exactly where Jackson is on a map, but as for cutting cross-country, I don't know the doctor, so I can't speak to why he wouldn't follow a road. Just because you found his glasses—assuming they *are* his glasses, which we don't know for sure—doesn't mean anything sinister is going on." Dennis levered himself to his feet. "I know you've got reason, with the way the world's been going since the EMP, but I think you're being paranoid."

"*You're* the one who told me I need to think about these kinds of things now that everything is different!" she yelled at him and threw her hands up in the air.

She wasn't getting anywhere with him. And arguing wasn't going to change his mind. She needed more proof that something was wrong with Humboldt in general, or Lewis Danville in specific. She heaved a sigh. "Whatever." She eyed the sun in the sky. It had crossed the zenith at some point and was now sinking toward the western horizon. "We should probably be getting back to town."

Dennis checked his watch. "You're right. It's going to take a while to get back, and it wouldn't do to be trying to make the trek after dark."

"Or get in after curfew." Kim said. She couldn't help the jab.

169

"That too." Dennis didn't rise to the bait. He just hitched his bag up onto his shoulders, got his crutch under his arm, and began to head back toward the road they'd left when heading for the river. Kim followed, trusting his navigation skills and what he'd taught her of orienting herself in the wilderness. It wasn't much, given that they'd used the roads most of the time, but she'd learned a little.

The bag had to be heavier with the weight of the butchered rabbit in it, but Dennis didn't seem to care. Maybe it was balanced out by the gun and knife he still hadn't taken back from her. Or maybe he was trying to be stoic. Or he was just being his usual stubborn, bullheaded self. His face seemed paler than she would have expected. There was a tightness to his face and the set of his shoulders that she thought she recognized.

"You okay?"

"I'm fine. Just more tired than I expected. Might have got a little too much sun." Dennis's voice was gruff, sharp with strain.

He didn't sound fine. Or look fine. But she wasn't going to press the issue. She knew Dennis had his pride, and there was no point in confronting him, not when they still needed to get back to town. If he really seemed to be having trouble, she'd ask again once they returned to the house.

They emerged onto the road a minute or so later and started back toward Humboldt. Dennis did a little better on the level ground, but she kept an eye on him anyway. She didn't want him to collapse and possibly hurt himself further. The bruises he'd acquired coming to find her in Murray had mostly faded to pale brown and yellow-green, but she didn't see any reason to let him add more to the collection.

The lines on his face were getting deeper with every step. Kim cast about for some way to distract him. She knew pain was could be magnified by thinking about it too much. She said the first thing that came to mind. "So, when do you think you'll be ready to get back on the road? You seem like you're doing better."

Dennis grunted. "Better. Not great though."

"Better is still progress. If you're not getting sick anymore, maybe we could head for Memphis the day after tomorrow?" She wanted to say tomorrow, but he looked like he might need a day of rest. He was clearly far from well, despite his earlier good humor.

"Maybe. Might need a few more days." There was an edge to Dennis's voice. "There's no rush. Memphis will still be there whenever we get that far."

Kim felt a rush of dismay followed by anger. "The city might be there, but what about my family? What about Aunt Carol and Uncle Bruno? What about my mother?"

"You don't know that she's heading to Memphis."

"She has to be. I know she stayed in WitSec, and she thought she had to stay away, but she wouldn't..." The words stuttered to a stop.

She wouldn't abandon family? But she'd gone into WitSec and left all of them behind. Kim had spent years resenting her for it, and she was still angry about it. She knew, from her brief holiday visits and more frequent phone calls, that Aunt Carol felt the same way. She swallowed hard.

"She'd come to Memphis to be sure we were okay." The words weren't as strong or as sure as she wanted them to be, but at least she was able to say them.

"Then she'll be there when we manage to make it there. In fact, with the distance she'd have to travel, any delay makes it more likely that she'll get there before we do, so you won't have to wonder and wait," Dennis said.

She glared at him. "Why are you so interested in staying here? Because of Lewis?"

He paused for a second, staring at her with hooded eyes in a worn face. There was anger there, but even stronger was a sort of bleakness that reminded her of those nights when she was sitting in her apartment, just after she'd been emancipated, wishing with all her heart for her mother and the comforts of her home and the life she'd known.

After a moment, he turned away with a breath that seemed to come from the bottom of his gut and carry a world's worth of exhaustion with it. "Lewis is a good man, and I think you're wrong about him. But Kim, I'm tired."

He began walking again, and Kim fell into step beside him. "Okay. So you rest tonight and tomorrow, and you'll feel better then."

"It's not that simple. Not that easy. Detoxing is harder than you think. And I've still got to deal with the injuries. Don't you understand that, Kim?"

"I do. But you're tough. You're Super Soldier Sullivan. You can—"

"I found them!" The voice was loud and startled Kim. "Someone call Militia Leader Danville. I've found the young doctor and her friend!"

Kim and Dennis both stumbled to a stop. They'd arrived back at the outskirts of Humboldt. Kim hadn't registered it, and she wasn't sure Dennis had either, with his focus on their argument and putting one foot in front of the other.

Even so, they'd managed to cross the border of the town. Now they were staring down the barrel of a rifle in the hands of a young man in the semi-uniform of the town militia.

Kim took a step forward then stopped as the gun lifted in warning. "What's going on? Is someone hurt?"

"You went missing. Militia Leader Danville ordered us to look for you." He stepped forward, his expression threatening and cold. "He'll be here soon, and when he gets here, he'll want to have a word with you."

Crap on a cracker and dogs in a dung heap, to borrow some of the colorful phrases she'd learned among the Black Rats and in some of her history classes.

Somehow, she didn't think having words with Militia Leader Danville was going to be a pleasant experience.

20

KIM NAKAMURA

L ewis Danville arrived fifteen minutes later, red-faced with anger. He jumped out of his truck and stalked toward them with a scowl that made some of the militia members shrink back.

Kim hadn't been looking forward to the confrontation to begin with, but Dennis was flagging, leaning more and more on his crutch as his expression tightened with pain. Lewis didn't look inclined to be even marginally reasonable.

He stormed up to them. "Where in tarnation have you been?"

Kim bit her tongue on the urge to say something flippant like "None of your business" and opted for an honest answer instead. "I asked Dennis to take me hunting."

"Hunting where?"

Mutt bristled and began to growl at his tone, and Dennis dropped a hand to her head to settle her. "Toward Lake Humboldt. We stopped along the Forked Deer River. We weren't in any danger."

"I decide who's in danger. You don't know what sort of perils there are out there," Lewis snarled. "You're in no shape to protect her, Sullivan, and Kim's skills are too important to risk." He whipped back to face Kim. "I thought you understood that. I thought you were smart. Clearly you don't have a lick of common sense, or you would have known not to go wandering off!"

"I just wanted to learn how to hunt." Kim tried to sound confident, but Lewis looked manic to her. Manic—and dangerous.

"While you were out there learning to hunt, you weren't *here* helping Joan like you should have been. Did you forget you need to help Mr. Craig with his diabetes? Or Mark Cardney with getting his ankle back into working shape? What about helping Joan with the livestock and taking care of other injuries? One of the men had a shelf fall on his head. Joan had to try to diagnose him, but she can't tell me if he's concussed or not and if it's safe to let him go back to work. That's three people who needed *your* expertise, girl, and they didn't get proper help because you were out learning to hunt!"

"Joan was gone when I checked in earlier, and hunting is an important skill." She tried to defend herself.

Lewis was in no mood to listen. "It's a skill that dozens of young men in this town are better equipped and better trained to make use of than you. I've got plenty of young bucks who can handle a gun, or a bow and arrow if comes to that. But you and Joan are the only ones with any medical knowledge, and you're the only one with proper training."

Kim kept her mouth shut and her rebuttal to herself. It was clear that nothing she said was going to make any difference to the enraged militia leader.

Lewis glared at them both for a moment. "Were you seen?"

"Seen? By who? There's no one around." Kim frowned.

"You see anything out there? Smoke, fire, traces of campers?"

"Nothing but each other, Mutt, and a rabbit or two." She set her hand on Mutt's back, close enough to Dennis's to feel his fingers through the fur. She needed the reassurance of his presence and Mutt's strength. The dog leaned closer to her, as if sensing Kim's unease and fear. Despite Dennis's unspoken command, she hadn't relaxed. Smart dog.

"You leave any traces of your presence?"

"Nothing but the place where we butchered a rabbit." Dennis shifted his weight. "Lewis, what's all this about?"

Lewis flicked a glance of mingled disdain and fury in his old comrade's direction. "This is about the safety of Humboldt and protecting valuable community assets. Which, clearly, you aren't fit to do, since you let her go wandering off into the wilderness."

"I didn't wander off," Kim countered, "and Dennis was with me. I was—"

"You were putting the whole community at risk is what you were doing!" Lewis stalked forward. It was all Kim could do to hold her ground. She was beginning to understand why even tough guys like the militia men would obey this man without hesitation or argument. "You don't know who's out there, or what." He raked them both with his gaze. "Ever since the EMP, we've been seeing roving gangs of looters. And a few loners, but they aren't anything to laugh at. They're tough folks, and most of them are meaner than snakes. They'll rob you blind if you're lucky, kill you or worse if you're not. Sullivan, you aren't in any shape to stop them. You can barely stand on your own two feet, and you're shaking like a snowstorm victim."

Dennis looked like he was about to protest, and Kim wanted to say that the danger was part of why she'd wanted to learn hunting and

176

shooting. Lewis didn't give them any room to speak as he continued his tirade.

"A lone man would have been bad enough in that we could have lost Kim and her skills. But what if you'd encountered a marauding band of pillagers? They could have forced you to reveal the status of our little town, or they could have waited and followed you back here. Your actions could have put all of Humboldt at risk. Do you realize that?"

Dennis was frowning at his old friend. "Lewis, I know you have to protect your people, and I respect that, but I think you're being a little too protective. You sound like you're getting paranoid in your old age, Sergeant."

"And you clearly aren't thinking straight if you think I'm not doing exactly what I need to be doing." Lewis faced Dennis, and there was more than a hint of a sneer in his words as he spoke. "You've only been clean for a day or two, Sullivan, and you think your mind's recovered from the way those drugs addled your wits? 'Cause I sure don't, or you'd be keeping the girl in town and yourself in bed, where you obviously belong."

Dennis flushed red as the verbal blow hit home. His hand clenched in Mutt's fur, and Kim felt herself wince in sympathy. Worse, she saw the barely hidden sneers on some of the militia men surrounding them, the scorn. Dennis could probably see it too.

Anger followed sympathy, comforting in the warmth of it, even as she gritted her teeth in frustration at being unable to think of anything to do. She didn't like that Dennis had been a drug addict, but announcing it to the whole militia? Treating him like he was brain damaged or slow-witted because of his condition?

She thought Lewis had understood that Dennis was in rough shape, that he'd cared about his old friend. But he clearly cared less than she'd expected, and what he'd just done was despicable. She might have been peeved at some of the actions addiction had driven Dennis to, but she'd never have encouraged him to stay in Humboldt and get clean here if she'd known his supposed friend would undermine his recovery and confidence like that.

Kim was tempted to tell Lewis exactly what she thought of his behavior. But with several militia men surrounding them, she forced herself to stay silent. She and Dennis stood in place while Lewis directed his men to form a squad and take them back to their house. Then Lewis turned back to Dennis. His temper seemed to have cooled, but Kim wasn't sure she liked the grim determination in his expression any better.

"We'll see you back to your house for tonight," Lewis said. "Kim, there are people who need your assistance, so I hope you'll be reasonable and not make them suffer for this unpleasantness." With that, he turned away and stomped off to his truck. It roared to life, and he drove away a moment later.

Kim scowled after it. "Could have given us a ride back, you jerk." She wasn't too concerned about herself, but Dennis was turning paler by the second, and the lines of pain were getting deeper in his face. He was still upright, but she wasn't sure how much farther he could make it.

Dennis must have caught a glimpse of her concerned stare, or maybe he was still stinging from Lewis's words, because he braced himself on his crutch and forced himself to stand a little straighter. He limped forward with grim determination. "Come on, Kim. We don't want to keep these men away from their posts. Besides, curfew will be soon, and we've still got dinner to cook."

Kim fell into step beside him, trying to ignore the loose guard of militia men that walked alongside them, blocking any chance to change course. She was glad for the reassuring bulk of Mutt padding between her and Dennis. The dog's head was swiveling from guard to guard, and every so often a discontented rumble, like the beginning of a growl or a deep-throated bark, would vibrate through her chest. Kim knew the dog was probably only responding to the unease she and Dennis were projecting, but she was the tiniest bit gleeful to see some of the militia members eyeing Mutt warily, as if she might bite. Perhaps it was petty of her to find amusement in their discomfort, but she'd take what enjoyment she could get, given the circumstances.

They arrived at the house just as dusk was beginning to settle into twilight. Kim ignored the militia members at her back as she unlocked the door and let the three of them into the house. Once Dennis had staggered past her, she slammed the door shut and locked it. Then she went to a nearby window and peeked out.

She'd hoped the men would leave after they were inside and go about their business, but apparently Lewis had given them different orders. Two of the militia had set up a slow circling patrol around the house, and another man remained on guard by the front door.

She turned back to Dennis, who'd collapsed in his usual chair. "They've got guards patrolling around the house like we're criminals!" Her voice rose as she vented the fury she'd felt earlier. "Hunting us down and lecturing us about 'town safety' and 'civic duties' just because we decided to go hunting without his express permission? It's not like we're kids, or helpless. And he's not our boss!"

"He is in charge of keeping his town safe, and he's not wrong about the dangers out there. I've seen some of them myself, and so have you." Dennis sighed. "I understand what Lewis is doing may seem harsh or unreasonable to you, but he has a lot of responsibilities, and it's a difficult job."

Kim rounded on him. "So you were okay with the way he talked to you? Like you were brain damaged? You were okay with how he told

179

everyone you were an addict and made you sound like you were barely a step up from a village idiot? Because I sure wasn't. He had no right to say those things to you—or about you."

Dennis flushed. "I can't say I appreciated that, no." His expression darkened. "I told him about my condition in confidence, and I don't like the fact that he disregarded that."

"So you agree that he's out of control and out of order?" Kim felt a brief moment of hope. If she could convince Dennis to leave Humboldt, they still might have a chance to escape before Lewis tried to make them prisoners within the town.

Her hope shattered when Dennis shook his head. "I don't agree with how he handled things, but we have to remember that Lewis was upset. And worried about us. I suspect he'll apologize once his temper cools."

"Being upset doesn't justify treating us like prisoners."

"I know, but he'll probably stop being so restrictive once he's calmed down and thought things through." Dennis said. "Just be patient with him, Kim."

"Whatever." She could tell by the expression on his face that the argument was going nowhere. He was too loyal to his old friend to think clearly regarding his behavior. Or perhaps it was some remnant of his training and time in the Marines: a commanding officer must be obeyed. Either way, she'd need more proof, or else a compelling argument, to change his mind.

She changed the subject. "We can decide what to do in the morning. For now," she dropped her pack and collected his from where he'd set it down while she was checking the window, "what's the best way to cook a rabbit?"

"Well, there are a number of ways, really." Dennis started to stand, then he crumpled back into his seat. His face went white and his jaw clenched. Kim could see the pain sweep across his features as he tried to soothe his leg. "Ahhh…"

The spasm held him for several minutes while Kim watched powerlessly, cursing the fact that his recovery meant there would be no painkillers to help ease the throbbing. By the time Dennis finally relaxed a bit, he was sweating. She felt sick to her stomach with concern for him.

When she was sure he was at least a little better, she stepped forward. "Is there anything I can do for you?"

Dennis shook his head and shoved himself slowly to his feet once more, leaning heavily on the chair and the crutch as half-voiced curse words spilled from behind clenched teeth. Once he was upright, he gave her a pain-filled grimace. "I think I just need to rest."

She nodded. "What about dinner?"

"I'd never be able to stomach it." He sighed. "Sleep's the best thing for me, and a chance to rest the muscle. You can cook the rabbit pretty much any way you'd like with whatever we have in the kitchen. Though you might clean the bones and start a soup stock with them. Just simmer them nice and slow."

"Okay." She watched him slowly drag himself up the stairs. Then she turned and looked at Mutt, who was lying across the edge of the back door. She scowled. "I hate this place, Mutt. I hate that we're stuck here until he's feeling better, and that there's no telling when that will be."

She took the rabbit meat out of the bags. She put some of it in a pan to cook with a little oil, salt, and pepper. She started simmering the bones on a low heat, as Dennis had suggested, with a little more salt and pepper. She gave the remainder of the meat to Mutt, who wolfed it down as soon as it hit the floor.

Twenty minutes later, her meal was done. She carried it into the living room so she could flop across the couch as she ate. While she chewed, she thought about her experiences in Humboldt so far.

Something was wrong with this place, and it all tied back to Lewis Danville and his militia. She was willing to bet the missing Doc Kennedy—she couldn't make herself believe he was simply absent after she'd found his glasses—was a part of the story surrounding the problems in the town.

She wouldn't find the proof she needed to convince Dennis or the answers she needed to satisfy herself while sitting in the house. Luckily, Lewis had given her the excuse she needed to gather information and search for clues. If she was serving as the town's doctor, she'd have free run of the place—or at least as close to freedom as she was going to get here.

Tomorrow, I'm going to find a way to get the truth about what's been going on in Humboldt, no matter what it takes. She finished the rabbit and took the plate to the kitchen, then headed for her room to get some rest.

21

BILL WHEELER

S hannon's fever was down. Bill finished winding the bandages around her shoulder and sat back to look at his handiwork. They'd been in the emergency care center for several days—long enough for him to use most of the available bandages and medications —but he was cautiously hopeful that things were finally turning around.

The first two days had been touch and go. Shannon's fever had hovered at the edge of dangerously high, and delirium held her firmly in its grip. For a while there, he'd been afraid he hadn't acted in time to stop the blood poisoning from turning into gangrene.

But the antibiotics had done their work, and the angry red lines had started to recede. Each time he drained the wound, there was less gunk to drain from it, and the smell of poison and rot began to lessen. Shannon wasn't out of the woods by any means, not just yet, but he was beginning to hope she might come through all right.

He went out to the entryway where he'd made his own sleeping area and collected the can of broth he'd prepared. It was thin enough to be good hot or cold, and it was about all Shannon had been able to swallow, besides water and the sports drinks she'd carried with her. It wasn't enough. She'd lost weight she really didn't have to lose, but at least it had kept the fever from drying her out completely.

Bill took the broth back to the treatment room, trying not to think too much about the problem he'd discovered the day before. But he couldn't stop thinking about it: they were running out of medical supplies. Packing and wrapping the shoulder multiple times a day had used up far more gauze and bandages than he'd realized. Yesterday he'd discovered he only had one package of sterile gauze and three rolls of bandages left.

They were also low on antibiotics, or at least anything he recognized as such. There might be other types of antibiotics here, but he wouldn't know them by their labels. There wasn't a ready-made reference source handy for him to consult, not that he was sure he'd be able to make heads or tails of it even if he found one. Medical terminology could be confusing, as he'd discovered while caring for Edith during her illness.

They needed more bandages, at the minimum, but he had no idea where to find them. He also wasn't sure about leaving Shannon alone and unconscious. What if more looters came and tried to break into the truck? What if they broke into the emergency care center and found her while she was helpless?

Bill grimaced as he entered the room. He didn't like thinking such thoughts, necessary though they might be. He'd been raised to think the best of his fellow man, and even all the catastrophes of the past weeks couldn't shake that lingering sense of trust and respect.

He approached Shannon's bed, elevated it with practiced motions, and tipped her head back to allow the broth to go down easily. He carefully poured a small swallow of the liquid down her throat.

Shannon coughed. He started to adjust the angle of her head, but Shannon pulled away from him. Bill froze, uncertain if the motion was an unconscious instinct or a deliberate movement. Shannon coughed a few more times, swallowed, and relaxed against the bed. Her head lolled on the mattress, then she faced him. Her bleary eyes opened for the first time since the accident and focused in his general direction. A weak, croaking voice, raspy with disuse, uttered one slurred word. "Bill…"

Bill wanted to whoop with joy and jump into the air like a jubilant teenager. He restrained himself with an effort and kept his voice quiet. "Hey there, Shannon." He held up the broth. "Can you drink some more? You need liquids."

Shannon stared at him, clearly not quite awake. Then she gave the tiniest of nods and opened her mouth. Bill slid a hand carefully behind her head to help steady her and put the can to her lips. He again poured it slowly, taking utmost care to avoid choking her by accident.

Shannon swallowed several sips of the broth, then pulled away. "Water." Her voice was still raspy, but stronger. Bill hurried back out to the waiting area, grabbed a fresh water bottle, and brought it back to her.

Shannon drank roughly a quarter of the bottle before she pulled away. Her eyes gained some clarity, and she blinked and looked slowly around the room. "Where?"

"We're in an emergency care center in Stuttgart. You passed out behind the wheel of the truck."

Shannon frowned, then looked at him. "I had…fever…shoulder…"

"Your shoulder got infected, and the infection turned to blood poisoning. You've been out for days—feverish and delirious. I've been taking care of you." He didn't see any reason to give her the gory details, not at that moment. Details could wait until she was feeling better, if she insisted on knowing them. Bill knew he'd be just as happy if she never asked and he never had to relive the experience.

Shannon didn't say anything for several moments. She already looked tired, even though she'd been awake for less than half an hour. Finally, she managed one more word: "Supplies?"

Bill had to smile. Pragmatic Shannon, always thinking of their situation and their survival. "We've got plenty of food and fuel, as near as I can tell. Might need to get some more medical supplies, but that can wait until you're feeling better."

Shannon shook her head, just the smallest of movements. "No." She coughed, then winced as the movement jarred the still-healing shoulder. "Don't wait."

"I don't want to leave you by yourself when you're still feeling poorly. Now that you're on the mend, you'll be ready to go in a few days. We can look for more supplies then."

Shannon shook her head again. How she managed to look stubborn and determined with her eyes drooping and exhaustion stamped on her face, Bill didn't know, but she did. "Don't wait." Then her eyes slid closed as exhaustion claimed her once more.

Bill watched her sleep for a moment, his emotions churning in a mix of relief, fondness, and consternation. He knew Shannon was still ill and weak, and not really in any condition to make decisions or give orders. All the same, he felt like he ought to follow her direction and do as she'd asked, despite the potential risks.

He went back to the waiting area, turning the matter over in his mind as he ate some of the broth, drank a bottle of sports drink, and cleaned up the trash.

Yes, there was a risk that looters might come by and try to break into the truck or the emergency center. They might even find Shannon. But if he didn't go out to hunt for supplies, he was guaranteed to run out of bandages and antibiotics. How did he know if the medicine he'd given her was enough? Doctors always said you had to take a full course of antibiotics, or the illness could come back. Was it the same for infections? Bill wasn't sure, or what the full course of antibiotics was for the medicine he'd been using. It wasn't like the prescriptions he'd taken for illnesses, where there was a bottle or a panel with the instructions written out for dosing. He didn't want to find out he'd guessed wrong by trying to nurse Shannon through another infection.

No matter how he looked at it, the risk of looters attacking the emergency center and finding Shannon was lower than the danger of the infection returning in full force. She was right—he couldn't put off going to look for more bandages, gauze, and medicine.

Bill pushed his makeshift bedding to a place where it couldn't be seen from the doors if someone looked inside. He didn't want people seeing signs of habitation and trying to come in. Then he tucked Shannon's knife into his belt along with a flathead screwdriver that could serve as a tool or a secondary weapon if he needed it. He also emptied Shannon's bag and adjusted the strap to hang it crosswise over his chest.

Once he was sure he had everything he needed, Bill checked for signs of anyone watching, then slipped through the doors, which he shut and locked behind him. He rattled the door to make sure it was secure, then went around to the back of the truck to make sure it too was firmly locked and bolted. Once he was certain everything was locked down, he made his way across the parking lot beyond the emergency center to look at the street.

The emergency center was on the edge of a suburban neighborhood, with houses across the street and to the left, where the three boys had disappeared when he'd sent them away. To the right there were still a few houses, but there were also larger buildings he thought might be shops or businesses. Bill turned his steps in that direction. He hoped he wouldn't have to go far. The sooner he could get back to Shannon, the better.

He'd barely crossed the first street when a shout came from behind him. "Hey, buddy! Hey!"

He turned to find a stocky man wearing stained jeans and a battered hoodie waving at him. "Yeah, you! Hold up a minute!"

Bill stopped and waited as the man jogged up to him. He was surprised a complete stranger would call out to him, but he wasn't going to ignore someone who needed his attention. And maybe he could get some information.

"Who are you?"

"Name's Jay. Just Jay." The man stumbled to a stop, breathing heavily. "Was hoping to catch you." He frowned. "At least, I think I was."

"How do you mean?"

"Well, I heard about a fellow with a truck parked near the urgent care center. Since you seem to be the only man nearby and the only stranger, I thought it might be you." Jay took a deep breath and straightened up. "So was I right? You're the fellow with the truck?"

Bill nodded. "I am."

"It's your truck? Like, you've got the keys to the cab, and to the trailer?"

Tension gathered in Bill's shoulders. There was something about the man's questions that made him uneasy. Still, he supposed it was only reasonable for people to be curious about a truck that had been parked in their neighborhood for several days. And he'd brought the keys with him. They were always deep in his pocket, so they'd be safe. "I do."

"Great. That's great." Jay reached back, hand pressing into his lower back as if he had a backache. Without warning he whipped out a long, heavy hunting knife from the back of his belt and leveled it at Bill's torso. "Since you've got the keys, you can give them to me."

Bill jerked back, his hand going to Shannon's knife. "Excuse me?"

"You heard me. Give me the keys to that truck, or I'll take 'em from you and leave your guts on the ground." Jay stabbed at him, and Bill jumped back reflexively, avoiding the blade.

Bill whipped out Shannon's knife and flicked it open, adjusting his grip as the blade clicked and locked into place. He held it out in front of him and stepped back, putting some distance between himself and Jay. "What do you want with the truck?"

Jay snorted, his expression and voice derisive as he spoke. "Are you kidding? I saw those kids coming back from that truck the other day, carrying all that food. Mitch and his family live next door to me, and with a little prompting he told me all about it. That truck is full of supplies. Enough food to last forever, maybe even until the Army comes and fixes things."

"The Army ain't coming. There was an emergency broadcast." Bill spoke softly. "They issued the announcement over a week ago, Jay. They said everyone's going to have to fend for themselves for a while."

"Then that truck'll set me up with all the provisions I need for a good long while." Jay stalked closer. "What do you need it for, anyway? Where do you think you're going to go? What does one old guy like you need a truck full of supplies for, huh? I can put it to better use."

Bill backed up, one eye on the knife and the other on Jay's face, which was twisted in a mask of determination and avarice. "Look, Jay, if you need food or supplies to tide you over for a while, I don't mind giving you some things. Enough to last a fairly long time, until you can grow your own food or barter with your neighbors for something more sustainable. You just put that knife down and I'll take you back to the truck, and we'll get you some food."

"Why would I want to take a measly armful that will run out soon when I could have it all and set myself up as the center of the community—make everyone come to me? I could take over if I had all that food. Not to mention a working vehicle—those are worth their weight in gold these days. I could live like a king." Jay's eyes glinted. "Come on. I can tell you're no fighter. Just give me the keys, and I'll let you walk away from this. I might even leave you some food."

Had he been alone, Bill might have given in. But the truck wasn't his to give away. It was Shannon's. It was her only way to get to her daughter and her family in Memphis. He wasn't willing to betray her by giving up the keys, no matter what the consequences. He shook his head. "Afraid I can't do that."

"Your loss." Jay lunged and slashed at him. His movement was swift and sure, that of a man who was no stranger to handling a blade.

Bill dodged out of the way and swiped back at the man. His reach was longer and his reflexes were sharp, a legacy of years in a mechanics bay where accidents could happen at any time. At the last moment, he twisted his wrist, aiming to hit Jay with his fist and the metal handle of the knife. He didn't want to accidentally hurt Jay, the way he had the boys in the previous confrontation.

He realized his mistake a second later. Jay took advantage of his hesitation to drive in. The blade sliced through Bill's shirt and cut a shallow groove along his side. The burning shock of pain made him stumble. He tried to recover, but Jay was a practiced fighter and gave him no time to regain his balance.

Bill backpedaled and brought his knife up in desperate defense as he tried to get the screwdriver free or stanch the bleeding from his side.

Time moved strangely, the way it had when Barney killed Noah. He couldn't get his bearings or think straight. The strap of the bag across his shoulder and chest tangled his elbow and inhibited his movement, but he didn't dare take his eyes off Jay long enough to remove it.

Bill dodged another slashing stab of the knife, only to run right into a sucker punch from Jay's left fist that doubled him over. That was followed by a kick that knocked him to his knees. Bill dropped his knife as he reached out to break his fall with his hands.

Jay grabbed the collar of his shirt and twisted hard, getting him in a chokehold. Bill coughed as Jay set his knife next to Bill's jaw and spoke. "Last chance. Give up those keys, or I'll take them from your corpse."

"Can't." Fear flooded through him, tangled together with pain in his gut and his leg. His hand scrabbled across the ground in an attempt to find the handle of the knife. His screwdriver was in the pocket next to Jay. He didn't think he could get to it before Jay dug the blade in. "I can't give you those keys."

"I'd say it's your funeral, but no one really does those these days. Too bad." Bill felt sick with terror and fought to keep it from his expression. He might have failed Shannon, and he might be about to die, but at least he'd end his life with dignity.

A thundering boom shattered the air nearby. Jay jerked back with a yelp as something cracked into the concrete and sent shards flying into the air.

22

LEE KINGSTON JONES

L ee managed to find an old tarp made of that all-weather woven plastic-type material in a small storage bin tucked away in a corner near the garage. He carried it into the yard, laid it out, and rolled the body awkwardly onto it. His stomach churned and threatened to regurgitate his meager breakfast as his hands came in contact with the blood pooled around the man's head. The smell stung his nose, and the feel of the tacky, red liquid made him want to scrub his hands in the dirt until every particle of red was gone. The splatters across the concrete, like some demented artist's work, hit him in a way no turkey shoot or hunting kill had ever done.

He wrapped the tarp around the body of the homeowner Andre had killed in a sloppy bundle and dragged it farther away from the pavement, wincing at the weight of the stocky frame. Dead weight. The morbid joke made him want to smack his own head against the brick house. Then he stopped, a grimace crossing his face as he realized he'd forgotten something: he should check the guy's pockets for anything useful. Andre would expect him to do that.

He unwrapped the body and frisked it, trying to ignore the queasiness in his stomach as he dug through the pockets to come up with a set of keys, a wallet with ID and money that was next to useless these days, and a thin, three-inch pocketknife. He rolled the guy back up with a sigh of relief, then paused, uncertain of his next move.

He didn't have enough strength to lift the guy into a garbage can. And there was no running water at this house—at least, he assumed there wasn't, since he hadn't seen a place yet that had water still flowing—to wash the blood off the concrete.

It felt like he ought to give the guy a burial, if only so he and Andre didn't have to look at the body or smell it as it began to decompose. With a sigh, he went looking for a shovel. Andre didn't say anything to him, not even to ask about his progress as he went from the back door to the indoor garage entrance. Nor did he offer to help when Lee came back through with the shovel. He didn't even acknowledge it when Lee stopped and set down the stuff he'd retrieved at Andre's elbow.

I shouldn't have expected anything else. I failed him. Of course Andre wouldn't offer to help me. At least he's not chucking beer cans at my head.

Digging a man-sized hole in the ground was a lot harder than it looked, and Lee was soon dripping sweat, despite the cool spring air. The rough handle of the shovel scraped at his palms and threatened to raise blisters, but he kept working. Andre had told him to take care of the body, so he would. A few blisters would be a small price to pay for regaining Andre's approval, or at least lessening his disdain.

He dug until he'd created a hole about two feet deep, as far as he could tell. He'd heard somewhere that you had to dig a hole at least six feet deep to keep animals from smelling a body, but he didn't think he had the strength for that. Besides, he was only about five-foot-six, so how would he get out of a hole that deep anyway?

Lee levered himself out of the shallow grave and shoved the body into it with a grunt. Filling the hole back in took forever, but eventually he was done. He swiped one grubby arm over his forehead, then went to put the shovel back and look for something to clean himself up.

Andre was sitting on the couch, drink in hand and shoes off, relaxing. The wallet, keys, and knife had disappeared, and Lee hoped for a moment it meant Andre had forgiven him.

Andre looked up, his eyes cold and his expression dismissive. "Are you done?"

"Yeah. I guess. Buried the guy in a shallow grave." Lee shrugged awkwardly, wincing at the soreness in his back.

Andre noticed the wince, and his lip curled. "Clean yourself up, Lee. You look like you've been rolling through the muck."

Lee flushed at the rebuke, wondering why it stung so much. He turned away to put up the shovel and look for some bottled water. He found a stash of it—either the house owner he'd just buried had liked bottled water, or he'd been lucky enough to stockpile some in the early days of the disaster—and took two. One Lee drank. The other he used to wash his hands, arms, and face while standing hunched over the sink.

Andre coldly studied him as he wandered back toward the front room with his hair dripping. "I suppose it's too much to assume you'd use the bathroom." He waved Lee away. "Go find a clean shirt. You have to be smart enough for that."

It felt weird, not to mention wrong, to dig through the dead guy's clothing, but Lee did it anyway. Anything to take some of the contempt out of Andre's expression. He even managed to nerve himself up enough to take a clean pair of underwear and a jacket that sort of fit.

He hoped for some sort of acknowledgment from Andre, but the man barely looked at Lee, and he didn't say a thing when Lee produced a meal of sandwiches and chips for both of them. He simply took the food, curled his lip at it, and ate, all without ever once acknowledging Lee was there.

He wanted to apologize, but he'd learned a long time ago that apologies didn't mean a thing and didn't get him any clemency. Back at home, if he tried to apologize, it was more likely to earn him a backhand across the face and a snarled admonition to "Quit your useless sniveling and act like a man, for once."

Andre might not be as ready with his fists as Max Jones was when his mood soured, but his words were more cutting than anything Lee's father could ever have managed to produce. The weight of his disdain was almost physical, like sandpaper against Lee's gut. It made it hard to eat, or think, or do anything, for fear of angering the other man even more. He settled for sitting quietly and waiting for Andre to make the next move.

Hours passed. Andre appeared to be napping for a while, but Lee didn't dare go to sleep in case Andre woke up and got angry at him for it. He nearly jumped out of his skin when Andre opened his eyes, stretched, and rose from his seat.

"Come."

Lee shoved himself upright so fast he nearly fell over. He barely slowed down to grab the knife he'd set aside while washing up as he followed Andre out the front door. He wanted to ask where they were going, but Andre's dark mood kept him from opening his mouth. It didn't look like the older man was interested in answering questions, and asking might make things worse between them.

Lee followed his mentor through the dusk-filled streets as they moved from the residential area into a rougher part of town. Derelict mechanic shops and stores with bars on the windows lined the streets, most of them deserted. The few that weren't deserted weren't exactly welcoming. More than once, Lee saw men and women with tough-looking faces and forbidding expressions watching them from windows or doorways. It made him nervous, but Andre ignored them, so Lee did his best to pretend to do the same.

Finally, Andre paused across the street from a dingy doorway and hunkered down to watch the building. Lee studied it too, trying to figure out what was so important about this particular location. He'd have asked Andre, but he wasn't sure if asking would get him an answer or a backhand to the mouth, like Max Jones would have given him.

A weathered sign over the door identified it as the Black Roads Watering Hole. It looked like a dive bar being kept open by virtue of a coughing, rusty, decades-old generator that powered weak, flickering lights.

Two minutes later, maybe fewer, a guy with tangled, greasy hair under a bandanna, two-day stubble, and worn, stained jeans sauntered around the corner and toward the door. His denim jacket carried several patches, the most prominent of which was a name—Lee was too far away to be able to read it—over the logo of a large black rodent on a motorcycle.

Lee recalled that Andre had mentioned being a member of a motorcycle gang called the Black Rats. Maybe this was one of his former associates. He wondered how Andre had known the man would be there.

The second question was partially answered over the next few minutes as other men in similar outfits arrived and made their way inside. After the fourth or fifth man entered, Andre started forward, Lee close behind.

He wasn't technically old enough to enter a bar, but Lee wasn't going to bring it up if Andre wasn't. He figured being in a bar with a bunch of temperamental bikers was still safer than being alone in the streets. Besides, he couldn't watch Andre's back or prove himself to the man if he hid outside like a whiny kid.

He stayed close as Andre shoved the battered door open and strolled inside. The big man acted like he owned the place, and Lee did his best to imitate Andre's confidence. The door slammed shut behind him, effectively silencing the muted discussion as the patrons of the bar turned toward the door. Peering around Andre's arm, Lee could see at least half a dozen bikers, all wearing the Black Rat patch somewhere on their clothing. Three were at the bar—two with beers in hand and the third with an empty shot glass. The rest of them were slouched around a threadbare pool table.

Andre broke the silence, his voice smooth but threatening. "Good evening. I wonder if one of you gentlemen can tell me if Sarah Naka-mura Atkinson has arrived in town and where she might be."

One of the men, a slightly younger fellow with scraggly brown hair, shifted away from the bar. "Who's asking? Don't know you, and I don't think you belong here, pal."

Lee had moved to Andre's side. He saw the slow, predatory shark's smile that swept across Andre's face. "You must be new to the Black Rats, boy. I assure you, I do in fact belong here. Sarah was my wife, and I know she's a member of your gang."

"No, she ain't. And you ain't either, Andre." An older man stomped forward from beside the pool table. "Sarah disappeared, and no one knows where she is, not even Bruno and his old lady. As for you—" The man spat at Andre's feet. "I remember you. You nearly brought the whole gang down, between murdering that fellow and all your drug dealing and heroin trafficking. It was hell when the Black Rats Motorcycle Club straightened themselves out and went mainstream, and a lot of that is down to you and blackguards like you. Nearly got us all arrested for your crimes, you punk."

Andre turned his shark gaze on the man. "Your mind must be as rusty as your bike, old man. I brought money to the Black Rats, and connections. Which is more than a yellow-bellied, ham-fisted, drunken old weakling like you can say."

"You watch your mouth, Atkinson. You aren't a big shot around here like you thought you were, and you sure aren't welcome." The older man glared. "In fact, you've got about ten seconds to take yourself out before I send you on your way with some bruises and spilled blood."

"You have no control here." Andre stepped forward, hands curling into fists.

"He don't, but I do." The bartender came around the bar, eyes hard. "And I'm of a mind to agree with James. Get out of my bar, Atkinson, and don't come back. I don't hold with murderers and drug traffickers in my establishment."

Andre's whole body stilled, and Lee could feel the tension in the air. "I was welcome enough before."

"You had a patch on your shoulder, and no record, and Bruno's support before. None of that's true now. So get out."

Andre stared at the man, all tight stillness, and Lee didn't know how these other guys couldn't feel it. "Well," Andre said. "If that's your decision."

Lee knew he should have expected it, but he still jerked backward as Andre whipped toward the bartender, snatched an empty bottle off the bar, and slammed it across the bartender's face in a shower of shattering glass. He followed it up with a well-placed blow to the gut that doubled the man over and sent him reeling to the floor.

The Black Rats leaped forward with shouts of indignation and rage, converging on Andre's tall frame. Lee shrank back against the wall as a full-scale brawl erupted. The space in front of the bar turned into a whirlwind of flying fists and shouts. Blood splattered across the scuffed concrete floor and the nearby barstools, the ones that hadn't been sent flying, at least.

The fight was one of the most chaotic and violent Lee had ever seen, and Andre was right in the thick of it. His mouth was twisted in a manic, cruel smile as he dealt blows—punching, kicking, and attacking with whatever weapons he could get in his hand. He slashed a broken bottle into the cheek of the man who'd first addressed him—James, Lee thought—and kicked one of the patrons from the front of the bar so hard Lee could have sworn he heard something crack.

Another man lunged at Andre with a pool cue. Andre caught it and twisted sideways, ripping the cue out of the man's grasp before he hammered the wider end between the biker's legs. He followed through with a swing like a pro baseball player to the man's temple. The pool cue broke in half, and blood surged from the wound as the man collapsed bonelessly to the ground. Andre seized the other half of the cue and spun around to engage the next opponent, heedless of the blood splattered across his hands, his face, and his clothing.

Andre's eyes shined with the violence he was committing. Lee watched, both mesmerized and repulsed by the raw viciousness of the combat.

Movement caught Lee's attention from the corner of his eye. He jerked around just as one man—he thought it was the guy who'd been drinking shots at the bar, but he wasn't sure—lunged at him, fists upraised and bloodlust in his jaundice-yellowed eyes.

Lee yelped and ducked out of the way of the swinging fists, his hands searching for a weapon. He thought of the knife at his belt but couldn't bring himself to draw it. He dodged another swipe of the man's fist and found himself backed against the bar. He slid sideways, and one hand brushed the cold glass of a beer bottle.

Lee seized the bottle, slid out of the way of a short, charging rush, and brought the bottle down as hard as he could against the man's head. The bottle shattered, and the man collapsed against the wooden bar top then slid to the floor. Lee nudged him with a foot, but the guy's eyes were closed. He looked like he was out cold.

Lee grinned, exhilaration taking the place of his earlier fear and trepidation. He'd done it. He'd defended himself and actually won a fight with a larger guy. Not just any guy, but a biker, a tough guy like Andre.

He turned to look for Andre to show him what he'd done. To show him he could fight, that he wasn't useless when it mattered.

Andre was flat on his back across the pool table, one-half of the broken cue serving as a fragile barrier between him and a massive man in a Black Rats vest. Lee didn't remember seeing him before. He might have been out back and come in during the fight.

The man hammered a kick into Andre's knee, and Andre grunted, losing some of his balance and leverage. The cue inched closer to his chest. Then Andre spotted Lee.

"Lee." His name was spoken in a grunt as Andre strained to dislodge his attacker, but it was all the command Lee needed.

There weren't any more broken bottles around, and he couldn't knock the guy over the head with one anyway. He'd get glass in Andre's face, maybe even in his eyes. Lee yanked the hunting knife out of his belt and moved closer. His knees felt weak, and his hands were suddenly sweating.

"Hey! Get off of him!" Lee said. "I'll stick you if you don't!"

The biker ignored him. Either he was too interested in taking out Andre or he thought Lee was no threat.

Lee didn't feel like a threat. He was barely half the size of either of the combatants and nowhere near as strong. He forced himself to step closer. "I'm warning you, let him go."

Andre managed to push back, only to grunt as the man reared back and punched him hard in the ribs, twice. The biker lifted his fist and hammered it toward Andre's face. The former prisoner managed to block, but he couldn't turn the tables. Bent back over the pool table, he didn't have the freedom of movement he needed to fight properly.

"Lee."

Images of the officers Andre had shot, the man he'd beaten to death, and the blood on his hands earlier in the day danced in front of Lee's eyes. He clenched his hand tighter on the knife, his mouth dry.

Now or never. I gotta...I gotta help him. I can't disappoint him again. I can't keep being useless in a fight. I have to do something. Just...just cut him. I can just cut him, and he'll back off, and Andre can finish him.

He could see Andre's cold expression, the one he'd worn all afternoon. The disdain that cut like knives. The contempt that made him feel lower than a worm.

He remembered the way Andre had called him son and told him "Well done." He recalled his pride at being able to impress a tough, powerful figure like Andre.

There was a roar of fury, and the biker jerked Andre up and slammed his head against the pool table. Lee heard the grunt of pain and the harsh exhalation as the air was shoved out of Andre's lungs.

The biker pulled back for another attack, and Lee reacted, driven by his desperation not to lose the only man he'd ever considered a mentor or anything remotely like a father.

He took three running steps forward, knife upraised, and plunged it down just as Andre's opponent slammed him against the pool table once again.

Lee had meant to hit the biker's arm, or maybe his shoulder—a wound that would make him let go of Andre, but not necessarily a fatal one. But the biker's move had put the blade level with his neck.

Lee watched, equal parts amazed and horrified, as the blade plunged into the biker's throat. The man's neck erupted in a spray of red as he jerked reflexively backward.

Lee kept his grip on the knife as the keen edge slashed through the inside of the neck. The man scrabbled at the wound for a moment, blood fountaining over all three of them. Then he collapsed with a final, gurgling breath.

23

BILL WHEELER

In the second following the small explosion of concrete chips and dust, Bill took the opportunity offered by Jay's loosened grip and jerked himself free. It didn't take much—his assailant was as startled as he was. He didn't notice as Bill escaped his choke hold and scrambled to put some distance between them. The move cost him a slight cut from Jay's knife, but he barely noticed the sting as he rolled away across the rough ground and sat up to search for the source of the noise as well as the knife he'd dropped. He managed to close his hand around the handle and get back up to his knees and braced in a defensive posture just as a strong feminine voice rang out.

"That's enough of your nasty behavior, Jay. You back off, or I'll put the next bullet somewhere you won't like it and leave you to crawl back home."

A woman emerged from a doorway across the street. Her long graying hair was tied in a sloppy ponytail, and she held a shotgun firmly in both hands, cocked and ready at her side. She wore sturdy outdoor clothing, complete with boots and a no-nonsense expression on her face.

Jay scowled, but he lowered the knife. "He's got supplies. I was just—"

"You were just being a bad-tempered bully, Jay Carmichael, and you and I both know it. Just like you know Genevieve would have your hide if she knew what you were about. Threatening people with knives and fighting in the street." The woman gestured up the street with the shotgun. "You apologize to that man and get back home, or I'll tell her myself—after I've helped you along with a boot in your backside."

Jay flushed, but he sheathed the knife and yanked his sweatshirt back over it. Bill rose to his feet, knife in hand, as the man turned back to him.

After a moment, Jay shook his head, and his expression turned shame-faced. "Sorry, buddy." He sighed. "I don't know what's wrong with me. I just saw those boys, and heard Mitch's story, and it was like the devil got in my blood."

Bill wasn't sure he believed the apology, but there was no point in quibbling about it. "Fair enough. It's strange days, and you're not the first I've seen get snake-mean under stress. Probably won't be the last either."

"Yeah. Well." Jay hesitated, then shot a look at the woman with the shotgun. "I'd best get going." He turned and hurried down the street. Bill watched him go with a sense of relief. He didn't put his knife away until the man disappeared around a corner.

Once Jay was gone, Bill turned to his rescuer. She'd walked across the street to him, shotgun balanced easily on one shoulder. "Thank you, Miss…"

"June. June Richmond." She held out a hand, and Bill shook it. "Sorry I didn't intervene sooner, but I had to go get the shotgun and load it first."

204

"Bill Wheeler, and it's not a problem. You helped, and that's what counts." Bill lifted his shirt to examine the shallow gouge Jay had managed to inflict. It stung, but he'd had worse, and the bleeding was already stopping. "Thank you."

"You're welcome." June offered him a regretful smile. "I hate to ask it of you, given what he just did, but I hope you'll forgive Jay. He's a bit of a twit sometimes, and an idiot at others, but once you get past the rough edges, he's not a bad guy. Just desperate, like most of us."

Bill nodded. "Times are rough, and I don't think anyone's at their best."

"No, they aren't. And I'll be honest with you, I can't entirely fault Jay for his actions. We're all a little out of sorts."

"I think most people are since the EMP went off," Bill said. "I think lots of people were expecting the government to do something, but they can't do much, or they won't."

June's expression turned bitter. "As if we'd want help from any so-called government now. We'd probably just get another bunch of self-important, arrogant, entitled muscleheads with weapons they shouldn't be allowed to use who'd take all our food and water and leave us starving and desperate while they 'protect' us."

Bill frowned at the anger in her voice. "Did something happen recently?"

June grimaced, and her hand tightened briefly on the butt of her gun. "Two days before you and your truck rolled in. There's a militia base a few miles out of town, and they've got those old diesel Jeeps without roofs. Cars that still run, at least. They rolled into town with their weapons and their cars, talking about protecting the citizens and establishing law and order. At first, we were happy to see them. We thought things were getting back to normal, or at least they'd get better."

Bill remembered Barney and his pseudo-military cult following—and all the trouble that had resulted from it. "I'm guessing it didn't go the way you expected."

"They went door-to-door and demanded most of the food and water people had saved or scavenged. Anyone who protested or argued got threatened. A couple people got knocked around a bit. They broke one man's arm and said if he didn't settle down, they'd shoot him in front of his kids." June's voice was heavy. "I wanted to fight them, but I live alone, and I didn't have enough shotgun shells available to take on a group like that."

"I know the feeling. I've been on the wrong side of something similar myself. I have a friend, Shannon, who got shot in the shoulder by a man like that. Nearly got killed." Just remembering it, and what had happened only a short time after with Connor, made his throat tighten with regret and sorrow. "Though she was lucky. Two others were actually killed."

"It's bad out there," June agreed.

Bill looked sideways at her. "I'm a bit surprised, with things like that happening, that you'd go out of your way to help a stranger. I could have been another one like those militia men."

"Could have been, but I knew you weren't." June smiled at him, and the expression transformed her face, adding warmth and good humor. "I live right across from the urgent care center, just over there." She pointed to a house. "I've been watching you. I saw you when you pulled in, you and that girl who looked to be in such bad shape."

"Shannon. She's my friend who got shot."

"I wondered. I saw you then, and I saw you a couple days ago, when those kids tried to steal your supplies. Most would have run them off as soon as they had the upper hand, but you were kind to them. You gave them food, took care of them. Seemed only right someone should return the favor when you were in a bind."

"I appreciate it." Bill sighed and rubbed the back of his head. "Don't suppose you know where I could find any medical supplies? I left the center because Shannon needs more antibiotics and bandages."

"What happened? Besides getting shot, I mean." June tipped her head. "If you don't mind my asking."

She looked sincere, and she'd helped him. Bill decided to go ahead and tell her the truth. "She's got blood poisoning—well, she did have. I'm not sure if it's gone completely or not."

June made a sympathetic grimace. "Ouch. It's in the shoulder?"

"Yes." Bill said. "I've given her all the antibiotics I could find, and drained and cleaned the wound, but I can't be sure she's fully recovered yet."

"Well, I can tell you two things: there's a vet clinic two streets over that should have bandages and might have some amoxicillin, or cephalexin and clindamycin. They'll be animal dosage levels, but you can make do if you have to."

Bill nodded. "You said two things?"

June pursed her lips. "My mom and grandma were old-fashioned natural healers. Believed in using natural remedies any time they could get away with it. And my grandma, she always told me that you used honey to fight infections and onions to draw poison."

"Honey and onions?" Bill raised an eyebrow.

"Yep. You cut the onions and heat them till they're soft, then lay them over the wound like a poultice, and they'll change colors as they draw out the poison, and maybe infection too. Then you clean the wound and pack it in honey. It's a natural antibiotic and anti-inflammatory."

"I hadn't heard of that." Bill said. He was intrigued. There was a good chance there was honey somewhere on Shannon's truck, with all the supplies she had. If he could find an onion, he might be able to speed up the healing of her shoulder.

"Like I said, it's an old family practice. I don't know that many people would use it if they've got antibiotics on hand, or that it's ever been mentioned in anything other than word-of-mouth traditions. But I figure, times like this, there's no sense in ignoring anything that might help, whether it's printed in medical journals or shared among family," June said.

"Speaking of information, there's a market three blocks beyond and two over from the veterinary clinic. Militia cleaned it out pretty thoroughly, but you might get lucky. Just be careful you don't try to use a rotten onion."

"I'll be careful." Bill said. He looked at the sky. It had been about noon when he'd walked out the clinic doors, and time was passing. "I'd best be going if I'm going to get back before dark."

"I can come as well, if you want a guide," June offered.

Bill considered the idea, then shook his head. "I reckon I can find my way well enough. But Shannon's resting in the care center, and I'd feel easier if I knew there was someone to make sure no one could disturb her."

"That's a good idea," June agreed. "You get going. I'll keep an eye on your truck and your friend while you're gone, so don't fret about that."

"Thank you, June." Bill exchanged a smile with her, then turned and headed in the direction she'd indicated, intent on finishing his errands as quickly as possible.

The veterinary clinic was easy enough to find. It wasn't large, but the sign was a bright red and white that stood out against the pale blue of the spring afternoon sky. The lock wasn't a difficult one to open either. Less than ten minutes after he'd spotted the clinic, he was inside, inhaling the stale smell of sick animals and medicines.

The cages were open, all the animals gone. He was grateful for that. He made a methodical search through the offices, opening every cabinet and exploring the contents. He found gauze and bandages in each of the four treatment rooms, along with alcohol swabs. All of that went into the bag. In a back room, he found extra supplies and half a dozen bottles of cephalexin. All of that went into the bag as well. Once he'd finished his search, he closed everything back up and left the building. He locked the front door behind him, then turned his steps in the direction of the supermarket June had described.

He found it half an hour later. Windows were broken, and most of the shelves were bare. Bill made his way across the broken glass cautiously and slipped inside to search for anything looters or militia might have overlooked.

There wasn't much. The small half-aisle of books, toys, and greeting cards was virtually untouched. So was the aisle full of cleaning supplies. Bill helped himself to some of the multipurpose cleaner. In the health section, he unearthed some hand sanitizer that had rolled under a shelf and took that as well.

There was nothing left on the shelves of the dry food aisles and only scattered bottles of condiments. Bill took them, including a small bottle of pear blossom honey. He wasn't sure if the pear blossom would affect the healing properties of the honey, but it was still worth using.

Most of the food that remained in the produce section was going soft and inedible, spotted with mold and places that squished unpleasantly under his fingers. He was about to leave when a thought occurred to him.

The supercenter had a lot of stock in the back storage area, and it was harder to find things back there, as he knew quite well from his few days locked inside the supercenter. It might be the same here. He searched and found a door into the food storage areas in what had once been the meat department.

Someone had come through and taken a lot of the stored items in back as well—either that, or the store had simply not received its delivery before the power went out. There wasn't a lot there. Bill searched among the tossed-aside boxes and crates anyway, unearthing items here and there. Most of it wasn't particularly noteworthy, but under a stack of plastic flats, he found a small onion that he thought might be useful. It wasn't in the best condition, but it still smelled all right. It wasn't moldy, soft, or sprouting, nor was it turning black.

The sun was low in the sky when he emerged. Bill's wounds ached, especially his much-abused knee, where most recently Jay had kicked him to the pavement. The bag was heavy, but the weight reminded him of the good luck he'd had hunting for supplies. He'd have to tell June about it before they left.

He made good time back to the urgent care center and spotted June standing in the doorway of her house, gun at her side. She waved at him, then vanished inside. Bill watched the door shut before turning to enter the clinic.

"*Son of a rattlesnake and a mud worm.*" A familiar, rough voice met his ears as he crossed the threshold. Bill dropped the bag and hurried toward the treatment room where he'd left Shannon.

Shannon lay on the bed, cursing a blue streak in a weak, rasping voice, her good hand clutching her shoulder. From the state of the sheets, it looked like she'd tried to get up and had no luck.

Bill moved forward to help raise the head of the bed, then turned to grab the bottle of sports drink he'd opened for her earlier. "Sorry, Shannon. Didn't mean to be gone so long. Have you been awake awhile?"

Shannon drank several swallows then shook her head. Her eyes were tired, but far clearer than they'd been earlier that day. "Where have you been?"

"I was getting more bandages and medicine for you. We ran through all the stock here." He held the bottle for her to drink some more.

Shannon frowned. "Why?"

"Because your shoulder got infected, and you darn near got gangrene, being stubborn about it. I've been draining and tending the wound, and I'll be doing that again as soon as we've both got some food in us." Relief that she was finally awake and talking combined with the worry he'd felt over the past several days and made his voice sterner than he meant it to be.

Shannon's eyes widened, but she leaned back into the bed. "Okay."

"Good. You rest, and I'll get some grub for both of us." Bill turned away. He was almost to the door when Shannon spoke.

"Thank you."

"You're welcome." Bill stopped and gave her a reassuring smile, then he went out to see what could be made for dinner. He had his own wound to tend, and an onion to heat for the drawing poultice June had described, and supplies to sort through and put in order.

He was also tired, hungry, and sore. Despite all that, he couldn't stop the smile that swept across his face. His heart felt lighter than it had in days.

Shannon was awake, and it was beginning to look like she might make a full recovery after all.

24

LEE KINGSTON JONES

L ee stared at the dead biker. So did everyone else who was still conscious. Lee couldn't bring himself to care about that, or about the fact that the fighting had ceased when the man fell. All he could do was stare at his blood-drenched hands and the red ruin that had once been a living man's throat.

He'd done that. He'd sliced a man's throat with his own two hands. It didn't seem real. It was like a bad dream he was waiting to wake up from.

He was startled out of his daze by a heavy hand clapping him on the shoulder. "Very good, Lee. I knew you could do it."

Lee turned his head. Andre looked like a war refugee with his torn, blood-splattered clothing, bloody nose, and faint bruises already appearing across his face and arms. The makeshift bandages Lee had wrapped around his arms that morning were no longer green, so much blood had coated them. Lee stared at them in a numb haze.

I should probably offer to change those out when we get a chance. Andre might get an infection otherwise.

He watched as Andre strode across to the bar, carelessly stepping on bodies as he went, and grabbed the dark-haired biker Lee vaguely remembered being the first one they'd watched enter the bar. The man whimpered as Andre grabbed a handful of his vest, heaved him upward, and slammed him against the nearest wall.

"Stop whining." Andre's words were cold and flat. "You'll live, unless I decide otherwise—which I may do if you continue to try my patience."

The man gulped and went quiet. Andre nodded. "Very good. Now, tell me anything you know about Sarah Nakamura."

The biker blinked, confusion written across his battered features. "Who?"

Andre lifted a fist. The man jerked his hands up. "Wait! Wait! Please! I really don't know who you're talking about. I've only been in the Black Rats for like, maybe a year. I don't know any Nakamuras."

"What of a woman with the name Atkinson?"

"No sir, don't know anyone by that name either. On my honor as a Black Rat." The man shook his head frantically, as much as he was able with Andre's grip threatening to choke him.

"Gardena, then."

"Bruno Gardena's boss of the Black Rats, and his old lady's name is Carol. Don't know anyone else with that name."

Andre scowled. "And you have never heard either of them speak to or about a daughter, niece, or great-niece?"

"No. Haven't heard of anyone like that. Honest I haven't." The Black Rat cowered away from the expression on Andre's face.

"You're useless." Andre pulled back then slammed his head against the other man's face. Lee heard the muffled crunch as the man's nose shattered, along with some of his teeth and possibly his cheekbone.

The biker passed out. Andre stared at the limp body for a moment, then dragged the body to the door and heaved him into the street. Lee winced. Being handled like that, if the guy didn't have a busted face and ribs before, he probably did now.

The numbness was fading, and the magnitude of the fighting and its aftermath crashed over Lee's awareness. Red splattered practically every surface, splashed across walls and tables and the top of the bar, and in viscous pools on the floor. The air was filled with the iron tang of it, mingling with the smells of unwashed bodies and spilled drinks. There were low whimpers and liquid, gasping breaths from a couple of the men, one of whom was the bartender. The rest were still.

Too still. One man looked like his skull had been cracked, and another seemed to have got one end of a broken pool cue in the gut. Lee didn't want to look any closer to be sure. His eyes slid back to the man he'd killed and the jagged red gash carved into his neck.

All of a sudden, the room was too small, too hot. The air was choked with scents he didn't want to smell, the bodies of the bikers mingled with the memories of the two men Andre had shot outside Tunica. He heard whimpering and couldn't tell if it was his own.

Andre was rooting around behind the bar. Lee stepped back, then turned and bolted to the door, desperate to reach the clean, cold air outside.

He staggered out the door and nearly tripped over the still-unconscious biker lying on the pavement. His knees felt weak, and he dropped into a shivering crouch beside the wall of the bar.

I killed a guy. I—I ripped his throat out. There's so much blood, and I spilled some of it. And that dude I hit with the bottle—he wasn't moving. Did I kill him too?

His stomach rebelled, and Lee gagged, coughed, and proceeded to be violently sick all over the concrete in front of him. He threw up until his arms could barely support him, until there was nothing left to come up, not even bile.

Once he was done, he wiped his mouth, spit a little to get rid of the burning, acrid taste, and pushed himself to his feet. Part of him wanted to just stay there, curled into a ball. But Andre was inside, and he might need help. He'd gotten pretty banged up by the big biker before Lee had killed the guy.

Lee took a deep breath and stuffed his hands in his pockets to hide the trembling. When he was sure he didn't look too much the worse for wear, he turned and headed back to the bar to see what he could help Andre with.

Andre was sitting at the bar, a bottle of Jack Daniels Black Label open in front of him. He looked up as Lee entered. "Ah, Lee. Come join me."

Lee made his way over and settled onto the bar stool next to Andre. The older man poured a tumbler full of whiskey and pushed it toward him. "Here."

He stared at the drink, perplexed. "I'm not old enough to drink."

Andre waved a red-stained hand dismissively. "Rules regarding alcohol are for children, not men. And you proved yourself a man tonight."

Lee blinked. "I did?"

"Of course." Andre indicated the dead biker.

Lee gulped. On one hand, Andre's praise made him feel confident and powerful. On the other hand, he still felt kind of queasy. After a moment of hesitation, he reached out and took the glass. He sipped the amber liquid and nearly spat it back out as it burned down his throat.

The heat of it calmed his stomach a little and cleared his head. He looked at Andre. "I didn't even know I was gonna do it until the knife cut into him."

"That's natural, especially since it was your first. But you must remember two things, Lee. It was him or us, and you were defending me. Remember, too, that only the strong survive in this world, the strong and the ruthless."

Andre took a swallow of his drink and fixed Lee with a level stare. "Tell me, Lee, would you rather be the predator or the prey? The victim or the victor?"

Put like that, there was no question. "I don't want to be a victim." He glanced at the body on the floor. "Just…it gets easier, right? Like hunting turkeys?"

Andre's brow creased in thought. The big hands toyed with the glass, leaving reddish smudges across the surface. For a minute, Lee thought he wasn't going to answer. Then Andre spoke, his voice quiet and still and empty of emotion. "Yes." Andre offered him a rare smile, one that just barely touched his eyes. "You'll be an adept student now that you've cleared the first hurdle."

Lee wasn't so sure about that. He wasn't sure he even wanted killing to be easier. Then he looked at Andre's face, at the smile. The pride. There was no trace of the cruel, dismissive man who'd shared a house with him this afternoon or brought him to the bar.

The look on Andre's face was everything he'd ever wanted to see in his father's eyes.

He didn't want that to disappear. Andre's approval was like a drug, and he wanted more. As much as he could get. He wanted to feel the pride, the sense of accomplishment and self-worth he'd experienced earlier when he'd successfully defended himself.

"Yeah." He raised his glass in salute, then tossed back the contents. He ignored the way the alcohol burned and made his eyes water, and he held out his glass for a refill. "You're right. That dude got what was coming to him. Next time, I'll be able to help you even more. You'll see."

Andre nodded. "I'm counting on you, son."

25

BILL WHEELER

Dinner was chicken noodle soup and crackers dug from the truck. Bill heated the soup painstakingly in the can with his lighter. Once it was hot enough, Bill took the two cans, along with two more bottles of sports drink, back to the treatment room. He handed a can to Shannon. "Here. You can sip it slowly, straight from the can."

He cracked open both drinks then suited actions to words. The broth was more concentrated than he was used to, salty and strong, but tasty nonetheless. Shannon followed suit. She drank slowly, and her hand was shaky, but he was glad to see a little bit of color in her cheeks that wasn't the flush of fever.

After they ate, he helped Shannon sit up a little further and started to unwind the bandages from her shoulder. Shannon watched, jaw clenched against the pain, as she followed his directions to shift one way or the other.

The red lines of blood poisoning had mostly disappeared, but the wound was still inflamed, with a suspicious whitish area around the edges. It was far better than it had been, but Bill could tell it needed to be drained again.

Shannon eyed the raw edges of the injury. "Looks worse than I thought."

Bill prodded her shoulder, feeling the heat still present in the wounds. "It looked a lot worse when we first came in here."

As he'd done before, he slipped on some gloves, broke some of the scab over the wound, and applied pressure, grimacing as yellowish-white liquid oozed up. Shannon let out a hiss of pain. "Skunks and stomachaches, that hurts."

"I know it does, but I have to drain the infection, unless you want to have another round of blood poisoning. I'm sorry, but you're just gonna have to put up with it." He pressed down more firmly.

Shannon grimaced, and her good hand clenched tight on the side of the bed, but she didn't try to escape or push him away.

Bill drained as much gunk as he could from the front of the wound and cleaned around it with an alcohol swab. Then he helped Shannon turn over so he could repeat the process. Shannon made a few pained noises and cursed under her breath, but she let him work.

Bill was impressed at her fortitude. "You're doing great, Shannon." He stopped when his hands ached and the discharge was mostly blood red. He discarded his gloves, then grabbed the onion.

Shannon eyed it. "You're hungry?"

"No. Not for onions, at least." Bill used the knife he'd borrowed from her to cut the onion in half, then began to heat it over the lighter, the same way he'd done with the soup. "I heard from a lady that you could use a warm onion to help draw out infection and poison. I figured it couldn't hurt, and it might save us some time, resources, and pain."

Shannon eyed the onion. "I guess it's worth a try." She paused, then asked, "How are we on supplies? Medical and otherwise?"

"I just scavenged a bunch of bandages and some antibiotics from a veterinary clinic down the street. We should be good for a while on that front. Food..." Bill hesitated, then decided to tell her the truth. "Aside from what we've been eating, I gave away three boxes to some kids that live nearby."

He'd been worried it might anger her, but all Shannon did was nod a little and say, "All right."

The onion was beginning to get soft and translucent. Bill shut off the lighter and came back to Shannon. "This might be a bit uncomfortable."

"Can't be worse than what you were doing before." Shannon shifted to get a little more comfortable, then leaned back. "Go ahead."

He plastered the onion slices—they'd come apart during the heating process—to the wound and wrapped a cloth over them. "We'll leave that for a few minutes. Then we'll clean the wound out again, put on a fresh bandage, and give you a shot of antibiotics."

Shannon sighed. "Well, why don't you tell me what's happened since we arrived here and maybe take care of those cuts on your side and your neck. That will help pass the time."

Bill had nearly forgotten about the gouge Jay had given him, but Shannon's words brought his attention back to the wound. He lifted his shirt and eyed the injury. "It's not that bad."

"Yeah, that's what I said." Shannon gave him a wry smile and tilted her head at her injured shoulder.

She made a good point. Bill sighed, then turned around and collected another alcohol swab. He cleaned the slash and applied a series of medium-sized butterfly bandages to bring the edges together. He wrapped a length of bandage over top of it to prevent any contamination and tucked his shirt back in. The cut to his neck was barely more than a graze, and no worse than nicks he'd gotten while shaving. He cleaned it with an alcohol swab and left it at that.

"How'd it happen?" Shannon frowned. "I didn't think you got hurt at the supercenter, and it looks too recent for that anyway."

"It happened earlier today." Bill perched himself on a nearby bed. "I got on the wrong end of a man with a knife."

"Start at the beginning," Shannon suggested.

Bill proceeded to tell her all about the last few days. The nerve-racking drive into Stuttgart. His frantic efforts to stem the tide of infection and sepsis in her shoulder. His decision to sleep in the waiting room and why. The kids, the fight, and how he'd given them supplies. And how that action had triggered Jay's attack and June's intervention.

He finished the story with a sigh. "I'm sorry I wasn't careful. I didn't think about what might happen when I gave those kids the food. I should have realized, after all that happened at the supercenter, that they'd tell other people. And that it might lead to people trying to take our supplies by force."

"You didn't know." Shannon shrugged her good shoulder. "You did what you thought was best."

"I shouldn't have taken the supplies and given them away without asking you first." He hadn't thought about it at the time, but it felt a little bit like stealing now.

"Why not? Not like anyone's waiting for the inventory. These days, the truck's as much yours as mine. Besides, you did a good thing. You said yourself that because of it, you made an ally who helped you out." Shannon shifted on the bed then looked at the onion poultice. "Think it's been on long enough?"

"I'd give it a little longer." It hadn't quite been twenty minutes, by Bill's reckoning. He folded his hands together in front of him and winced as the movement made his injured side throb. "Maybe I did the right thing for those kids, but I don't mind telling you, when they pulled that gun, I just about had a heart attack. And I'd probably be dead if June hadn't stepped in with Jay today."

"But she did step in, and you're not dead. So why are you worried?"

Bill took a deep breath and voiced the thoughts that had been drifting about in his mind since the encounter with Jay. "Because I'm not like you. I'm not a fighter, I'm not as tough as you are, and I hate being involved in conflict. I'm no good at it."

"Not everyone is."

"Yeah, but..." Bill searched for words for a moment. "I just don't know how long I can survive the way the world is now. How many times have one or both of us been in trouble, and I couldn't do anything? Too darn often."

"Not true." Shannon used her good hand to scoot up a little on the bed. "You're strong when you need to be. If you hadn't knocked Barney out that night in the supercenter, I'd have been strangled to death. If you hadn't hit Connor with the truck, we'd both be dead." She paused. "You're kind. Kindness is hard, especially in times like these. Harder than being tough or fighting. To be able to be generous and caring in days like these, you have to be strong. So quit beating yourself up or thinking you're weak."

Bill considered the words. Shannon had a point, but he still felt like she was giving him too much credit. "That didn't make me strong. I just couldn't stand to lose you. I didn't want to face the world alone. Heck, I was set to go mad with no one to talk to these past few days.

The quiet messed with my head. It was too much like when Edith—" he broke off. The familiar lump of grief lodged in his throat.

Shannon's expression softened. "Edith. Your wife?"

"Yeah." Bill swallowed and took a deep breath to regain his composure. He rose. "Reckon it's about time to take a look at that shoulder of yours, see if the onions have done their work."

Shannon sat up a little so he could get to the wrap. "You don't talk about your wife."

"I don't. She's passed away, so there's not much point." Bill peeled away the wrapping and the onion layers. The onion had taken on a strange, nasty color and a smell that made him wrinkle his nose. "Looks like it worked. It did something, at least."

"I'm glad. I'd hate to ruin a good onion for no reason." Shannon hesitated. "You told me once that your wife was a good baker."

"She was." He cleaned the wounds with yet another alcohol swab. "She loved making pastries of all kinds."

"What was your favorite?"

Bill considered for a few moments as he finished cleaning her shoulder. "Apple pie, straight from the oven with cinnamon and sugar and a little bit of whipped cream." He went to get the honey and brought it back. "She made it every year for my birthday and our anniversary, and sometimes for Thanksgiving and Christmas too, if she didn't decide to try something else."

Shannon blinked. "When is your birthday? I don't think I ever asked."

"September eighteenth."

"I was born on April fifteenth." Shannon eyed the honey as he opened it. "What's that for?"

"Honey's a natural healing remedy. Helps prevent and stop infections and the like." He helped her shift forward a little and carefully upturned the bottle to dribble the thick, golden liquid into the wound. "Might as well use natural remedies and save the stronger stuff for emergencies."

For a few moments, there was quiet as he focused on the task at hand: honey on the entrance wound, then a pad to keep it sealed. Repeat for the exit wound. He grabbed a fresh bandage and wrapped the whole shoulder in clean, white cloth.

Once Bill had finished, he rummaged in the bag for a bottle of the cephalexin pills. They were smaller, designed for animals that weighed far less than a human, so he took two and brought them back to Shannon. "Antibiotics to help fight any remaining infection."

Shannon downed them with a swallow of her sports drink. Then she looked at her shoulder, shifting it a little bit to test the comfort and range of motion. "You're good at this."

Bill shrugged. "Had some practice. There's always accidents around a mechanic's shop. And I did a lot of the home care for Edith." He hadn't meant to say that, but for some reason, he couldn't take his mind off his wife. Being in the urgent care center brought the memories closer to the surface of his mind than usual.

Shannon reached over and touched his hand with her good one. "Wanna tell me what happened?"

"Not much to tell." He tried for a nonchalant tone but couldn't seem to manage it.

"Still might help." Shannon offered him a small, crooked smile. "I'm a good listener."

Do I really want to talk about Edith?

The truth was, he hadn't much thought about it, not since his wife's funeral. There hadn't been anyone to really talk to, or with. He was retired—no coworkers to speak to. Neither he nor Edith had much in the way of family left. He hadn't felt like talking to the neighbors, most of whom had been Edith's good friends and were struggling with their own grief. He wasn't the sort to talk about such personal matters with perfect strangers.

But Shannon wasn't a stranger, not anymore. She was willing to wait quietly for him to gather his thoughts and decide whether he wanted to talk to her or not. Oddly enough, that made him want to confide in her.

He settled back on the bed he'd been perched on earlier and picked up his drink. He took a long swallow and began to speak. "Edith and I, we met young and married young, in our early twenties. She was a generous, loving woman, always helping out at church or baking stuff for school bake sales, even though we didn't have kids. Or she'd help folks in the neighborhood. She could be a little absentminded, but she was a good woman."

Another gulp of his drink. "We thought she just had pneumonia at first. It was a bad cough that seemed to never go away, but we just figured it was one of those drug-resistant diseases. But then it started getting worse, so we checked again."

His throat hurt, and his eyes were stinging. "Lung cancer, the doc said. Advanced. It was a shock, because Edith—she didn't have any of the risk factors, as far as we knew. Didn't smoke. Didn't work around hazardous materials like asbestos. She wasn't sick that often, never showed any signs of any sort of risk."

He shook his head, chest aching as the thoughts and memories continued to flow out of him like a river whose dam had burst. "You worry sometimes, about breast cancer, or maybe a tumor in the brain. Random things that can get anyone. But lung cancer, in a woman with no history of risk factors, and no family predisposition—we didn't see that coming."

"I'm sorry." Shannon's eyes were compassionate.

"That's what the doc said." Bill took a deep breath and swiped at the tears threatening to fall from his eyes. "She started chemo a week later. Chemo, surgeries, more therapy—we tried everything. Did everything. The first round, she went into remission for two years, and we hoped it would be the last of it. But then the next year, it was back, and worse than ever."

He focused on Shannon's face, knowing that if he closed his eyes or looked away, he would see Edith lying in a hospital bed or in a lounge chair at the treatment center they'd gone to. "We kept trying. Kept trying for another three years. Sometimes she was so sick she couldn't eat, or hurting so bad I had to knock her out with meds to let her get some rest. She needed help to eat, help to drink, help to bathe or go to the restroom. I didn't mind that so much—I promised for better or worse—but seeing her face, seeing her in pain and so nauseous that even water would come back up, that broke my heart."

The memories danced in front of his eyes, inescapable and more painful than the knife wound Jay had given him. "She got worse, and the cancer metastasized. Doc said there was nothing else he could do." He remembered the agonizing hopelessness of that meeting. "I was all for looking for another doctor, a second opinion, a drug trial— anything that might help her."

He could barely swallow with the lump in his throat and the ache in his chest. "Then Edith told me she was tired. Just like that. 'I'm tired, Bill.' And I knew. She couldn't fight any more. If nothing was going to save her, then it was cruel to put her through more tests and radiation and pain. So I…" His voice cracked, and he forced himself to finish the sentence. "I brought her home and made her comfortable.

Took care of her. Then one day, little over a month ago, she fell asleep and didn't wake up. She was gone."

The words choked him, and he bowed his head, grief like a weight on his chest and shoulders.

The sound of feet hitting the tiled floor reached his ears, and seconds later a slender arm wrapped gingerly around his shoulders. "I'm sorry for your loss."

Tears stung his eyes and fell down his face. He didn't bother to wipe them away this time. "I miss Edith. But I know—I know—if she'd lived to see days like this, she would have wanted me to help you. You're a good woman, and you're a friend. Closest thing to family I got now." He shuddered.

"You're family to me too. And I want to thank you for taking such good care of me."

He shook his head. "I couldn't lose you. Not now. I lost Edith; don't think I could handle losing someone else without shattering to little pieces. I wouldn't be able to live with myself if I'd failed you too."

"You didn't fail Edith, and you certainly didn't fail me. I'd be dead if it weren't for you." Shannon's arm squeezed his shoulder in a one-armed embrace. "I'm sorry for what you lost, but I'm glad you're here with me, Bill. I couldn't ask for a better person to be at my side."

He couldn't answer her. He'd gone so long trying not to think about or feel his grief and the crushing weight of bereavement. Shannon's unwavering support and quiet presence—especially after so many days of fearing he'd lose her too—was like a key to a floodgate. He couldn't stop the rush of tears and sorrow, and he didn't want to.

The world might be shattered, but for the first time since his wife had died, Bill thought he might have a chance to eventually heal and become whole.

26

KIM NAKAMURA

K im woke with the sun in her eyes and a goal firmly in mind. Today she was going to get some answers about how things really were in Humboldt, not the sanitized "everything is good" version Lewis kept trying to hand her.

Dennis was still asleep and resting fitfully when she peeked into his room, so she let him be. The day before had obviously been too much for him, and the more rest he got, the sooner he'd recover. The sooner he recovered, the sooner they could leave Humboldt behind them.

She dressed and fixed herself a bowl of oatmeal and some tea, then she let Mutt out to do her business. When the dog came in, she gave Mutt some of the rabbit bones and a fresh container of water. She pulled her hair into a sloppy ponytail and yanked her shoes on. Then she grabbed her backpack and meager supplies, including the gun Dennis had given her. He hadn't asked for it back, and now that she knew how to handle it, she felt better for the added protection.

She still wasn't sure she could shoot someone, or anything that wasn't inanimate or food. But she knew she could buy time and bluff. A gun might make someone pause if they tried to accost her.

She also carefully tucked the broken glasses she'd found the day before into her jacket pocket.

She walked down toward the Danville house but stopped before she reached it. She wasn't interested in another confrontation with Lewis. She didn't trust him, and she was tired of his constant hints that she ought to stay.

After about thirty minutes, the Danvilles' door opened, and Joan emerged, her work satchel slung over her shoulders.

Kim hitched her bag higher and walked forward as if she were just now coming down the road. "Hi, Joan."

Joan looked up and smiled at her. "Kim. I wasn't sure you'd be joining me today. Lewis said he talked to you, but I know you're caring for Dennis."

Kim almost choked on the scathing response she wanted to deliver regarding Lewis Danville and their supposed "talk." Instead, she shook her head and readjusted her pack. "Dennis is resting. I figured I ought to let him sleep and recover."

"Sleep is the best medicine," Joan said. "But it's time we got started on the rounds to see to the individuals who need a little more help."

Kim fell into step beside her and searched her brain for something to say, to start the conversation she wanted to have. Her instincts told her Joan was her best source of information, but she wasn't entirely certain how to go about convincing the older woman to tell her the truth.

To her surprise, it was Joan who broke the silence between them. "I heard about your confrontation with Lewis last night. Some of the things he said. I'm sorry if he was overly harsh or said things he shouldn't have."

"You mean like telling the whole militia Dennis is a weak-minded drug addict?"

"Among other things, yes." Joan sighed. "I know Lewis has a temper, and he often lets it get away from him. But he's a good man. He's just under a lot of stress."

Kim scowled. "Everyone is under a lot of stress. The world pretty much ended two weeks ago."

"It's not the same." Joan shook her head. "Lewis is responsible for keeping Humboldt safe and running smoothly. He has to train the militia, keep track of the rations, patrol the borders of the settlement, and make the administrative decisions. It's a lot for one man to handle."

"He could delegate."

"That's not Lewis's style, I'm afraid. He's used to taking charge. Part of his military training, I believe."

Kim thought about it for a moment. "I can understand that, but I guess I'm a little confused. You say he makes decisions and trains the militia and all that. But what does that mean? What are the borders? How tightly does he have to monitor the rationing, especially when you have gardens in almost everyone's backyard? And training the militia—is that teaching them how to shoot, or safety protocols, or—"

"Enough." The single sharp word was enough for her to fall silent. Joan flashed her an irritated look. "I told you, Kim. It's not wise to ask questions. Don't go prying into things that aren't your responsibility. It's not healthy, especially if the militia catches wind of it." Her gaze flicked to a nearby guard. "Best to keep your head down and stay out of trouble."

She wanted to protest, but Joan's hesitation made her stop. The older woman was clearly spooked. Pressing her too hard, too soon, would most likely make her refuse to talk at all.

They made the rounds in a sort of uneasy, unspoken truce, working together to take care of patients. Mrs. Morgan was doing well, her heart still working exactly the way it was supposed to. The guy with the concussion was on the mend, but he was still having headaches, so Kim suggested he rest another day or two.

Then they arrived at Mr. Craig's. Kim stepped inside and felt an immediate spike of concern. The older man looked unwell. She led him to a chair as soon as they were through the door and crouched in front of him.

"What's wrong?"

"I'm not feeling too well." Mr. Craig swallowed. "Been having headaches, and my vision's all strange, blurry-like. Thirsty too. Real thirsty. Hard not to drink my entire water ration as soon as I get it." He sighed and slouched back as if he could no longer sit up straight. "And I feel so dang tired…"

None of that sounded good. "Have you been doing the things I asked you? Eating a high-protein diet, drinking plenty of water, keeping a food journal? Did you do that?"

Mr. Craig blinked slowly as if he'd lost interest in the conversation, but Joan answered her. "I know you suggested a different diet to help balance his sugar, but I'm afraid the change in his rations hasn't been approved."

Kim felt like she'd been doused in ice water. "What? Why not? If I'm right about his symptoms, he's close to developing ketoacidosis, if he hasn't already crossed the line. If he can't get his blood sugar down, this could kill him."

Joan reached out and put a hand on her shoulder. "I understand you're upset. But you have to understand—Lewis didn't feel we could make those exceptions without causing discord. If we make special concessions for one person, no matter why we do it, then everyone will want to have their own special privileges. Eventually, we'd have to draw a line in the sand, and who knows what would happen?"

"So he thinks this is better?"

"Of course not. But…" Joan trailed off. "Please, Kim. We'll all do the best we can, but there's only so much we can give and so many accommodations we can make."

A fury she hadn't felt since her mother disappeared into Witness Protection erupted inside her. On the one hand, she understood what Joan was trying to tell her. But Lewis and Joan had been so adamant about needing a doctor or someone with any medical training at all. What was the point if they weren't going to listen to what she told them?

She took a deep breath. "Can we at least get him some more water?"

"We can try."

"Right. We should do that. And maybe get one of those people who aren't working to help care for him and monitor his condition. The guy with the sprained ankle might be the best choice." She didn't want to suggest Mrs. Morgan. The older woman had more time and mobility, but with her weak heart, a shock might give her a heart attack. Kim wasn't sure they could risk it.

"I'll tell Mark. Is there anything else?"

Kim thought for a moment, then rose to her feet. "Let's go over to the clinic. I can look at the records and the supplies, see if there's an alternative treatment we can use to stabilize him."

She didn't wait for Joan's response. She went to the kitchen, grabbed a bottle of water, and brought it back to Mr. Craig. She helped him drink, then set the half-full container on a side table. "You should get some rest. With any luck, you've peaked, and your sugar will start going down."

Mr. Craig nodded weakly. Kim made him comfortable, then followed Joan outside. Her stomach churned with anger and a sick sense of helplessness. She might not be a full-fledged doctor, but she could recognize the signs of severe hyperglycemia. She'd had the bad luck to see the side effects when one of her dormmates had developed early onset adult diabetes without knowing it. She knew how bad it could get. But at least Cassie had been able to get help in time. She wasn't sure Mr. Craig would have the same opportunity.

Kim barely paid any attention to the visit with Mark Cardney. His ankle was healing on schedule, and he was happy to help out with Mr. Craig. That was all she could bring herself to care about when her brain was clouded with fury and resentment.

She followed Joan into the clinic, then closed and locked the door. "You said Lewis was in charge of the welfare of the people of Humboldt. He's been all about needing a doctor, even though I've told him I'm not fully trained. Or even half-trained. Now you're both ignoring the advice I gave you, and you're putting a man's life in danger."

Joan stilled, her hand on the door to the back rooms. "I understand your frustration, Kim. But you have to understand—"

"No. I don't. I don't have to understand anything. Especially when you've been lying to me. To me and Dennis both." She pulled the glasses out of her pocket and held them up. She watched Joan's eyes widen. "I found these while we were out hunting."

Joan gaped, then shook herself. "They're very interesting, but—"

"They're exactly the same as the glasses your former doctor wore. I saw them in the picture in his office. These frames are old-fashioned, not the kind most people wear. I'll bet there's no one else in Humboldt who has glasses like this."

Joan shifted, and Kim saw her swallow nervously. "Well, it's possible Dr. Kennedy might have dropped them."

"Sure it is. Only Lewis told me Dr. Kennedy went to see his daughter in Jackson. But Jackson's in almost the opposite direction of Humboldt Lake, relative to the town. I checked a map. It's south of here, and Dennis and I went northwest, toward the lake and hatchery." Kim slapped the frames down on the counter and folded her arms. "There aren't any militia here. Just us. I want the truth. Otherwise, you and the rest of Humboldt can go drown in the lake for all I care."

For a minute, she thought Joan might prevaricate again. Then the older woman's shoulders slumped, and resignation crossed her face. "I should have known you were too smart to take anything on Lewis's say-so." Joan moved and sank into one of the chairs.

Kim settled in next to her. "What happened to Dr. Kennedy? Lewis told me he decided to leave for Jackson because they didn't see eye-to-eye."

"They didn't. Dr. Kennedy didn't agree with a militia, or centralized supplies and rationing. He didn't think Lewis could keep corruption from creeping in. He said Lewis was too much of a stubborn hothead to be a good community leader."

No arguments there. Kim didn't voice the words, but her expression made her feelings clear, because Joan gave her a pained smile. "What happened?" Kim asked.

"They argued. Two days after Lewis formed the militia and named himself the leader, about half the residents of Humboldt—this side of it, anyway—left. Some of them were looking for family. Others said they refused to live under martial law. Most of them, Lewis didn't give a half-cooked dandelion about. Couldn't have cared less. But then Dr. Kennedy said he was leaving too. He was the only doctor still here, and Lewis was furious that he'd leave the community without a medical professional."

"I know that feeling." Kim clenched her hands in her lap. "Did he yell at him too?"

"Frequently. They might have talked it out eventually, but Lewis went and put a guard on him. Dr. Kennedy told him flat out that he refused to be treated like a prisoner. The very next night, he made a break for it."

"And?" Kim asked. "That can't be the whole story."

"It isn't. The militia went after him. One of them men—I never did learn who—fired at him. Lewis said it was supposed to be a warning shot, but who really knows? All I know is Kennedy was killed by that shot, out by the Forked Deer."

"Where I found his glasses."

"Most likely." Joan took a deep breath. "Lewis covered up the murder. Said he couldn't let it get out and cause a riot. Or an insurgency. He wouldn't let anyone speak against him on the matter."

"That's wrong." Kim bit her lip. "And it isn't everything, is it? The militia, it doesn't seem to be well-organized. I mean, I don't know how a militia is supposed to function, but the way you were looking at them and the way you talked about them—they aren't just guards, are they?"

Joan let out a bitter laugh. "Of course not. Most of those boys never had a day of training, and they're strangers to any real discipline. Lewis doesn't care. He wanted militia members who could shoot and fight and look tough to discourage any trouble. Didn't matter if they were good men or had a lick of sense. As long as he could make them follow his orders without question. That's hardly a problem, of course, when he lets them have free rein in the town. As long as patrols are walked and trouble reported, Lewis will ignore everything else."

Kim's stomach clenched. It sounded way too much like the gang she'd grown up in, before Carol and Bruno had decided to go straight. "It sounds like they're just a bunch of bullies with weapons."

"They are. They have no problem beating up anyone who doesn't agree with them." Joan's lips thinned. "The man with the concussion...I know what you were told, but that wasn't a job site accident. He ran afoul of one of those militia boys when the boy was in a bad temper, and he got injured for not moving out of the way fast enough."

Kim flinched in horror. "That could have killed him."

"I know."

"Lewis didn't do anything?" She couldn't quite believe it. "How is letting something like that happen taking care of the community, or the people?"

Joan's eyes flickered with resignation and pain. "I know. I've tried to bring it up to him, to get him to talk to the men and rein them in. Enforce some rules to keep them from hurting people. He always brushed me off, said that young men were rough around the edges, and they'd settle down once they got used to their new responsibilities. Then I found out he was actually ordering some of the attacks against people who tried to oppose him or question his rules."

Kim felt sick. "This is really bad, Joan. You have to see that, right?"

"It doesn't matter. Unless Lewis says otherwise, it's not wrong." Joan sighed. "I did try to talk to him about it, ask him to be more tolerant. But…" She trailed off, and Kim saw her rub one arm absently.

It was a gesture she recognized from watching her mother throughout her childhood. "He hurt you. That's what those bruises are from, isn't it? Because he hit you when you questioned him?"

Joan didn't answer, but Kim didn't need a verbal response to see the truth in her face. Joan's expression was a mirror of the one her mother had worn when Kim was nine or ten and had innocently asked if she'd fallen, and why she and Daddy liked fighting so much.

"I'm sorry. I'm sorry you have to go through that. It's not right that you're being punished for standing up for people and trying to do the right thing." Kim reached across and took Joan's hand. "You shouldn't have to put up with that."

Joan didn't pull away, but her lips curled in a soft, sad smile. "It is what it is, and I do all right. Lewis is a difficult man, but I do love him, and I'm sure he'll do the right thing eventually. It just takes patience."

"You sound like my mother. She talked like that when I was a kid. She was always making excuses for my dad's behavior, even when he bloodied her lip or cracked her ribs. I used to be afraid I'd come home and find her dead because of him."

She hadn't thought about that for a long time, but it was the truth. She'd loved her father, but she'd also been afraid of him. The older she got, the harder it was to ignore what was happening—and what it meant.

She looked Joan in the eye. "I was scared for her. But my mom—she had lines she wouldn't let him cross. And when he did, she walked away. She turned him in to the police and made sure he got put away." She still remembered standing outside the courtroom and watching as her father was dragged away. The venom in his expression and her mother's unflinching resolve.

Joan tilted her head. "Your mother must be a very brave, very tough woman to be able to do something like that. It takes a lot of courage to stand up to someone you love and to stick to your guns. I don't know that I could do it."

"I think you could if you had to. But you're right. My mother is an amazing woman. Tough as nails and solid as steel. She stood up for what was right, even though no one else agreed with her. Even though it meant she had to leave and go into Witness Protection. She's so strong. Even when I was angry at her, I knew I wanted to be that kind of person. Strong and sticking to my principles. I'm proud to be her daughter."

I just wish I'd told her that more often. I hope I get a chance to see her and tell her again.

"You're a brave girl." Joan squeezed her hand. She paused, then spoke softly. "Truthfully, I've known for a while that Lewis is out of control. And I've thought about leaving. I even have a bag packed, if he ever goes completely crazy. And a car I asked him to give me in case I needed to lead a foraging or scavenging expedition in another town." The sad smile reappeared. "I've thought about just hopping in the car and never coming back, but I haven't been able to make myself go."

"I know the feeling. It's hard. But if you wait too long—don't wait too long. Lewis is dangerous, and if he's already hitting you, then the next time he loses his temper he could do a lot more damage. You won't be able to do much, or hide it, if he breaks bones."

"I know." Joan rose and looked at Kim, her eyes dark and solemn and wary. "I'll be honest with you. You need to follow your own advice and get out of town soon. I know Dennis isn't at his best, but the longer you stay, the harder it will be for you to leave. Best you get out before you wind up the same as Dr. Kennedy, or worse."

27

BILL WHEELER

"I'm fine. We need to get back on the road."

Bill scowled at Shannon. A full day of rest had given her more color in her cheeks and a voracious appetite. She no longer wavered on her feet, and she had managed to eat her food and go to the bathroom unassisted the day before. Her shoulder was still far from fully healed, but the angry redness of infection had given way to the color of typical healing. When Bill applied pressure, the fluid that emerged looked like normal blood.

They had the antibiotics if she needed more. They had the remains of the honey and a solid supply of bandages and gauze. Shannon was clearly energetic enough to argue.

"Fine. But I'm driving. You're not going to be handling the wheel until we can be sure you won't tear your shoulder open." He gave her a stern look. "I'm not letting you ruin all my hard work."

Shannon was on the verge of pouting, but she was the one who looked away from their staring contest first. "Fine. You're the driver."

"Good. Let's clean up and get out of here." He was worried about her shoulder and her health, but Bill had to admit he would be happy to see the last of the urgent care center. All the time spent in medical facilities with Edith had given him a strong dislike of anything resembling a hospital, and Shannon's recent illness and narrow escape from death had only reinforced that feeling.

They cleaned up the used bandages and trash and disposed of it, then went to the entrance. Bill eyed the mattresses he'd purloined. "We've got some space in the truck. Bet we'll be able to use those when we get where we're going."

"Couldn't hurt," Shannon said. "They'll be more comfortable than the trailer floor or sleeping in a seat."

Shannon began picking up pillows. Bill grabbed the mattresses and hauled them outside. He was just about to open the truck when he spotted a familiar figure in the doorway across the street. June was watching him. He waved to her then paused as a thought struck him.

They had a whole truck full of supplies. And June had helped him, not just by driving Jay away, but also with her advice and home remedies. He also knew the people in the neighborhood were desperate and hungry.

"What's up?" Shannon emerged from the care center laden with bedding. She spotted June. "Is she the woman who helped you?"

"Yep. I was thinking I might give her some supplies as a thank-you for her kindness and a helping hand for the people around here. From what she told me, they could use it."

Shannon nodded. "We've got plenty." She looked back into the center. "You'll be able to haul a lot more if you use those gurneys you took the mattresses from."

That was a good idea. Bill smiled and opened up the truck, then turned and went inside the building. He came back with the two rolling bed frames he'd set aside days before. While Shannon dragged mattresses and pillows and sheets into the truck, Bill unloaded boxes of supplies. He stacked the carts with as many boxes, bags, and containers as he could make fit, reaching around and through the pallets to provide a wider variety of foods.

He managed to get most of a pallet onto the carts before he had to stop, afraid that one more box would send the stacks crashing down. He grabbed the first makeshift cart and began to wheel it carefully across the street.

June stared at him, eyes wide, as he guided the gurney to the door. Bill grinned and offered her a little bow. "Special delivery for you."

"You...I...This is..." June swallowed hard, her eyes bright. "You didn't have to do this."

"That might be true. Doesn't mean I didn't want to. I figured people around here could use the supplies, and Shannon agrees with me that we've got plenty to spare." He tapped the cart. "I don't know where everyone is or who needs what. I trust you to see that folks get what they need."

"Of course. Of course." June blinked, then stepped back. "Just let me open up my garage, and we can store everything there."

Unloading the gurneys went faster with two people, and soon the boxes were stacked neatly along the walls. Bill swiped the sweat off his brow. "That ought to feed folks for a good long time."

"It will." June reached out and gave him a rib-cracking hug. Bill suppressed a wince as the pressure made the stab wound throb and returned the embrace. "Thank you for being so generous. You and your partner both."

"You're welcome." Bill hugged her back. "You should know I didn't clean out everything in the urgent care or the veterinary clinic. There's some medical supplies available if you need them."

"Thank you." June hugged him again, then stepped back. "I guess you and your friend will be moving on then?"

"Yeah. She's got a daughter she needs to find, and I'm along for the ride."

"Well, you be careful, and you be safe. The world's a dangerous place, and folks like you are too rare these days. We need more of your type, helping out and reminding folks what's really important in life."

"Same goes for you, June. You take good care of yourself. And tell those boys I said to behave, if you see them again."

"I'll do that."

"Bill!"

He turned to see Shannon standing at the back of the truck. She didn't look too impatient, but it was clear she was done loading the supplies and eager to get on the road. Not that he could blame her. He'd checked the maps, and by his reckoning, they weren't more than a few hours out. There was a good chance they'd be in Memphis by nightfall.

He offered June a final smile of farewell before jogging back to the truck. He pulled down the door and latched it, then went around to the driver's side and heaved himself up into the cab. He leaned over toward the passenger side. "You okay getting in, or do you need a hand?"

Shannon eyed the door and the step. She planted one foot on the thick rubber of the tire and shoved herself up. She caught the handhold with her good hand and dragged herself into the cab beside him with a grunt of effort. She scowled at her arm, once more in a sling. "I hate this thing."

"Better that than the consequences of you tearing that wound and making it worse." Bill smirked at her exasperated expression as they both buckled their seat belts. He ran through the checklist as Shannon had taught him to do, then stuck the key in the ignition, and the truck roared to life.

He guided the vehicle out of the emergency bay and through a careful turn toward the road. Two minutes later, they were cruising down the highway past the buildings he'd explored two days before.

They rode in comfortable silence for a while. Bill waited until they'd cleared Stuttgart and the inevitable crash zone on the edge of town before he voiced the question he'd been thinking about since they left Oklahoma.

"When we get to Memphis, where are we going? And what can we expect when we get there?"

Shannon's brow creased. "Assuming they haven't moved, my aunt and uncle will be living next to their scrapyard on the northwest edge of Memphis."

A scrapyard sounded promising. As a mechanic, he knew scrapyards were a goldmine of parts for any number of vehicles or devices. "What about your parents? Or siblings?"

Shannon shook her head. "I don't have siblings, and my parents died when I was a kid. My aunt and uncle raised me after that, with the help of the Black Rats."

"The Black Rats?" He'd seen the patch on her jacket and the tattoo on her shoulder. "I'm not familiar with the name."

"It's a motorcycle club based out of Memphis. My aunt and uncle are the leaders of the club. At least, my uncle was the boss the last time I spoke to them."

Bill mulled that over as he worked the truck around a tangle of metal that had once been two or three sedan-style cars. "I don't know much about motorcycle clubs or riders. Nothing outside of what you see on the TV, really." He glanced at her. "Tell me what they're like?" He pitched it as a question to let her know she didn't have to tell him more than she felt comfortable revealing.

Shannon bit her lip, then reached into her bag and pulled out some candied ginger, which she popped in her mouth. "Biker culture is complicated. Hard to explain if you've never lived it. Like any other group, you've got good folks, decent people, and a share of bad apples." She swallowed the ginger and dug out another piece. "I grew up as a member of the Black Rats. Got my first motorcycle when I was fourteen, along with my rider name and my jacket." She eyed the battered and stained denim ruefully. "My uncle wasn't the boss then, but he and Aunt Carol were pretty well respected. Which was good for me, because I wouldn't have made it into a one-percenter gang without that."

"One percenter?" Bill frowned. "I'm not familiar with the term."

"Ninety-nine percent of MCs are law abiding, and one percent are not." Shannon had a fond expression on her face. "That's the quote anyway, as best I can remember it. It isn't always true, though it was for the Black Rats back then. I thought it was great."

Bill couldn't see the appeal himself, but then he'd never had much wanderlust in his soul, and he was a peaceable fellow by nature. He'd never had any desire to do more than get a decent education then find a job where he could work with his hands, a lady to share his life with, and a home to call his own. His greatest ambition had been to be a solid, honest, working-class citizen, like generations of Wheelers before him. But as his mother had always said, it took all kinds to make a world. So he listened as Shannon described the life she'd grown up in.

"I loved all the traveling, being on the open road. I knew every inch of my first Harley like the back of my hand, down to the scrapes in the paint from my first crash. Of course, I was a kid in the beginning, so my participation in club activities was kind of a gray area. But I got to help with charity work when we went out on drives for food and toys. I was the kid-friendly face that made people feel a little safer, I guess."

Shannon sighed and leaned back against the seat. Her eyes stared into the distance, into old memories. "Back then, my name was Sarah. Sarah Nakamura. My dad was a Black Rat out of the Roswell area, and my aunt and uncle were based in Memphis. It was a big change when my dad died in an accident and I had to move, but Aunt Carol took good care of me. She made sure I didn't go too far out of line. She did a fair job, too, until I met Andre."

"You've mentioned him. Your ex-husband," Bill said.

"Yeah. Only a bit older than me, but he was—well, he was the sort of huge, muscled guy no one wants to cross. He talked like he was educated in a posh school, and he could charm a cat out of a creamery when he wanted to. He worked as a cook for his day job and rode with the Black Rats nights and weekends and his occasional day off. When we first met, he was good to me, made some of the nastier fellows stay away. He seemed like the kind of guy who had it all—steady job, connections in the Black Rats, enough muscle and smarts to make good, and even some skills, like cooking. I thought becoming his old lady was better than finding gold."

"His old lady?" Bill frowned. Shannon was barely half his age, as near as he could guess. Far too young to be anyone's old lady. In his experience, the term was usually used in reference to one's mother, possibly grandmother.

"Biker term. Someone's old lady is their wife, or significant other. Step up from being just 'property of' or 'so-and-so's woman.'" She made a wry face. "Or other, less flattering terms." Her hands traced over the patches on her jacket. "In some motorcycle clubs, women are riders, and they have a voice. But in a one percenter, being someone's old lady is as good as it gets. A woman's rank is determined by her husband and her blood family."

"Sounds a mite barbaric." Bill tried to keep his voice as neutral as he could.

"Maybe. But it's what I grew up with, and it's what I knew. A lot of bikers and motorcycle clubs take good care of their brothers and their women. Most of the Black Rats were decent folk, underneath the cursing and propensity for fighting." She turned to Bill with a strange little grin on her face. "You were talking the other day about me being strong, being tough enough to fight, to almost hold my own against Langmaid. The Black Rats taught me that."

Put like that, he could see the benefits in the way she'd grown up and how being in a motorcycle gang had been good for her. It still wasn't the sort of life he would have chosen, especially not if he'd been born female, but he could see the attraction.

Which really left one question. "Why'd you leave?" Shannon gave him a startled, incredulous glance, and he clarified. "I know you told me about your husband, how he was a drug smuggler and he killed someone. But it sounds like you had a community that could have helped you if you'd stayed."

The bitter laughter that answered him was almost painful in the raw nature of it. "You have no idea. Testifying against Andre made me persona non grata. Not even being Bruno and Carol's niece, or pseudo-adopted kid, could change that. Andre was a snake in the grass, and he got booted for the murder, but there are still unspoken rules. Speaking against him broke those rules. If the club had taken me back after I testified against my own husband, a brother in the Black Rats, they'd have lost half the membership or more, just on principle. I wouldn't have lasted a day on my own. Andre had a lot of friends, inside and out of the Black Rats, and a lot of clients who were ticked I put their favorite runner and handler away."

"I'm sorry to hear that." It was such a cliché and pointless thing to say, but it was all he could think of.

Shannon shook her head. "I made my choice, and I have to—had to, I guess—live with it. Staying would have torn the Black Rats apart from the inside out and put a lot of innocent people in the line of fire, including my family. So I went into WitSec."

"You ever go back to Memphis, even just passing through as a truck driver?"

"Nope." Shannon shook her head. "Never could risk it."

Bill nodded, but his mind was on other things. "You're certain your family are still in Memphis? If it's been five years?"

"Sure. Carol and Bruno were senior members of the Black Rats Memphis chapter. They wouldn't just up and leave their territory. Besides, Uncle Bruno owns the scrapyard where the club meets, and he wouldn't leave behind his bikes, his special projects, or his investment."

"A scrapyard?" Bill frowned. The scrapyards he was used to were huge, sprawling open areas of land, sometimes part of someone's yard, with a million ways to get in or out and precarious piles of metal in the process of rusting away. As a mechanic, he considered them a treasure trove, but in terms of a place to settle in and make camp, he wasn't nearly as certain of the viability. "Are you sure it's safe?"

"Safe as anywhere. Uncle Bruno's scrapyard has an eight-foot corrugated metal fence around most of it." Shannon saw his expression, and her own went tight. She reached out and put a hand on his arm. "Look, I understand your reservations. But they're family. Bruno and Carol especially, but all the Black Rats are family in a way, even if half of them would rather spit in my face than admit it. I can't just abandon them after what's happened. I've got to at least see if they're okay and do what I can for them."

Bill understood her feelings and her determination, but it didn't stop him from having serious concerns.

They hadn't been safe in a supercenter with four walls and locked doors. They hadn't even been completely safe in a medical facility, as his stinging neck and aching side could attest. Their truck, for all it was a godsend in terms of supplies, was also one giant, rolling target.

A scrapyard didn't seem like the safest place to settle down, and a bunch of bikers of questionable character didn't seem like the best guards. Especially since Shannon hadn't parted with them on the best of terms.

A lot could change in five years, for better or for worse. And a lot *had* changed in the past two weeks. Even if the members of the Black Rats had remained exactly the same as Shannon remembered before the EMP, they were certain to have changed now, like everyone else in the world.

But Bill could tell that Shannon wouldn't be deterred, and he couldn't fault her determination to find and take care of her family. He'd have done the same if he'd had anyone to go to—anyone aside from the stubborn, tough-as-nails figure sitting beside him, still pale from blood loss and convalescence but determined to keep going.

Bill released a carefully inaudible sigh and pushed away any further protests he might make. They'd just have to handle the situation as they found it. He'd be there to help Shannon talk to her family or to support her if circumstances made talking impossible. That and driving the truck was all he could do.

The miles slid by in silence, broken only by the exchange of drinks and snacks, and the occasional stop to take a leak and stretch tired limbs. The sun drifted through the sky with excruciating slowness, highlighting the miles of accident-choked roads and small ghostlike towns.

They got onto the highway for the final stretch and cruised past the mile markers without comment. In the passenger seat, Shannon grew more tense with every sign.

When they crossed the bridge into Memphis, Bill sat up a little straighter and scanned the road in front of them, which was clear of cars. He'd known from the emergency broadcast that small towns were on their own, but Memphis was a metropolis with a population of more than a million inhabitants. Perhaps the Army or another government agency had moved in to take care of the large population center.

This looked promising.

Except everything was quiet. Too quiet.

Shannon fidgeted next to him, and Bill slowed the truck down, scanning left and right as he drove.

They approached the city proper, and Bill strained to see some sign of habitation, maybe government and military occupation. Even a police presence would have been a welcome sign of law and order.

There was nothing. The town was like a scene out of an apocalyptic movie. Trash littered the streets. Papers and plastic bags swirled and drifted in the intermittent breeze. Buildings were boarded up and locked down, and many of them had broken windows gaping open in mute and jagged evidence of looting.

The area was eerily quiet. If there were people, they were staying out of sight. Bill's mood worsened with every street they passed. They'd passed enough near-abandoned towns that he should have been used to it, but somehow it was worse to see what had once been a thriving and bustling city reduced to a silent shell of itself.

It was heartbreaking. Bill and Shannon traded a look, but neither of them spoke. There was nothing to say. Bill turned his attention to the road and focused on threading his way through parked and crashed cars with a single-minded intensity he hadn't needed in days.

Shannon finally broke the bleak silence. "You'll want to turn left onto Thomas Street. It's also labeled Highway 51. We'll take that up to the neighborhood that houses my uncle's scrapyard."

Bill nodded to show he'd heard. He didn't trust himself to speak.

28

KIM NAKAMURA

B y the time rounds were over, Kim was wound tighter than a spring and ready to bolt at the slightest hint of danger. If she hadn't been concerned for Dennis and Mutt, she'd have taken her chances and made a break for it. But she couldn't leave the former marshal behind.

It had been Dennis's idea to come to Humboldt, but she'd been the one to encourage him to stick around while he went through detox. She felt she owed it to him to warn him what kind of man Lewis had become and to own up to her mistake in supporting Lewis's suggestion that they remain in town.

Dennis was in the kitchen when she arrived at the house they'd been given. He still looked pale and tired, with pain lines bracketing his mouth, but he was upright and standing at the stove. His hands were steadier than she'd seen them in a while. He offered her a crooked little half-smile as she came in.

"Hey, Kim. Good job on the soup stock. It's coming along well. Should make a great dinner this evening."

She hated to be the one to shatter his current good mood, but Joan was right. The longer they waited to leave, the harder it would be. She dropped into the nearest chair and braced herself for the discussion to follow. "We've got a problem."

Dennis gave her his full attention at once. His eyes were sharp as they checked her for injuries. "What happened? Someone hurt you?"

"Not yet." Kim took a deep breath. She didn't want to be the one to tell him this. She knew how hard betrayal could hit. She also knew she might be the only one who could prod him into action. Dennis had already proved he'd do a lot for the sake of keeping his promise to her mother. "But Lewis is…" She trailed off, uncertain how to phrase it. "…dangerous."

Dennis frowned. "I told you, he's just under a lot of stress and short-tempered."

"He killed the previous doctor when he tried to leave, then he covered up the murder. Since then, he's been ordering the militia to beat up people who disagree with him and allowing them to do whatever they want outside of patrolling and reporting to him," Kim said in a rush.

Dennis went absolutely still, as if she'd delivered a football-style kick straight to his groin. Then he stumbled forward and collapsed into the other chair at the table, his eyes wide with shock. "That can't be right. You have to be mistaken."

"I wish I was." Kim leaned forward and put a hand on his arm. "I know he's your friend, and I wish I didn't have to be the one to tell you this, but it's true. I heard it from Joan Danville. I asked her about the glasses I found."

Dennis shook his head. She thought it was the sort of last-ditch denial people had when they were trying not to understand something they already half-knew was true. "I can't believe it. There has to be some sort of mistake. Some explanation. The Lewis Danville I knew wouldn't do anything like that."

"If there's an explanation, it isn't one I know. Or that Joan knows." Kim thought about telling Dennis about Joan's bruises, then dismissed the idea. As much as she respected Dennis, she knew if she brought up the abuse, he might latch onto it as an excuse—claim Joan was telling tales as revenge for a fight between her and Lewis.

She'd seen—and heard—such arguments and denials all too often when her mother had been in the Black Rats. Dennis might be more levelheaded and realistic than the average biker—though his recent addiction made her wonder if that was really true—but Lewis was his friend. It was only normal he'd try to defend him.

She watched Dennis wrestle with her words, trying to find an explanation that would make sense. "That doctor—"

"He and Lewis disagreed over the militia and Lewis leading the town after the EMP. He tried to leave, and the militia chased him down and shot him out near the Forked Deer River."

Dennis shook his head. "I can't believe it." He abruptly shoved himself to his feet, a look of grim determination on his face as he collected his shoes and shoved his feet into them. "I need to talk to Lewis. I need to hear what he says."

Kim swallowed. She didn't think it was a good idea. On the other hand, it might be the only thing that could convince Dennis they needed to leave Humboldt. "Do you know where he is?" she asked.

"No. But I know how to find out." Dennis turned and stumped his way toward the door.

Kim took a moment to make sure the soup stock wouldn't boil over, then followed him. Mutt rose to her feet with an inquiring look, but

Kim shook her head and the dog flopped back down. As much as she would have liked Mutt's large and reassuring presence at her back, she was pretty sure things were about to get ugly.

Dennis stalked out the door and made his way toward the first militia member he spotted. Kim stayed close. She didn't like the look of faint contempt in the younger man's eye, and after what Joan had told her, she didn't trust anyone wearing the quasi-uniform of the enforcers.

The enforcer stiffened, visibly on guard as they approached. "Militia Leader Danville said—"

"I know. I'd like to have a word with Militia Leader Danville. Where is he?" Dennis's voice snapped like a whip, and the younger man's spine straightened automatically.

Kim felt a sense of appreciation. If this was how he'd been when he was in the military, she could see how he might have gained the reputation he'd had.

The militia man hesitated, and Dennis glared at him, hand tightening in unspoken warning on his crutch handle. "Where is he, boy?"

"Watering Hole. Four streets over." The young man recovered his previous demeanor with visible effort. "He doesn't like to be disturbed when he's there. Not unless it's an emergency."

"I know his habits. Doesn't mean I care." Dennis shook his head. "What's the name?"

"Humboldt Watering Hole." The young man shifted in place. "We'll have to escort you."

Dennis's gaze raked over the youth, his stare hard enough to make the young man flush uncomfortably. "You even legal? You don't look it. Or does Lewis make the mistake of thinking a gun in your hand makes you old enough for anything?" His voice was almost snide.

"I'm twenty-five." The young man scowled back, his pride visibly stung. "And Militia Leader Danville makes the rules."

"Fine. Let's get going then." Dennis jerked his head, and the militia man waved over one of his companions. Together, they trooped through the early evening dusk. Kim took the opportunity to sidle closer to Dennis.

"The Watering Hole—is that what I think it is?"

"If you think it's a bar or other alcohol-selling establishment, then yes." Dennis grunted as he took a rough step and stumbled a little.

"He's got rationing and farming and martial law, but he's got a bar open?" Kim made a face. "Why not put people to work on other things if he has the resources to have a booze joint?"

"Because alcohol's a fairly cheap vice, and a little booze and tobacco go a long way toward making people feel easier about the situation. It's one reason why soldiers used to get a pack of cigarettes and a bottle of beer most evenings, before health officials convinced the brass that the risks outweighed the benefits." Dennis growled the words. "A bar, even if it's a cheap, tacky hole in the wall, gives people a place to go and grouse and socialize, and feel like the world can't be that bad, 'cause at least we've got indulgences like that left."

It made sense. Kim recalled from school that alcohol was a depressant and a relaxant. It would make people mellow and slow, except for those who became angry or aggressive drunks.

How many incidents between the militia and the townspeople were being brushed off in the name of an alcohol-induced misunderstanding? She chilled at the thought. Like having rough edges and being under stress, being a little drunk was the kind of excuse most people would brush off. How many times had she heard people say, "You'll have to excuse him, he's just a little drunk"? How many times had she seen the injured party go from angry or upset to nodding and laughing it off? It was exactly the kind of excuse Joan might offer so she could forgive and forget the bruises she got from Lewis. The idea that Lewis might actually encourage that sort of thinking made Kim a little sick.

She forced the thoughts away as they rounded the corner. The Humboldt Watering Hole was easy to pick out from the rest of the storefronts. It was the only one lit up and occupied. Dennis limped his way toward it and through the door with single-minded determination.

Lewis was sitting at a booth near the back with militia members scattered around the room. There was a bottle of whiskey on the table in front of him, already open and partially emptied, and a glass with an inch of amber liquid inside. Lewis's cheeks already had a slight flush, which Kim suspected indicated intoxication. Kim swallowed hard.

If Dennis noticed anything about Lewis's condition, he didn't show it. He stalked straight up to his old friend and slid into the seat across from him, leaving Kim to take a seat at a nearby two-person table. She was close enough to help if needed yet still gave the two men a semblance of privacy.

"Hate to trouble you, Sergeant, but we need to talk."

"I told you, I'm no sergeant anymore, Dennis. Just Lewis Danville." He snapped his fingers at the bartender. "But since you're apparently feeling better, let me get you a drink. On the house."

"I'll take water or soda. I'm not sure I want alcohol just now." Dennis waved away the offer of whiskey. "I could, however, use some answers." He kept his voice low, a soft conversational mutter just above a whisper. "I've been hearing some funny rumors."

"Yeah? What sort of rumors?" Kim saw the way Lewis's shoulders tensed and his expression closed down, and she was pretty sure Dennis saw it too.

"I heard there was a doctor in town after the EMP hit. Now, I know you told us the man went to Jackson, but I've heard he was heading for the lake. Might have met with an accident." Dennis kept his voice low and easy, but Lewis's hand tightened on his glass.

"You know there's always rumors. One man gets a little discontented and leaves town, and the next thing you know, half a dozen people are swearing he's everything from living as a hermit with a mistress to murdered by gangs. Nature of the beast, and all that." Lewis spoke casually, but his voice had deepened and carried a hint of irritation.

Dennis shrugged lightly. "Sure, I know all that, Lewis. But you've got some young guns in your militia. I remember my first tour and the way things could go in a hot zone. Hard not to let your temper get the better of you, or your nerves."

The thud of Lewis's glass on the table made Kim jump. "What do you want me to say, Dennis? You've been in a war zone, and the whole darn country's as good as one these days. You know how crazy it is out there."

"Yeah, I do. I really do. I'm just a little confused. See, you told me one thing, and the rumors say another. Normally, I'd believe you, no question. But Kim found the doc's glasses up near the river. And that's a problem compared to what you told me."

So he had looked at the map. Kim felt a brief surge of pride and happiness. Despite how dismissive he'd sounded the day before, Dennis had actually cared enough to check Lewis's story against the facts they had.

Her happiness disappeared like a match in a monsoon as she noticed Lewis's darkening expression. His voice was a low growl, his irritation turning to anger when he spoke. "Look, Dennis, the man was a malcontent, a dissident, and a fear-monger. Normally, I wouldn't have cared, but he was the only doctor we had, except for Joan's veterinary training. I tried to reason with him, but he wouldn't hear a word I said, so I had to take care of him another way. Couldn't have him stirring up trouble."

"Did you send him away?" Dennis said. His voice had a slightly sharper edge.

"Why the heck would I do that? We needed a doctor. Still do. No, I didn't send him away, but I had to make sure everyone knew who was boss. Including Doc Kennedy." Lewis scowled over the top of his glass. "Don't give me that disapproving look, Sullivan. You know how important discipline is during troubled times."

"Discipline, yes. But a town isn't a dictatorship, and you ought to know it. There's a fine line between discipline and tyranny, just like there's a line between keeping the peace and being the oppressors. You ought to know that, Lewis Danville." Dennis's voice was stern. "We talked about it often enough when we were in the Corps."

Lewis's free hand slammed onto the tabletop. "I did what I had to do." His voice rose toward a shout. Then he visibly controlled himself. He took a deep breath and poured himself a generous measure of whiskey. "This town was becoming a lawless wasteland of anarchy when I stepped in." He swallowed a good third of his drink and gave Dennis a heated glare. "Now, I won't say mistakes haven't been made, but it's been chaos since that attack, or whatever it was. I got people organized. I set up security measures. I arranged to make sure everyone had enough food and supplies. I'm the one who made this town a haven instead of just another ghost town full of frightened people and violent thugs."

"Maybe not a ghost town, but you've still got frightened people and thugs. You call them citizens and militia." Kim spat the words from where she sat, interrupting before she could stop herself. Dennis reached out and set a hand on her arm, but her anger had ignited. "You told me the guy with the concussion had an accident, but I know he was attacked by one of your wannabe soldier boys. And what about Mr. Craig? He's dying because you won't give him the care he needs for his diabetes."

"It isn't possible. Special diets and all that—we don't have the resources. We've got to save the resources for people who it'll do some good for." Lewis took another drink and gave her a look of mingled pity and condescension. "I know your training as a doctor, or a nurse, means you don't like to think like that. But as a leader, I've got to think of what's best for everyone. Got to consider the greater good, you might say."

"In a pig's eye." Dennis's voice was lower than Kim's but just as heated. "You know better than anyone what a trap that kind of thinking is."

Lewis twitched his gaze back to Dennis. He looked like he was about to speak, but Dennis shook his head.

"As Marines," Dennis began, "we knew not to leave a man behind. Semper Fidelis, remember? How many times did you stand beside me, or behind me, while we made sure every man in patrol was safe?" He looked so disappointed Kim wanted to shrink in her chair, and she wasn't even the target of his anger.

"It's easy to say when you aren't the one responsible—"

"Don't give me that load of horse hocky. Leaving a man to die without even trying to save him, or attacking a defenseless citizen for disagreeing with you, is barbaric, and you know it, Danville." Dennis snarled the words. His face was flushed, and Kim could tell he was trying hard to hold onto his temper. "You were quick enough to tell Kim all those stories about what a super soldier and leader I was in the military. I'm telling you, *Sergeant*, that if I were in your company now, I'd be lobbying to call a mutiny or a Code Red on you."

"I'd see you horsewhipped and put on half-rations if you tried!" Lewis slammed his palms on the table as he stood, heedless of the way the table rocked and his drink sloshed. "You're out of line, Sullivan!"

"You're not my sergeant or militia leader, Danville." Dennis gestured for Kim to stand and pushed himself free of the booth as soon as she was upright and away from her chair. "Not even my town leader. I'll say what I think, and I'll say it plainly. Right now, that's the best respect I can give you."

He turned, then stopped, frozen in place by the multiple guns pointed at him. Kim flinched and just barely controlled the urge to duck behind him.

Lewis's voice was poisonous as he spoke. "I won't be shown such attitude in my own town, Sullivan, old military friend or no. I can't have people sowing dissent and disrespect. The two of you are going to be confined to your house until I decide what to do with you, or until you calm down and realize how unproductive your attitudes are."

Kim whipped around. "You can't do that!" She took a step forward before Dennis grabbed her arm and pulled her to a stop. "I have to find my family in Memphis!"

"I know what you want, but as long as you're in my town, you'll play by my rules. I won't have you trying to undermine me by telling stories and running off whenever you like." Lewis sneered at her. Then his gaze flicked over her shoulder to the men still guarding them. "Take these two back to their house. Set a minimum six-person squad to guard them and make sure they don't get ideas. Oh, and be sure the dog is contained as well."

Kim wanted to punch the smug look off his face, but Dennis pulled her back further and shook his head in warning. With a final glare,

Kim subsided. The militia men fell in around them and prodded them toward the door.

Dennis didn't say a word as they were marched back to their home, now more of a prison. He didn't speak as they were shoved inside and the door locked behind them. Mutt whined, sensing his distress, and Dennis put a hand on her head. Then he looked at Kim, regret in his eyes.

"Kim, I'm sorry. I should have paid more attention to your concerns."

She appreciated the apology, but she couldn't let him take all the blame on himself. "It's not entirely your fault. I was the one who suggested we stick around long enough for your detox."

Dennis sighed. "I know, and I appreciate that. But I was still the one who wanted to linger past the worst of it. We could have been on the road two days ago if I hadn't been so poorly." He stumbled to his preferred chair in the living room and fell heavily into it. "I wouldn't have believed it if I hadn't seen it. I never thought a good Marine like Lewis Danville would fall prey to the tyrant's delusion."

"Tyrant's delusion?" Kim settled across from him.

"Old concept I read about when I was younger. I can't remember the exact quote, but it was something like, 'The worst tyrant is one who acts in the belief that he does so for the greater good, for then his conscience is complicit in tyranny, without even the stirring of self-doubt to check his excesses.' It was something like that, anyway, though I can't swear I remember the exact wording. It's been a long time since I read that book."

She was curious about the source, but she couldn't deny the relevance. "Is there any way to bring him to his senses?"

"Not with the way he was acting. In that mood, you'd have better luck moving a hundred-year oak tree with your bare hands."

"Then we need to find a way to get out of here before it gets worse." Kim scowled at the door. "Since we're currently under house arrest with guards on all the doors, how do we make our escape?"

Dennis gave her a bleak smile. "Well, we start by getting some food in our bellies. Which means heating up and finishing that soup stock you started. After that," he tipped his head to study the house, "I have some ideas."

29

BILL WHEELER

By the time they turned up Highway 51, Bill had come to the conclusion that driving in the city was a lot harder than driving on the open roads. There was more debris to avoid and more obstacles to try and guide the truck around. The grim mood inside the cab didn't help.

Bill was trying to find a way to break the silence when he noticed a store. It was a clothing store like several they'd passed, but a sign in the window drew his attention like a magnet: Jerry's now has Big and Tall!

He started to guide the truck in that direction. Shannon turned to look at him. "We're not there yet."

"I know, but I could use some clean clothes. It's been a while since I had anything other than the one shirt and pair of pants I'm wearing, plus that set of scrubs I put on while helping you." The scrubs hadn't fit that well, and he'd trashed them after Shannon's recovery seemed certain. They were so covered with blood and other fluids he hadn't thought them worth salvaging.

He indicated the store with his chin. "I saw the sign, and it occurred to me they might have clothes that actually fit me."

Shannon eyed the store thoughtfully then nodded. "I guess a few more minutes wouldn't hurt." She looked down at her own grimy, blood-stained, and well-worn clothing. Bill had made some efforts at cleaning and patching her jacket during their time on the road and their emergency stop. Even with his best efforts, it was worse for the wear, along with the rest of her clothes.

The truck pulled up to the store, and Bill took a moment to be glad for the mostly empty parking lot. He parked the vehicle, and the two of them descended from the cab and picked their way over the well-worn and uneven asphalt. The store windows were broken—evidence of looters—but they were also boarded up, as though someone was making an effort to keep it secure. Bill wondered who would be protecting the store, given the lack of nearby houses and the generally deserted feeling of the town.

With Shannon's wounded arm still tucked into a sling, it fell to Bill to get the door open. Fortunately, the lock was an easy one, and with a few quiet tips from Shannon, he got the door open. The two of them slipped inside.

They both had sturdy shoes on, scuffed and dirty but still in overall good condition. Bill made straight for the men's section to search for the larger clothing sizes. He bypassed slacks, polo shirts, and button-down options and went straight for the t-shirts, sweatshirts, camou-flage gear, jackets, and basics like underwear and socks. He wanted heavy-weather gear and clothing that could withstand the stress of the world they now lived in.

He found some heavy jeans and shirts in his size and bundled them into his arms along with a package of clean undergarments. He hauled the entire bundle to the set of dressing rooms in the back.

The stall was on the small side for a man of his size, but Bill couldn't find it in himself to care as he tugged on the first clean and truly comfortable clothing he'd had since the EMP had destroyed all electronics and a good measure of sanity in the world. It didn't do much for the dirt under his fingernails or the oily state of his short hair, but it was a miracle for his mood. He tried on a few sets of clothing then folded everything together and exited.

He walked out, intending to find a jacket to go with the rest of it when he saw Shannon standing stock-still in the middle of the room.

"Shannon?"

"Don't move, old man, or you'll regret it."

Bill stiffened as a figure holding a gun emerged from a corner he hadn't paid attention to.

The man was a rough-looking character with tangled, stringy black hair tied back under a well-worn bandanna. His jeans were ripped and smeared with oil stains, and his shirt was wrinkled and stiff with sweat and dirt. His belt was heavy, studded leather, scarred and decorated with a chain that looked like it looped around to a back pocket. It matched the buckles across the tops of his boots.

The heavy denim vest was what caught Bill's attention though. It was decorated with patches, including a name—Rough Rider Rick—and a diamond with a 1% on it. There was a prominent patch above it: a black rat on a motorcycle. The same patch Shannon had on her jacket. "You're a Black Rat?" Bill asked.

"Don't act like you don't know." The pistol wavered in Bill's direction. "This store's in our territory, and you two were looting it. We're not gonna let you get away with stealing from us. I got a bunch of brothers coming any second now."

"Hey." Shannon moved forward, and the gun immediately swiveled back to point at her. "I know this is Black Rats territory, but we weren't out to steal anything. We can pay for our stuff."

"Money ain't worth spit."

"I know. We've got food supplies, and I'm happy to pay you guys back for the clothing. I've got plenty of other stuff I'd be happy to donate to my brothers."

"We aren't your brothers! You don't call us that when you're not one of us!" The Black Rat looked furious.

"But I am. I been out of territory for a while, but I was a part of Carol and Bruno's club. I'm their niece, Shan—Sarah. Sarah Nakamura, used to be Atkinson."

The Black Rat snorted. "Please, everyone who knows the Black Rats has heard about Andre the snake and his old lady. Only an outsider would be dumb enough to try and convince us to trust you using those names."

"I'm not trying to give you the run-around. It's true. When I was a kid and running with the club, they used to call me Smart Aleck Sarah." Shannon looked frustrated. "I still have my jacket, even after everything. It's in my truck."

"Anyone can put patches on a piece of denim. Takes more than stitches on fabric to make a member of the club. It's about blood, and brotherhood, and family."

"I know that. I do. Look, if you could just let me talk to Bruno—" Shannon was interrupted by several engines revving in the street. She and Bill both tensed.

Seconds later, a gruff voice came echoing through the door, followed by an older man in jeans and a leather jacket over a stained t-shirt and scuffed work boots. Behind him, Bill saw another man in similar

268

attire who stopped at the doorway and leaned against the frame with the attitude of a guard.

"You better have a good reason for sending up sparks, Jackalope, or I'll see you licking tar off my wheel wells for a month." The man came to a stop and stared at the two of them, Shannon especially. His eyes widened, and his whole posture stiffened. Seconds later, his expression went blank. His voice was carefully expressionless when he spoke again.

"Sarah."

Shannon's back was stiff and straight as a board, and Bill saw her swallow nervously. "It's been a while, Uncle Bruno. You're looking well."

"You look like you lost a fight with the Bloods." Bruno's tone didn't change at all. Bill felt a tendril of unease at his stony demeanor.

"Life's been rough the past few days."

"Life's been rough the last five years here in Memphis. We had to go straight, and your husband's actions caused a huge stink. Darn near got us completely cut out of any legit groups, and a lot of our business ventures dropped us. Not that you'd know anything about that, with the way you vanished." There was a hint of anger there.

"I'm sorry, Uncle Bruno. Andre's got friends in a lot of places. I got shipped off to WitSec."

"Got shipped off? That's not the way I heard it. I heard you went willing. You certainly left Kim in our care quick enough. You never tried to contact us after that, not even when we looked for you."

Shannon winced, and Bill felt a pang of sympathy for her. She'd done what she thought was the right thing, but the consequences were staring in her face. It looked worse than he'd thought it would.

Five years could change a lot.

Bruno tipped his head to the biker who'd stopped them and the three men hovering by the doorway that Bill hadn't even noticed arriving. "Bring them and their vehicle to the scrapyard. We'll talk more there."

He turned and walked away without another word. Bill exchanged a look with Shannon, and the two of them followed her uncle.

Bill just hoped the look on her face—like she'd been shot again—wasn't a precursor of literal wounds to come.

30

KIM NAKAMURA

K im had hoped the lack of formal training or discipline among the militia would result in lax guards and perhaps an opening for escape. But apparently whatever rules Lewis used to enforce his commands were forceful enough to keep a consistent six- to ten-man guard on the house. Two men each watched the front and back doors, while the others did a roving patrol to keep an eye on the downstairs windows.

After the first few hours, Kim was ready to scream with frustration. Dennis, on the other hand, remained calm. He ate his share of the stew, then went upstairs to look outside. Kim finally lost patience and joined him.

"I thought you had some ideas on how to get out of here," she said.

"I do, but we're not going to get anywhere by rushing things. With someone like Lewis in charge, we're only going to get one chance to make an escape." Dennis frowned at the window. "I think I've got an idea we can make work, but it'll be difficult."

"How difficult?"

"Easier for you than for me. Mutt could go either way." Dennis pointed out the window. "Tell me what you see."

"Garage roof. Yard. Shed where you were puking. Fence. What's your point?"

"What you don't see: militia guards." Dennis grinned. "Never thought I'd be happy for having spent several hours puking my guts out, but I'm betting it stinks to high heaven out by the shed."

Kim took a second look. He was right. There weren't any militia men near the shed. She looked back at Dennis. "Okay. How does that make any difference?"

Dennis pointed. "Garage roof to shed roof, and shed roof to the fence, and the fence to the ground. It's not the easiest route, but it's doable."

"Even with your hip?" Kim was pretty sure she could make the trip, and even Mutt might not have too much trouble. But Dennis was more likely to fall off the roof than be able to walk across it.

Dennis grimaced, and his hand rubbed the injury absentmindedly. "I've had some time to rest, and I'm through the worst of the detox, so I can manage it. It won't be easy, and I'll have to do without the crutch. But my knee's had time to recover too, so it's not impossible." He gave her a faint smile. "I've been learning the past couple of days that a lot of things aren't as impossible as I thought they were."

"Glad I could be of help." Kim smiled back. "So, I guess we'd better do this at night? Take advantage of the limited visibility?"

"Makes the travel harder, but it does give us an advantage." Dennis nodded. "We should pack up our bags, then get as much rest as we can. We'll go in late night or early morning. Between midnight and dawn is when most people tend to relax."

"So we go across the roof, down the fence, and sneak out of town to head for Memphis?" Kim itched to leave immediately, but leaving at night was smarter. Knowing they had a concrete plan made the waiting a little easier.

Together, she and Dennis cleaned up their dinner dishes, just in case someone was watching through a window or crack in the door and reporting their actions. They packed their bags, then went upstairs and retired to their rooms as if going to bed. It all seemed a bit pointless to Kim, trying to mimic a normal routine, but she trusted Dennis's judgment on the matter—that it was better to be paranoid than too lax. Kim forced herself to lie down and relax, but she couldn't sleep. The simmering coil of anger at Lewis and the excitement of a midnight escape with Dennis kept her from dropping off.

Finally, the soft knock she'd been waiting for came. She shoved her feet into her shoes, tied them tight, and grabbed the bags. She would be responsible for carrying them, since she had better mobility and balance. Dennis would be responsible for getting Mutt onto the roof and keeping her going.

There were still no militia men near the shed when Kim opened the window. She tugged the bug screen out of place and turned it diagonally to set it to the side. Then she swung a leg out the window and ducked down to ease herself through the opening. It wasn't comfortable, and she didn't envy Dennis the task of trying to get his larger and more injured frame through the same opening. Once she got her footing on the slanted roof, she reached back in and grabbed the bags, then slipped out of the way.

Mutt came through next, wiggling and huffing quietly. Her paws skidded a little as they dislodged grit from the rough surface of the roofing shingles. With Kim on one side and Dennis shoving her through from behind, the big dog managed to climb through and mince her way across the roof to a more stable location.

Then it was Dennis's turn. Kim saw him wince and bite his lip as he swung his bad leg through the window and crouched to ease himself through. His muscular frame was no advantage in such tight quarters, and she heard him grunt as he squeezed himself into a folded position to fit. He staggered a little as he got his body free of the opening, but he grabbed the windowsill with both hands and kept himself upright as he pulled his other leg through. Then he collapsed to lean against the windowsill, breathing hard.

Kim waited, her nerves humming with every second they were delayed. Mutt picked up on her anxiety, or perhaps it was Dennis's discomfort. The dog fidgeted in place. She seemed to be as eager as Kim was to get a move on.

Finally, Dennis straightened and turned around so he was facing her. He nodded. Kim tightened her grip on the bags and began to make her way to the edge of the roof. The slope was tricky, but as a kid, she'd specialized in sneaking around whenever her mom and dad were arguing. She made it to the edge, gauged the distance, and took a short hop.

She landed with a dull thump and crouched, waiting to see if the guards heard her. They were all either very inattentive, or they were determined to avoid the disgusting smells emanating from the ground near the shed. Kim wrinkled her nose at the acrid stench, then focused on getting over the edge of the shed roof to the top of the fence so she could make a step down.

Behind her, Dennis was quietly coaxing Mutt over to the edge of the garage roof. The dog wasn't too thrilled with the direction she was being pointed, but at last she moved toward the edge with cautious steps. Kim moved out of her way as the dog bunched her muscles and made a leap onto the shed, then kept going to bounce over Kim's head to the ground. The noise she made was a lot louder than Kim's descent. She and Dennis held their breath to see if the sounds attracted the men.

Minutes crawled past, Mutt remained silent on the ground, and no one showed. Kim breathed a little easier. Dennis waved for her to follow Mutt. She stayed where she was long enough to see him sit down to navigate the shingled slope, then followed his directions. She hopped down the top rail of the five-foot-high chain link fence to land next to the dog. Mutt whuffed softly, and Kim put a hand on her head. "Quiet, Mutt."

There was a dull thud above them, and minutes later Dennis's face appeared over the edge of the shed roof. He gauged the distance between the roof and the fence, as well as the size of the top bar, made a disgruntled face, then disappeared. Seconds later, his feet came over the edge as he began to descend.

Kim saw the disaster unfolding seconds before it actually happened. Dennis couldn't see the fence properly, and he wasn't lined up the way he needed to be. She started to call out a warning, but it was too soft or she was too late.

Dennis's foot hit the top of the fence. The fence wobbled, and it threw off his descent as his bad leg landed on the top bar. His weight shifted, and his bad hip gave, and Dennis fell at an awkward angle. To add injury to insult, his bad hip slammed into the top of the fence. Dennis crashed the rest of the way to the ground with a strangled sound of pain. His jaw was locked, his shoulders tight, and his face a mask of agony as he rolled onto his back. His breathing was quick and shallow, and even in the dim light, she could see how pale he was.

She shifted closer and sat at his side. "You okay?"

"Have to be." Dennis gritted his teeth. After a moment, he rolled to his good side and carefully pushed himself up into a sitting position. "Son of a biscuit with bread and butter."

Even in the dire circumstances, Kim had to smile. "You sound like my mom."

"Hah." Dennis barked a low laugh. "Your mom swears like me. Marines are supposed to be good influences, so we get creative with our swearing. Besides, it's kind of fun seeing who can come up with the best curses without using the kind of words our mothers would have washed our mouths out for saying." He gave her a stern look. "Stop trying to distract me while I recover. We don't have time."

Kim rose and offered him a hand. Dennis took the hand and a grip on the fence to heave himself up off the ground with another muttered stream of invective. Once he was upright, the three of them slipped through the short stretch of grass that separated the fenced-in back-yard from the open side yard, and from there into the next yard over. That yard was surrounded by a wooden fence, which made it easy to pass through the yard to escape notice by the militia perimeter. From there, they began the trek across the town, eyes searching every shadow and corner for signs of the militia or Lewis's battered old truck.

Avoiding the patrols required several detours away from the western edge of town, where they were headed. Kim's nerves were drawn tight as wires, and she couldn't even imagine how Dennis was feeling. Whenever she looked at him, his expression was tight and pale. He was limping heavily with his hand burrowed as deep as it could go in Mutt's short, thick coat.

They left the densely occupied area of town, and Kim found herself breathing easier. It wasn't necessarily safer, but at least there was less chance of being caught.

Then they turned a corner, and she spotted a familiar truck and real-ized her mistake. She remembered they hadn't been in the occupied area of Humboldt when Lewis had first picked them up, and Joan had mentioned foraging and scavenging expeditions. Kim swallowed hard.

"Just keep moving, and keep an eye out." Dennis had seen the truck too, and his expression was grim. "We can get past him if we're careful."

They started to move among the empty houses bordering the street separating the residential neighborhood from the first set of shop fronts. They kept one eye on the truck while looking for movement nearby. It was hard to see, the darkness obscuring their vision and making strange shadows around them.

She was so busy looking out for Lewis that Kim walked right past the doorway of a store and would have ignored it altogether if a voice hadn't said "Kim?"

She turned around. Dennis stopped with a stumble and a startled exclamation as Joan appeared out of the store.

"Joan," Kim whispered.

"You're not supposed be out here. Lewis told me you were confined to the house." Joan's eyes were wide and nervous.

"Yeah, well, Dennis and I decided to take your advice. Dennis is over detox; time to move on."

"Lewis will be angry." Joan's gaze was darting around the area. Even in the dimness, Kim could see the fear on her face. "He'll be so angry."

"He doesn't need to know you saw us. No one else did." Kim's heart hammered in her chest.

"I can't let him get angry. He was furious after how Dennis talked to him at the Watering Hole. He was...you've seen his temper." Joan shook her head. "Wait a few days. He'll cool down. You can talk to him. If you apologize and promise to stay, or maybe to come back as soon as you've seen your family, it'll be fine. You'll see."

Kim paused. She knew the signs of a battered wife determined to reconcile and reduce the chances of taking another dose of her husband's temper. Sometimes it was better to pretend to agree and go along with it—then run away fast.

But that wasn't her way, and it wasn't Dennis's. He spoke up before Kim could decide what to do. "Sorry, but we can't do that. Kim's got family to find, and I'm not about to apologize for speaking the truth. I didn't in the Corps, and I won't now."

Kim knew it was a mistake the second the words were spoken. "Joan. Joan…"

Joan stepped back. "Lewis! Lewis! Dennis is taking Kim away! They're trying to leave!"

Lewis erupted from a nearby building, and so did half a dozen men of the militia, guns at the ready.

Kim and Dennis both lunged to get away, and Mutt surged forward with a menacing woof.

Dennis's bad leg slowed him down, and Kim found her path blocked by Joan. It was only a few seconds, but it was enough.

Mutt vanished into the darkness as the men surrounded them. Dennis swore. And Kim fixed Joan with the most poisonous scowl she could muster.

31

BILL WHEELER

The last leg of the drive to the scrapyard was suffocating in its silence. Shannon—Bill wondered if he should start calling her Sarah—looked pale and lost. Her arms were wrapped close around her torso, and Bill didn't think it was just the pain in her shoulder that was causing her to curl up.

He supposed it was natural for there to be a bit of coldness between family members, given the circumstances, but the harshness of Bruno's response had clearly hurt her. She hadn't looked that shaken since the fight with Langmaid.

They pulled into a large scrapyard, big enough to house a neighborhood in a pinch. It was full of winding paths through heaps of debris. Bill chose the widest path he could find. He nudged the truck along until the last of the trailer was through the pitted, rust-streaked gate and one of Bruno's bikers had shut the portal behind them. Then he put the truck in park and opened the door.

Bikers emerged from stacks of metal and crushed cars like ants emerging from a kicked-over anthill. Most of them were men of various ages in denim and leather and worn clothing that would have made Edith start lecturing and stealing shirts for laundry if she'd been around to see them. All of them wore a jacket or vest with the black rat on it, and most of them wore the diamond 1% patch.

A few women were among the men and dressed in similar clothing. In the lead was a smaller, older woman with some of Shannon's features and gray hair tied back in a heavy braid. She spotted Shannon climbing down from the truck and, like Bruno had, stopped dead.

Shannon—or Sarah, Bill still hadn't got that straight in his mind—took a deep breath and a step forward, shoulders squared. "Hello, Aunt Carol."

Dark eyes flicked between Shannon and the truck. "See you traded your bike and your membership for a big rig."

"It wasn't my idea. I had to go into Witness Protection. Andre had too many friends, and the Black Rats—"

"Black Rats would have stood by you if you'd asked us. You're blood. And we were already tossing Andre when you spoke out against him. You'd have had to find someone else, or come under Bruno's wing again, you and Kim, but you could have come to us."

Carol's expression was tight, but where Bruno's had been an expressionless mask, hers was full of anger and pain, and a sort of injured pride. Bill thought of speaking up for Shannon but held his piece. This wasn't his world; it was hers.

"I thought I'd be a pariah, not to mention put the family in danger. Didn't want to put you and Kim through that." Shannon looked as if she'd rather be anywhere else. Or anyone else. "I'm sorry. I didn't think I had a better option."

"You thought we were good enough to leave Kim with. Just not good enough to stay with yourself." Carol shifted her weight, and her gaze flicked to the truck. "We can discuss that later. Right now, we have to deal with that monstrosity you brought into our yard."

Shannon raised her chin. "Truck might be a monster, but it's a good haul, especially with everything that happened two weeks ago." She came around to stand next to Bill and held out her hand. Bill gave her the keys. She turned and tossed them to her uncle, who'd been watching with folded arms and a grim expression. Bruno caught them with a faint look of contempt.

"There's enough food in the back to feed the entire club for a month, if it's used right. Plus extra mattresses, some medical supplies in the cab, and some tools. Bill and I drove it all the way here to help the family."

Bruno blinked, then moved to the back of the vehicle. Bill heard the back liftgate rattle open. He heard a whistle of appreciation and a wave of murmurs pass through the assembled bikers. Then there were muffled thumps and the sound of the door coming back down.

Bruno came back. "Lots of food back there."

"Plenty for the club?" Carol asked.

"Plenty for the club." Bruno nodded. "It's a solid gift."

"So what? We letting this chick buy her way into the Black Rats' territory? Her and the old man?" The nasal, sneering voice made Bill's shoulders tense up. It was too much like Barney Langmaid. He turned.

The man who stepped forward was close to Shannon's age, perhaps a little younger. He had a crooked nose that looked like it had been broken once or twice, and dark, dirty-blond hair that had probably been cut short before the EMP. His expression was twisted with contempt. "They aren't part of the Black Rats, and we got enough of our own to worry about feeding."

"Shannon's blood. Maybe she's not been around, and there's some bad history, but she's still kinfolk. And she did bring us a truck. In these times, that's a long way toward making amends." Bruno's voice was considering. "Man's another matter."

"His name's Bill Wheeler, and he saved my life. Twice." Shannon spoke sharply. "He drove the truck after I got shot by a lunatic."

"That's a good thing to do, but these days, we can't just trust the club to what people have or haven't done in the past. We have to look to the future." Carol moved closer, sizing Bill up with cool eyes.

Bill maintained eye contact, not wanting to seem weak. He had no idea what the older woman was looking for, but whatever it was, she didn't seem to find it. Her expression was hard.

"You know how to ride?" she said at last.

"No. Never had the inclination." As tempting as a lie was, he knew he'd be caught in a minute. What little Shannon had said was enough to tell him how out of his depth he'd be trying to bluff his way in.

"Can't ride. No affiliations. Too old and too soft to be walking as a guard. And you aren't a fighter, that much is obvious."

Bill wondered how Carol knew that but didn't see any point in asking.

"Even with Shannon's truck," she went on, "we don't have the supplies to feed an extra mouth who can't give anything back. Especially someone who's not family." Carol tipped her head, a gesture so familiar it made his heart ache. That was Shannon's expression, clear as day. "You did right by Sarah, and I appreciate that, but the Black Rats can't support you."

"I can earn my way."

"Unless you've got skills other than being a warm body in the kitchen or on the scavenging team, you've got nothing we need. Now, I'd be willing to set you with a house in the territory and leave you some supplies to start with, but Black Rats don't need a roadblock in the path."

"Bill has skills." Shannon stepped forward again. "He's a mechanic. Good one."

"Everyone here knows how to maintain a bike." That was the blond man again.

"What about how to modify it to run on fuels other than what comes from the pump? What about knowing how to get gas out of a tank without using a siphon and frying your throat and lungs? Or how to fix the more complicated things, besides tires and basic maintenance?"

"You saying this old man knows how to do all that?" There was clear skepticism in the biker's voice.

"Sure." Shannon slapped the side of her truck. "Modified the entire transmission so it would run after the computers in most motors got fried. He's the reason the truck runs, and he can drive it too, which means he can help you salvage more than you could on a bike. Haul bigger cargo around your area. He can also fix any of the bikes that need it."

Carol turned back to Bill. "You can do that?"

"Sure. I was a mechanic for a long time, and even after I retired, I kept my hand in when I could. Shannon's telling the truth about the truck." Bill glanced around the scrapyard. "With the tools in the trailer and the stuff you got here, I reckon I can do anything you need, as long as it doesn't involve a fresh coat of paint."

"We do our own paint jobs." Carol said, but her expression was thoughtful. She seemed less stern and closed off than before. After a moment, she looked at her husband. "Bruno? What do you think?"

Bruno stared at him like he was trying to read his soul. Then he nodded. "Probationary. For now."

Carol hummed agreement. "You heard him. We'll see if you're as good as you say. For now, you stick to the clubhouse and mind your manners." Her gaze flicked to another biker. "Austin, put them up in a couple of the open bunks."

"Why should I? They're nobodies." Austin was a lean, rangy fellow with a sharp, weasel-like face and dark hair tied back in a messy ponytail. His mouth was twisted in a sneer, and his hands were stuffed in his pockets, every inch of his posture radiating distrust and dislike. "Strangers."

"Told you already, Sarah's blood, and Bill's on probation as a club mechanic. We keep family and assets here. So help them find a bunk."

"All I'm saying is that we can do our own repairs well enough. We got guys who can learn anything this old man knows. And you can call the girl family all you want, but she's been gone a long time— first I've seen her since I joined four years ago. She's a grown woman, with no brothers vouching for her. Why should we take her in, even if she got us a truck?"

"She's my niece. Unless you're claiming I'm not a brother." Bruno's voice was hard and menacing.

"Sure, sure, I got that. But she's not got a man, you know? She's not anyone's old lady or even a hanger-on," Austin said. "What makes her so special? There's other kids belonging to the club who are grown up and got cut loose."

"She's still connected. Her daughter is in my care, and she hasn't disaffiliated. Means she's got family from past and future. That's good enough. And we do need a mechanic, with all the trouble around town these days." Carol stalked forward. "You've got your orders, Austin. So step off and do what you're told."

"Why should I? You're not the boss. Bruno's the club leader. You're just his old lady, and that don't count for much." Austin's lip curled.

Carol stood her ground, but her face was tight. "This isn't that kind of club, and you know that. You got a beef with me, you stand up like a man, not like a soft, spoiled socialite who wishes he was a brother."

"Who knows what kind of club this is now? Huh? World's been shot to pieces, law and order's a joke, and we're doing the jobs of a gang and a police force both. Why should we? We're the one percenters!" Austin thumped his hand on his chest.

"One percenter means you answer to your own law, not that you're a thug. In a one-percenter club, leader rules apply, and I'm the boss's woman. So unless Bruno speaks against me, I'm speaking to you and telling you the way it's gonna be."

Shannon spoke up before Austin could argue further. "She's right. Until Brute Bruno steps down or gets taken out, then he and his old woman are the law." She stepped forward until she was in the biker's face. "I know men like you. My former husband was one like you, before he got the boot for being a murderer and a drug runner. You're a skunk, Austin. You need to clear the stink and get cleaned up before you drag the rest of us into the garbage. Or you get thrown out like trash."

Austin jerked back. Then he rallied and looked around. Bill followed his gaze. He saw several men looking anticipatory, a few wary, and a couple predatory. He focused on the predatory ones, trying to burn their faces into his memory. If worse came to worst, he was going to get Shannon's gun from the truck and shoot those men first. If he had to.

Austin's gaze finally went to Bruno. "You gonna let this broad get away with talking to me like this, Brute? Or your old lady? You know how things are supposed to go—brothers first."

"Family first. And blood is thicker than water, unless it proves otherwise." Bruno shook his head. "You've been given your commands, Austin. Do what you're told, or answer to me."

Austin scowled, his shoulders hunched against Bruno's implacable stare. "Fine. You wanna back some freeloaders on your sour old broad's say-so, fine." He jerked his head at Bill, angry and sullen. "Come on. Clubhouse is this way. Bunks in the back. Then you can come back and help unload." His gaze was scornful as he looked at Bill. "If you got the muscles for it, I mean. Since it's clear that you," his gaze switched to Shannon, "are gonna be about as much use as a flat tire on a freeway."

Shannon twitched and flushed under the assessment but didn't argue. She went to grab their bags from the cab then followed the man as he turned and slouched away.

Bill turned to Carol. "Thank you."

"Thank Bruno. His word. We'll see if you make it good." Carol walked away, headed for the opposite side of the scrapyard. Bruno gave Bill a searching look, then went after her.

Bill took a deep breath and hurried to catch up to Shannon.

They had shelter, a place to stay, and food to eat. They even had clean clothing. He just couldn't help wondering what else they'd picked up with their accommodations—and what the price would be.

32

KIM NAKAMURA

The men closed in around them, and Kim glared as Lewis came to a stop outside the ring. "Let us go," she said. "I've got things to do."

"I understand you have concerns about your family. I truly do." The false sympathy and condescension in Lewis's tone made her teeth ache. "I wish we could just let you leave, but we can't. I'm sorry, but I'll need you to return to your house for now."

Two men grabbed Kim by the arms.

Dennis exploded into action. He hammered a punch into one young man's face, then grabbed the gun and hit the man who tried to grab him with the butt of it. It connected with his face, and he lurched backward with a busted lip and missing teeth. Dennis whipped around and raised the gun to point it at one of the men holding Kim.

Then Lewis strode forward, raised his foot, and slammed the sole of his boot into Dennis's wounded hip with the kind of force Kim suspected would break bones or dislocate joints.

Dennis collapsed with a howl of pain. The rifle he'd snatched fell from his hands as he clutched at his leg and writhed on the ground in helpless agony. One of the men moved to scoop up the gun. Two others moved to stand guard over him.

Lewis stepped forward and crouched down to look at his old friend's face. "I am sorry, Dennis. I really am. I wish I hadn't needed to do that." He sighed, but the look on his face was more satisfied and vindictive than anything else. It turned Kim's stomach.

"Why, then?" Dennis ground the words out.

"Because Kim has valuable skills—skills this community needs. She might not be a fully trained doctor, but she's got a lot more training than Joan or anyone else. And she's got the resources to learn more, with Dr. Kennedy's old office and all his supplies. She can do a lot of good here. A lot of good. We need her to stick around."

"That's my decision, not yours." Kim spat the words at him. She tugged at the grips of the men restraining her, but she had no momentum and no leverage, and they were both stronger than she was. "Why would I want to work for you?"

"I understand why you might feel that way, but this is my town. I'm not really giving you a choice. After all, if you don't work—or don't have a good reason for not working—then you don't eat. You'll be under guard until I feel like I can trust you to do the right thing. So you do the job, or you suffer the consequences."

"You've got no right to treat us like this!"

"Sure I do. Humboldt's my town, and it's my job to do what's best for the townsfolk. If that's making sure we have a doctor in the house, by whatever means, then that's what I'll do. It's that simple."

"Yeah?" Dennis coughed and glared at his old friend from his position on the ground. "I guess I'm just gonna…be collateral damage? Like your old doctor?"

"It'd be easier for me to handle you that way, I'll grant you." Lewis stood up. "But we were friends once, Dennis. I haven't forgotten the first rule of the Marines. Semper Fidelis, as you said. That's why you'll be going to jail rather than serving as a public example of the consequences of insurgency."

"You'd just kill him?" Kim felt sick. "Are you serious?"

"Rules and discipline have to be enforced." Lewis stared at her, his gaze empty of anything resembling compassion or even basic humanity. "Examples have to be made so people understand that there are real penalties for disorderly behavior."

He shook his head with another show of mock sympathy as he looked at Dennis again. "I was going to let that outburst at the bar slide since you're new to Humboldt. I thought you just needed time to settle in. But trying to take a valuable resource is a different story. I can't let you get away with that."

He looked toward his men, dismissing Dennis as beneath his notice with a contempt that made Kim want to bite him. Or ram his gonads through his larynx. "Take my old friend to lock-up and make sure he's well secured. I don't want to take any chances he'll get out."

"And the girl?"

"Take her back to her house for now and keep her under guard."

The two men holding her nodded and started to drag her away. Two other men jerked Dennis roughly to his feet. "Come on, old man."

Fear clawed at Kim's throat as they started to haul him in a different direction. The idea of being without her protector made her stomach clench. "Dennis!"

Dennis looked up, his eyes still dark and hooded with pain, and locked gazes with her. His jaw clenched, and she saw anger and something fierce and dangerous light his expression.

Kim saw the muscle in his good leg tense. That was all the warning she or anyone else had before he exploded into motion. He tore himself free of the men holding him, then launched off his good leg to deliver an incredible uppercut to one man's jaw. He grabbed the man's rifle on the retraction and whipped it into his gut, a move he'd taught her but that she'd never seen in action before. His bad leg swept the man's feet as his elbow whipped back to slam into the second man's sternum.

The second man fell, and Dennis snapped a punch into a third man's jaw. Then he bolted toward the woods as fast as his wounded leg would allow.

Lewis swore. "Get him!"

The men who weren't holding Kim went after Dennis. Dennis pushed himself harder and made it to the tree line just as the first few men started to close in on him. Kim thought she saw him shift and what might be the glint off a rifle. A shot rang out, and the men closest to the trees flinched. Kim grinned, remembering how Dennis had tried to train that flinch out of her.

Then Dennis was gone, and Lewis was snarling in frustration. "You lousy, weak-willed, molasses-slow, dumb-as-rocks morons! How'd you let one crippled old drug addict get away from you?"

"You didn't tell us…" One of the men started, but that was as far as he got before Lewis backhanded him across the face.

"I shouldn't have to tell you anything, except to give you orders and see them carried out! You're militia, and you should have pinned him, kicked his leg out from under him—heck, he was attempting to escape! You could have shot him, and it would have been fine with me!" Lewis was red-faced and shouting.

The two men holding Kim started to drag her away, only for Lewis to turn on them. "Not her house! Did you not just see Sullivan escape? He knows that house, and if he broke out, he'll be able to break back in." He exhaled hard, and Kim briefly entertained the idea that he might have a stroke due to high blood pressure. It was more fantasy than hope, but she was feeling vindictive. "Take her to my house and keep her under guard." The last word was spoken in tones of disgust. He started to turn away and spotted Joan. "Go with them, Joan. Make sure she stays put."

"Of course, Lewis." Joan nodded. "I'll walk back to the house with them."

"Good. Good. If she tries to make a break for it, break her knee." Lewis eyed Kim. "She doesn't need both knees to do her job. And you know how to tend that well enough."

"I understand." Joan's head lowered, then she shook her hair back with a deep breath. "I'll see to it." She turned and walked over to take a grip on Kim's jacket. "Come on, Kim."

She wanted to try and run, the way Dennis had. But she couldn't do it. She knew Lewis was cruel enough to break her knee without hesitation, and his men would do the same. Joan might be less coldhearted, but she'd also been the one to rat them out. Kim settled for giving Joan the hottest glare she could muster.

She had to bide her time. Opportunities would come. Dennis had told her that. She just had to trust his advice and be ready to take the first chance she saw. Right now, that meant walking along and not fighting too hard. She didn't have to act happy about it, or even resigned to it, but she could act like she wasn't going to fight too much.

Joan and the men dragged her to the Danville house, and Joan opened the door, then motioned for the men to bring Kim inside. The men shoved her through the door but didn't follow.

Joan led Kim to the kitchen. "Have a seat, Kim." Kim complied sullenly. "Would you like something to drink?"

Kim stared at her. She felt anger and fear, but over both was a searing contempt she hadn't known she was capable of. Not even Dennis at his worst had inspired such utter disgust and loathing.

Joan flinched under her gaze. "I know you're angry, but—"

"Angry? You were the one who told me to get out, and then you turned around and turned us in!" It took everything she had not to scream the words, but Kim didn't want to draw the attention of the guards outside. "You're no better than a back-stabbing hypocrite."

"Kim, I know it's upsetting. But please understand. Lewis is, well, when he's in a temper like this..." Joan trailed off, rubbing her arms with a grimace.

Kim could feel some sympathy for the older woman, but it didn't hold a candle to everything else she felt. "So what? You were talking about getting out. Didn't it occur to you that you could have just asked us to take you with us? I would have, and I bet Dennis would have too. We could have used your help with his hip, and you could have gotten away from that beast."

"Lewis is my husband."

"Yeah. My mom used to say that about my dad. But she never helped him hurt people, and she had the guts to walk away when he started killing. You can't say the same."

"Lewis didn't kill Dr. Kennedy."

"It doesn't matter if he pulled the trigger or not. He covered it up, and he gave the orders for others to be hurt. You told me that. He lets the militia men do whatever they want, even if that includes terrorizing other people."

Joan sighed, looking older and defeated. "I don't know what you want me to do." The words were a whisper.

"I want you to do the right thing. Help me get out of here. Help me find Dennis and leave town. Come with us if you want."

"But Lewis is my husband. And Humboldt is my home." Joan shook her head. "I can't just leave."

"You could. Dennis and I would help you." Kim stopped, seeing the slump of Joan's shoulders and the expression on the older woman's face. She folded her arms over her chest. "But you won't. Because you're all talk. You haven't got the spine to stand up for yourself or for the things you believe. You didn't even have the guts to step aside and let us go when it wouldn't have cost you anything."

Joan only stared at her with tired, tragic eyes. Kim turned away, but not before delivering one last, scathing comment. "I hated what Dennis did when he was suffering from addiction. But you? You're a thousand times worse, and you don't even have his excuse."

"Kim—"

"Unless you're going to help me, don't talk to me. Don't offer me a drink or something to eat. I'd rather stick my hand in a wood chipper than take anything from you."

She knew she was being harsh. But they'd been so close to getting away, and Joan could have helped them. Lewis wouldn't have even needed to know she'd seen them. But in the end, she'd let her fear overpower her sense, and her principles.

Kim understood what it was like, living with an abusive man. She knew how terrifying it could be, for all that her mother had tried to shield her from the worst of Andre's rage. But she couldn't excuse Joan's actions, and she couldn't accept them.

Silence fell, thick and heavy, over the kitchen. Kim ignored the woman at the other end of the table and settled back to think.

Dennis would probably try to help her, since he was free. But she couldn't just wait for him to come for her. She had to try and find ways to help herself, since no one else in the house would. She needed to plan, and now was the best time. After all, it wasn't like she had anything better to do.

33

BILL WHEELER

The scrapyard and the Black Rats weren't the most welcoming lot, and Bill had never felt more like an outsider, but at least they had a roof over their heads and a place to sleep. Sure, it was a cot covered by one of the thin hospital bed mattresses they'd brought with them, but it was better than being outside in the dirt.

Or under the dirt. Bill had no doubt that there were Black Rats who would have happily put them both six feet under and taken the truck for themselves. Fortunately, those weren't the people in charge. The bad apples seemed to have scattered as soon as Bruno had laid down the law. Even Austin had made himself scarce after he'd shown them to the clubhouse.

The clubhouse was a large, weathered building that had probably been the office and garage at one time before expanding into what it was now. Someone had added a lounge room, a bunk room, a dining room, and a kitchen. Everything was well-worn, and some of the items had clearly been salvaged from outside.

All in all, it reminded Bill a bit of the garage where he'd worked and a bit of his favorite place to get parts, with a little bit of home mixed in.

He might have found it comfortable had it not been for the wary stares he got from every biker he came across.

I'm a stranger, and they're wary of strangers. I just have to give it time and show them I can pull my weight. They'll warm up and settle down, and I can settle in.

The words in his head helped, but it was still unnerving. He'd never faced such suspicion and distrust—except from people like Barney Langmaid—and he wasn't used to the feeling.

He helped the men unload the truck and store the supplies while the women worked on a meal. The scrapyard had a generator, so there was a limited amount of power available for cooking. One of the younger Black Rats, a quiet fellow with bruises on his face, showed him where he could get water and heat it for a quick wash.

"You wash up before meals?" Bill couldn't hide his surprise.

The Black Rat gave him a disbelieving look. "Bruno won't let us spoil a meal with motor oil and stuff on our hands. Says we don't need folks getting sick on top of everything else."

Bill had to wonder if that was Bruno's command or Carol's. It didn't seem prudent to ask, not when he was a guest. He apologized for any offense, thanked the man, and made use of the facilities. Then he followed the Black Rat back to the dining room, where Carol and Shannon—he knew he was going to have to get used to calling her Sarah at some point, but she was still Shannon to him—were setting the table. Bruno was already seated.

Bill started to take a seat next to the Black Rats leader, but Shannon caught his arm and steered him to the other end of the table. "Club hierarchy. We're new, and we're only here under voucher, so we don't sit near the boss."

It didn't make sense to him, but he knew better than to question her. He just nodded and took his seat. He was handed a beer, lukewarm but still wet, and watched as the bikers who were still in the scrapyard wandered in to sit around the table. Once all the men were seated, the women brought food—a stew and bread—and took their own seats.

The soup was simple but good. It went well with the beer and the bread, a heavy sourdough. Good, solid fare to fill a man's belly. Bill dug in with a will.

Once the bowls were emptied, Bruno kicked back. "Report."

"Not a lot of action today, and no sign of the guys from last night, as far as we can tell. Biggest thing was picking up these two at the clothing store," one of the older men at the table said.

Shannon sat forward. "Uncle Bruno, I know I've not been back long, but could you tell me what's been happening since the EMP?"

"EMP? What's that?" The young man with bruises on his face spoke up.

"It's what blew the electricity all across the country. We managed to catch an emergency broadcast on a ham radio that Bill put together," Shannon answered.

"Dang. We thought it was just Memphis or something." The young man sat back.

Bill shook his head. "It's countrywide."

"Whatever it was and whatever it did to the rest of the country, the fact is the city erupted into chaos," Bruno said. "Law enforcement stopped enforcing any sort of law within the first day or two. At least, outside the rich folks' neighborhoods." Three of his men twisted and spat, making their disdain clear. "Black Rats stepped in for their territory, and we've been policing ever since. Running patrols, trying to keep a lid on looting, and all that stuff."

Carol spoke next. "We were doing all right, with only a few minor scuffles, until last night."

Bill didn't think he was imagining the way Shannon's back tensed and her expression went still, the way it had when they'd heard about Hank Nilsson's death. "Last night?" he asked.

"Someone busted up one of our hangouts. Three Black Rats dead, plus the bartender, and it was messy. Floor was crimson with the damage. Doberman Doug had his throat practically ripped out."

Shannon blanched. "Doberman ate it? Not many could take him down."

"We know. That's why everyone's on edge and ready to ride or shoot today."

That explained the level of suspicion Bill had noticed. It made him feel a little better about some of the sideways looks he'd been getting. "Was it maybe another..." He had to pause to think of the correct terminology. "...motorcycle club, or a street gang?"

"Not much chance. Everyone these days has too much trouble in their own territories to go hunting more. We've actually been luckier than most. Most people respect the patch." Bruno said. He sighed. "But I'm afraid this incident might be a sign that things are about to get hotter. This attack felt personal."

Shannon spoke again. "Which bar got hit?"

"Black Roads." That was the young man with the bruises.

Shannon went so pale Bill almost feared she'd torn her wound open again. "Black Roads." She whispered the words. Then she rallied. "Anyone see the guys that busted up the place?"

"Sprocket did." Carol indicated the bruised biker.

"Can you tell me?"

298

Sprocket looked at Bruno. Bill saw the club boss nod, and the young man turned back to Shannon. "There were two of them. One was a big guy, almost as big as Doberman, white, middle-aged, muscled. He had cold eyes, and Devildog didn't like him. Said he wasn't welcome or wanted."

"What about the other guy?"

"Just a kid. Young and wet behind the ears, looked ready to soil himself. African American boy, followed the big guy and acted like a kicked dog—right up until he knocked me over the head with a bottle and took Doberman's throat out with a hunting knife."

"Doberman got taken out by a kid?" Shannon looked shocked, and a little sick. Bill wondered how long she'd known the aforementioned Doberman, and how well.

"He was pinning the big guy on the pool table. Kid came at him from the side."

Shannon took a deep breath. "Get a name, Sprocket?"

"Wasn't listening when Devildog was yelling at him." The young man shivered. "Sure was when the big guy busted me up against the wall though. He was asking about Bruno and Carol, and some chick named Sarah. When he realized I didn't know nothing, he knocked me out and tossed me in the street. By the time I woke up, they were gone, and the bodies were cooling."

Shannon swayed in her seat. Bill reached out and put a hand on her shoulder. "What's wrong?"

"Black Roads was where Andre and I first met. Noticed him because he was too suave for that joint. The big guy in the bar sounds like him, and it would be like Andre to brainwash a kid into tagging along if he got the chance." Shannon's hands clenched into fists, but Bill saw a fear in her eyes that not even Langmaid and his gun had inspired. "I was suspicious when I heard the bar name, and the description, but asking about Sarah? That makes it certain."

She swallowed hard, and the next words were spoken in a bleak, sick tone that reminded Bill of the way he'd felt when he'd heard Edith was dying. "Andre's back in town. And he's looking to settle old scores."

"Fudge nuggets," Bruno swore, then followed it up with several less repeatable terms. "That's all we need."

Bill kept silent, but he felt cold, and the food was suddenly heavy in his stomach. He might not know Andre personally, but he'd heard enough from Shannon to know one thing.

If Andre was in town, then so was trouble, with a capital T.

34

LEE KINGSTON JONES

Lee woke up with a headache the size of Memphis and a sour taste in the back of his mouth. He groaned, trying to remember if that was the booze or the bile, then gave it up. It wasn't like it mattered.

He'd drunk enough at the bar with Andre for the world to go all fuzzy and start tilting at the edges. He hadn't even protested when Andre had made sure of the remaining Black Rats and the bartender. Somehow, with a third of a bottle of Jack Daniels in his gut, the smell of blood and the crimson puddles in the room didn't seem so bad. No worse than a good turkey shoot.

Walking back to the house had been an experience, and the fuzzy, spinning feeling had turned into nausea. He knew he'd puked again, and Andre had clicked his tongue in mingled disapproval and amusement. The older man hadn't offered him help getting back, but at least he'd slowed down and stopped when Lee had to throw up or wandered too far off course.

Eventually, they'd made it to the house, and Lee had staggered in to collapse on the couch. If Andre had said anything, he'd passed out before he'd heard it.

Now his head was throbbing, his stomach was churning, his mouth felt like he'd been chewing on vomit-flavored cotton balls, and the light of the sun might as well have been needles in his eyes. He winced and shoved his head into the couch cushions.

"Stop being so melodramatic, Lee. It's only a hangover."

Andre's sarcastic voice hit his ears like a battering ram, and Lee winced again. Still, he managed to lift his head and squint in Andre's direction.

"I feel kinda sick," Lee admitted. He dragged himself into a sitting position. "Didn't think I drank that much."

"A third of a bottle of whiskey? Of course it was a lot for a first-time drinker. There are many hardened alcoholics who would be swaying in their seats with that much whiskey. It's eighty proof."

Lee blinked. "Umm, that's like—forty percent alcohol?" Now that he was sitting up and sitting still, the nausea was subsiding.

"Indeed. But quite impressive nonetheless." Andre threw him a packet of crackers and a bottle of water. "Still, we have work to do. The water and the food will help. Get your head together and be ready to go. The sun is setting, and we have some walking to do."

Lee started. He hadn't realized it was quite so late. "Sure." He opened the crackers and took a cautious nibble. Andre was right. The crackers and the water helped settle his stomach. By the time he'd finished the water, he didn't feel so queasy, and his headache had gone from excruciating to aching the way it sometimes did after a row with Max. He could live with that.

Andre came back from where he'd disappeared into the garage. He was carrying his usual bag, but it looked a little heavier than usual. "Come, Lee."

Lee stood up and followed the other man out into the street. The sun was low in the sky and stabbed Lee in the eyes. He squinted and trotted after his mentor.

Andre led him toward the outskirts of Memphis, moving confidently through the streets like he'd been born there. Maybe he had. Lee had no idea how Andre had grown up or where. A few times, they skirted different areas marked with graffiti that Andre pointed out in passing. Finally, Andre turned and led him to the doors of a large outdoor and home improvement center.

Lee stared at it. "What are we gonna get here?"

He couldn't see Andre doing much with gardening tools or construction supplies, and power tools were pretty useless these days. There were plenty of hand tools that could be used as weapons, but why travel so far to get them?

Andre didn't give him an answer, too preoccupied with the broken window. "It appears someone has beaten us here. Well, perhaps they will not have taken what we need. I would hate to have to resort to crude measures to gather supplies."

Andre broke out the remaining glass, then strode inside. Lee followed him as he grabbed a large flat cart and wheeled it toward the gardening section.

"See if they have any large buckets, Lee, and motor oil."

"Buckets and motor oil?" Lee blinked. "How much?"

"As much as you can carry." Andre turned to study him. "As much as you can carry in two trips. Perhaps three."

Lee nodded and winced, as it made his head spike with pain, then took off in what he thought was the most likely direction. He found motor oil, though it was a severely depleted supply, in the same section as lawnmowers. Finding buckets took a little more time, but he located a few five-gallon buckets and loaded the bottles into them. Then he hauled them back to the gardening center. They were heavy, and his arms were burning by the time he made it back.

Andre was loading bags of fertilizer onto the cart. He gave Lee a look of approval. "Excellent. I'll also need some matches or a lighter."

Lee remembered seeing those near the registers. He went and grabbed two of the long-wand lighters and a box of large matches for good measure. He eyed the fertilizer. "Can I ask what all this is for?"

Andre thumped another bag onto the cart. He studied it for a moment, then nodded with satisfaction. "Fertilizer and motor oil make fairly good bombs. Not always high yield, of course—nothing like weapons-grade explosives—but they make a loud bang, a decent amount of fire, and an impressive amount of smoke."

"Bombs?" Lee's stomach lurched again. "We're gonna bomb something?"

"In a matter of speaking." Andre's eyes were hooded, but there was no hiding the anticipation in his gaze or the lazy, predatory nature of his expression. "The Black Rats are based in a scrapyard not far from where we're currently staying. I visited while you were sleeping and had the pleasure of seeing my former wife arrive. I was hoping she'd be thrown out of the yard, but no such luck."

Lee didn't know the woman, but he would almost feel sorry for her if he hadn't heard from Andre what a witch she was. That didn't change the apprehension that was creeping into his veins like ice water. "You're gonna bomb her ride?"

"Nothing so wasteful." Andre snorted. "She drove in a truck, which is invaluable in more ways than one. No, I thought I would borrow an idea of yours."

"An idea of mine?" Lee blinked, distracted from his worries. "I don't remember any ideas I had about…that." He wasn't sure how to define Andre's plan.

"Your turkey hunting idea. You used noise and alarms to startle a turkey out of the undergrowth, yes?" Andre smirked and patted the fertilizer. "Fertilizer bombs in strategic places will cause a panic. If we block the exits—and I know where they are—then they'll have no choice but to run through the main gate. When they do, we can simply pick them off with the guns we've stockpiled from the home's former occupant and the denizens of the bar last night, not to mention the other weapons I've managed to procure. It will be as simple as a turkey shoot, and far more enjoyable."

Lee wasn't sure it would be either of those things. In fact, he was pretty sure it wouldn't be simple or fun. Killing a guy in the heat of a fight was one thing. Planning a bunch of murders in cold blood was something else altogether. "Why not just shoot your ex? I know she deserves it."

"As do the rest of the Black Rats, for abandoning me, turning me out of their club, and for sheltering her instead of throwing her out as they should have for being a traitor to her husband." Andre's expression went cold. "Among gangs of any kind, loyalty is all. She should have been punished for speaking against me and stealing my daughter."

"Yeah. Okay, I can see that." It made a kind of sense.

Andre's icy gaze turned to him. "I trust you are not harboring disloyal thoughts, Lee?"

"Of course not. I knifed a guy for you last night." Lee swallowed hard and lifted his chin. "I'm loyal to you, Andre. You know that. I just don't know that I'm ready for something like this." He was pleased he managed to keep his voice steady.

Andre, however, didn't look nearly so pleased. "Second thoughts, Lee? Now, after this past night? I thought you had learned your lesson, learned the value of a good kill."

"I did. I did. I just think—well, I haven't quite got my mind to make the leap from killing in defense to shooting panicky people who are running from bombs. Or, you know, setting bombs in the first place."

Andre sighed and shook his head, his eyes full of that disappointment that made Lee's stomach twist in funny directions. "Lee, I thought you were smarter than this. I thought you knew how to look at the big picture."

"I am. I'm working on it. But I only got past the killing thing last night."

"Nonetheless." Andre moved around the cart and set a heavy hand on Lee's shoulder, his grip tightening like a vise until Lee winced. "I won't tell you again. This world is kill or be killed. Be the predator or the prey, the victim or the victor. You chose when you killed that man last night and broke the other's head open with a bottle."

His next words hit Lee like a ton of bricks and destroyed whatever haze was left from his hangover. "You're a killer now. You must learn to act and think like one, in any situation. You must learn to anticipate and to keep your composure. Even enjoy the hunt, if you can." His voice went low and menacing. "To do anything else is to reveal a lie about your original decision. And I don't like falsehoods, Lee. Or failures."

Lee gulped. "I understand you, Andre. I got it."

"Very good." Andre smiled and released him. "Now help me with this

306

cart. I want to take it back to the house before we begin the bomb assembly."

Lee took his place at the push bar without a word and put his back into it when Andre told him to. Inside, his mind was buzzing worse than any alcohol could cause.

35

KIM NAKAMURA

J oan eventually left the kitchen. Kim stayed where she was, fuming and feeling her nerves getting tighter with every passing minute. She wanted to do something, but she wasn't sure what, and she knew she couldn't rush it.

It was just like the hunting lessons. Patience was required, but waiting was the hardest part. Only this time, it was more nerve-racking than boring.

Kim nearly jumped out of her skin when the front door slammed open. She watched as Lewis stormed in, his face set in a furious scowl. Kim could guess the reason behind the thunderous expression, and she smirked at him. "Dennis got away, didn't he?"

"One crippled old man who was a drug addict and hopping on a crutch two days ago, and not a one of those lackwits can follow his trail."

"That's what happens when you use untrained, hot-tempered muscle-heads with the brains of lemmings as soldiers." Kim sneered. "He might be old, retired, and wounded, but you forgot what you called him. He's Super Soldier Sullivan. The guy who led soldiers and won fights single-handedly. Thanks to you, he's not drug addled anymore. Sharp as he ever was." She laughed. "You're never gonna catch him."

"I'll catch him. He might be clean, but he's still weak and damaged. And he's alone. We'll run him to the ground soon enough." Then Lewis smiled coldly. "Of course, that's assuming he's still clean."

Kim glared at him. "What's that supposed to mean?"

"He's hurt, and he doesn't have you to keep him on the straight and narrow. He's just barely coming out of detox. Odds are, the second you were gone, he went looking for some pills or cough syrup. That's what junkies do."

"He's not like that."

"Sure he is. He's gone soft, and after the way I hammered his leg, he's got to be nearly blind with pain. Even if he thinks it's just to get him back on his feet, he'll pop a pill. Then it will be another, and another, until he's flopped up in an alley somewhere, drugged out of his mind. And then it won't matter whether we find him or not."

Kim felt her stomach flip, but she kept her chin up and her expression defiant. She wasn't going to give Lewis the satisfaction of seeing her worry, nor was she going to start doubting Dennis. He'd shown up for her, and he'd come this far with her, and he'd gone through detox when she asked him to. He'd stood up to his friend on her say-so. She wasn't going to give up on him that easily.

Lewis must have guessed her thoughts, because he snorted. "You're loyal. I'll give you that. Pity you've placed your trust in the wrong man."

"Even if I did, you're not the right one," Kim sniped back.

"It's too bad you think that, because now I'm all you have." Lewis gave her a cold smile. "Whether you like it or not, Humboldt is where you're going to be living from now on. And in Humboldt, my word is law. I decide how safe you are. Or how uncomfortable you are. You want to stay safe, you're going to have to play nice with me."

"You sound like my dad. Dennis helped lock him up." Kim stood up and met his gaze, arms folded and stance firm, the way her mother and Dennis had taught her to stand up to bullies of any kind. "I have to say, I hope he does something a little more permanent with you."

"I told you, he's long gone." Lewis took a step toward her, one hand raised to strike. Kim forced herself to stand without flinching.

They both jumped when glass shattered and a rock bounced off the sink. Lewis immediately spun, hand on his gun. Kim tensed and considered bolting, but Lewis was between her and the exit. She didn't have good odds for escaping. She stayed where she was.

After a moment, a familiar, gruff voice rang out. "Lewis. I know you're there with Kim. Bring her out or lose Joan."

"You're bluffing," Lewis snarled.

"Come on out and see. Bring Kim."

Lewis glared at the window, then stalked over and grabbed Kim's arm. Kim let him. She knew he'd never let her go through that door without some kind of hold on her, and getting outside meant she had a much better chance of escaping. Especially if Dennis really did have a plan.

Together, they marched out into the early morning dimness, the promise of dawn showing the first hints on the horizon. There were three militia members hovering in the yard with their weapons in hand. Kim barely noticed them. She was too busy staring at Dennis.

He was there. One arm was around Joan, holding her tight. The other hand had his second pistol against Joan's temple. His eyes were fierce.

He was still clenching his jaw, and she could see tremors of pain in his expression, but he was there. The fire in his eyes was all the proof she needed to know that he wasn't drugged. He looked like a man who might be called Super Soldier Sullivan.

He met her eyes, and his voice was firm as he addressed her. "Kim, are you all right?"

"I'm good. A few new bruises, but nothing serious." She doubted he could say the same, but she wasn't going to bring that up in their current situation.

"Good." Dennis turned his attention back to Lewis. "The deal is simple. Kim for Joan. You let her go, and as soon as she's past me, I'll let you have your wife. You try to stop her, try to sneak a man up on me, or try to send one of your would-be soldiers to intercept, and I put a bullet in Joan, then you, then as many of your men I can shoot before I can't shoot any more." His tone was deadly serious and left no room for doubt or negotiation.

Lewis looked as if he'd swallowed a barrel full of lemons and live frogs, but he finally nodded. "Deal."

Kim jerked at her arm, and Lewis let her go. She stumbled a bit, then hurried toward Dennis. She would have run, but she didn't want to trip or fall. She just wanted to get out of there—and out of Humboldt.

Dennis lifted an elbow subtly into her path, and she stopped. Dennis twisted his head and whispered into her ear. "Thirty yards into the woods, straight back, I've stashed the bags. I grabbed them from where we dropped them earlier. They're under a big oak surrounded by yaupon. Grab them and get out of sight. I'll follow as I can."

Kim jerked her head in a tiny nod to show she'd heard, then headed for the tree line. Her spine itched with the feeling of being watched, but she didn't dare turn around.

She ducked into the undergrowth and behind a tree, then turned around to watch the scene unfolding beside the Danville house.

Lewis was glaring at Dennis. "Girl's free. Now release my wife."

The militia men were inching forward. Kim stuffed her hand into her mouth to stifle the urge to shout a warning. Dennis could see the men as well as she could, and any outburst on her part would only give her away and distract Dennis.

The night was heavy with tension and clear as the smell of dirt. Kim had to lock her muscles to keep from running down to help her mentor.

Then Dennis shifted his grip and shoved Joan forward, down, and away from him and out of any line of fire. Lewis shouted, and the men surged forward. Dennis shot the first one straight in the face, and the man fell to the ground without even time to scream. The gun fell from his nerveless hand. Dennis moved to snatch it up and started backing up toward the tree line. His eyes—and his gun—were trained on Lewis. The former sergeant had stopped only a few yards away with a look that promised murder.

A moment too late, Kim remembered the fence and the misstep Dennis had made earlier that night. She remembered the way he'd fallen and how Lewis had kicked his recently healed knee out from under him.

She saw him stumble over an uneven patch in the ground and started to stand up. She was too slow.

Dennis staggered. She heard the sound of pain he made as he landed awkwardly. His hip and knee gave out under him, and he fell hard. A strangled yell ripped out of his throat, and he lost his grip on the gun.

It was a fraction of a second. Then he was moving to stand up again, pistol in one hand as he shot a second militia man. His feet dug furrows in the dirt as he tried to get up despite the pain that whitened his jaw and his knuckles.

He didn't make it. Lewis covered the distance between them, and his knee hammered into Dennis's face. He broke his nose with a crunch Kim could hear from where she was huddled, frozen in place.

Dennis fell back, but even then, he was still trying to fight back. Blood poured down his face, and his jaw clenched in agony.

Lewis kicked his wrist hard enough to rip the gun from his fingers and possibly break his hand. Then he snapped his foot back and hammered it into Dennis's bad hip—hard. Dennis went limp, and Kim thought he might have passed out from the pain. His eyes snapped open not five seconds later, but that was enough time for the remaining militia man to pin him to the dirt with both hands wrenched behind his back and a knee on his good leg.

And still he tried to get away. But the man's grip was too strong. Lewis stepped forward and did something that made Dennis flinch and shudder.

Silence fell, broken only by Kim's heavy breathing and the low moans from Dennis as his chest heaved. He glared up at the man he'd once called friend.

Lewis stared back. Then he motioned to the militia man and two more who'd appeared, probably drawn by the shots. "Get him to his knees."

Kim watched in mounting horror as Dennis was hauled into a kneeling position then pinned there by the men. One tied something around his wrists then stepped back. Kim saw him plant a foot on Dennis's lower legs at the knee joint and press, making the older man hiss with renewed pain. The other two men took firm grips on his shoulders and held him in position.

When Dennis had been secured, Lewis stepped forward. He shook his head, an expression of regret on his face that Kim didn't trust one bit. "It really is a pity, Dennis. We were friends, teammates back in the Marines. I was sure that once you'd cleaned up your act and come to your senses, you'd be an asset to the community. Maybe not the man you once were, but an asset nonetheless. But you're too stubborn. And too blind."

"You killed a man and kidnapped a girl." Dennis's voice was hoarse, but strong. Kim hoped that meant he was thinking of a plan to escape his predicament.

"I keep the peace, and I keep Humboldt safe and secure. I make sure we have what we need. I'm sorry it's not what Kim wants, but Humboldt needs a doctor. She's just too valuable to let go wandering off into the wilds."

"You could have picked another way."

"Not really. You think she would have come back after she got to Memphis? Assuming she made it that far? Not a chance. No, the only surefire solution was to keep her here. But you had to interfere."

Lewis moved forward and unholstered his pistol before he crouched in front of his old friend. "You know, I thought you'd be too drug addled to move this fast. Then I thought the drugs had made you soft in the head and in the body. So, I'll have to admit, Dennis, I am impressed with how well you've done. I am." He shook his head again. "I wish I could just let you go or lock you up. But you're too unpredictable, and too dangerous."

He stood again. The expression on his face made Kim feel like ice and lead had been dumped into her veins. Her fingernails cut into her palms as he continued speaking.

"As much as I admire you, Dennis, and despite our old friendship, I can't afford to have Super Soldier Sullivan running around and messing up my plans. So, I regret it, but this is goodbye."

Joan spoke up. "Lewis, there might be another way. Maybe we can use him as a hostage, use him to draw Kim out. She'll be easier to catch off guard, and she's a soft-hearted girl. She'll probably surrender to save his life. You don't have to…to do this."

Lewis's tone was unyielding as he answered her. "You're wrong, Joan. There's no other way. I made the mistake once of trying to go easy on him. I won't make that same mistake twice."

The pistol rose. Alarm bells went off in Kim's mind. In the gray light of dawn, Dennis looked pale and proud and fearless, every inch the warrior he'd once been. But he wasn't escaping. He wasn't fighting. He didn't move as the pistol came to rest, pointed at his forehead.

36

KIM NAKAMURA

The next few seconds were like a nightmare come to life—passing in slow motion, but completely inescapable.

Dennis looked up at Lewis, defiant even in his disadvantaged position.

Lewis stared down at the man who, only a few days ago, he'd embraced and spoken of with pride and respect. His finger slid from the barrel of the pistol to the trigger.

Kim lurched forward, not even knowing what she intended to do but knowing she was too far away, that it was a futile gesture, and unable to hold back as horror clawed at her throat.

Lewis pulled the trigger. The sound of the shot exploded into the air, far louder than it had seemed in the woods hunting only days ago.

Dennis's head snapped back. A shower of red mist blasted into the air behind him, coating the three men holding him with crimson gore.

Dennis's lifeless body slumped to the ground, no longer supported by his captors, or any sign of vitality.

A scream shattered the air, shrill and piercing, a high howling sound of pure anguish. "No! No! No!"

Kim's throat hurt, and she realized, with a sense of distance and shock, that the voice filling the air was her own. Those screams were hers, frightened and full of the same pain that was ripping her chest apart and tying her stomach into knots that would never come undone.

She felt numb and sick and twisted up inside, full of guilt and horror and rage. She could scarcely breathe with the ache of it.

Then she saw Lewis turn to look in her direction, and realized she'd broken from her cover, stepped out from behind the tree she'd huddled next to. The first rays of sunlight had come over the horizon, and she was clearly visible.

The slow motion feeling shattered like glass under a surge of panic as Lewis waved for the men to move in her direction. She felt paralyzed by grief, but she couldn't stay where she was.

Then she saw the red splattered across the nearest militia man's uniform. Dennis's blood, still gleaming wet. The sight shocked feeling back into her legs, and she bolted for the undergrowth again. Branches whipped at her face, arms, and legs as she drove herself deeper into the woods. A part of her feared that she was leaving a trail for the militia to follow, but she couldn't bring herself to stop, or slow down, for fear of being caught.

She stumbled into an area of thick yaupon holly surrounding a gnarled, towering oak tree. Dennis's last words to her echoed in her mind. Kim dove into the holly, hands searching frantically for the rough cloth of the heavy-duty canvas pack Dennis had carried or the fabric of her own bag. For a moment, she thought she might have misremembered the directions Dennis had given her.

Then her hand closed around a bunch of canvas, and she sobbed with relief. She tightened her hand on Dennis's backpack and felt around for her own. Once she had both of them, she hesitated a moment, then shoved her way haphazardly through the tangled boughs to the small, cleared space where the holly circled the tree. The heavy bushes around her offered a place of concealment where she could stop to breathe and gather her thoughts.

It was only when she'd curled into an uncomfortable ball against the roots of the oak that she realized she was crying silent, hot tears, and her throat ached with holding back moans—or screams. She wasn't sure which.

She folded her arms around Dennis's backpack, holding the bundle tightly to her chest as she muffled her sobs with the fabric. Now that she wasn't running for her life, her mind was frozen, thoughts circling in a loop like a scratched record.

She kept seeing those last moments, when Dennis had fallen and Lewis's men had trapped him. The proud, stern expression on his face, despite the pain he was in. Then the thunder of the gunshot and the spray of red…

She choked back bile, her stomach churning as she relived Dennis's death over and over in her head.

Dennis was dead. He'd been killed because he'd come back to rescue her, to help her escape Lewis. It had happened so fast—she'd had no time to do anything, and yet her heart insisted that if she'd just moved faster, thought quicker, or done something different, she could have saved him. What she could have done, alone and unarmed, she didn't know, but it didn't change the aching helplessness, irrational anger, and certainty that she'd failed him.

It hurt. Everything hurt, a deep and raw sensation worse than anything she'd experienced since her mother had gone into WitSec and she'd been left as an emancipated minor fending mostly for herself with the help of her great-aunt. If she hadn't been so terrified of being caught and dragged back to Lewis, she would have been howling with grief. But all she could do was cling to the backpack, breathing in the last remnants of Dennis's gunpowder-sweat-dirt-leather scent, with a faint trace of dog.

Kim shuddered, wishing she could rewind time to save him. Or go further back, to before she'd suggested they stay in Humboldt long enough for him to detox. As much as she'd hated watching him sink further into addiction, at least he would be alive if they hadn't stopped, or if she'd never let it slip that she'd had medical training.

Kim took deep breaths and tried to focus. The yaupon hid her well, but she couldn't stay here forever. As much as her heart ached with loss, she couldn't afford to get lost in her grief. She had to figure out an escape plan.

She needed to get out of the woods, then out of Humboldt. Or the other way around, whichever kept her safer. She needed to make tracks for Memphis as fast as she could travel.

Lewis knows I'm headed for Memphis. What if he comes after me? His truck moves faster than I can go on foot—he could cut me off.

Kim chewed on her lower lip, ignoring the heavy ache in her chest, the raw, scratchy feeling in her throat from crying, and the tears drying on her cheeks. Lewis's truck represented a problem she wasn't sure she could circumvent. She wasn't skilled enough in tracking and orientation to travel cross-country, let alone foraging the way she would need to. Trying to hunt would not only be difficult, but time consuming.

First things first: she'd need to wait for the search to peter out. Otherwise, there was too much risk that she'd be caught before she could get very far.

As if her thoughts had been a signal, the yaupon rustled. Kim froze, sitting still as a frightened rabbit while the branches all around her thrashed and quivered under the onslaught of an unseen figure.

Then she heard a low *whoof*, a sound she recognized. She leaned forward to part some of the brush. "Mutt!"

It took several minutes of effort, but the dog finally wriggled into the small space between holly and oak tree with her. Kim coughed as the dog's large bulk pushed her against the tree and almost smothered her in a wall of warm muscle and fur. The dog settled onto the ground, her head in Kim's lap. Kim scratched Mutt's ears, then curled forward to bury her face in her coat. Fresh tears soaked the short fur, but the warm, heavy bulk was comforting in her arms and across her legs.

Mutt didn't fight. She was more likely to run. Even so, her presence was helpful. She could be used to intimidate militia members. She made Kim feel safe, like an extra layer of protection within her hiding spot.

Kim stayed where she was for a long time. Long enough for the sun to penetrate her little safe space, for her grief to fade to numbness and then to hunger. She ate some of the food in the packs and drank a little water before taking an inventory of what she had available.

Dennis had taken the guns, both of them, and one of the knives. That left her two knives, plus medical supplies, clothing, food, and water. She also found two clips of spare ammo and felt a brief moment of frustration that she didn't have a weapon to go with them. Then the feeling was swallowed up in numbness once again.

The light began to fade into early evening. Kim swallowed the last of a bottle of water. Night offered a good chance to escape notice, but it also meant there were more chances she could get lost.

Kim bit her lip. The fact of the matter was that she couldn't make a move until she knew more about what was happening beyond her hiding place. After a few deep breaths to steady her nerves, she struggled to her feet and began to shove her way through the bushes. Mutt was right beside her, and the dog's burly shoulders helped clear a path faster than Kim could have managed by herself. When she stumbled free of the yaupon, she looked around.

There was no sign of anyone else in the woods nearby. If the militia was still searching, they'd moved far beyond her current location or gone in a different direction entirely. After a moment, Kim settled the packs across her shoulder and began to creep back the way she'd come. Not only would it be the direction that no one would expect her to go, but a peek at the Danville residence might give her some idea of what was going on.

She shuffled carefully back toward the house, taking a path that was on an angle from the one she'd traveled previously. She made sure to follow all the warnings and tips she'd ever heard about traveling undetected. Minimize noise, try not to disturb the vegetation too much. Stay low, so she was more likely to be mistaken for a wild animal. Beside her, Mutt seemed to have picked up her mood and was slinking along like a dust-colored shadow.

She reached the edge of the woods near the Danville house and circled around the garden and chicken coop until she could see the house while remaining under cover. There were no visible guards, but Lewis's truck and a car she assumed was Joan's were both parked nearby. Then her eyes locked on something that made her blood boil.

Dennis's body was still lying in the yard in a crumpled heap, as if he'd been discarded trash. Kim clenched her jaw until she felt her teeth grind, and her shoulders stiffened with a rush of fury that burned every sense of numbness away. She wanted to storm up to the house, call out Lewis, and punch him until he apologized or died. She wanted to scream and curse until she couldn't scream any more.

Focus on what you need to do. It was a voice that sounded like Dennis's, only in her head instead of her ears. Kim blinked back a sharp prickling in her eyes. He'd told her that so often. Focus on what you need to do. Feelings and thoughts could come after she'd achieved her objective.

Her objective was to escape Humboldt. Her problem was that she knew her pursuers—one of them at least—had a car, which she couldn't outrun on foot. There were also dozens of men looking for her, and she had no idea where they were, or how they were stationed, or what Lewis had them doing, which meant they'd be hard to avoid.

Her eyes focused on Joan's car. Joan had told her that she kept the car ready to go in case Lewis's abuse ever became too much and she decided to flee. At the very least, it would have gas, and it would get her out of town fast. If Joan kept it supplied the same way Dennis had talked about stocking the SUV he'd wrecked, then it might be full of useful items as well, like extra food and water.

Joan's car was the answer to her conundrum—if she could get to it. Under different circumstances, she would never have considered stealing a car, much less from a woman who was trapped in an abusive relationship and might need a way to escape. But now she felt no compunction.

Joan had betrayed them to Lewis. She was a large part of the reason Dennis was dead. As far as Kim was concerned, Joan Danville deserved whatever her husband dished out.

The late afternoon air, just turning to twilight, offered her the best chance to get to the car and steal it. The light was fading enough to make perception difficult, and the sunlight slanting into the yard would reduce visibility. At the same time, there was light enough that she wouldn't need to turn on headlights to betray her presence. Of course, starting the motor would likely alert Lewis, Joan, and whoever else was around, but that split second of extra time would be all she needed.

It was the best plan she could think of, but the idea of actually executing it made her mouth go dry. She'd have to get far closer to the Danville house than she wanted to risk approaching. But there were no better options. After a few moments of deep breathing to get her emotions under control, she crept forward.

Mutt came with her, and Kim froze as her heavy paws cracked dried twigs and broke branches. The sound echoed in Kim's ears like miniature gunshots. She turned to the dog. "Stay, Mutt. Stay."

The dog whined softly but lay down in the undergrowth. Kim scratched her ears and resumed her stealthy progress toward the car. She hesitated at the edge of the yard then started forward at a quick shuffle, trying to be as quiet as possible. She also tried to keep one eye on the car and one eye on the house, in case Lewis or Joan left. She was almost halfway to the car when she stumbled over something and looked down.

There was a gun lying in the grass—one of Dennis's. It must have been thrown there during the fight. Kim stared at it, then bent to scoop it up.

Something hit her hard in the back and knocked her to her knees. She fell and rolled to her back. Her blood went cold. Lewis Danville stood over her, a smirk on his weathered features.

"I thought you might come back. You're too soft-hearted and loyal to leave Dennis."

Fear and rage pounded through her like a heartbeat. She did the first thing she could think of—she raised the pistol in one hand, arm shaking slightly with the weight, and pointed it directly at the militia leader's face.

37

KIM NAKAMURA

K im stared at Lewis down the length of her arm and the barrel of the pistol, focusing on the sights like Dennis had taught her. Her breath was fast and her heart was pounding. She raised the other hand to steady the gun in her grip.

Lewis laughed. "You really think I feel threatened by you holding a gun? Come on, Kim." His voice dripped condescension. "We both know you don't have the guts to fire a gun. At least not at a person. A human being is very different from a rabbit."

Kim swallowed hard. "Yeah. The rabbit's defenseless. I won't make the same mistake about you."

Lewis sneered. "Maybe, but that doesn't mean you can pull the trigger. Why do you think Dennis didn't leave you with a gun in the first place?"

The words hit like bullets, but Kim kept her aim steady, letting her anger drive the fear from her mind. "You'd have taken it."

"If she won't shoot, then I will." A third voice intruded into the conversation.

Lewis was just turning toward it when a shot rang out and made Kim's ears ache with the thunderclap. Lewis staggered and went to one knee, a hand clutching his shoulder. Kim flexed her hips then rolled into a crouching position. She nearly dropped the gun in surprise.

Joan was standing there, a pistol in hand and an expression of loathing on her face as she stared at her husband.

Lewis's voice was a pain-filled wheeze when he spoke. "Joan...why?"

"Because I should have put you down a long time ago." Joan's aim didn't waver and neither did her expression. "You always were a stubborn, bad-tempered mule of a man. I put up with it as your wife— figured I knew what I was getting into, and you'd mellow out eventually. But then this disaster happened, and you became a dictator and the worst thing that ever happened to this town."

Lewis coughed, his shoulder and side turning slowly crimson. "I brought order—"

Joan's laugh was harsh, grating, almost hysterical. "You didn't bring order! You brought in a bunch of young thugs with guns that you thought you could control. Then you railroaded everyone else into doing things your way, and to blazes with anyone who said different!"

"It was necessary."

Joan's expression twisted. "Necessary? Was it necessary to give Thomas a concussion because he didn't move out of the way fast enough? Was it necessary to cut people off from medicine? And start rationing before the first month was even out and the spring growing and harvesting hadn't even started?"

She took a step closer, and Kim had to fight not to back away at the bitter, self-loathing, and hate-filled sneer that transformed Joan's features into something that wouldn't have looked out of place in a horror movie. "I put up with that, just like I put up with your tongue-lashings when things didn't go your way and the back of your hand when you'd had one too many whiskeys and a bad day. But then," her voice cracked with grief and rage that Kim recognized all too well, "but then you drove away Doc Kennedy. I could have lived with that, except you had him killed because he wasn't willing to stay under your thumb."

Kim shifted sideways, choosing a path that would get her closer to the car, further from Lewis, and out of Joan's line of fire. From the side, she could see the disbelieving and baffled fury on the militia leader's face.

"We needed a doctor," he wheezed.

"Killing him was your solution? Then kidnapping a half-trained young woman who was trying to reach her family, and *then* killing a good man?" Joan stalked forward another step. "You killed Dennis for protecting Kim! He was a good man. Not long ago, he was your brother in arms. You could have done a dozen other things, including driving them to Memphis and back, if it mattered so much to have her here. But no, you couldn't accept any challenge to your authority." The venom in her voice would have made a scorpion run in terror or keel over dead on the spot. "So you killed two good men in your blind determination to be unchallenged, right or wrong. Killed two men and terrorized the entire community with your heavy-handed ways. And I've had enough. Enough of it, and enough of you."

It was like watching a movie in slow motion. Kim saw the words hit home, saw Lewis turn from uncomprehending anger to uncontrolled fury. The spark of unreasoning madness she'd seen before in the bar lit his eyes as his face turned purple.

Lewis roared, an incoherent, angry snarl of protest, and lurched to his feet, toward his wife.

The sharp report of the gun cut him off as Joan fired, this time into his chest, then again into his face. Kim recoiled with a gasp as blood sprayed outward.

Lewis collapsed like a puppet with cut strings to lie motionless in a slowly expanding puddle of red. Kim stared.

She'd been ready and willing to shoot him, or thought she had. But the reality of it was raw, brutal, and impossible for her mind to fully process. Fallen, Lewis looked too much like Dennis, all the vitality gone from his slack features—those that hadn't been obliterated by the gunshot.

"Go." Kim jumped and nearly lost her balance as Joan spoke, her voice harsh like a crow's cawing. "Get out of here."

Kim blinked, feeling as if she'd been hit over the head. Joan's words didn't make sense. Then Joan made a sharp, angry noise and stepped toward her. Kim flinched, and the paralysis broke. She scrambled to her feet.

"Keys are in the ignition. Get out of here." Joan pointed to the car. "Militia will be on their way back, so get gone. They're likely to try and take vengeance on you for Lewis's death if you're still here."

Kim shivered as her gaze went involuntarily to Lewis's body. "What about you?"

"I gotta stay. Got things to take care of here." Joan gave her husband's body a disdainful look. "One more mess of his to clean up, and then— well, we'll see. But you get going."

Kim hesitated and Joan shouted. "*Go!*"

Kim bolted for the car. "Mutt! Here, girl!"

The dog came bounding out of the woods at her call. She stopped at Dennis's body and sniffed, and Kim heard a soft whine. She would have loved to stay, to mourn alongside the dog. But the militia was coming, and she couldn't risk it. "Mutt! Come on!"

Mutt came. Kim opened the door to the back seat and let the dog clamber inside while she tossed the packs into the passenger seat. She shut the door and turned to Joan one last time.

The older woman didn't let her say a word, saying again, "Go."

Kim wrenched the driver's side door open and slid into the seat. As promised, the keys were in the ignition. A single twist made the engine roar to life. Kim slammed the door shut and shoved the car into gear. Then she hit the gas.

Her last sight of the Danvilles as she pulled out of the drive and made her way toward the highway was Joan lit by the taillights and staring at the body of her husband on the ground.

38

LEE KINGSTON JONES

The scrapyard was a confusing mass of metal and meandering, half-cluttered pathways, all surrounded by rusted, corrugated fencing. Personally, Lee thought it looked ready for a bulldozer or two rather than a bunch of low-grade fertilizer bombs, but Andre's word was law.

Andre wanted bombs at any escape routes and hard-to-see locations so he could drive the Black Rats out like rats abandoning a sinking ship—bad joke intended, he said. Then he could shoot them and watch them panic, caught in the middle of bombs and bullets, and forced to decide between a slow death by fire or a quick one by gunshot.

Lee didn't know anything about making fertilizer bombs—or any kind of bombs, really, not even Molotovs—so Andre had sent him with a notepad and a pencil to sketch out the scrapyard and find some likely spots for their plans to be enacted.

Not that Lee knew much about the best place to put an explosive either. The only thing he really knew was that Andre wanted to set up the shooting station at the front gate. Lee had scoped that out first and pinpointed the best spot. Then he'd sneaked through a hole in the fencing and started to survey the yard. All the bikers had gone inside for the evening, which made it easier.

He wondered if the biker Andre had tossed out of the bar was here and if he'd recognize Lee. He hoped not. The idea of trying to take on one or more Black Rats without Andre made him queasy.

The truck that Andre said his ex-wife had driven in looked like a good place to put one or more of the explosive devices. It was big, it had a lot of places to hide things, and if everything went right, it might even start some fires when the fertilizer blew. Andre would like that. Lee made some notes and moved on.

He wandered around toward what was clearly a working repair station with multiple bikes in various states of disassembly. He was so absorbed in his work that he didn't realize he wasn't alone until a voice spoke up and nearly startled him out of his skin.

"Who are you?"

Lee jumped and clutched his notebook to his chest, heart hammering as he looked around. After a moment, he spotted a man in the shadows of the repair bay, wiping his hands on a stained towel as he ambled forward. He gulped.

The man wasn't wearing Black Rats insignia, but that might be because he'd clearly been working. Aside from that, he was big, almost as big as Andre, and his skin was a few shades darker than Lee's own. He was older, his hair a pale gray in the evening light, but his arms were muscular, and Lee was willing to bet the man's shoulders under his loose shirt were the same.

The man came closer and addressed him again. "Who are you, young man?"

He couldn't refuse to answer. If he tried to run, the man would know he wasn't supposed to be here. He'd probably chase him down. He might kill him. Lee swallowed a couple times and took a deep breath to steady his nerves before he answered. "I'm Lee."

"Bill Wheeler." The man set down his rag. "You look a little young to be a Black Rat."

Did gangs have age requirements? He didn't know. It occurred to Lee that this man didn't seem to know if he should be a Black Rat or not. Maybe he was new to the gang or something. The thought gave him a little more courage. "Uh, yeah, well...I got family in the gang."

"Thought it was a club." One eyebrow rose.

"Uh, sure. Yeah. Motorcycle club. I'm always getting that confused. My old man says I watch too many TV shows." Lee chuckled weakly. "Probably why I'm not really a member yet."

To his surprise, Bill chuckled. "That makes two of us."

"You're not a Black Rat?" Lee blinked in surprise. He hadn't thought there would be any outsiders here. Andre had made it seem like they were a pretty closed-off group, with the exception of people like his treacherous ex-wife. "What are you doing here then? I thought no one but crew and family was allowed."

"I guess I'm a special case. On probation as their new mechanic after helping the boss's niece drive in." Bill laughed again. "Probably gonna stay that way too. I can't see myself joining, if I'm honest."

"Why not?" The words escaped before Lee could keep them back, and he cursed himself for his curiosity. What if Bill got angry about his questions and wanted to take him to see his "family" in the crew? They'd know Lee was an impostor. "I mean, you don't have to tell me. I was just curious. I've heard it's like a family."

He'd learned during their travels that the closeknit community was part of why Andre was so angry at the Black Rats—his family and friends had rejected and betrayed him to side with his ex-wife.

"It might be. But I guess not everyone fits into every family." Bill shook his head. "I came out here to work on the bikes because it isn't exactly the most comfortable environment for me in there."

"You don't like bikers?" Lee frowned. *Could this be an ally for Andre, maybe?*

Bill gave him a rueful smile. "It isn't that I've anything against bikers, and I'm sure these fellows are friendly enough. It's not easy being a stranger in a strange place, or trying to fit into a group and a culture you're not used to. I'm just a good old country boy from the south-west plains, born and bred for wide-open spaces and a patch of land to keep and call home instead of cities and being on the road all the time. These guys aren't familiar with me, and I guess I'm a little too sensitive to their suspicion. Shannon warned me they'd be a little wary, but it still rubs me the wrong way."

"I guess I can understand that." Lee nodded agreeably.

"Thanks." Bill frowned. "Not that I mind talking to you, Lee, but you're out kind of late for a lad your age. I would have thought you'd be at home."

Lee flushed. "I'm just running some errands for my—for my dad." The word felt strange on his tongue, especially applied to Andre rather than Max Jones. "He needs some parts for repairs. I said I'd check around here, see if I could find them."

Bill's expression softened with approval. "That's admirable. You're a good kid, Lee, but you ought to get on home. It'll be dark soon, and the streets aren't likely to be safe, from what I've heard."

Bill moved closer and laid a gentle hand on Lee's shoulder. Lee controlled the urge to flinch away with effort. "You tell your dad that if he wants, he can come by tomorrow and ask to talk to me. I'll point him toward any parts he needs, if I can find them, and help out with the repairs if he wants some assistance."

Lee's mind went blank, his reply swallowed up in an unexpected and crushing wave of guilt. Bill seemed so kind and so sincere that the truth of his errand and what it would mean for the man suddenly felt like it was choking him.

"Yeah. Bye." Lee forced the two words out, then turned and bolted from the scrapyard before Bill could say anything else—or worse, ask him more questions. The notebook was clutched tightly in his arms, an almost forgotten weight as he hurried down the streets, back toward the house he and Andre were occupying. His head hurt as doubt crept in and hammered at his thoughts.

Andre had told him all about the Black Rats. How they'd betrayed him, cast him out. How they were a bunch of amoral thugs. Lee had been prepared to encounter someone like that. Someone he could despise. But Bill—Bill acted like the type of man Lee had always dreamed of having as a father. He wanted to believe it was fake, just a mask over a cruel nature, like the face Max Jones had showed people when he and Lee were out in public.

But what reason would Bill have had to lie? He didn't know who Lee was. He hadn't given any indication that he knew what Lee's real purpose in the scrapyard was. He just seemed like a genuinely nice guy who happened to be there at the same time Lee was snooping around.

Lee was so wrapped up in his thoughts that he barely noticed when he arrived back at the house. Andre was in the garage, working by the light of a battery-powered lamp he'd found while Lee was sleeping off his hangover. He looked up with a pleasant smile as Lee approached, his mood no doubt improved by the three finished units he'd stacked to one side.

"Welcome back, Lee. I trust you have the information I asked for?" His smile was a lazy, contented one, rather like a well-fed cat's. Lee's shoulders relaxed a little.

"I have a few ideas. That big truck they have in the front is a good place to stash a few bombs. If we can get the fuel tank, the fire's guaranteed to make them panic."

Andre frowned thoughtfully. "While you make a valid point, there are better uses for a vehicle like that than explosive power. I would rather place the explosives closer to the main clubhouse and other structures that might offer them shelter. Did you determine the best locations?"

Lee looked down at his notepad and his shoulders tightened again as unease filled him. Talking to Bill, he'd completely forgotten about the task he was supposed to be completing. The drawing he'd made wasn't finished, and he'd never gotten up the nerve to go close to the main buildings.

He didn't remember the layout clearly enough to make quick notes now either. Which meant he didn't have the information Andre wanted. And Andre had said many times that he didn't tolerate failure.

"Lee?"

He wanted to lie, to make up something. But if he got anything wrong, Andre would know he'd lied, and Andre had said more than once he disliked liars as much as he disliked failures. Lee took a deep breath, bracing himself for more of Andre's cutting anger as he raised his head. "Sorry. I don't know."

334

Andre's jovial expression evaporated like ice on a hot stove. "You don't know. Why not, Lee?"

Lee felt his shoulders hunching. The urge to make himself smaller, to try to hide, was almost unbearable. "I…I got spotted. Ran into a guy. I had to get out of there, and I didn't get a chance to finish."

"You got spotted. So you fled like a coward and did not even make an attempt to circle back and complete the task you were given." Andre's voice was cold, and his expression made Lee want to back away—or run. It was the same expression he'd had when he was talking to the Black Rat in the bar the night before.

"I mean, I didn't want him to raise the alarm. I figured, with the truck and the gates, we had enough info—"

Whatever else Lee had planned to say, he forgot as Andre took two quick steps forward and lashed out, backhanding him across the face with enough force to split his lip and make him see stars. Lee stumbled backward and fell on his tailbone. His hands hit the pavement hard enough to bruise as he caught himself, staring wide-eyed at the man he'd called his mentor and pseudo-father for the past few days. "Andre?"

"I do not tolerate failure, Lee."

Andre grabbed the notepad Lee had dropped, then bent close and grabbed Lee's collar in a tight grip with his other hand. Lee choked as Andre hauled him roughly upward, dragged him to the door, and tossed him into the driveway, heedless of the gravel Lee landed in.

Lee coughed. His ears were ringing, his heart hammering, and his lungs burning as he gulped in air and tried to fight back the all-too-familiar fear, shame, anger, and hurt.

The notepad and pencil hit him in the chest. "Go back and finish the job." Andre gave him a look that made Lee cold. "Do you understand?"

Lee didn't bother with words. He wasn't sure he could speak with blood dripping from his lip and his cheek throbbing from the blow. He nodded, grabbed the notebook, then shoved himself to his feet and darted down the street, determined to put as much space between himself and Andre as he could.

By the time he stopped to catch his breath, his shirt was dotted with crimson spots of blood. His hands and forearms hurt, both from the first bruising impact and from the raw scrapes he'd collected when Andre tossed him into the gravel. His lungs burned, aching for air. No wonder, since he hadn't managed a proper breath since he'd first seen Andre in the garage.

He reached up to touch the aching, swollen place on his lip, then pulled his hand away to stare at the red on his fingertips. Beneath the pain of his new injuries, he felt a deep sense of betrayal and shame. Somewhere inside, he'd started to believe that Andre might be cruel with his words, but he'd never hurt Lee—at least not with his fists the way Max Jones used to.

He'd been wrong. Andre wasn't any better than his father. In fact, he might be worse.

Lee shook his head, trying to shake the thought away. He'd known from the start that Andre was violent. It wasn't Andre's fault he'd deluded himself into thinking otherwise. And it wasn't Andre's fault that he hadn't finished the task he'd been assigned, despite knowing how much his mentor disliked failures.

Andre was still the toughest guy Lee knew. He'd taught him a lot about survival and taking care of himself. And he was the best protection Lee had—his best chance to make something of himself.

He'd just have to work harder and avoid failing in the future. Lee gripped his notepad and started back toward the scrapyard. He loped down the road and tried to ignore the heaviness in his heart and the stinging in his eyes.

39

BILL WHEELER

B ill waited a few minutes to see if the young man would return, but he didn't. Eventually, Bill decided the youth must have taken his advice and returned home. He hoped the boy had found what he needed or was on his way home to tell his father there was a mechanic available to assist him.

In the meantime, the light was fading, the evening air was getting colder, and the boy's intrusion had broken his concentration. He was also tired from the driving and unloading he'd done earlier in the day. Bill wiped his hands once more on the stained cloth he'd found, then started back toward the main clubhouse.

He was almost all the way there when the sullen glow of an ember caught his attention. He focused on it and saw Carol leaning against a wall and puffing on a cigarette. The older woman spotted him at the same time and inclined her head. Bill took it as an invitation and went to stand next to her.

"You're out late." Carol's gruff observation broke the silence.

"I had a feeling people might be more comfortable talking without me, so I thought I'd come out and see what I could do on the bikes that need repair." Bill rolled his shoulders. "Don't know where the spare parts are or how they're organized though."

"They aren't really. Just got piles of metal and mechanical stuff lying around. The boys take the cars apart as they need things and dig through the rubble and equipment till they have what they're looking for."

"I kinda guessed as much." Bill scratched through his hair, trying to see if he'd managed to get any oil in it or in the stubble of his beard. "Would anyone mind too much if I tried to set up a system?"

"Probably not, so long as you don't mess too much with the bikes and where they're parked." Carol eyed him laconically then stubbed out her cigarette and lit another. "You being the mechanic, you've got a certain amount of leeway in that area." She held out the cigarette. "You smoke?"

"I'm afraid I don't." Bill emphasized his refusal with a shake of his head.

"More for me." Carol shrugged and took another drag.

They stood in silence for a moment before Bill spoke. "You helped raise Shannon?"

"I've always known her as Sarah, but yeah, Bruno and I raised her after her parents died. She was a handful."

"I don't doubt it, but you should know, she's an amazing woman. Tough as nails. Right after the EMP hit, she kept things together and made sure everyone got food and medical attention."

"She's that kind of girl, I guess." Carol looked sideways at him. "Makes me wonder how she came by those injuries. And how bad they are."

Bill winced. In the fuss of their arrival, they'd never found time to tell anyone about the events that had led to Shannon's injuries. "Healed— or mostly healed—concussion. A few bad cuts. The worst one, the one I'm still keeping an eye on, is the through-and-through bullet to her shoulder. That one was…" Bill trailed off, uncertain how to phrase it.

"That one got infected, which turned into blood poisoning, which nearly killed me. But Bill got me to a medical facility, found supplies, and treated the wound until I recovered." Shannon came to stand beside her aunt, her face pale and her arm tucked close to her side.

Carol jerked the cigarette out of her mouth. "Blood poisoning? Sarah Nakamura, why didn't you tell me sooner?"

"Because you and Uncle Bruno were too angry to listen. And because I can tell everything's not all right here." Shannon—Sarah—gave her aunt a solemn look. "That Austin guy, for example. There was a time when you'd never let a low-rank brother talk to you like that."

"I know. And so does Bruno." Carol drew in a deep breath of cigarette smoke, then let it out in a slow sigh. "After you left, we went straight. No drugs, no big-time criminal stunts. But lately, we've been getting more guys like Austin, riders who want to go back to the old way. It's made things difficult."

Carol took another puff, then met her niece's gaze. "You should know, Bruno's taking a lot of heat for taking you back in, even under a probationary status. You might be family, but there's more than one newcomer who thinks you might be a WitSec informant. A few old-timers too."

Shannon scoffed. "You know me better than that. Besides, even if it was true, the disaster two weeks ago was nationwide. There isn't even a WitSec to report anything to, as far as I know. For that matter, there isn't even a government, according to the emergency broadcast Bill managed to tap into. I'm not sure there's even a military left."

"Maybe. Doesn't stop the boys from being suspicious. Some are even saying you were given the truck as a goodwill gesture to lower our guard. Trojan horse kind of thing." Carol stubbed out the second cigarette.

"That's not true."

Carol shook her head. "Doesn't matter, Sarah, and you know it. Words won't help. It'll take time and actions, assuming we have enough of either to make a difference."

"What do you mean?"

"I mean the young toughs and rougher brothers are getting edgy. They want some action. They want to assert their dominance, make a stand, make a statement. Bruno's holding them back, but he's older, and he's had to make some compromises. I might be the president's old lady, but these days, that don't count as much as it did last month."

"But Uncle Bruno's still in charge?"

"He is. As long as you two make yourselves useful and keep your heads down, we all ought to be okay. Speaking of which," Carol pointed toward the main building, "get some rest, both of you. Bill, we need you to get to work early to fix some of the bikes for our boys. Sarah, you need to keep up your strength and finish healing. Last thing anyone needs is you getting sick or getting blood poisoning again. So you two head inside. I'll check around the perimeter and follow you in."

Shannon nodded obediently, and Bill fell in step beside her as she made her way inside. "You okay?" he asked.

"Mostly. Worried about things here. And worried about Kim. I hope she's safe and doing all right," Shannon said.

"If she's half as tough as you, I'm sure she's doing well." Bill gave her a quick hug, and the two of them retired to their bunks.

341

40

LEE KINGSTON JONES

F inishing his surveillance didn't take that long, not with the fear of Andre's disapproval following him like a wolf at his heels. By the time Lee returned to the house, he was tired, and his arms, hips, and face were all aching. He gave Andre the notepad, then went inside to grab some food and water, maybe scrounge a painkiller or two.

He had no luck with the meds, but the food and water helped. Andre ignored him, so Lee took the opportunity to stretch out on the couch and close his eyes. He'd slept a lot, but being unconscious with a hangover wasn't the same as a proper rest. He wanted to be as ready as possible when Andre called on him again.

He woke up to Andre's hand shaking his shoulder roughly. It felt like almost no time had passed, but night had fallen, and only a flashlight in Andre's hand gave him any visibility at all. He blinked. "Andre?"

"It is time. I spotted Sarah in the compound." Andre's voice was sharp, but Lee couldn't tell if it was anger, anticipation, or something darker that tinged it. The flashlight beam distorted everything. Seeing Andre's face cast in shadows from below made Lee shiver.

He looked kind of like a demon out of the stories Lee used to hear at church, back when his mom had been alive to make all of them go.

"Okay." Lee got up as quickly as he could. "Can I ask what the plan is?"

"The plan is simple." Andre handed Lee a gun and an ammo clip. He was holding a second one, and a rifle Lee couldn't remember seeing before. Lee had no idea where he'd gotten them and was fairly certain he didn't want to know. "We will set up the bombs around the edges of the scrapyard, where the exits are and the metal is thinnest, as well as near any spots where there are vehicles that might also explode. On my signal, you will light the fuses, then join me in shooting the Black Rats as they flee the compound. We will take out anyone and everyone who is not my treacherous ex-wife."

"I thought you wanted to kill her." Lee blinked.

"I do. But I want her to suffer first. I want her to see her entire world burn, her family dead, and everything she cherishes in ashes. Then I want to make her beg for death until she is no longer capable of speaking." Andre's voice was cold and thick with what Lee could only describe as bloodlust.

The idea of setting off bombs and shooting helpless, panicking people made Lee a little sick. But the idea of facing Andre's wrath made him feel worse. Lee accepted the gun Andre handed him and stuffed it in his belt, tucked the spare ammo into a front pocket of his jeans, and shoved the lighter Andre gave him into a hip pocket. Then he followed Andre out to the garage and helped him gather the home-made explosives into the wheelbarrow.

Andre took the lead, and Lee tried not to think about what they were about to do. The gun and bullets felt heavier than usual, weighing down his steps.

The scrapyard was quiet when they arrived, though it looked like the club had a generator to provide a little bit of light. Lee was grateful for that, since it meant he could see and the light from their lantern wasn't so obvious.

He and Andre set the explosives around the chained back gate and two places where the metal of the fence had rusted through. Lee edged his way through a gap to put a bomb near a stack of partially rusted cars. He followed Andre's instructions to guide a fuse across the ground to the outside, then followed his mentor to another spot to continue laying their traps.

When all the explosives were set, Andre pushed the empty wheelbarrow out of the way. "I need to go around to the front gate. I'll fire a single shot when I reach my position. When I do, start lighting the fuses, then join me."

Andre slipped away. With his pockets full, Lee folded his arms and stuffed his hands into his armpits. He was shivering, and it wasn't entirely from the cold. He didn't want to be there, standing in the dark, about to commit what amounted to an act of terrorism.

It was dark. He could run away, the way he'd run away from home. He could flee into the night and not stop moving until he was out of Memphis. Maybe until he was out of state entirely. Andre wouldn't know he was gone for a while. Lee would have the gun and the ammo and lighter to make his life easier, along with the knife Andre had given him.

He could hunt. If he moved quickly, he could even get back to the house and grab supplies, like extra clothes and food that was already dead and processed. And some tools. Whatever he could carry and still move quickly.

It was tempting. The urge to bolt was like a siren's call in his head.

But his feet wouldn't move, not with the overwhelming fear that also ran through him.

Andre had traveled from Mississippi to Memphis to punish his ex-wife. He was violent and unpredictable, as the bodies in their wake and Lee's swollen lip could attest. And Andre didn't like lies, betrayals, or failures.

What if Andre got angry enough to come after him? For the knife, or just because he was furious and wanted vengeance? The idea was terrifying, especially given the ideas Andre had expounded on regarding his plans for his ex-wife.

Lee thought of the things he'd seen Andre do. The beatings. The cold-blooded killing. The way he'd utterly destroyed the bikers in the bar would give Lee nightmares if he hadn't been too drunk, then too tired and too terrified, to have any sort of dreams at all.

He couldn't face that. His arm still ached with a phantom pain when he thought about the way Andre had nearly broken it in their first meeting. The thought of inviting worse made him nauseous, even worse than the idea of shooting at defenseless bikers.

Lee swallowed hard and pulled the lighter from his pocket. He clicked it a few times to make sure the reservoir had fuel and was working. Then he settled in to listen for Andre's signal, hoping against hope that it would never come.

41

BILL WHEELER

One minute he was dozing fitfully. The next, a sound like a gunshot or an explosion shattered his rest and sent him bolting upright in his bed. The second after that, he was scrambling to right himself as he fell off the narrow mattress and thudded into the floor with a jarring crash that woke him up fully.

Shannon joined him a moment later. "Bill, are you okay?"

"Fine. Fine." Bill dragged himself upright. "What was that sound?"

"I don't know. Might be a—" Whatever she was going to say was drowned out by another louder, much closer explosion. The rest of the bikers who were resting in the room were rousing. Bill and Shannon exchanged a look, then hurried for the door just as another explosion rocked the scrapyard.

Carol met them outside. "Something's exploding outside the fence. Metal's flying, and there's fire—" A third explosion—or was it a fourth?—went off.

There was an orange glow in the air that made Bill's gut clench. Around him, the Black Rats were muttering in fear and uncertainty. A few of them were making their way toward the bikes, obviously intending to flee.

Then another explosion, this time from a different direction, blew hot, sharp metal across the scrapyard. For many of the Black Rats, that was the last straw. They broke and ran.

Bruno's voice cut through the din, as strong and commanding as his niece's had been in the supercenter over a week ago. "Quit panicking, you fools! Form up, get the sandbags and the extinguishers! Make sure there aren't any fires burning among the derelicts. Get moving!"

It didn't stop all of the men from running, but it stopped enough of them. Bill joined a group of men as they grabbed buckets of sand and helped haul them toward the nearest glow.

There was a sharp crack, quieter than the one before it, from beyond Shannon's truck. Then another. One of the Black Rats came stumbling back, splattered with red. "Someone's out there! Someone's shooting at us!"

"Who?"

"Can't tell. I couldn't see them." The man's ragged breathing was wheezy with panic.

Another shot, and the man jerked, then fell. Blood stained a rough hole in the back of his vest, glittering darkly in the firelight.

Someone was picking them off as they tried to escape. Bill felt sick and cold and angry all at once. He wanted to do something, but he wasn't sure what. He didn't have a weapon, and even if he did, he couldn't have attacked or defended against an enemy he couldn't see.

All he could do was work with the remaining bikers to try and contain the fires caused by the earlier explosions and stay out of the potential line of fire as best he could. He dumped a bucket of sand over a smoldering pile of metal. Shannon brought him another bucket, carried in her good hand. They swapped buckets, and Bill made his way toward the next location.

A spark caught his attention as he headed toward the back of the scrapyard. He turned his head to look just as the spark reached an unassuming bucket. The bucket exploded, sending him reeling amid smoke and the pungent smell of fertilizer.

Fertilizer bombs in buckets. That's what they're using to smoke us out and start the fires.

He needed to tell someone, but his ears were ringing. He'd lost track of Shannon, Bruno, and Carol. He didn't know anyone else well enough to approach them.

Another smell, this one just as pungent and far more familiar, stung his nose. The fact that it managed to penetrate the smell of fertilizer was almost as alarming as his recognition of it. "Gasoline...there's gasoline leaking somewhere."

That was all he managed before one of the derelicts exploded and threw him backward. Bill hit the ground with bruising force and gasped as the air was knocked out of him. He choked against stabbing pains in his ribs as he rolled and fought his way clumsily to his feet. His ears ached, and he couldn't think through the pain, the high-pitched noise that filled his skull, and the feeling of being wrapped in lead and cotton.

There was fire roaring in several places now and fewer Black Rats trying to fight the fires. Bill looked around, wondering where his sand bucket had gone. The smell of smoke and fuel, oil and fertilizer all mingled in the air, clogging his nose, throat, and lungs.

Something cannoned into him and dragged him toward the truck they'd driven into the compound. He had just enough time to see

Shannon's soot-streaked face before another blast threw them both forward. Bill rolled over to see that the place he'd been standing was littered with smoking debris. If Shannon hadn't grabbed him, he would have been cut to ribbons by the hot metal.

"Move toward the front! Some of the wrecks have gas in them! They're going up!" Bruno's strong, steady bass voice echoed over the sounds of fire and people trying to escape or contain the blaze. "Move toward the front gate, but watch out for the shooter."

Bill and Shannon stood up and staggered toward the truck and the gate beyond it. Shannon was using various piles of junk, as well as the shadow of the truck, to avoid being a target. Bill followed her lead. He crouched low and tried to clear the ringing in his ears and the pounding in his head. The world was wavering, and everything was fire and smoke, darkness and light intermingled.

He was a few yards from the gate when several things happened at once.

He saw someone slinking in the shadows, and he thought he recognized the boy from earlier, carrying something dark in his hand.

Another crack of gunfire sounded, then a series of shots. Several Black Rats fell, some still and quiet, some screaming in pain.

Then, as he and Shannon stopped a moment by the side of the truck to prepare to run for it, he saw Bruno. The Black Rat club president had moved forward to see to one of his riders. It looked like the young man with the bruises. A bullet had caught him in the shoulder, or a little lower, and he bent over, moaning in agony.

Another crack and the man fell backward, blood trickling from his face and what looked like a bullet hole. Bruno started to rise.

Another shot rang out, and Bruno jerked and spun partially around. Blood spurted from a wound high on his chest, near the hollow of his throat. It looked horribly like the wound that had killed Noah Mochire just over a week before. Bill lurched forward, already planning to help.

Bruno fell, eyes glassy. He was dead before he hit the ground.

42

KIM NAKAMURA

Kim made it halfway to Memphis before she had to pull over. Her throat hurt, and her vision was blurred by tears she couldn't stop and didn't really want to. As the first sob escaped her, she pulled the car over, hiding it somewhat between two wrecks. Only then did she give vent to the grief she'd been trying to ignore while she drove.

Dennis was dead. Murdered. Two weeks ago, a month ago, she wouldn't have cared much. But now all she could think of was how he'd dragged himself on his busted hip and knee to her dorm. How he'd let her talk him into detoxing in Humboldt, despite the pain and his awareness of how miserable the process would be.

She remembered how he'd given her little tips on the road. The peaceful day when he'd taught her how to shoot. The way he'd praised her for getting the rabbit then taught her how to field dress and cook it.

She thought of how, less than twenty-four hours ago, he'd climbed out onto a roof in an effort to help her escape so they could get to Memphis.

She'd been so angry and dismissive of him. She'd been disgusted by his addiction and nursing the remnants of her grudge against him for tearing apart her family.

Dennis had come to her high school graduation, even though he had to stay far away from Carol and Bruno because they hated law enforcement officers and him in particular. He'd helped her work through college applications, guided her through applying for financial aid, and written her letters of recommendation. Bruno and Carol and the older members of the Black Rats had helped her move to college, but Dennis had been the reason she was able to go.

It had been so easy to be angry at him all the time. Now all she could think of were the missed opportunities.

Regret felt like knives in her heart trying to tear her apart. One sob became several, and before she knew it, she was doubled over, howling out watery, painful cries of grief and loss and rage, all mingled together in a stew of hot tears and raw pain. She cried until she screamed nonsense sounds that conveyed nothing but her pain. Then she cried some more, until her throat was raw and her eyes were dry and sticky. She felt broken inside.

She had no idea how long she sat there, lost in her grief. Eventually, the tears passed into numbness. The next thing she was aware of was a warm tongue licking across her face and slobbering into her shirt and jacket. She took a hiccuping breath and turned her head.

Mutt looked back at her, big eyes soulful and sad. The dog whined as their eyes met and licked Kim again.

Kim managed a weak, painful smile. "Hey, Mutt."

The dog nudged her big head against Kim's, a noiseless gesture of companionship and comfort. Kim ran her hand through the dog's fur, then scratched her ears. "I guess you're right. Can't sit here crying forever. We've still got to get to Memphis." She took a deep breath, scrubbed her face dry, and sat up. After a final pat to Mutt's head, she nudged the dog back and reached for the keys in the ignition. Two minutes later, she was on the road again.

Dawn was breaking by the time she reached the outskirts of Memphis, and she was exhausted from being up for two days straight. It was only nervous energy and the desire to see her family that kept her going over the last miles of desolate, trash-strewn pavement.

The sun rose, staining the sky red and orange and yellow, save for a patch of cloud-choked sky. Kim frowned at it.

Then she realized what it was. Not clouds but smoke, rising in a sporadic, patchy plume of gray smudges. She was driving almost straight toward it. Unease made her heart speed up.

Please don't be another disaster. Please.

She turned down another street, then another. The smoke kept getting thicker and closer.

She made another turn, then slammed on the brakes so hard she almost gave herself whiplash. Mutt whined from the backseat. Kim blinked and scrubbed a hand over her eyes, then looked again.

The scene didn't change. A thin, dark-haired fellow with a weaselly face was riding his motorcycle down the road. He wore a vest with the Black Rats logo on it.

Kim put the car into park and stuffed the keys in her pocket. She jumped out.

"Hey! Hey! Wait up!"

The guy stared at her, clearly debating the merits of riding away. Kim tightened her hand on the knife she'd stuffed in a pocket while she was in hiding the day before and resolved to use it if the rider didn't

353

stop. What exactly she could do with it, she wasn't sure, but she would do whatever she had to in order to get information.

Something of her feelings must have showed in her face because the biker slowed his ride and came to a stop, engine running. "What? Make it fast, girl, I got places to be."

"You're a Black Rat. My aunt and uncle—great-aunt and uncle, really —they run the crew. Bruno and Carol Gardena. Last I heard, Brute Bruno was the club president."

"Yeah? And who are you supposed to be?"

"Kim. Kim Nakamura. Used to be Little Kim."

The biker's expression twisted as if he'd bitten a lemon. "Heard of you." He spat to one side. "What you want?"

"What's going on? Black Rats still based at Bruno's scrapyard?"

The man cackled a sharp, almost hysterical laugh. "Don't you know, girl? Black Rats of Memphis are toast, at least as far as I'm concerned. See that?" He pointed toward the smoke. "That's the scrapyard going up in smoke. Some lunatic bombed it real good and opened fire on us when we ran. Those of us that got out are gonna keep going. Least if they got any sense. Me, I'm for anywhere that ain't here, and any one-percenter club that'll have me."

Kim nearly staggered as her mind processed what he'd said. The scrapyard was going up in smoke? They'd been bombed? Shot at?

"What happened to Bruno and Carol? And was there anyone else—a woman named Sarah, maybe? Did they get out?"

"Heck if I know, and I couldn't give two bird droppings either." The man spat again, his expression bitter. "We were in trouble from the minute that Sarah witch came into town. Bar got smashed up, guys killed, and now this. And Bruno and Carol trying to act like she was

354

family when they ought to have tossed her out. Maybe there'd still be a Black Rats Memphis chapter if they had."

Sarah—her mother—had made it to Memphis. The relief Kim should have felt was entirely overwhelmed by the news that the scrapyard had burned. She had a thousand questions and couldn't seem to voice a single one.

The Black Rat took her silence as the end of the conversation. He kicked the brake stand up and rode away. Kim watched him go, then turned and dove into the car. She nearly broke the key in her rush to jam it into the ignition and was lucky not to shear it in the steering column with how fast she twisted it. The engine roared to life. Kim pushed the gear into drive and stomped on the accelerator with a force that made the car jump forward like a startled horse. The tires squealed, and she was pretty sure she left twin streaks of black rubber on the road as she peeled out. She didn't care.

She drove until she was within a block of the scrapyard, close enough for the smoke to look black and thick as thunderclouds. She parked the car, threw her pack over her shoulder, and tucked the keys into one pocket and the gun into her belt. She opened the door and let Mutt out of the car, waited for the dog to have a brief squat, then turned and marched toward the wreckage of one of her childhood safe havens.

Her jaw was clenched so hard it hurt. Grief had been replaced by rage, cold and all-consuming.

Someone had attacked her family. Whoever it was, they were going to regret it.

43

LEE KINGSTON JONES

The explosions were terrifying. Lee couldn't help flinching with every one that went off. He jumped and instinctively ducked when the first car blew up. Then another exploded, and Lee suppressed the urge to cower against a structure and hide until it was all over. But Andre was waiting for him, and he didn't dare disappoint Andre.

Lee forced himself to put the lighter away and draw the gun as he moved toward the front gate. His hands were numb, disconnected from him. Everything felt strange, even more than it had the night he'd killed the biker.

Andre was standing about fifty yards from the gate and watching like a hawk. Then he took aim and fired. Someone inside screamed, and Andre grinned in smug satisfaction. He fired again, then frowned.

"Lee."

Lee forced himself to move closer. "Yes sir?"

"Go around the side of the truck. Start shooting to drive the survivors toward the gate." Andre scowled. "My wife is a small woman with one arm in a sling. If you see her, make sure to frighten her."

Lee thought the woman was smart, maybe smarter than he was. He wanted to refuse Andre's order, but he couldn't. He just ducked his head in something that Andre might have considered a nod and skulked away through the gate. He circled around to get beyond the truck cab. He spotted a figure and raised the gun.

He couldn't pull the trigger. He tried, but his fingers wouldn't move. He couldn't do it. He was stiff with fear, and his hands were shaking.

He wanted to pull the trigger. He didn't want Andre to be angry. But his hands seemed to be disconnected from his brain. The muzzle of the gun dropped.

I gotta do this. I gotta do this. Andre's counting on me.

Movement caught his gaze. He turned his head to see the big man from before and a smaller woman who matched Andre's description. Sarah and the mechanic—Bill, or whatever his name was.

Lee stared at them. He knew he should raise the pistol and shoot them. Or at least shoot toward them. But all he could do was stare at them.

Then the mechanic turned, and Lee saw the man notice his presence. He was on the verge of bolting, though he wasn't sure whether he wanted to run toward the gate, deeper into the scrapyard, or toward the mechanic. Before he could decide, another explosion rocked the scrapyard, this one much closer to the gate. Lee jumped backward, then dropped the gun and bolted back toward the opening he'd come through moments before.

He couldn't do this. Even a beating from Andre was better than staying here to get caught by the bikers or the explosions. He could survive broken bones and bruises and bleeding. But explosions and burns were way beyond him.

Another boom, and Lee barely managed to skid to a stop as red-hot metal flashed in front of his face. He flinched, staggered backward a few steps, and stopped in horrified shock as fire bloomed into the space in front of him as something ignited. Lee yelped as the heat washed over him.

He tried to move forward, but the fire moved faster than he did and cut him off. Lee froze. He stared at the fire.

He saw a figure moving on the far side of the blaze, a familiar figure with broad shoulders. "Andre! Andre, help me!"

The figure stopped. Andre stared at him over the leaping flames. Lee waited for Andre to tell him what to do, to give him orders. He waited for Andre's contempt, or his anger. He didn't care what Andre said or did, as long as the man helped him escape.

But Andre didn't say anything. He didn't step forward or step back. He didn't shout, or even glare. His eyes were cold, empty, and disinterested, as if he didn't care at all that Lee was trapped by fire with the people Andre had been shooting at moments before.

Maybe the smoke was too thick for Andre to be sure it was him. Lee coughed, then raised his voice to shout, "Andre! It's Lee! Help me! I can't see how to get out. How do I get out of here?"

Andre just stared at him. Then, without a word, he turned away, as if Lee was a stranger.

Lee's stomach lurched. "Andre! Andre!"

The man disappeared into the smoke and shadows. Lee stared at the fire, a burn that had nothing to do with the flames ripping through him. Betrayal. Loss.

It hurt. Everything he had done for and with Andre, and the man was abandoning him to die like a stranger, or a dog. Lee's eyes stung with tears, and he wanted to blame them on the smoke. The gun fell from nerveless fingers as he stared in the direction Andre had disappeared.

Andre had left him to die. That was the only thought in his head, pushing out the fire coming closer and the danger he was in.

Something else exploded, or burst into flames, and the heat hit him like a battering ram. Lee staggered, blinded by fire and smoke. He heard a loud crackling, roaring noise, but couldn't figure out which way to turn or where to go for safety. "Help! Please! Someone!"

The smoke burned his nose and throat. His skin felt like it might be burning too, as if he'd jumped on top of a stove. Someone grabbed his arm, then the shoulder of his shirt, and dragged him sideways, swearing softly as they did. Lee followed blindly, too weak, confused, and shattered to do anything else.

Fire stung his free arm, and he yelped with pain. The someone slapped the injured limb to put out a spark that had landed on his skin, he realized with hazy appreciation. He blinked and scrubbed at his eyes as he was dragged into shadows that were somewhat cooler than the rest of the scrapyard.

Bill was holding his elbow and supporting him as they both moved into a safe space on the far side of the truck. Lee stared at him dumbly. "You…"

"You're all right, kid. You're all right. You're safe now."

"You're not—Bill, what the heck? You've been burned. Look at your leg and your arm." Lee stared at the blistered skin with a sort of stupe-fied fascination.

Bill had saved him. Andre had abandoned him, but the man he'd only met once and actually helped attack and almost blow up had saved his life.

He'd run through the fire to save him. Lee swallowed twice, coughed out some smoke from his burning lungs, and managed a word. "Thanks."

"Not a problem."

"It is with those burns." The voice was a woman's. He thought it might be Andre's ex-wife. Lee frowned.

He didn't have any more time to think about it though, as gunfire erupted from beyond the gate.

44

ANDRE ATKINSON/KIM NAKAMURA

The attack had started well. Explosions had shattered the peace of the scrapyard, and the fires and panic that had followed had been absolutely glorious. He'd even managed to shoot Bruno, one of his three main targets.

Then things had gone wrong. He hadn't been able to find an angle where he could shoot Sarah or the strange man who accompanied his ex-wife. He'd lost track of Carol as well. And Lee, the weakling, couldn't even do as he was told and help with the shooting. Then the foolish brat had gone and gotten trapped. He'd had the audacity to shout for Andre to help him.

As if Andre didn't have anything better to do. He'd turned away from the pathetic, cringing form of the boy who'd followed him from Tunica. Lee had proven to be a broken reed, unreliable and unable to adapt to the way of life Andre preferred. At least the boy had been of some minimal use in getting food and shelter. But now he was more trouble than he was worth. Andre had no intention of wasting any more time on him.

Several more of the Black Rats had managed to get out of the scrapyard and shove the gate farther open while he'd been distracted. Andre fired at one of them, and the man fell. Then he had to take cover as one of the bikers drew a weapon and fired back.

As if that had been a signal, some of the others also pulled out guns and opened fire in his direction. Andre realized then what the glow of the fire had hidden from him before. The sun was rising. He was no longer covered by the shadows of night.

It was time to cut his losses and run. He could come back as soon as he had a new attack plan. He paused to shoot one last survivor who had emerged from the gate and was limping to one side.

Before Andre could pull the trigger, another shot rang out, and a trail of fire seared across his ribs. He staggered back, shocked by the pain. He twisted to look at where the shot had come from, one hand across his side.

Carol stood by the gate, next to the body of her husband. Her face was twisted in a grim mask of anger and grief. "That was for my Bruno, you sonuvagun." She raised the gun to fire again.

Andre raised his own gun and pulled the trigger, but it clicked on an empty magazine. With a curse, he threw the gun aside and turned to run, dashing for the smoke so it would obscure his form and make him harder to hit. Another shot rang out but didn't hit him. He fled, frustrated and angry.

The attack had failed, and he hadn't managed to kill or capture Sarah. He'd only managed to kill one of his three main targets. It was infuriating.

He emerged from the smoke, clutching his side and seething as he considered his next steps. A return to his safe house was the first, followed by tending his wounds.

Running footsteps made him stop and slip into the shadows of a nearby building. His first thought was to wait until the figure passed.

Then he realized the footsteps were running toward the scrapyard, not away. Seconds later, a slight figure appeared, followed by a large, mixed-breed dog. The dog huffed in his direction, and the slim figure slowed, then stopped to scan the area with tired eyes.

She was familiar.

Kim.

Somehow, his daughter was there in the streets of Memphis with a survival pack on her back, dirty clothes cloaking her frame, and a dog at her side.

She looked dependable. Strong. Useful. Andre smiled. His daughter—he knew how to handle his daughter. Surely, she missed her father. With luck, she blamed Sarah for his disappearance and would be angry enough to come with him without question.

Not only did he know how to manipulate her, but she had his genes. She could be molded into the perfect subordinate Lee had failed to be. She could be the perfect blend of ruthlessness and respect that he required. All she needed was his guiding hand.

He stepped forward. "Kim? Is that you?"

His daughter stopped and stared at him, her expression filling with uncertainty. "I…Dad?"

"That's right. It's me." He moved forward, ignoring the dog, who began to growl at him. He didn't care about the dog. He allowed himself to adopt a woebegone expression. "I'm sorry I've been gone."

"You've been in jail for committing murder." Kim's voice was cold.

"I know. But you don't know the whole story. Your mother…she betrayed me, made it look like murder when it was really just self-defense. Just now I was going to the Black Rats to ask for shelter and help, but she ambushed me. She shot me—"

"She shot you?"

"Yes." Andre moved a step closer, watching her. A few more yards and he'd be in range to grab her. Then he could force her to come with him. He'd have both his helper and a hostage against any potential retaliation by Sarah or Carol. "She attacked me. She didn't even give me a chance to explain, to try and talk to her." He let his expression become more distressed. "You'll talk to me, won't you? You'll listen to my side of the story?" He added a little pleading. "You'll help me?"

"I…I…I could help you…" Kim's voice wavered.

Then her expression turned grim, and she raised a gun and pointed it at him. "I could help you to the afterlife."

Of all the people Kim had expected to encounter, her father had been the last one she'd even considered. But there he was, emerging from the shadows like a demon. Kim stared at him, listening as he spun his tale of ambush and betrayal, his eyes full of remorse and fear and pleading.

Under the false emotions he was showing her, she saw anger, frustration, and calculating avarice. The pleading was a lie meant to make her trust him, like the words he was speaking in his faux-reasonable voice.

There was a part of her, the part that remembered being a scared, hurt, and angry sixteen-year-old, alone and homesick, that wanted to believe he was telling the truth. That wanted to run to his side because he was family, and he was familiar. If he'd showed up at her dorm a week and a half ago, she probably would have done it. But that was then.

She'd seen a lot since then. And learned a lot about people—and about herself.

Her father was just another Lewis. Selfish, arrogant, and murderous. In fact, he might be worse, because he was motivated by greed and cruelty and self-interest, whereas Lewis had at least been marginally motivated by community needs. At least he had been before he'd lost his head on a power trip.

Andre wasn't trustworthy. She knew that. Even Mutt knew that. The big dog, usually so placid, hadn't stopped growling since Kim's father had appeared.

Andre's false expression of sorrow had disappeared into shock when she raised the pistol. "Kim. What are you doing?"

"What needs to be done." Kim sighted down the barrel of the gun as Dennis had taught her. This time her hands were perfectly steady. "Why don't you tell me what you're really doing here and what really happened."

"I did tell you, Kim. Your mother ambushed me."

"Yeah, right." Without thinking, Kim dropped the angle of the muzzle and fired, sending up chips of broken concrete into Andre's face. Her father recoiled. "The real story."

Andre's expression darkened with rage. "You little—"

She fired again, this time higher. Andre jerked backward as the bullet grazed his cheek and ripped away a chunk of his ear. His hand shot up to cover the wound. Then he turned and ran away.

Andre vanished into the morning haze and smoke. Kim watched him disappear, then flicked the safety on and tucked the gun into her belt.

Weapon safely stowed, she turned and resumed her trek to the scrapyard, her heart in her throat.

45

SHANNON GRAYSON (SARAH NAKAMURA)

The explosions eventually stopped. Shannon and Bill joined the few Black Rats who remained in putting out fires and assessing the damages. The kid Bill had rescued followed them around like a puppy, dazed and confused.

Eventually, Carol joined them, her expression soot-stained and marked with tear tracks that all of them studiously ignored. Uncle Bruno's body had already been moved and draped with a stained tarp, to be buried when they had more time and a place to do so.

A lot of the piles of wrecks had been demolished by the explosions. The repair shed was completely gone, and one side of the main house was blown inward. The fence that had once surrounded the scrapyard was so many chunks of burned, rusted, and twisted metal, utterly useless for anything other than scrap. Some of the supplies they'd unloaded and the bikes that had been parked around the clubhouse had been destroyed as well.

The truck was dented and scorched, but Shannon hoped it was still drivable. It might also offer shelter for the night if they weren't able to seal off the main house before nightfall.

Bill's burns looked painful, and he occasionally looked a little hazy, as if he might have a concussion. But he insisted on helping out and getting treatment for the others before he took care of himself.

They'd just finished putting out the last of the fires when running, uneven footsteps made Shannon whirl around to look at the barely standing gate. Through the fading smoke and dust, she saw two figures coming closer. One was a slender figure, about the same size as Carol and Shannon herself. The other walked on four legs, loping forward with easy strides. Then the figures resolved into a dog nearly the size of a Shetland pony, and...

"Kim?" The word emerged, broken and surprised. "Kim, is that you?"

"Mom?" Kim staggered to a stop, staring at her. "Mom? You're here?"

"Kim." For one frozen moment, they stared at each other. Then she was moving forward, and so was Kim. A second later, her daughter was in her arms, both of them gripping each other tightly as if they'd never let go. Her eyes felt hot, tear-filled, and she allowed the tears to fall without thought. She was too relieved to do anything else.

"I was afraid you wouldn't be here."

"So was I."

Kim moved back and looked at her. "You're hurt."

"I'm healing. I feel much better now." Shannon managed a weak smile. "I was so worried about you. I couldn't contact you, and I didn't know if I could find you. All I could do was come here."

"I know. I felt the same way. But Dennis..." Kim stopped, choking on something that sounded like a sob. "Dennis helped."

"I'm glad." She wondered where Dennis was, but now didn't seem like the time to ask. There was too much else going on and more important things to focus on.

Carol and Bill came to join them, the kid still following Bill. Carol wasted no time hugging her great-niece. Once she stepped back, Bill stepped forward. "Bill Wheeler. You must be Kim. Your mom's told me a lot about you." He grinned, and he and Kim shook hands.

The kid stood there awkwardly, letting the dog that followed Kim sniff his hand. He looked desperate to be included somewhere, and Shannon suspected Bill would adopt him within the day if he hadn't already.

She also wondered what he'd been doing in the scrapyard. She added that to the list of questions she needed to ask once they'd sorted out shelter, injuries, and food for everyone.

Shannon threw her good arm around her daughter and faced her aunt. "What next?"

"Next? Next we rebuild and make Andre pay for the damage he's caused and the lives he's taken. Anyone fool enough to stand with him will pay alongside him." Carol's expression was grim and determined, and there was a dark promise in her voice.

"Sounds like a plan." Shannon smiled grimly. "You in, Kim?"

"Definitely." Her daughter looked as tired as Shannon felt—and as ready for a fight. "I owe him for a lot more than what happened here."

"Good. Then let's get to work." Shannon turned to the still-smoking scrapyard and the hulk of the partially destroyed living area rising up in the back. She would have loved to simply stop and collapse. Or find someplace quiet to bask in the joy of finally having her daughter back at her side after five long years. But there were things that needed to be done, and no time to waste, not if they wanted food and shelter and safety by the time the sun set once more. "We've got a lot to do."

For now, they'd lick their wounds and mend their fences. But as soon as they got back on their feet, they wouldn't wait for Andre's next move.

Once they'd had a chance to catch their breath, they'd take the fight to him, whatever that entailed. Shannon just hoped she'd be the one who got to crack the monster's skull in the end.

END OF FRACTURED DAYS
AFTER THE END BOOK 2

Trapped Days, August 7, 2024

Fractured Days, September 4, 2024

Final Days, October 9, 2024

PS: Do you enjoy post-apocalyptic fiction? Then keep reading for exclusive extracts from *Final Days, Toxic Tides* and *Broken World.*

THANK YOU

Thank you for purchasing 'Fractured Days'
(After the End Book 2)

Get prepared and sign-up to Grace's mailing list
to be notified of my next release at
www.GraceHamiltonBooks.com.

Loved this book? Share it with a friend,
www.GraceHamiltonBooks.com/books

ABOUT GRACE HAMILTON

Grace Hamilton is the prepper pen-name for a bad-ass, survivalist momma-bear of four kids, and wife to a wonderful husband. After being stuck in a mountain cabin for six days following a flash flood, she decided she never wanted to feel so powerless or have to send her kids to bed hungry again. Now she lives the prepper lifestyle and knows that if SHTF or TEOTWAWKI happens, she'll be ready to help protect and provide for her family.

Combine this survivalist mentality with a vivid imagination (as well as a slightly unhealthy day dreaming habit) and you get a prepper fiction author. Grace spends her days thinking about the worst possible survival situations that a person could be thrown into, then throwing her characters into these nightmares while trying to figure out "What SHOULD you do in this situation?"

You will find Grace on:

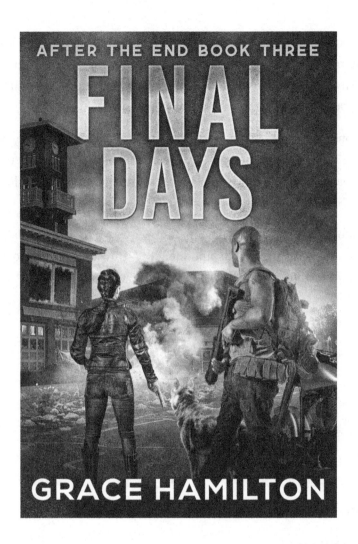

BLURB

In the shadow of a fallen world, law and order are just memories. Only survival remains…

Shannon Grayson had made it through the brutal early days of the EMP apocalypse. Despite suffering a bullet wound in her shoulder, she's managed to reunite with her daughter, Kim. And she's found a safe haven at the Wander Motel.

But tensions are rising in her group of survivors. Kim struggles with the aftermath of Dennis's death and the brutal trials she's been forced to endure. She needs to be at her best to survive and lead in this harsh world, but her past haunts her every step.

Shannon, Kim, and their newfound community aren't the only people fighting to survive in the post-EMP world. Andre, Shannon's ruthless ex-husband, is out of prison. He's rebuilding his motorcycle gang. And he's coming for Shannon and Kim.

Both mother and daughter have paid a heavy price for survival. They need time to heal, physically and mentally. But with Andre closing in, the Wander Motel is no longer a refuge—it's a trap.

Get your copy of *Final Days*
Available October 9, 2024
(Available for Pre-Order Now!)
www.GraceHamiltonBooks.com

EXCERPT

Chapter One

Kim Nakamura

"I swear, Mutt, it's like my mom thinks I'm still a child—like the kid she used to try and protect from my dad, or the teenager she left behind." With a grunt, Kim Nakamura straightened up from where she'd been digging through a pile of debris.

Beside her, Mutt woofed encouragement. The large mixed-breed dog butted her head under Kim's hand in silent demand for a scratch behind the ears. Kim grinned ruefully and obliged, ruffling the dog's short fur.

Then Mutt licked her hand and went off to nose about another tangle of cars and trash, looking for food or something that smelled interesting to her, though Kim couldn't imagine what that might be.

It had been a week since she'd faced down her psychotic father and been reunited with her mother outside the remains of her aunt and uncle's bombed-out scrapyard. That week had only served to make her life more confusing than before the disaster had wiped out the United States power grid and driven her to seek out her family in Memphis.

She'd thought being reunited with her mother, Sarah, would make the world seem...better, she supposed. But it hadn't been that simple. Nothing was.

To start with, her mother now went by Shannon, the new name she'd been given in WitSec.

To make it worse, thinking of WitSec only reminded Kim of the man who'd given his life to try and reunite her with her mother. Like the gun she carried on one hip, the knives she had stashed in her boots and the small of her back, and the worn, military-grade backpack on her shoulders, the name Shannon evoked memories of Dennis Sullivan.

She still saw his face in her nightmares most nights. Sometimes it was scrunched with pain, the way it had been when he'd been trying to detox. But most often, she remembered the way she'd seen him last: sprawled lifelessly on the grass with a neat red circle in his forehead and a puddle of red around his head and shoulders like a macabre halo.

Her feelings about Dennis had been complicated, but she mourned him and missed him with an intensity she never would have imagined a month ago.

Unlike her mother, Dennis would have trusted her instead of feeling the need to watch over her and coddle her. There were so many times in the past week she'd wanted to scream something like that at her mother and her aunt, but every time, she found herself unable to speak, because then she'd have to tell Shannon what had happened to Dennis.

She shook herself out of those thoughts before she could drown in them.

Kim watched Mutt go and sighed. "At least someone in my life is easy to please." She hefted her pack higher onto her shoulder and jogged after the dog.

After a week of wariness, arguments, and far too much tension on both sides, she'd finally managed to convince Shannon and Carol she would be safe searching for supplies on her own. Her mother had driven with her to the area around Horn Lake but finally relented enough to let her slip away to search another section of the highway by herself.

It's not like I don't know my father's still out there and still dangerous. I do. I'd never have made it this long or this far if I was as naive as she thinks I am.

Kim paused to take a deep breath and loosen some of the tension coiling within her. It wasn't entirely Shannon's fault she was so stressed these days. The events of the past few weeks aside, she just wasn't used to being around so many people all the time, and she needed space to breathe.

Like now. She knew Shannon and Bill were only a shout away, but it was still a relief to have some time alone, without other people hovering around her. She'd grown used to being mostly solitary over the years, and the constant presence of others at the motel the Black Rats were using as a temporary base had started to grate on her nerves. The walls were thinner than even the walls in her college dorm room had been. The privacy of her motel room didn't keep her from hearing far more than she wanted regarding the lives of her great-aunt's crew of bikers—men and women alike.

Her mother's constant hovering didn't help either. Especially now, when she didn't want the older woman to know what she was really looking for—besides cars with partially filled fuel tanks and basic supplies.

She was looking for cake ingredients. Anything that could serve to help produce an appropriately sized sweet pastry. Shannon's birthday was less than a day away, and Kim wanted to celebrate it. After all, it had been five years since her mother had gotten to enjoy any birthdays or holidays with her family, and Kim wanted to change that. They might all be struggling to cope with the disaster that had struck almost a month before, but to Kim, that made the celebration *more* important, not less.

She'd started her search four days ago, going out on scavenging missions with whoever was on the prowl at any given time. So far, she'd found more frustration than she had anything else. There was no milk because anything that might have remained in a store or someone's home had spoiled ages ago. Eggs were less perishable, according to Bill Wheeler, but also in short supply. If you weren't a farmer and didn't have access to livestock, you were pretty much out of luck on either front. Things like flour and sugar were rare. Most of it had been looted, and some of what she'd found had been infested with mold or bugs.

When all was said and done, she'd managed to locate enough flour for a moderately sized cake—of sorts: water, some sort of fake egg mix someone had missed or left behind, and maybe a cup or two of sugar. She'd also scrounged some frosting, mostly because it was less practical than many other food items, along with ginger snaps and ginger flavoring.

Her mother loved ginger. Kim figured she could slather vanilla frosting and powdered ginger over the ginger snaps, if all else failed. It wouldn't be great, but it would be better than nothing, as far as she was concerned.

"—elp!" The faint sound jolted her from her thoughts and made her straighten. She stopped searching and listened carefully.

"Help!" This time she heard the word clearly, spoken in a voice that was definitely not her mother's or Bill's, or anyone else's she could recognize.

That didn't mean it wasn't someone from the Black Rats. Even if it wasn't, Kim couldn't bring herself to ignore a cry for help. She slapped her thigh twice to get the dog's attention, using one of the signals she'd been training Mutt to respond to. The dog looked up at once, then loped toward her. Kim grinned fondly at her. "Come on, Mutt. Sounds like someone's in trouble."

She jogged toward the source of the noise and found a man leaning against a burned-out shell of a car. He was doubled over with his arms wrapped around his gut like he had a stomachache. The man looked up at her approach. "Help me, please! I've been...been..." He coughed sharply and hunched further in on himself.

Kim hurried forward, ignoring the way Mutt stopped and made a low growl in the back of her throat. Mutt didn't like strangers.

She was just out of arm's reach when a sense of unease caused her to falter. A voice oddly like Dennis's whispered in her thoughts.

Something's not right. Look at him.

She wanted to dismiss the thought, but years of having to watch out for her father's uncertain temper, along with the lessons she'd recently learned on the road, made her hesitate.

The way he's standing says it's a gut wound. But there's no blood. Can't be a shooting or a stabbing. And a blunt-force wound bad enough to need help would make it near impossible to talk, let alone shout for help loudly enough to get your attention. He doesn't look sick enough for that to be the problem, and there's no sign of him throwing up. He's not acting like he's got cramps either. It doesn't add up.

Kim stopped and watched the man carefully as she addressed him. "Sir, where are you hurt? What happened?"

"I…I've been…" The words sounded forced, but now that she was paying attention and close enough to hear him more clearly, Kim noticed the lack of wheezing that would indicate difficulty breathing. "…attacked…"

"By who, sir? And how are you hurt? What are your injuries?" Kim stayed where she was, her muscles tensing and her hand dropping to the weapon at her belt as the man's behavior raised more red flags.

The man looked up at her. "I was…" He trailed off, and his expression changed, from one of pain to one of annoyance and mild disgust. "I knew I should have gone with a broken arm or a head injury." He scowled. "Whatever, just don't give me too much trouble and neither of us has to leave here injured."

Then he lunged at her.

Get your copy of *Final Days*
Available October 9, 2024
(Available for Pre-Order Now!)
www.GraceHamiltonBooks.com

Toxic Tides

BLURB

In a world ravaged by drought, family is all that matters...

Eighteen-year-old Hazel refuses to become another wife and brood-mare to the prophet of the Wellspring cult. She's determined to find a safe haven for her younger brother, Caleb, in a world where 80% of all fresh water has been contaminated by an algae bloom. But if they're going to survive, they'll need help.

Scientists Emily and Sam, and wilderness guide Bash, might just be the kind of people they can count on. But a lifetime of isolation makes it near impossible for Hazel to trust outsiders. Even if they may be her only hope of breaking free from the prophet's clutches.

A remote forest cabin seems to be the perfect base of operations to plan their escape. But when the cult's soldiers come searching for them, Hazel must draw upon all her strength and skill to protect Caleb.

With her brother's life hanging in the balance, she'll risk everything to save him - even if it means taking on the maniacal cult by herself.

Get your copy of *Toxic Tides*
Available February 5, 2025
(Available for Pre-Order Now!)
www.GraceHamiltonBooks.com

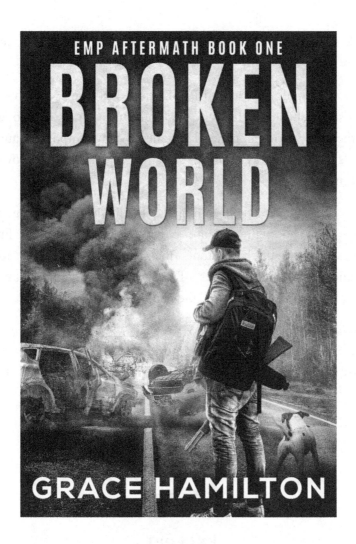

EMP AFTERMATH BOOK ONE

BROKEN WORLD

GRACE HAMILTON

BLURB

No power. No law & order. No safety net. The world as everyone knows it is over.

Laurel is stabilizing a patient in the ER when the power goes out. As she struggles to keep her patients alive, she faces an ugly truth—the world as everyone knew it is over. The smart thing to do is run and try to survive, but Laurel refuses to leave her patients behind—least of all her sick mother. There's only one choice to make. She'll have to stay and fight.

Bear is done fighting. War and PTSD have cost him everything—his job, his self-respect, and his wife - Laurel. But when he can no longer deny the old world is gone, he gains a new purpose. Laurel is hundreds of miles away from his mountain cabin, but he knows she needs him.

After so long being a lost soldier, he finally has something worth fighting for. The highways are clogged with dead cars. Frantic survivors want his truck, his tools, his supplies. He'll face treachery, desperation, and endless miles of unforgiving wilderness, but he's going to find his wife. Together, they can survive anything.

He just has to reach her.

EXCERPT

Chapter One

Laurel

"What have we got?" Laurel rushed forward, clutching the tablet she hadn't gotten used to using yet. Casting a hurried glance at the triage area, she pushed her glasses up the bridge of her nose and pinched it between her thumb and index finger. Too many patients, not enough staff. South Minneha Hospital was supposed to be different, yet just a week after opening, they were running into the same old problems. Plus some new ones.

In front of her, a female paramedic gestured to a gurney. Laurel couldn't remember her name. A young male was strapped to it, barely conscious, eyes rolling as he grappled for the oxygen mask on his face. Blood trickled from a gash on his forehead, which clearly wasn't his biggest problem.

"Twenty-three-year-old male, Tommy Jones, front passenger seat, collision with a truck, signs of internal bleeding."

As the paramedic reeled off the boy's stats, Laurel's mind was already three steps ahead. "He's going to need a chest tube," she said loudly. "Bay Three!" She gestured to the biggest of the empty bays as her team gathered around her. Two nurses and a resident. Allison Park. Not the worst resident she'd ever worked with, but not the best either.

As Laurel pulled on a gown and gloves, Park took the tablet and started to swipe at it. She was attempting to enter the patient's information. A step suggested by the bureaucrats who ran the new, extra high-tech hospital that Laurel had found herself working in.

"It's not connected—"

"Leave it," Laurel snapped. "You think we have time for that? Gown up, Park."

Taking a second to gather her breath, Laurel made herself look at the boy in front of her—really look at him. For just a second, she allowed the weight of the responsibility she held to crush her. Then she shook it off, opened her palm and said, "Scalpel."

A longer-than-usual beat passed. Laurel looked up.

"I can't find—" One of the nurses, Janet, was scrabbling in an instrument drawer. "It's not where it's supposed to be."

"Help her," Laurel gestured for Park to look too, but as the resident moved away, a series of alarms began to sound. "He's in v-fib! Crash cart!"

Laurel started compressions, heaving her entire body weight into the movement, thankful—not for the first time—that she still worked out six days a week.

"Where is that crash cart!" She looked up, over the top of her glasses. Park was staring wildly around the room as if the cart might appear from somewhere.

"It's not here. I thought we were supposed to have one in every room?" Park's expression froze as the color drained from her face; she was beginning to panic.

"What is *wrong* with you people!" Laurel glared at Park. "Take over," she growled, then ran from the room. There was a cart in Bay Two, she'd used it yesterday.

As fast as she could, she lurched out of Bay Three, into the bay next door, and grabbed the cart. When she returned, the alarms were still ringing. At this rate, they'd lose the kid before they even got him to an OR.

"Charge two-hundred," she yelled, slapping pads onto the boy's chest. "Stand clear!"

After the third charge, the alarms stopped. Instinctively, Laurel held out her hand and, this time, Janet pressed a scalpel into it.

With Tommy finally on his way to surgery, Laurel put her hands on her hips and marched back into Bay Three.

"That was an absolute disaster!" she yelled. "What was that? We could have lost that kid, all because no one knows their ass from their elbow! I shouldn't have to run out of the room to grab a crash cart. It should have been there. *One of you* should have noticed it was missing." As Janet, the two other nurses—Sandra and Maggie—and Park blinked at her, Laurel continued. "I was a field medic in Iraq for three years, and never had to put up with performance as dreadful as this." She paused. Janet was shaking her head. Park looked like she was about to cry, Sandra and Maggie were blushing. She was being too harsh. This wasn't her usual management style. She was good with people. She didn't shout or scream. Something about this place, though, was getting to her. Just a week in, and she was beginning to realize that South Minneha wasn't as shiny and perfect as she'd been promised it would be.

Opening her mouth to speak, Laurel noticed Janet narrow her eyes a little. The gesture made her stop, press her lips together, and leave before she said anything else.

Twenty minutes later, she was waiting in line for the coffee cart when Janet lightly touched her elbow. "Tough day?" she asked, raising an eyebrow to indicate she was not sympathetic.

Laurel sighed. "Coffee?" She'd reached the front of the line.

Janet nodded and allowed Laurel to buy her a double-shot latte, and then the two of them headed over to a bench nearby. Positioned under a large tree, looking out at the impressive fountain at the front of the hospital, it was a beautiful place to sit. Yet, somehow, it made Laurel uncomfortable.

"I think I'm having a hard time adjusting," she said as Janet sat down beside her. "All this." She gestured with her coffee-holding hand to the neatly manicured lawn, which had clearly been designed to convey the idea that South Minneha was not a run-of-the-mill hospital. This place was something special. Something *new.* "I said no to another tour so I could work here." Laurel shuffled uncomfortably in her seat and sighed a little. "I'll admit it, I was swayed by the Board's proposal. Brand new equipment. State of the art facilities. The kind of resources I'd only ever read about in medical journals."

"But—" Janet added, pausing for effect.

"But it's so different from what I'm used to. I used to enjoy my work, but here it feels like I'm fighting fires I shouldn't have to be fighting. Does that make any sense?"

After sipping her coffee, Janet nodded. "If you don't like it, why don't you leave? You don't *have* to stay here."

Laurel hesitated for a moment. She hadn't told anyone about the real deciding factor in her move to South Minneha.

Watching her, Janet sighed, then straightened her shoulders and sucked in her cheeks. She was a friend, but not the kind of friend to tolerate poor behavior or excuses.

"Look," she said, folding her arms in front of her plump stomach. "You made a choice. You *chose* to come work here because the money's good and because they promised you a bunch of shiny toys."

Laurel nodded, pushing her glasses up the bridge of her nose.

"From where I'm sitting, that's exactly what you got."

"What's the use of shiny toys if we can't get the basics, right?" Laurel almost laughed.

"Okay, so some things need work. We're *all* new here, Laurel. But I'm telling you now—you're not going to make any friends if you carry on like this." She paused, softening her tone slightly. "Let's be honest, there's no way you're quitting. You're not that kind of person. So you should probably start thinking about taking a different approach. The nurses are doing their best. Even Park is doing her best." Janet stood up, clearly not in the mood to sit and make further conversation. "You're in charge of the ER. You want things done differently? Then screw the Board and do them differently. Just don't take it out on us."

Laurel was about to apologize—a sincere apology—when a noise near the entrance interrupted. Following Janet's gaze, she rose to her feet.

"Great," Janet said through gritted teeth. "Looks like more inmates have arrived."

"More?" They started to walk back toward the entrance, watching as a prison transport pulled up and three large guards piled out onto the sidewalk.

Banging a fist on the side of the van, one of them yelled. "Shut up! We're here. No nonsense or we'll take you straight back."

The van doors opened just as Laurel and Janet drew level with them. Inside were two gurneys, each with a prisoner handcuffed to it.

"We were told there'd be a maximum of six per week but that's got to be…" Laurel trailed off as she tried to recall how many had arrived yesterday and the day before. Janet was chuckling. "What?" Laurel turned to her. "What's funny?"

"Haven't you figured it out yet?" Janet stopped and looked up at the imposing white building in front of them. "The only thing the people in charge of this place care about is *money*. They didn't build this hospital because they wanted to use the wonders of modern technology to help people. They built it to bring in big bucks from big donors, big pharmaceutical companies, and big-pocketed patients. More prisoners in the inmates' wing equals more *money*."

"If you're so skeptical, why are *you* here?" Laurel asked, folding her arms in front of her chest, tilting her head as she waited for Janet's answer.

"Same as you. Money. Fancy equipment." Janet glanced back toward the coffee cart. "And I like the coffee." Without offering a smile, she tossed her empty takeout cup into a nearby trash can and stalked back inside, sashaying a little as she walked.

As Laurel finished her own coffee, she watched the prison guards wheel the inmates inside. Straight through the main entrance, despite Robert Sullivan's promises about them being kept completely separate from her ER.

Taking out her phone, she flicked to Robert's name and typed out a quick message: *Need to talk ASAP.*

He'd avoid her, of course he would, but she wasn't going to let him get away with this. Janet was right; Laurel was in charge, so she darn well needed to act like it. Normally, she'd never even dream of kowtowing to someone like Robert—nice but, ultimately, interested more in the hospital's bottom line than anything else. The problem was, after everything Robert had done to get her mother into the trial —the only one in the country getting results for her type of cancer— she felt indebted to him.

Somehow, she needed to draw a line between the two things. Robert did her a favor, but she did him a favor too by agreeing to head up his fancy new ER. She was good, and he knew it, or he wouldn't have gone to the lengths he had to secure her. It was about time she reminded him of that.

Grab your copy of *Broken World* (EMP Aftermath Book One)
eBook
Paperback
Audiobook
www.GraceHamiltonBooks.com

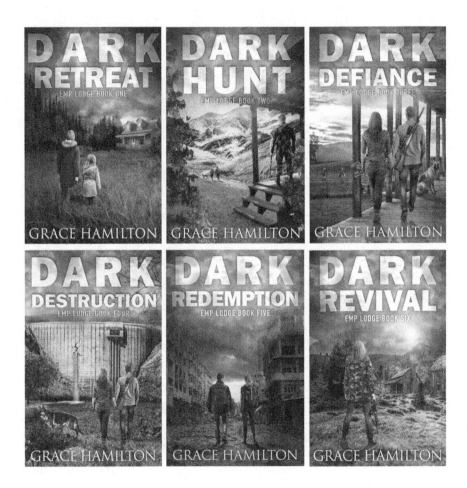

Made in the USA
Monee, IL
19 October 2024

68258746R00223